MW01503045

Dark Passions

Love Is A Many-Splintered Thing

A. J. Ciulla

Writers Club Press

San Jose New York Lincoln Shanghai

Dark Passions
Love Is A Many-Splintered Thing

Published by Writers Club Press
an imprint of iUniverse.com, Inc.

For information address:
iUniverse.com, Inc.
620 North 48th Street
Suite 201
Lincoln, NE 68504-3467
www.iuniverse.com

ISBN: 0-595-01069-5

Printed in the United States of America

by the same author

PAPA WAS A RIOT

EL PESCADOR

Acknowledgments

To my departed uncle, Sam Arena, I owe much. His tales as a fiddler in the roaring twenties allowed me to log on to his added years of recall, giving me some insight as to what made that unforgettable decade roar.

To my brothers, James and Sam, who have gone to their eternal rest, as well as to brothers Joseph and Louis, I must confess the essence of what each of them were is strewn throughout this narrative.

To Earl Vanderbilt and Elwood Stafford, I can't fully express what their friendships meant to me. I can't fully thank them for being my gurus, my Jiminy Crickets, my turnkeys keeping me confined to my desk when I would have preferred to ditch this entire project. They are gone now but not forgotten.

Table Of Contents

Prologue

Mr. McGregor helped Jennie from the shay, depositing her before the Woolworth Building. She watched him dab his eyes with a large red-and-white bandanna. Never before had he given any indication of affection, and that added to her gloom.

Mr. McGregor scrambled back onto the shay, and, without a backward glance, reined the horse around the corner. Jennie motionlessly stared at the corner as if waiting for him to return, pick her up, and take her back to the home.

Fear immobilized her legs. By edict of mind over body, she propelled herself to the massive door, slipping and sliding on the wet confetti underfoot, remnants of the mad celebration after the armistice.

At the door, she paused once more and spied the poster, centrally located on the pane of the main door, depicting a dirty, bandaged, fatigued doughboy. The words above the picture echoed the nation's newfound pride—*And they thought we couldn't fight!*

It might've been the message of the poster that gave Jennie the courage to open the door and walk into a bustle of activity. She stood there, lost and clutching her carpetbag, buffeted by shoppers scurrying from department to department.

A tall woman with an authoritative look noted her bewilderment and approached her. "May I help you?"

"Yes," Jennie replied. "I've come to see Mr. Willoughby."

"Is he expecting you?"

"I think so," she said uncertainly.

"Come with me."

Jennie followed her to the small office in the back of the huge store.

Mr. Willoughby wasn't there. The woman left Jennie standing by the desk and suggested she wait.

Jennie looked about the room, bare but for a desk, two chairs, and file cabinets along the wall. At the home, where austerity showed everywhere, the office in the administration building was opulent by comparison.

Turmoil filled her on that day, her eighteenth birthday. It was incongruous that she suddenly thought of a cake.

For the first time in Jennie's life, Mrs. Trimble failed to bake a birthday cake for one of her wards. There was a new little girl in administration waiting to take Jennie's place, and she felt annoyed with herself. Why should she think of cake at such a time?

Mr. Willoughby's entrance did nothing to allay her fears. He looked like a martinet, which added to her anxiety. He was almost courtly as he offered her a seat.

"Are you Mrs. Trimble's charge?" he asked kindly.

"Yes, Mr. Willoughby," she said in a small voice.

Cosmo Willoughby appraised the slender young woman before him. She wore a drab dress to her ankles, exposing ugly, utilitarian brogans. He shook his head at her dress—a sack of potatoes had more form.

From the beginning, the interview went badly. He tried to draw her out, but, to every question he posed, he received an incomplete reply—or none. She knew little of the war that just ended and less of the efforts to ensure lasting peace. He asked about movies, books, and music, but it was as if Jennie came from another planet.

Willoughby then tried women's fashions, because that had a direct bearing on Woolworth's business, but again, he drew a blank. He became worried, and, as he talked, trying to establish some sort of rapport, he wondered how he could renege on his promise. Then he realized he couldn't do that to the nice old woman at the home.

"Is Jones your family name?" he asked.

"No, it was given to me by someone I never met." For the first time, she showed a little animation. She hated her name, and, on several occasions, confided her hatred to Mr. McGregor, who, in her limited circle of friends and acquaintances, was the smartest person she knew.

"Jennie Jones is short and curt," Mr. Willoughby said. "It has a lilt to it."

"The man who named me Jones had a simple mind," Jennie told Mr. Willoughby.

His eyes opened wide. "How's that, Jennie?"

"He probably named his horse Dobbin and his dog Fido!"

Mr. Willoughby burst out laughing, suddenly feeling better about the interview. "Dobbin and Fido!"

"I don't appreciate being called Jennie, either."

"Why?" He was eager for her reply.

"A jenny is a female mule."

Willoughby laughed so hard, he held his sides. "I must tell that to my wife's arrogant niece. We call her Jenny. You don't have to use that name."

"I don't?"

"No. Jennie is a familiar form of Jane."

Jennie considered that. "I supposed Jane comes with the name Doe?"

"Jane Doe! Priceless! Tell me, why in the world would they spell Jenny with an IE, instead of the usual Y?"

"I don't know, Mr. Willoughby. Probably, he didn't know how to spell." She hadn't intended any levity but was stating her opinion.

Willoughby smiled. The young woman certainly made his morning. He looked into intelligent eyes and was pleased by the timbre of her voice.

Jennie felt the interview had gone badly—Mr. Willoughby must've discerned her inadequacies and wouldn't hire her. She was surprised when he said she had a job, but she was filled with misgivings. How could she possibly function in that inferno of activity?

Back on the street, Jennie took out an envelope from her carpetbag. In it was a ten-dollar bill, with which Mansfield discharged its obligation for her survival. She wondered how far the money would go. To her surprise, there was a new change purse in the bag, too, with some change inside, probably from the generosity of Mrs. Pringle.

Although the housemother at the home arranged for a single roommate without parents, the realities of what lay ahead for someone earning a five-and-dime clerk's pay were grim. Jennie took her bearings and walked east on Main Street. University Avenue was five blocks away. There she would meet her roommate and see the apartment they'd share.

Chapter One

Jennie heard her husband at the door at the bottom of the stairs. Evidently, he'd shaken free from his cronies at the bar. She waited anxiously, as she did every night, for a sign indicating whether she'd be ravaged. If his climb was noisy and uneven, and if, despite the iron rail for support, his condition buffeted him from wall to wall, she earned another reprieve.

Somehow, he'd reach the top landing, and Jennie would take over, helping him into the apartment and leading him to bed. She'd remove his shoes, then, steeling herself, pull at his socks, damp and pungent with perspiration. Stripping him down to his long underwear, the open slit in the back exposing flabby buttocks, she would unceremoniously drop him onto his side of the bed.

That wasn't how it would be. His steps were regular, and he didn't collide with the walls. He walked into the kitchen unassisted and managed a bit of levity that was out of character. It had become such a ritual, she knew what he was going to say and how.

"Do you know what time it is, Jennie?"

"What time is it, Gus?"

"Why, it's half-past kissing time. Time to kiss my gal!" He kissed her mouth, and the smell of stale beer, as always, nauseated her.

"I'm going to bed." He disappeared into the bedroom.

Jennie went into the bathroom, disrobed, and pulled on her nightgown. Gus was already under the sheets when she entered the bedroom. She turned out the light and slid in next to him on the large bed.

Gus leaned over and kissed her face, and she counted. It was always five—no more, no less. That never varied. Then, having accomplished the preliminaries, Gus went to work. He grabbed the hem of her gown and roughly lifted it up until it gathered under her chin and around her neck like a loose collar.

He straddled her and covered her breasts with his huge hands. Kneading her breasts, he rocked back and forth, priming himself. When he was ready, he slapped her thigh, indicating the time had come, and Jennie spread her legs to allow him to enter.

Jennie took her responsibility to care for Gus seriously. Her anxiety to get home before him wasn't because she feared his reaction to her going out dancing alone and without his knowledge. He was past caring. By getting home when she did, she could catch the last set of the fine band at Martino's.

Sitting at the window, two houses from the speakeasy, she waited for Jazzman Caruthers. He was her counselor, and he understood her. He talked to her through his horn, from which came soulful sounds with a profundity she comprehended, and he understood her, for those almost-human sounds seemed directed to her. Jazzman Caruthers would pander to her self-pity, adding to her despair, plumbing the depths of her sadness, then his horn would suddenly blare triumphantly, indicating better days were coming.

No sooner had she found one shaft of light in her situation, which was the infrequent demands on her body, than she learned she was pregnant. She wondered how it happened, then remembered Mr. McGregor once saying, "Even a blind hen gets a kernel of corn now and then."

Jennie didn't spare Gus. She berated him constantly. Most of time, he didn't comprehend. His condition was noticeably worse, and he needed help getting off to work. When he stirred his coffee at breakfast, the spoon rattled in his cup. Her concern was more for herself than for Gus. She had new priorities. Without him, all would be lost. She married Gus out of despair. With him, despair turned to security of sorts, but, with a child and Gus' problem, it was a concern.

With deeper understanding, she viewed the strangers who gave birth to her and left her for others to raise. She tried to keep that thought away but failed. In a desperate enough situation, she, too, would abandon a child.

The baby arrived with no trouble. It was a boy, and to Jennie's eyes, there was no fairer child. Having a baby was expensive, with diapers, powders, salves, a wardrobe, milk, and corn syrup. Later, when the baby started eating solids, the situation would worsen.

As a toolmaker, Gus' wages were more than sufficient, even with his drinking. Suddenly, without apparent reason, Gus cut down on the money he allotted her for household expenses. A nightly search of his pockets revealed less money than usual, too. Something was wrong.

"Gus," she asked one morning, "with the baby, we'll need more money. Why are you giving me less? I think I deserve an explanation."

"We're in a period of austerity at the shop. We've all been cut back."

That closed the subject, but Jennie didn't believe it. The Harding-Coolidge prosperity was gathering momentum.

Jennie managed to survive only by depleting the nest egg she built up by stealing from Gus' pockets while he slept.

One day, with the weather cold and damp, a slender man, shivering in his great coat, knocked on Jennie's door and introduced himself as Toomey, Gus' foreman at the shop. She hurried him into the kitchen and shut the door behind him, cutting off the draft from the stairway.

Toomey refused the chair she offered and stood near the door. "I have Gus' check with me."

"Is he all right?"

"Don't be alarmed. He's OK. He left without his check."

"Why would he do that?"

"Perhaps because he left before quitting time. He's done that twice this week."

"That's odd."

"Is Gus on the hard stuff?"

"Hard stuff?"

"I mean liquor."

"Oh, no. He has enough trouble with beer."

"Strange behavior," Toomey mumbled. "To tell the truth, I came by to learn why he's not waiting for the quitting whistle." He fumbled with the doorknob.

Jennie glanced at the check and saw Gus had told her the truth. They'd cut his pay. "Mr. Toomey?"

He turned and stepped back into the kitchen. "Yes, Mrs. Rhinehardt?"

"How's business at the shop?"

"We're booming," he said enthusiastically. "We're thinking of adding a third shift."

"I don't understand. Gus said you're having an austerity period at the plant, and that's why his pay has been cut." She waved the check.

"Doesn't he discuss important family matters with you?"

"Evidently not."

"This is awkward. It has to do with his condition."

"You mean his alcoholism?"

"Mrs. Rhinehardt, Gus was an excellent tool man. He was a superb craftsman, but toolmakers work within close tolerances. Gus is a bundle of nerves and can't function."

"Are you going to fire him?"

"Why, no. He's been a loyal employee through the years, and we want to be loyal to him."

"If he can't function…?"

"Not as a toolmaker, but we have him in the tool crib, parts department, receiving, shipping, and maintenance."

"And, sometimes, he sweeps out the place?" she guessed.

"Yes. We try to keep him working. Naturally, his trade brought top pay. All those other tasks are nonskilled or semiskilled."

"I'm glad you stopped by, Mr. Toomey."

"Glad to have met you, Mrs. Rhinehardt." He left in a hurry, taking the steps two at a time.

When Gus got home, Jennie handed him the check, and he was crestfallen.

"Why didn't you tell me?" she demanded.

"I didn't want you to know how little I make."

"Don't you think I have a right to know?"

"I did my best. I gave you all the money I could. It hasn't cost me so much at the bar. I swallowed my pride and started cadging drinks."

"You don't realize how bad our position is, do you?"

"Yes, I do. After dinner, I'm going to Martino's to tell him I'm accepting that new job."

"You're going to tend bar?"

"Nothing like that."

"A waiter, perhaps?"

"Oh, no."

"You're not singing with the band, are you?" she asked sarcastically.

"Jennie, let me finish. Mr. Martino recommended me for a job with Fritz Kroger."

"Who's Fritz Kroger?"

"He's the brewer who furnishes beer for Martino."

"Isn't that illegal?"

"Sure, but the whole country's drinking these days. Everybody's illegal."

"Are you the new brewmaster?"

"Why don't you get serious? I'll deliver the beer to Kroger's customers."

"That's not much of a job."

"It pays better than toolmaking."

"It does?" she asked in surprise. "Let me guess. You'll be well-paid, but there's an element of danger, right?"

"Well, yes. There are rival brewers…"

"Bootleggers."

"Who offer competition…"

"Highjack."

"I only do the bull work. The driver takes care of the problems…"

"He does the shooting."

"I've given this a lot of thought, Jennie. I can't stay at the shop. In a short time, we'll go under."

"You're right there. We owe the grocer, and we're behind in our rent and utilities. There's the baby and his needs, too, and you and I aren't eating like we should."

"You see then, don't you?"

Gus looked so pitiful, her heart went out to him. He was a gentle giant of a man, but he was weak. She wished she could comfort him and tell him it was out of the question, but her fear of the future forbade it.

"Yes," she replied, "but I don't like it. You're all the little fellow and I have."

On Monday morning, a truck stopped in front of the apartment building, and Gus left for his new job.

Fritz Kroger kept Gus sober during working hours, but he made up for lost time at night. As a result, Jennie rarely saw her husband sober. Jazzman Caruthers still drew her to the open window and cast his spell on her. She named her son not Gus or August, but Jasmin, in deference to her guru. She dared not go so far as to call him Jazzman. As for Gus, he paid less attention to the child than before.

One afternoon there was a gun battle involving Gus' truck, and there were casualties on both sides. Gus stayed home that night.

"Jennie," he said, misery showing in his face, "I've made a terrible mistake. I work in a world inhabited by animals. I'm in terror on every trip."

After losing a good man to a bullet, Kroger wasn't thrilled by Gus' conduct during the battle. Gus wasn't someone he could count on, but he was honest, and that was rare among his soldiers. His size, coupled with a face that resembled Von Stroheim in the movies, made him look threatening. Kroger transferred Gus to collections, pairing him with someone named Conrad.

Jennie felt a little better about that, but she knew anyone involved in bootlegging was a poor insurance risk.

Like the rest of the city of Rochester, she had little hope that the city's police department would clean up the mess that was getting worse every day. For a city that held itself above neighboring Syracuse and Buffalo, Rochester's tolerance for its rising crime rate was strange. Perhaps it indulged itself in equivocality. There was nothing wrong with the City of Flowers. It was just the times.

Chapter Two

The violent wars in the major cities of the country for the lions' shares of the bootleg booty have been well-documented. No less violent were the barracudas in the lesser waters of upstate and western New York. The pundits in sociology pontificated, saying their fair city suffered from a malady transmitted by several other cities in the state. Certainly, Rochester was never like raucous Buffalo, stunted in its social growth. The malady in Niagara Falls was a curse even in the best of times.

Danny DeGeorge had few equals in public relations. He was smooth, almost unctuous, a good contractor who knew when to offer gratuities and when not to. The best friend in business was a highly placed government official.

Danny's considerable success should've satisfied his ego, but he quickly saw that the Volstead Act opened the country to new challenges and horizons for those with the courage to reach for them.

The illegality of what he contemplated bothered him at first, but he eased his conscience with the comforting thought that more than a few of the minions of the law were on the team.

His new enterprise was an instant success until the pressures of rival factions were felt. DeGeorge stayed away from the northside. It was wide open, with too many barracudas, hungry and slashing their way to a place in the sun.

DeGeorge's territory was too close to that of Fritz Kroger, who also had influential friends, and more importantly, a collection of violent men determined to keep the DeGeorge operation from expanding.

One evening, one of the trucks hadn't returned. Two days later, children playing in the high weeds at the circus grounds on the west side found the bodies of two men.

A meeting was scheduled for investors, who wanted better protection for their investment. One of the more important ones put it succinctly by saying, "Danny, you don't have the balls for this business."

Before long, some of the most violent men plaguing Niagara Falls came to Rochester. Those professionals reversed the fortunes of war, and the hunters became the hunted.

A mantle of gloom draped the Kroger organization. Three more men died that week, and Fritz gave Conrad and Gus unreasonable schedules. One would think the once-indomitable bootlegger feared there would be no tomorrow, and he had to gather as much money as he could. He'd learned a bitter lesson. Leopards could sometimes change spots, and pussy cats could turn into tigers. He'd badly misjudged DeGeorge.

Gus was tired, and he was near home from his last stop. He decided to forego supper and return to the Oasis, where he'd succumb to his body's demands.

When they walked into the speakeasy, Gus' drinking mates greeted him like a conquering hero, much to Conrad's resigned amusement. Gus refused the proffered drink, because he was still on duty.

Martino took Gus into his inner sanctum, where he opened a safe and drew out a stack of bills. He looked at the chit Gus handed him and meticulously counted out the amount. Gus signed the bottom half of the chit, tore it off, and jammed the rest of it, along with the cash, into his pocket.

When Gus returned to the bar, Conrad was waiting. He'd been irritable all day.

"Come on, Gus. Let's get the hell out of here. I want to go home."

"Hold your horses, Fella. I have to go to the john."

"No time for that. Fix the money belt in the car."

"To hell with the belt. I gotta piss."

"Jesus Christ! Wait here. I'll check the room first. You're carrying a lot of dough." Conrad found the men's room empty and stood guard while Gus went inside.

Since the stalls and urinals were empty, Gus took a moment to place the money in his money belt. Conrad could wait. When Gus came out, his friends had a beer waiting for him, and he didn't refuse. The demons inside him wouldn't allow it.

Exasperated, Conrad grabbed him roughly. "Come on, you lush! We're leaving right now!"

Martino stepped in. "Hold on a minute, Conrad. I'll send him out when he's through."

Conrad controlled his anger. It was no secret Martino had a vested interest in Kroger's operation. Gus took his beer and walked to the bandstand to tease Jill, Martino's chanteuse, who was getting ready to sing the first number of the next set. They laughed, which infuriated Conrad, and he stormed out.

Martino kept his word. Gus downed his beer and was ushered to the door. Conrad was in an ugly mood, but he had the motor running and the door open.

Before Gus reached the car, Conrad saw a touring car turn the corner and bear down on him. He roared off into the night, leaving an astonished Gus staring as the car disappeared.

"Conrad, come back!" Gus shouted.

The touring car roared past the Oasis, and the occupants started firing, some of their bullets hitting Gus in the chest. There was intense pain, and he realized he was dying.

Somehow, he got to his feet and staggered away, feeling a desperate need to reach his family one block away. It took a Herculean effort to get there. He managed to open the main door of the building, then he fell onto the bottom of the stairs.

Jennie heard the door open, followed by a thud. She ran to the landing and peered down at the figure sprawled at the entrance, then ran down the stairs to help Gus. The light, coming in through the glass from the street-light outside, showed he'd been shot, and she knew he was dying.

Jennie steeled herself and stifled a scream. If she made a sound, she'd alert Gus' assailants to his whereabouts, then they'd kill her, too.

Gus opened his eyes and saw her, giving her a wan smile. "It's the end, Jennie," he whispered, his face contorted in pain. His head fell back, and there was a terrible silence, then he called her name.

"Yes, Gus?"

"Take care of the little one."

Jennie cried softly.

Right before he died, Gus said clearly, "My waist!"

She was frightened. What did he just say? His wounds were in his chest. Gingerly, she unbuttoned his coat and felt his waist and the bulge under his shirt. She pulled the shirt out from his trousers and found the belt— Gus hadn't checked in with Kroger for the night.

The discovery galvanized her to action. She unlaced the belt and carefully pulled it free, then ran upstairs. When she reached the apartment, she looked wildly for a place to hide it. Rushing into the bathroom, she saw the diaper pail beside the commode and remembered it was filled with dirty diapers.

The baby was asleep in the crib beside the bed. Without disturbing the child, Jennie deftly removed the rubber sheet and ran into the bathroom, dumping the contents of the pail into the bathtub. She rolled the money belt into a tight ball and wrapped it in the rubber sheet, then carefully placed the package in the center of the pile of diapers, arranging them to hide the package. She remained calm and forced herself to be patient, then washed her hands.

Back at the foot of the stairs, she sat beside Gus and started tucking in his shirt, then stopped. An assailant, yanking the belt from Gus, wouldn't bother tucking in the shirt again.

Jennie summoned all her courage. With shaking hands, she gathered her husband's remains to her bosom. When she heard sirens, she was reassured—no assassin would come with the police around. The light from the street focused on Gus' dead eyes, and, in her terror, screams came easily.

Kravetz, the officer on the beat, was one block away when he heard Jennie's anguished cries. He ran toward the sound, and it seemed as if the entire neighborhood ran with him.

When he saw the scene on the lower step of the apartment house, he braced himself. Jennie clutched Gus' body, and she was drenched in his blood. In her grief, she gave no thought to modesty. She wore a terry cloth robe, and the belt kept it from falling away completely, but her exposed chemise was saturated with blood as well as the upper section of the robe. Her legs were fully exposed and bloody, too.

Reaching down, Kravetz pried Jennie from Gus' body, then pulled her robe closed and covered her. He closed Gus' eyes and went through his pockets, finding a wallet, some keys, and a bit of change. Those items were turned over to Jennie.

Then he felt a tap on his shoulder and turned to see a fellow officer.

"Who was it?" the man asked.

"Gus Rhinehardt," Kravetz replied.

"I know him. He was a toolmaker and a regular at the Oasis back when it was a legit beer garden. He got it in front of the speak. The front window's been shot out, and there's blood all over the sidewalk."

"Caught in a crossfire," Kravetz suggested.

"It's the damn bootleg war."

That was the judgment later when headquarters closed the books on Gus' murder.

Jennie locked herself in the bathroom, disrobed, and sponge-bathed herself thoroughly in the sink. She shampooed her hair and rinsed it, then rubbed herself dry with a thick towel and tried to do the same for her hair.

Taking a long flannel nightgown from the hook on the back of the bathroom door, she slipped into it quickly as a chill struck her. In the bedroom closet, she located Gus' coat sweater, which hung well below her knees. She left her hair uncombed, and it resembled a fright wig. With her swollen eyes and odd attire, she was repugnant.

A knock on the door startled her. Normally, she heard footsteps on the stairs. She was surprised to open the door and see Conrad, then resented the fact that he was still alive. Gus called him a gunsel, a troubleshooter whose job it was to protect Gus, because he carried the money. She wondered what went wrong.

A stranger was with him, a hawk-like man who looked as if he suffered from malnutrition. His darting eyes swept every nook and cranny of the cramped kitchen, and the visit brought Jennie to near panic.

"Mrs. Rhinehardt, we'd like to talk to you. I'm Conrad."

"I know. You worked with my husband."

"Fritz sent us. Otherwise, I wouldn't have intruded at a time like this."

"The dear man. You tell Mr. Kroger I'm touched by his concern. I don't hold him responsible. Gus knew what he was doing when he went to work for him. It was his choice."

Conrad was nonplused. The situation took a strange turn. Did that dumb broad really think Fritz gave a shit about her drunk husband? "Mrs. Rhinehardt, we're here for the belt."

"Belt? What belt?"

"The money belt. Gus was carrying a great deal of Mr. Kroger's money when he was shot."

"You must be mistaken. The police found no money belt on Gus."

"I know. I was in the crowd when the police came. The boss wants me to make sure Gus didn't hide it in the apartment."

Jennie started crying. "Poor Gus. His wounds were horrible. He couldn't have made it up the stairs."

"I know, Mrs. Rhinehardt. There was a trail of blood from the Oasis to the front landing of your building, but no blood on the stairs."

"We gotta search, anyway. Kroger's orders," the stranger added.

The possibility of the police returning and Jennie's crying made Conrad nervous. "Let's get on with it, Joel."

They made a thorough search of the apartment, looking in cabinets, drawers, and behind and under all the furniture. Conrad was in the bathroom, and Jennie heard him moving around. She held her breath and closed her eyes. If Conrad found the money belt, there was no telling what he'd do to her.

He came out holding his nose. "Phew! Don't you ever wash those damn diapers?"

Joel walked up behind Jennie and felt her waist, making her shriek. "Relax, Lady. I don't need a cheap feel. I was just makin' sure the belt ain't on you."

Then they left, and Jennie locked the door, letting Conrad and Joel grope their way down the stairs.

When they reached the bottom, they avoided the pool of blood that hadn't been removed.

"Knew it wasn't there," Conrad commented.

"Ugly broad. Gus must've had a chick on the side."

"You're right. What is it the French say? Find the woman. I know just the canary who's going to sing."

Strazzi was unhappy, and that didn't bode well for anyone who crossed him. His tension was shared by Danny DeGeorge, even though Strazzi was his underling. The import from Niagara Falls lived up to his reputation, and victory was finally within reach.

The action at the Oasis was botched. The hit was incomplete, and, to a perfectionist, unforgivable. How could Joe Chink have failed? Strazzi's top aide was his protegé, nurtured from his teens in the battlefields of Niagara Falls.

Strazzi couldn't remain silent any longer and shouted, "Get Chink in here!"

A young man sauntered into the office, unconcerned about his boss' ire. He knew what troubled Strazzi, but Joe feared no one, which endeared him to his boss.

Strazzi looked directly into his aide's eyes, made inscrutable by epicanthal folds. "What happened at the Oasis, Joe?"

"I know, I know. I didn't complete the job."

"Damn right you didn't. You took out the big guy, who wasn't a threat to us, and let Fritz' gunsel get away in the Studebaker."

"Couldn't be helped. They came out separately. That bothered me. When the big one finally came out, I gunned the motor and bore down on them, thinking I'd get them both, but the driver took off. I wasn't fast enough. That big six has a lot of guts."

"OK, Joe. I don't know how you could've done it differently. It's just a matter of time. We'll get them all."

Jill hadn't arrived, and Martino had never known her to be late. He was worried. He asked everyone if they'd seen or heard from her since the Oasis' early closing that morning. No one had, which alarmed him even more, because Jill was very gregarious, always talking on the phone to her friends. He called her apartment and didn't get an answer.

Martino took a waiter and went to Jill's apartment. To his dismay, the door was ajar, and complete destruction greeted him. Everything was broken or torn to shreds. Dresser drawers were emptied, and clothes were strewn about. Pictures were torn off walls and destroyed.

Jill lay across the bed, her blonde hair draped halfway to the floor, her eyes staring at the ceiling. Her normally fair face, because she was a true blonde, was already darkening in the hot apartment.

She'd been garroted, and the silk stocking was still around her neck. The coroner confirmed she'd been raped, too.

It became another unsolved murder. There was no reason to connect the gangland slaying of Gus Rhinehardt with the death of Martino's chanteuse.

Jennie accepted the news eagerly and completely. To do otherwise would've brought out a truth she couldn't live with—that the hiding of Kroger's money precipitated the death of a lovely woman Jennie adored.

Once Kroger's men left the apartment, Jennie was galvanized into action. She poured the dirty water in the diaper pail into the toilet bowl, then flushed the bowl. She partially refilled the pail and gingerly picked off each dirty diaper and dropped it in until she unearthed the belt. After cleaning it thoroughly, she placed it under the tub.

Finally, she luxuriated in a much-needed warm bath. When her hair dried, she combed it out—there was no time for curlers. She wove it into two braids and pinned them into a tiara.

Her mind wrestled with many thoughts. Slowly, she walked into the bedroom and stood naked before the full-length mirror on the closet door.

Joel was wrong—she wasn't ugly. She had a pretty face, and, although she wasn't a Gibson girl, no Gibson girl had a figure like hers. It all evened out.

She passed her hands lightly over her breasts. She wasn't buxom, but her modest breasts were delightfully sculpted. Her rib cage, large for a slender woman, enhanced an already fine figure. She had the legs of a professional dancer, and why not? Before her pregnancy, she was a habitue of the pavilion at Sea Breeze, where, in her opinion, there was no finer dancer.

When she reached for her cosmetic box for her lipstick, her mind stopped wandering, and she was brought up short. What kind of horrid creature was she? Gus was dead! The trauma of his burial lay ahead, and he deserved, if not undying love, respect and a grieving widow.

Jennie sat down heavily on the bed and cried. After the funeral, she could make plans for herself and Jasmin.

She knew at an early age that her life wouldn't be easy. She'd been released from the home at the age of eighteen, and she quickly learned that an orphan's progress was best served with a path-clearing machete.

Jennie was an optimist. From her bereavement, she knew, would come blessed sunshine. From her loss would come a widening of her horizons. She asked for nothing more.

First, she had to leave the neighborhood, which had once been respectable and now was vile and sordid. She would run and hide. Men like Kroger wouldn't take losses lightly. Although Jennie was absolved concerning the missing money belt, a mystery remained.

Martino was told to visit the widow to render his condolences on the death of her husband. Fritz Kroger felt Gus' internment would deplete what little money Jennie had. If unexplained expenditures showed, that meant she had money.

When Martino was ushered into the kitchen, he saw abject poverty. The kitchen was a disaster, with an unswept floor and pots and pans piled high in the sink. A child's cry grated on his nerves.

Jennie, her hair unkempt and eyes red with grief, wore a sweater that was much too large, tied at the waist with a length of rope. She spooned cold beans out of an open can.

The scene upset him, because it brought to mind his own miserable beginnings in a family with too many children and too little money. He was anxious to get away.

Jennie feared him. There were many stories about his past and the atrocities he allegedly committed. Looks were deceiving, because Martino looked like a benign grandfather.

"I knew Gus well," Martino began. "He was a good friend and valued employee. Fritz and I share your grief. We have the additional grief of losing Jill, who was like a daughter to me. She was once Fritz' girl. It's a cruel world, Mrs. Rhinehardt."

He reached for her and took her by the shoulders to hold her in a show of compassion. Jennie was terrified, because his coat touched Gus' sweater, which, in turn, touched her slip, and that covered the money belt.

Although weak-kneed, Jennie kept her composure and remained upright, holding onto the side of the table. Martino said a few more words and left.

The next morning, Jennie took a streetcar and went to a bank as far north as the streetcar would take her to deposit the money.

Chapter Three

It was spring, the season of rebirth and renewal when Jennie bought a house in a neighborhood in the city's extreme northeast corner. The hub of the neighborhood was the intersection of Goodman and Norton Streets. Norton Street was the edge of civilization—beyond that was the unincorporated village of Irondequoit. There, two eras and worlds met, and she could start a new life. With her husband interred, she'd bury with him all connection to the world of bootleggers.

The south side of Norton Street boasted social and cultural development. There was a speakeasy, not as elegant as the Oasis, but one with full service. There were also a barber shop, two grocery stores, and a trolley car terminal, which was nothing more than the end of a single set of tracks.

In addition to culture, there was religion in the form of a church in what had once been a farmhouse. Irondequoiters had no love for residents of Rochester. Perhaps they envied their indoor plumbing, piped-in water, paved streets and sidewalks, sewer system, and streetlights.

Goodman Street was paved with brick for three miles. For those three miles, there was one set of tracks. When the trolley car reached the terminus, the trolley, a long arm that received electric current from the overhead wire, was disengaged and its position reversed, so the car could make the return trip without turning. Three miles south of the terminus, the track blended into a double set.

In the other direction, Goodman Street, when it crossed into Irondequoit, dropped in social status and rank and became just another pathway without street signs. There, Goodman was a two-lane cow path with huge elms growing down the middle of the lanes. When it rained, Goodman became a quagmire. The mudstompers, a designation that fueled the animosity of both factions, trudged into civilization wearing boots and overshoes, discarding them outside the door of the corner grocery store. They retrieved their footwear on their return to the hinterlands.

Not all of Irondequoit was back country, however. Several miles north, closer to the lake, was a small community of *nouveau riche*, investors who made their fortunes riding the crests of the waves of Coolidge prosperity and the stock market. They huddled together, basking in their importance.

The house Jennie selected was on Goodman Street. Although it had a full acre of land, she vacillated. It was obviously the oldest house in the area, but the owners put on a new roof, new window frames, and renovated the interior. In the cellar, which had been a dirt floor for years, was a new furnace and concrete floor.

When Jennie finally gave the exasperated Mr. Blodget the go-ahead for the purchase, he nodded.

"The title search revealed it was built in 1830," he confided.

"Why, that's practically one hundred years old!" Jennie said.

"Only the red bricks, cellar walls, and heavy oak beams remain. Everything else is new. It had to be the only house in a heavily wooded area back then. Who knows? Maybe it was part of Frederick Douglass' underground railroad. You know, Mrs. Rhinehardt, that thought occurred to me when I first saw that old house."

Jennie was silent. She often complained that, despite being a bootlegger's wife, her life was drab, but there was nothing drab about owning a piece of Americana.

"It's not possible," she said, hoping Blodget would strengthen his conjecture.

"Why not? A nocturnal walk through the woods to Culver Road, a wagon ride north to Sea Breeze, then east on Lake Road to Pultneyville. From there, a boat to Canada and freedom."

"Why Pultneyville?"

"The town's history, showing it was the last station in that branch of the underground railroad, is well-documented. Besides, that's the only spot along the Lake Ontario shoreline where the water's deep enough for large boats."

What Blodget tossed out as a possibility, Jennie accepted as fact. For years, she entertained anyone who'd listen with tales of her station in the underground movement and how her house helped free the slaves.

Gathering Jasmin in her arms, she went outdoors to the back of the house. The child was only two, and it had been a long day. Blodget offered to carry him, but Jennie refused.

The entire yard was in bloom. She was paying $3,000 for the property, which she thought was high, but she had a full acre in which her son could romp.

Behind the old house was a barn the previous owners converted into a garage. Alongside the house were grapevines, and east of them was a row of pear trees. There was a peach tree behind the barn, too.

She turned toward the Realtor. "Mr. Blodget, I know I've made the right choice."

Jennie was safely tucked away from those who knew of her husband's associations, and her outlook improved. New confidence came over her. She felt God was on her side at last. Although she still lived in Rochester, being in a lightly populated outpost made her feel she had moved to a remote farm hamlet. To Jennie, the Goodman area was quaint.

There was a certain naïveté about the people. To be sure, signs of progress were there, too. There was a library available on Portland Avenue, if one cared to walk that distance, but there were no movie houses or taverns except the speakeasy on the corner. Other than two grocery stores and a barber shop, there was no commerce. The only drugstore was Hy Mandel's, on the corner of Norton and Portland, and, in the wintertime, that was a hard mile away. The trolley car, the neighborhood's lifeline, went south only.

The gang wars that were the focus of the city miraculously spared her new neighborhood. The only concern was the speakeasy. How it survived the violence around it was a mystery. Conjecture had it the owners were noncommittal in mob loyalty, succumbing to the pressure of whichever provider had the most muscle at any time.

It was a neighborhood to churchgoers, and that almost-bored tolerance seemed strange to Jennie. The large clapboard structure, unadorned with either cupolas or dormers, housed a bevy of courtesans of the second floor. Once a fine hotel, it now had no name. It was known simply as the *speak*, and it drew high rollers out on the town from great distances. Its anonymity made it an attractive watering hole.

The area was far from dry. It was fruit country, and most of the locals made their own wine and cider. It was the height of hypocrisy to judge those who concocted their own libations, when a woman had a husband who was a sot and a bootlegger.

Jennie knew the neighbors would've judged her corrupt if they knew where she got her money. She never wavered in her belief that the money was hers. Gus gave his life working for Kroger, and the money was Gus' legacy to her and Jasmin.

Except for the formalities on the dance floor, Jennie hadn't acquired the social graces that should've come to her naturally, having been raised among many. However, her home wasn't a finishing school.

She was at a loss as to how to approach her neighbors. Was there a certain protocol involved that the young must wait for their elders to make the first contact? Was there a social rule that said new arrivals wait for established residents to initiate the first meeting?

The old couple next door had an identical stretch of land. It was neat and orderly, and the vegetable garden was a farm to Jennie. It was obvious the crops were vital to their food supply, because the old man didn't work, and his slow gait indicated either poor health or an injury. The wife seemed robust enough, but she was home all the time.

Once, when Jennie went to retrieve her son, who had his face pressed against the fence, peering through the gaps between the boards, the old woman startled Jennie. She'd been kneeling against the fence, weeding her spice garden.

"Hello," she said. "I've meant to introduce myself since you moved in, but I hesitated, because I know how young people like to be left alone these days."

Jennie looked at her neighbor. There was a trace of an accent in her speech, but her English was good. "Oh, no. I've been dying to meet you. I've got no one, and I could use some adult conversation."

"Well, for starters, I'm Maria Martorana." She pointed to the old man some distance away. "That's my husband, Mateo."

"I'm Jennie Rhinehardt. This is my son, Jasmin."

"Oh, yes. My husband and I have been admiring him for some time. I've seen a lot of good-looking kids in my time, but I never saw a better-looking boy than your son. My husband's quite taken with him. We lost our son years ago, when he was three. Influenza took him, along with half the town. We came to America soon after."

"Were there no other children?"

"After my first child, I was unable to conceive."

"Oh. I'm sorry."

"Children would've been a comfort to us. He has no family, and all I have left is a brother in Italy who's forgotten he's got a sister."

"I'm an orphan, and now I'm a widow, too. Little Jasmin is all I have."

"He fits the name. Jasmin's a flower, isn't it?"

"At the time, I thought it was a great idea," Jennie said almost apologetically. "Actually, I named him after a musician I greatly admired."

Maria's eyebrows rose. "So what's in a name? In my country, I had a neighbor whose little boy was named Fiorello, which means *Little Flower.* Why, we even name our boys Angel and Saint."

"Why don't you and Mateo stop what you're doing and have tea with me?" Jennie offered.

"Mateo!" Maria called. *"Vieni qui!* Our new neighbor has invited us for tea."

In a short time, Maria came to love Jasmin as her own, but it was Mateo who took over completely. Soon, they were inseparable, and Jasmin spent more time on the Martorana grounds than his own. He followed Mateo everywhere. If the old man weeded his plants, Jasmin sat beside him, playing in the soil. When he watered, he let Jasmin hold the hose. Sometimes, Jasmin pulled up the wrong plant, but Mateo didn't care. To him, Jasmin could do no wrong.

They walked in the woods together, where he showed the child nature's wonders. When both became tired, the old man carried the child, enduring the pain of his legs and condition.

Weeks passed, and Jennie remained near home, fearing to venture out to seek employment. There were sufficient funds to sustain her and her child for a while, but that would end if she didn't find a job. Violence in the city escalated to the point where all citizens were on edge.

Kroger fought hard, but his rival, DeGeorge, had imported men from the Falls, led by the legendary mercenary, Strazzi, and his protegé, Joe Chink, who proved too fierce and cunning to defeat.

"Fritz," Gus once said, "is in over his head. Now we're the hunted."

While Jasmin slept in the morning, Jennie relaxed with a cup of coffee and the *Democrat* and *Chronicle.* The serenity of what had now become a bucolic life, although frustrating—it was two years since she last danced at Sea Breeze—was therapeutic. Whatever trauma remained from Gus' violent death faded with time.

If, however, someone delicately asked if she missed connubial bliss, Jennie would've been hard-pressed to reply. Certainly, Gus' frenetic and rapid-fire intrusions into her person, which she stoically endured, couldn't be construed as bliss. She knew very little about sexual matters. What little she knew came from Jill. The *chanteuse,* waxing philosophical in her basic but entertaining language, opined the union of man and woman was God's gift. If the union was right, it was the ultimate ecstasy.

Jennie felt bereft of that particular gift. She recalled many nights of sin—mental ones, not physical, but just as devastating—when she lay alongside Gus and fantasized. As Agnes Ayers, she enacted erotic scenes with the impetuous and hot-blooded Valentino, or, as Mae Murray, with a more subdued but equally passionate John Gilbert.

Things hadn't changed. She was still fantasizing.

Giving advice about someone else's child was always a delicate matter, but Mateo finally spoke up.

"Last week," he told Jennie, "me and the little one went to the corner for ice cream. A lady stopped me and said I had a beautiful granddaughter. See how long his hair is?"

"But it's beautiful," Maria protested.

"No matter. A boy is a boy, and a girl is a girl. I think he needs a boy's haircut."

Jennie pondered that. "Who knows how to cut hair? I don't."

"No," Mateo said. "No home job. A barber for the boy."

"Do you know him, Mateo? Is he good with children?"

"Mr. Belding is very good with children."

"How much does he charge?"

"Give him a quarter. He charges twenty cents, but sports, like Jasmin, tip their barbers, don't you, Jasmin?"

When they returned, and Mateo presented Jennie with her handsome son, Maria hugged and kissed him. Jennie simply patted his head. She knew her neighbors thought her cold. Perhaps that was because of her years of impersonal interaction at the home that made Jennie undemonstrative.

In the dark of the night and the privacy of her own home, Jennie's displays of affection were uninhibited. After bathing and drying Jasmin, she lay him on her bed and kissed his entire body. Then, before donning his pajamas, she removed her own clothes and lay on her bed in her step-ins. She set him on her breasts and reveled in the feel of him until he slept.

Jennie sat on one of her kitchen chairs, dealing with her loneliness, which was always more pronounced on the Sabbath, while Jasmin slept. She needed a job. In a place of employment, she might meet a gainfully employed man who could be husband, father, and lover. She had no illusions, though. With a child, she would have a hard time selling herself.

From her vantage point on the front porch, she watched the neighborhood come to life. Mateo and Maria came out of their homes dressed in their finest. They walked slowly, wearing, for the occasion, in addition to their fine clothes, a dignity befitting the Lord's day. She watched them walk along Goodman Street north to Norton, then turn right, walking toward the farmhouse turned church.

On schedule, Mr. and Mrs. Pittman came out of their house across the street with little Marvin between them. They, too, were going to church. The child was big for his age but was no older than Jasmin.

Her child stirred, and Jennie took her chair inside and fed him breakfast. She kept a vigil out the window until her old neighbors returned, then she and Jasmin went outdoors.

Mateo created an opening in the fence between the two properties. He built a gate that functioned simply enough for the youngster to open and close. Suddenly, Jasmin's horizons doubled. Mother and child walked through the gate.

"Who owns the old house where you and Mateo attend services?" she asked Maria.

"The diocese owns it, but it once belonged to Mrs. Hackman. She offered it to our bishop for use in the basement, and he, in turn, furnished Father Weideman."

"Can that be? Is it a proper church?"

"Wherever you put the tabernacle and have a priest, you have a church. You can have a proper mass even in a prison cell."

"Maria, you said the diocese owns the house now."

"Yes. Poor Mrs. Hackman. She died and left the house to the church. Then the bishop bought the lot next door."

"For expansion?"

"And parking space. This area will grow, and, sooner or later, we'll tear down the old house and build a fine church. What's your religion, Jennie?"

"I never knew my parents. I have no idea which religion I was born into."

"How about your husband, God rest his soul?"

"He never went to church that I know of. We were married by a justice of the peace."

"With a name like Rhinehardt, he could've been Lutheran."

"We'll never know. Frankly, I don't care."

"Weren't you exposed to religion?"

"At the home we had nondenominational services."

"Jennie, come with us next Sunday."

Jennie paused as if considering that, but it was exactly the invitation she'd been hoping for.

The congregation poured out of the old building and milled about the yard. Jennie appreciated Mateo's wisdom in suggesting a regular haircut for Jasmin. America was a land of millions of Jackie Coogans wearing bangs. Jasmin was the cynosure of all eyes.

There were many introductions. Jennie made no effort to remember names—she was interested in only one introduction. Her eyes followed a large woman who was obviously a leader, carrying an air of authority. Maria perceived Jennie's interest.

"That's Mrs. Belding, the president of the sodality," Maria whispered.

"The barber's wife?"

"Yes." She took Jennie to meet Ida Belding. "Ida, I'd like you to meet my neighbor, Jennie Rhinehardt."

"Mrs. Rhinehardt, how nice to meet you. The child's a doll. My husband was right. He certainly is good-looking. He was reluctant to clip his long hair."

"Are your children here, Mrs. Belding?" Jennie asked.

"No, no children. When I learned I couldn't have them, I threw myself into my work."

"Ida's a forewoman at the button factory," Maria explained. "Bossing men around is quite an accomplishment for a woman."

"The fact that I worked there since I was a little girl didn't hurt, either," Ida explained. "Mrs. Rhinehardt, I see you're in mourning. Did your husband pass away?"

"Gus died a short time ago. I was left with his child. I must get over my grief and continue. Gus' insurance money won't last forever. I must find employment before long."

"You poor child. When you're ready, see me. I may be able to help."

Jennie hated her black dress and stockings. She couldn't abide her self-imposed exile. She missed movies, especially since Rudy was back making them, but all she could do was read about them in the papers and magazines.

She missed Sea Breeze and its dance pavilion. That galled her more than any other deprivation. She kept abreast of music through her radio and records, but she feared she was missing out on all the new dance steps.

Mrs. Koven didn't attend the neighborhood church, which was why Jennie never met her. She hadn't enjoyed the company of young people since her carefree dancing days, which seemed a lifetime ago. Mr. and Mrs. Pittman, across the street, were much closer to her age than the Martoranas, but they were argumentative, which grated on her. She heard them bickering constantly.

Jennie stood on no ceremony and paid Dora Koven a visit.

"I'm Jennie Rhinehardt," she said. "This is Jasmin."

"I've wanted to meet you for some time," Dora replied, "but women in mourning seem to have a *Keep-off-the-Grass* sign on them. I'm Dora, and this is Tommy. This," she added proudly, "is my husband, Abel."

"Why, that dates to the Garden of Eden."

"Not really," he corrected. "It's short for Abelard. I could've gone the other way and become Lard."

Jennie laughed, feeling good about her newfound friends. Dora was a looker, with blonde hair, while Abel was slender as a reed, with a narrow face, hawk nose, and small chin above his ascot. Despite that, he presented an attractive appearance. He was as friendly as a pup and as bright as a silver dollar. The ascot was an affectation adopted from Clive Brook, the suave English actor, but he restricted it to his home while he wore pajamas and a robe.

Soon, the two women started trading visits. Jennie flattered them with her rapt attention to discourses on music—Abel was a fine saxophone player.

They sat in Jennie's parlor listening to some Jolson records when Abel left the room and came back with another record he wanted Jennie to hear.

"This is one of my most prized possessions," he explained. "It's King Oliver's *Chimes Blues.*"

"What makes it so special?" she asked.

"Two reasons. I know of no other recording that explains better what New Orleans jazz is about, and secondly, this music is going downhill. I'm hanging onto this one."

"That's hard to believe. It's all I hear on the air."

"True, but white bands are now making the money."

"Why should that be?" Jennie asked. "If you're good, you're good, regardless of color."

Dora nodded. "It's white patrons who pay, and they want music to dance and romance to. Henderson knows what the patrons want, great sound and show tunes like *How Come You Do Me Like You Do?*, *I'll See You in my Dreams,* and *Who?*"

Abel set the record on the turntable. "Listen to this intro. Oliver used it first, and now we all do it. Oliver and Armstrong start with two bars on their horns, followed by two bars of full ensemble."

The women were silent as they listened to the masters play.

"My, they *are* good!" Jennie exclaimed.

"That's Lil Hardin's chimes," Abel said softly. "Listen to Dodd on the wood block. Isn't it the cats?" His mouth moved, as he mentally played along on sax. "Notice Oliver's horn is muted, and Armstrong's isn't. That's jazz! Too bad times change. That's why Armstrong went with Henderson."

They sat in silence after the record finished. Finally, Abel stood and carefully slipped the record into its jacket.

"And I thought Jazzman Caruthers was good," Jennie sighed.

"What do you know about Jazzman?" Abel was stunned. "He never made a record."

"Oh, I listened to him often," Jennie blurted, then stopped, horrified. What had she just divulged? Her friends were silent, staring at the young woman in black in a new way.

"Was Gus a man of means?" Abel asked cautiously.

"What do you mean?"

"I can't afford to belly up to the bar, let alone sit at a table with Dora at the Oasis. Besides, I don't know Joe."

"Joe?" Dora asked. "Who's Joe?"

"You know. The same Joe in the password at the door of all speaks. You can't get in unless Joe sent you."

The women laughed.

"Yes, Gus was well-heeled," Jennie lied. Kroger's name throughout Monroe County was synonymous with corruption. Jennie would die if her neighbors learned Gus had been one of Kroger's soldiers. "He took me there often. You probably have wondered about my son's name. I admired Jazzman Caruthers, but I couldn't call my boy Jazzman, so I named him Jasmin."

"There's an awful lot about you, Jennie Rhinehardt," Dora said, "that I'm going to find out."

Chapter Four

Jennie's young neighbors seemed the ideal couple. She was happy for Dora, but she felt a tinge of envy slip past her guard when the two showed their affection for each other. Then Jennie felt sorry for herself. Why couldn't someone like Abel come along and sweep her off her feet?

She went to mass every Sunday, which was a much-needed diversion. There was also the possibility of finding a fine prospect for a meaningful relationship that would lead to marriage. Her prospects, however, were slim.

Straight from the cabarets of New York, Sophie Tucker lamented in one song, "a good man is hard to find." Certainly, there was a man who'd make Jennie a complete woman, despite her black stockings and black dress. In the dark of night, she sat Jasmin on her knee and discussed the matter with him even after he fell asleep.

Suddenly, there was a man sitting in the front pew every Sunday who intrigued her. He was tall and lanky, with a penchant for Harris tweeds that were too large. Occasionally, their eyes met, but she learned nothing from that. Always, after mass, he stood on the church grounds and lit his pipe. He looked like a country squire straight from the movies.

Week after week, all Jennie did was gaze at him from a distance. In her mind, however, she concocted all sorts of situations where they'd find each other.

Once, she carelessly asked Maria about him. Maria looked at Mateo, then said, "His name is Peter Ellers. He's Mrs. Pittman's brother."

That frightened Jennie.

"He's not married," Maria added.

What had she done? Jennie prayed the old couple wouldn't try to play Cupid. It was too soon. She was still in mourning.

It was early evening when Jennie heard a knock at her door. She opened it and saw Mrs. Pittman, and she almost gasped. She didn't know the woman, although they exchanged pleasantries from across the street.

"Jennie, do you play euchre?" The familiarity surprised Jennie.

"I've played it." She almost added that it was a tavern game, and her late husband was a tavern person.

"My husband, my brother, Pete, and I are tired of playing cut-throat euchre. We're dying for some real competition. Come across the street. I baked a pie."

Jennie thought about it, fighting the excitement rising in her. Mrs. Pittman accompanied her to the Martoranas, where they left Jasmin, then Mrs. Pittman put her arm around Jennie's shoulders, and they crossed the street like old friends.

Peter Ellers was the ultimate extrovert. His lively chatter put Jennie at ease. She enjoyed card games, and it was obvious from the start that her hosts were no match for Jennie and Peter. Jennie watched him closely. He seemed the perfect prospect.

As the evening wore on, however, little annoyances cropped up. The air was soon foul with tobacco smoke. Constant interruptions came in the game as Peter filled, tamped, and lit his pipe.

"Coffee's ready," Mrs. Pittman declared, kicking her husband under the table. "Come help me with the pie."

Ellers moved to the seat beside Jennie. Up close, she saw the lines of his face indicated he was older than she thought. His teeth were stained from constant smoking, and the smell of tobacco emanated from him.

Another Gus, she thought bitterly of the nausea of Gus' stench of stale beer when she'd been pregnant.

She listened to Peter talk about a fishing trip to Seneca Lake.

After the light repast and the table had been cleared, Jennie announced she was heading home. She thanked her hosts for a pleasant evening.

Peter leaped from his chair to accompany her across the street—not what she wanted. If he attempted to kiss her good night under the glaring light of the Martorana front porch while she still wore widow's black it would blight her reputation.

When they reached the old couple's house, Jennie ran quickly on the porch steps, leaving Peter standing on the walk. Without knocking, she opened the door, entered, and called softly, "Good night, Mr. Ellers."

Then she shut the door.

Tommy spoke in two- or three-word sentences, as did Marve Pittman across the street. Although Jasmin made a few sounds, none could be construed as speech. To have a beautiful child who was a slow learner would be a crowning blow to Jennie. She prayed her son be spared the failings of his parents.

She confided her fears to Maria and Mateo, and both rejected them emphatically. Children set their own pace when learning to talk, and that had little to do with intelligence. Still, the old couple didn't know Jasmin learned to walk long after his first birthday.

Jasmin soon proved them wrong, dismissing all doubts concerning his ability to speak. Distinctly and with a fine, resonant voice he would carry into adulthood, he asked Maria to, "Bake me a boy."

Maria hugged and kissed him, then hurried next door to Jennie's house, followed by Mateo, who also heard the boy's request. They overwhelmed him with attention.

Maria baked a little boy with outstretched arms. He wore a dunce cap, and she used foil for buttons and facial features.

Jennie visited the Kovens to ask Dora to go with her to the millinery near the bank. She wanted to discard her black clothing for Jasmin's special party. Dora was clipping Abel's hair, while Tommy sat on his father's knee.

"Climb upon my knee, Sonny Boy," Abel sang in a bad imitation of Al Jolson. He saw Jennie and stopped. "I know. It's a bad number. Cloying."

"I kind of like it," Dora said between snips of the shears.

"You would. You probably think *jada, jada, jada, jada, jing, jing, jing,* the height of sophistication."

Dora finished, and she chased father and son from the room. Abel carefully wrapped his ascot around his thin neck.

"Sit down," Dora commanded Jennie. "Look at your hair. It's a rat's nest. Jennie, when was the last time you did anything with your hair?"

"I combed it this morning."

"You're getting it cut right now."

When Dora finished, she said, "I missed my calling. That's a damn good job."

"Why, Dora, you made me look like Clara Bow!" By virtue of a series of provocative roles the past year, the It Girl of the silver screen had supplanted the naughty Colleen Moore as the personification of the modern flapper.

The notion of Jennie a flapper made Dora smile.

Jennie finally shed her mourning clothes. She was free after one year of mourning. There were those who said one year wasn't enough, but they could go to hell. She could wear colors that gladdened her heart again, sing songs that lifted her spirits, and resume dancing—the cruelest of her disenfranchisements.

Perhaps in defiance, she remained clothed only in panties and chemise. Taking Jasmin's hand, she led him to the bedroom, smiling at the reflection in the full-length mirror. Her body was her vanity, her son her pride. She donned a bright print dress and then dressed Jasmin in a sailor suit again. There was something about the child that was most captivating as a sailor.

Invited to the party were Tommy and Marve, Jimmy Logan and Sam Trippett from Norton Street, Antoinette Dubois from Yates Street, and little Carrie Evans from the house directly behind the Martoranas.

At the last minute, Jennie also invited Guy Lovell, whose family moved into the house beside the kovens just that morning. Guy was a bright child with lively eyes who seemed to appraise everything and everyone. He was accompanied by two older sisters. When the girls were invited to stay and help, they eagerly accepted.

The children were left to their own devices. They screamed and sometimes struck each other, establishing patterns of behavior that would remain for years.

The Rochester Button Company was housed in a large, two-story block building near the armory, with its cannon facing the railroad tracks. Just inside the gate was a guardhouse. Jennie said she had an appointment with the plant manager.

While she waited for an escort to lead her to G. T. Percell, her attention was drawn to the vast parking lot in back. A spirited crowd gathered in one corner, where a platform had just been erected.

G. T. Percell was a robust, heavy-jowled man with gray hair cut short in the Prussian style. Despite his size, he presented a neat appearance. His eyes followed Jennie in the room with obvious amusement.

"Sit down, young lady."

Jennie sat opposite him, experiencing the nervousness of all job interviews.

"I should save time and have one of the girls help with your application, then tell you to start work Monday."

"Oh?" Jennie was puzzled.

"Yes. You don't think I could face Mrs. Belding if I didn't give you a job, do you? Know what she's doing now? She's soliciting money, food, clothing, and medical supplies for the victims of the hurricane in Florida and Alabama."

"I read about that. The area was buffeted by the elements for eleven days."

"Two hundred forty-three people died, and far more were injured. Thousands lost their homes. Now they've got a full-blown epidemic. We give Ida a lot of latitude. She means a lot to us here. We remember she earned us a letter of thanks during the war from President Wilson for all the liberty bonds she browbeat us into buying."

He left his desk and told Jennie to fill out the application. When he returned, she was done.

"Mrs. Rhinehardt, you start Monday in packaging. You'll work with other young women."

Mrs. Belding left moments before Jennie arrived at the Martoranas. Maria waited for Jennie to speak. Ida had informed them Jennie was hired at the factory, and they knew what Jennie wanted.

"Jennie," Maria blurted, unable to wait any longer, "we'd be happy to take care of Jasmin when you start work Monday."

"How'd you know?" Jennie gasped.

"Mrs. Belding told us."

Jennie was upset and wondered why Ida would rush over with such news. "That was fast. I just got back from the interview."

"She didn't come here just for that. She asked me to help Father Weideman line up the men of the Holy Name Society for the rummage sale Sunday, after the twelve-o'clock mass. The sale will be in the church parking lot."

Jennie felt mollified. "Let me guess. It's to help the victims of the hurricane. I know it's an imposition to ask you to care for Jasmin, but desperation makes me bold."

"Don't say that. I'll be caring for my grandson."

"You're a dear." Jennie kissed the older woman's cheek. "I'll pay you something each week."

"No need for that," Mateo said. "I'd take that as an insult."

Maria opened her mouth, but Jennie said, "It has to be that way, or I'll make other arrangements."

"Well, in that case..." Maria looked at her husband.

"I've given this some thought. You can't deny you could use some financial help. It won't be much, but I'll give you something every week. It might vary, because I can only afford to offer ten percent of my income."

"That's too much." Mateo shook his head.

"I wish it was. I'm not getting much to start."

Dora had been married for five years, and she and Abel were still very much in love. He was a good provider. Days, he worked at the shoe factory. Nights, he played sax at various affairs. Sometimes, when he played at an elegant affair, Dora accompanied him. Several times, they invited Jennie, too, but she begged off each time, fearing a chance meeting with some of Gus' old associates. She wondered if anyone ever solved the mystery of the missing money belt and was looking for her.

"You're going to refuse again, I know, but Abel says to ask, anyway," Dora said. "He's playing Saturday night at the ritzy wedding reception at the Sagamore Hotel. Come on. Break out of your cocoon and come."

Abel walked in. "No fooling, Jennie. It'll be a doozy. I'll play with some really good musicians, and we'll make a fine sound. There's Rabbi on the horn, Frankie Dell on sax, and I'll be on clarinet. We picked up Hank Gordon on bass and Pippy Nardello on drums. If I may say so, we're among the best of the local talent. Rabbi has picked up a couple of out-of-town boys, a sharp ivories man from Syracuse and a great trombonist from Chicago."

Jennie craved the sound of a live band, and the urge to dance to a good beat was so strong, she had trouble saying no. The smart thing would be to refuse once again, but the urge overwhelmed her.

She thought hard. The reception was private, and the clientele at the Sagamore would be highbrow—not the kind of place to meet any of Gus' associates.

"What time do we leave?"

They were startled and looked at each other in silence.

"After the Martoranas have watched Jasmin all week, dare I ask them to ride herd on him again?" Jennie wondered.

"Why not? Wait," Dora said. "My mother's coming to stay the weekend. She can handle both boys."

"Are you sure?"

"I'm sure. That's one well-mannered little boy you've got."

The Sagamore was an old hotel, but it stood off Main Street on East Avenue like an old dowager, a landmark for Rochester society. The reception, by invitation only, was catered. The women walked in with the band, and there was no questioning their right to be there.

When the band started playing, Jennie was filled with almost uncontrollable excitement. Abel was right. It was a great sound. They started with a slow ballad, a record Jennie owned called *Moonlight and Roses*. It was the right day to end the ennui of her existence.

Dora danced with an usher, but no one invited Jennie to dance. Dora and her partner went to the center of the dance floor and danced blithely along. With the fingers of her free hand, Dora waved to Abel, and he winked back.

Abel's band lost no time playing the year's blockbuster hit—*Black Bottom*. Jennie was ready and jiggled to the beat like a Model T after it was cranked. She could've been ignored, because the guests were there for a wedding reception and weren't aficionados of that dance. Only three couples tried it, because Rochester was slow to accept it—the city was still mastering the Charleston.

A lithe young man saw the pretty woman with lovely legs and asked her to dance. Jennie had a natural aptitude for it and was endowed with choreographic skills. She thought the music deserved more than she'd seen at the movie at the Gaiety once.

Mixing her movements with artistry, she did side turns, stamps, skating glides, skips, and leaps. She was a whirling dervish, and, when she went into a rapid-fire slapping of both halves of her derriere, a gasp swept the hall.

Then the song ended, and there was applause and whistles. Jennie just showed Rochester how the Black Bottom was supposed to be done.

Abel was watching in amazement and turned to the drummer. "Jesus Christ!"

"That broad can really dance," the drummer said.

"That's no broad, Pip. She's my neighbor and a nice lady."

"Sorry. Hey! I remember her!"

"You do?"

"Yeah, maybe four years ago I played with Sax Smith at the Breeze Pavilion. She was a regular."

"Who was she before she moved next door to me?" Abel asked above the din.

"She lives next door? I don't know her past, but she's probably the best dancer in town."

"She sure ain't the mousy widow who moved into our rustic neighborhood."

"Mousy? You gotta be kidding."

The young man refused to release his find. To Jennie's delight he asked her to dance all night, and they did many dances, including the waltz, the two-step, the fox-trot, and the polka.

They were waiting at the streetcar stop. Dora had been distant all evening, and Abel, too, was quiet. That bothered Jennie.

"Anything wrong, Dora?" Jennie asked.

"You haven't been honest with us. Who are you?" Dora asked.

"What kind of question is that? I haven't deceived you. I'm what I always was, Jennie Rhinehardt."

"Are you someone we should know?"

Jennie became fearful. Had she made a mistake? Was there someone at the wedding who recognized her from her past?

The streetcar arrived before she could answer. All three walked to the end of the bus, and Jennie sat between them. She knew she had to pick up the conversation.

"Believe me, Dora, I'm plain Jennie."

Dora was silent.

"Jennie," Abel asked, "have you ever been on the Keith Circuit?"

"Me, in vaudeville? You must be kidding." She felt relieved that her life with Gus wasn't in question. "I'm beginning to understand what this is all about. Look, Abel, music is your life. I'm not a good homemaker, like Dora, or talented in music, like you, or smart like Mrs. Belding. My passion is dancing. The girls at Woolworth's taught me when I worked there. I certainly would've told you about it if I thought it was important."

By nature, DeGeorge wasn't a violent man. He hadn't anticipated the carnage his entry into the world of crime precipitated. He wasn't above bending the law when necessary, which was what he thought bootlegging was about.

The reality of bootlegging shocked him. He was willing to live and let live, to share the booty. Fritz Kroger declared all-out war.

There were times when the mounting casualties on both sides sickened him. If it were possible, he would've pulled up stakes and moved on, but his cohorts, appetites whetted by the fortunes their early returns presaged, wouldn't allow it. Of his partners, those elected to uphold and enforce the law were the most voracious.

He sat across from Strazzi, and his deep resentment of that terrifying man threatened to burst from him. They never had conversation. Strazzi simply lectured him, explaining, in simple terms, the realities of each day. DeGeorge felt like a child in the principal's office.

"Well Strazzi," DeGeorge began, fighting down a compulsion to address him as Mr. Strazzi. DeGeorge was the boss, not Strazzi. "We've won the battle. The committee met last night, and your fee for the job you did for us is ready. You've whittled Kroger down to where he's no longer a threat. We can carry on from here."

"Danny, Danny, Danny," Strazzi said in a patronizing tone that set DeGeorge's teeth on edge. "In this battle, there's no finish until there's a knockout. Split decisions come back to haunt you."

"You've taught us enough that our own people can keep Kroger under control."

"Trust me, Danny. I know people. Kroger's tough. My reputation's on the line. I don't want to return after he's gathered a new army. You won't sleep nights if you let him live. Have patience. I'll nail him soon. Haven't I done all I promised?"

"I don't have the Oasis," DeGeorge said petulantly.

"I see," Strazzi said in amusement. "The Oasis is the missing jewel in your crown as king of the hill? I can get you that anytime, but I'm keeping that avenue open. That's the link between Kroger and Martino. I remember Martino when he was younger, and he was one tough bastard. I'll have to nail him, too."

Chapter Five

Fritz Kroger's back was to the wall. He was a realist and fatalist. His minions scurried for cover, and so savage had the fighting become, that despite the carnage chronicled almost daily in both city newspapers, the readers were losing much of their initial shock.

He was willing to accept whatever fate had in store, but he had a slim chance. Just as Strazzi knew that it wasn't over until Kroger was dead, Kroger knew eliminating Strazzi would even the odds considerably. That would take some doing. David slaying Goliath was a fluke.

There was chaos in city hall, where public servants trusted no one. It was common knowledge that there were payoffs, bribes, and outright gifts, but from whom, to whom, and to what purpose? The situation was much the same with the police.

At every new atrocity committed by beasts on both sides, Jennie cringed. She was involved, even at a distance.

Fritz Kroger knew a lot about many things. He was a self-educated man and a voracious reader. History was his passion. He delved into religion occasionally, too, but it was almost too much to believe that he read the Bible, too, because it gave him a spiritual rush.

He enjoyed the ancient pageantry and exciting drama, now being recreated in movies, reliving the glories and foibles of mortals thousands of centuries before those of the present day, seeing a similarity in their weaknesses and strengths.

His organization, once extensive, was reduced to a small group of men hiding from their enemies. It wasn't loyalty that kept them together—there was more risk running than staying together.

Kroger was aware that Strazzi had a dossier on him that read like a biography. Both men played a deadly game of hide-and-seek.

There was grumbling among his men. Some couldn't understand why he was making a last-ditch stand. They could organize a convoy and slip out of the city in the dead of night.

Those who knew Kroger best understood. He couldn't live with the colossal failure that loomed almost as a foregone conclusion. He'd make a heroic stand, like Colonel William Barrett Travis at the Alamo. He vowed he wasn't through yet. He refused to continue fighting in the trenches, exchanging gunfire. His men would all become like Sergeant York, sniping at the enemy and picking them off one by one. Faced with no other choice, the others endorsed his plan.

Conrad, the maverick, who, with Joel, went to Jennie's apartment on his own initiative the night Gus died, was a sycophant, a bootlicker who repelled Kroger. Overnight, however, he became a favorite. He killed Sheik Loubet, a dapper killer with an angelic face and mad-dog disposition.

The fight crowd was filing out of Convention Hall, and Loubet, one of Strazzi's stalwarts, made a bundle betting on the main event. From across the boulevard and through a milling crowd, Conrad fired his rifle, shooting Sheik above the right ear.

It was a morale booster, and Kroger made plans for another, more dramatic, execution. For that, he enlisted Martino's aid. The plan evolved from a slender lead provided by an unlikely source. A habitue of the Oasis, who was a teller at the Rochester Community bank, mentioned, in idle conversation, of a small man in a green fedora who came into the bank every Friday like clockwork. He deposited a substantial amount to a bank account in his and his wife's names, with a Lewiston address. Lewiston was a suburb of Niagara Falls and Strazzi's hometown.

A quick check among the Kroger men established that a man of that description was among Strazzi's goons.

"It's your turn at bat," Kroger told Martino. "Can you still handle a shiv?"

"It's like riding a bike. You never forget."

"You get him when he comes out. Where you plan to hit him?"

"That depends. I like to go for the belly. My H. G. Long has a seven-inch blade, but I understand this guy's short. I don't like to enter at an angle, so I'll go for the heart. To get the stomach, I'd have to penetrate five inches, but the heart's only three and a half."

"You'll have trouble if you strike bone." No stranger to stilettos, he wasn't the knife man his partner was.

"I won't miss. The guy will lose consciousness instantly, and he's dead in three seconds."

The stage was set. Martino leaned against the bank wall, ostensibly reading the early edition of the afternoon paper. The big clock overhead was a landmark, a meeting place for the city. Clinton and Main was the hub, the most active intersection, in town. The bank was on the southeast corner, but it faced the intersection at an angle.

Martino was assured his prey was a punctual man, but two o'clock came and went without him. That bothered Martino. Then he saw his target.

He had spent too much time at the corner already, so he disobeyed Kroger and approached the man before he entered the bank. He slipped the knife through the newspaper firmly and accurately. The victim's mouth snapped open soundlessly, then he fell.

Martino was too frail to hold him, but Conrad materialized out of nowhere and kept the body erect as he withdrew the weapon and wrapped it in the newspaper. Together, they propelled the little man to the side of the building and set him there.

Joel rounded the corner in Kroger's Studebaker and whistled. "Get in!"

The car door opened, and Martino, spry for a man of his years, leaped in with Conrad right behind him.

Strazzi was humiliated. Both hits were headline news. It galled him that two members of his elite band were singled out for execution. If he'd been terrifying before, he became maniacal. Striking from ambush wouldn't affect the outcome of the war, but Kroger could prolong it for a long time.

He studied Kroger's dossier long and hard. Fritz covered his tracks well. The villa in Penfield was empty, but for an old couple left as caretakers. His barber hadn't seen him for a while, and no Kroger soldier was seen in his usual eating places. The brewery was shut down, and the Oasis was padlocked.

Kroger had disappeared. It was time to think. Somehow, he had to draw Fritz out.

Kroger was an avid reader, but the sentries at every library and bookstore came up empty, as did those watching picture shows. Kroger collected guns, too, but he had all the ones he wanted. His Luger collection was complete, with one from every issue down to the first. Strazzi despaired. How would he get that wily bastard out of hiding?

Then one day, Strazzi, the master of destruction, went through his first agony of self-doubt. Aimlessly turning the pages of the newspaper, he came across an ad offering a small curio shop for sale. He was amused. The poor slob had a white elephant on his hands, nothing to interest Strazzi.

When he saw it in the paper again, however, then again on the third day, an idea struggled to emerge. Kroger was an early riser, too, and read the paper at breakfast. It was a long shot, and Strazzi kept his speculations to himself, but he decided to try it. He bought the curio shop.

Then he disappeared, telling no one where he went. Joe Chink took over operations in his absence. Strazzi scoured the countryside, buying expended artillery shells from the French, German, and British forces. Kroger didn't need those, nor did he have any use for rifles, but Strazzi bought a Dandeteau 6.5 and a single-shot rolling block, both obsolete but put into action by the French at the beginning of the war, making them rare.

For handguns, he selected a 7.65 Biretta pistol from 1915, and the Webley-Foster automatic revolver, along with some Lugers.

Then he advertised a close-out sale. Each day, he offered a special, but Kroger, who read the ads with amusement, had no interest in the offerings. Strazzi counted on that. He went to Niagara Falls and met an old crony, a machinist who owed him a favor.

"I need a pearl-handled Luger," Strazzi said.

"Never heard or seen one."

"What do they use?"

"Bone, I guess."

"No. It's gotta be creamy white."

"I could use ivory, Straz. You gonna send me on safari for some?"

"Spike, Spike, Spike. What does a piano player do when he sits down to play?"

"I don't know. What does he do?"

"He tickles the ivories."

"I get it! I'll see the Kimball people in Buffalo first thing tomorrow. I'll jazz up the butt of a Luger on my lathe."

When Strazzi returned to Rochester, he brought back an ivory-handled Luger, a thing of beauty.

Kroger slouched over his coffee as he read the ad in the morning paper. An ivory-handled Luger from a dead German officer was being offered.

He bolted upright, spilling his coffee and called on his two bodyguards.

"Get the car, Boys. We're going shopping."

"Kind of early for shopping," one said.

"I want to get there first, before the city's awake. If that store's not open, we break in."

Strazzi's men were in place. Joe Chink was at the newsstand fifty feet from the curio shop. Across the street were two seasoned killers in a horse-drawn milk wagon. Strazzi sat in his car, rearview mirror focused on the shop.

Waiting was painful. So much rode on that sting. He had unanswered questions that plagued him. Did Kroger read the ads? Did he want the Luger badly enough to venture out to get it? Suppose he came later in the day?

Suddenly, Strazzi's heart sang. Through the mirror, he saw Kroger's Studebaker stop before the shop, and Fritz followed two burly henchmen out of the car. Strazzi's orders were to get them on the way out of the shop. His man in the shop was to be a shopkeeper, nothing more.

They were in the shop a short time, but, to Strazzi, it felt like eternity. Then they came out with Kroger in the middle, all three admiring his new purchase.

Joe Chink pulled a Tommy gun out from under a newspaper and sprinted up the steps. His initial burst obliterated Kroger's face. The two men in the milk truck fired a second later, but it all sounded simultaneous to Strazzi. The victims never reached for their guns.

Strazzi strolled to the shop, picked up the ivory-handled Luger, wiped it, and pocketed it. It was a pretty piece.

The headlines on the front page shocked Jennie. Gus had been prophetic after all. The war of attrition was won by the DeGeorge faction with unprecedented savagery in the city's history. All the souls she knew through Gus were dead. A few she didn't know managed to escape, leaving her with a constant source of apprehension.

She saw the pictures of Conrad and Joel and cried because the pictures of their bullet-ridden bodies in the quarry on Ridge Road brought back all the gruesome details of Gus' slaying. There was a picture of Kroger's body and his bodyguards, who'd been killed in the alcove of a small curio shop, where Kroger, the gun collector, bought a rare, ivory-handled Luger. A search of the area failed to locate the weapon.

Jennie understood the state of Gus' mind when he told her about the money belt around his waist as he lay dying. He knew Armageddon was at hand, and, whatever Fritz' destiny, the boss wouldn't need the money.

Martino, Kroger's partner and owner of the Oasis, was missing. The Oasis was still padlocked shut. Some said he couldn't be found, because his body lay at the bottom of Irondequoit Bay. Inexplicably, Jennie felt a trivial concern intrude—she'd never hear Jazzman Caruthers' horn again.

Danny DeGeorge, in gratitude, gave Strazzi a king's ransom. He took it to Chicago and was never heard from again. Joe Chink returned to Niagara Falls, where he built his own empire. He took with him a gift from Strazzi—an ivory-handled Luger.

The shedding of mourning clothes should've announced Jennie's availability, but there was no rush of swains vying for her affections. She became resigned to the fact that a new husband wouldn't come from the parish or neighborhood. There were sports who made discreet and immoral overtures, offering to make the widow merry, but she put them in their place with practiced sarcasm.

The factory was different. Over one hundred men worked there of all ages, sizes, and shapes. Surely, from many could come one who would fulfill her as a woman.

The packaging department was mostly women, who were considered more dexterous than men. Often, in a warm thaw, with the thermostat failing to guide the boiler, the room became unbearably hot. Then women rolled up their sleeves, unbuttoned a button or two to expose some cleavage, and pulled their skirts above their knees to capture a breeze. Suddenly, the traffic of male workers increased dramatically, every destination charted by way of the packaging department.

It became a game to which both sides looked forward. It was like a public market, with all the wares on display, and many trysts began that way.

Jennie observed the game between the sexes and studied the body language of the women, noting their stratagems. She listened to the seemingly aimless chatter between men and women, which was, in reality, a wooing, accompanied by acceptance or rejection.

At first, it seemed demeaning and crass, then she decided that, if that was what it took to get a man, she'd learn the rules.

At the time clock, she was approached by several men. Research on them wasn't necessary, because Ida Belding was always with her at punch-in and punch-out time. She knew all the employees, and, each time a worker approached, she shook her head slightly at Jennie.

Ida wanted what was best for Jennie. They'd become close, more than fellow workers, sodality sisters, or neighbors. Ida brought Jennie into the factory, and she protected her. A good husband would be a godsend, but Ida steered Jennie away from wrong choices.

Jennie was engrossed in securing a package when she heard voices start buzzing like bees in a hive.

"It's Travis Taylor!" the woman sharing her table whispered.

"What's that?" Jennie asked.

"It's a him. He's the cutest guy in the whole damn place. He's in the doorway. Oh, my! I think he's looking at me!"

Jennie looked behind her to the doorway. Travis Taylor was casual, almost bored, as he surveyed the women. Jennie had to admit he was special. He was tall, with a dazzling smile and classic nose. His hair was a mat of tight curls, and one stray curl fell to his forehead, giving him a rakish look.

He didn't return the rest of the week, and the women became resigned to the fact that there wasn't anyone among them who interested him. Travis was a hard man to forget. Jennie realized even the thought of him moved her.

To everyone's surprise, however, he returned the following week. He entered the large room and walked directly to Jennie, introducing himself before walking out. Jennie was ecstatic. She finally had something to dream and fantasize about.

Travis was in no hurry. He paid periodic visits to Jennie, much to the combined chagrin of the other women. When he put his hand on her shoulder the first time, Jennie froze. The next day, he put both hands on her shoulders. Before the week was out, he kneaded the muscles in her shoulders. Every time he touched her, she felt a thrill.

Jennie told Ida of the development of her relationship with Travis, but Ida had known from the beginning. She couldn't discourage it. Except that he was a favorite among the ladies, there was nothing negative she could say about him.

One Thursday, Travis made a date with Jennie to take her out to dinner Saturday night, then to the movies. The Gaiety was showing *Seventh Heaven.* Jennie told Dora and Abel about it, and they were happy for her. The old couple, when Jennie asked them to baby-sit Jasmin, were also pleased. She slept very little that night.

Friday, Ida Belding called Jennie out into the hall to talk privately.

"You know I know just about everything that goes on around here," Ida said.

"What are you getting at?"

"I hear things I'm not supposed to hear."

"Please, Ida. What are you trying to say?"

"I heard Travis Taylor bragging in the dye room about what he intended to do to you."

Jennie paled. "What did he say?"

"Something about taking you to bed."

Jennie's eyes narrowed, and her jaw tightened. It was hard to contain her rage. "What were his exact words?"

"I can't remember."

"Yes, you can. Out with it."

"He said he was going to bang you in your bed until your eyes turned cherry red. Colorful language, I must say."

"Colorful, shit! I'll kill the bastard!" Jennie ran toward the dye room.

"Hold on, Jennie! Hold it!"

Jennie ignored her and reached the dye room door. Finding it locked, she pounded until someone opened it.

Travis looked up in surprise when he saw Jennie hurrying toward him, and he smirked at his friends. The widow was seeking him out.

"You son of a bitch!" she shouted, slapping him hard enough to make him stagger and leaving a welt on his cheek.

His coworkers laughed as he lunged toward her, but he saw Mrs. Belding standing there and stopped short, then turned on his heel and stalked off.

Jennie cried all night. It was the most humiliating day of her life. She had urges too, and she knew they were healthy, but she vowed she'd never consider a liaison because of Jasmin. Her son was the most important thing in her life. Saddling him with a mother known for her promiscuity was the cruelest thing she could think of.

Percell roared his disapproval of the dye-room affair. Who would've thought quiet Mrs. Rhinehardt had such moxie? Was she another Ida Belding?

The next day, he called Ida into his office. "How's your young friend doing?"

"Humiliated, angry, and concerned about gossip."

"What can the harpies say about her? She reacted the way I hope my own daughter would in a similar situation."

"I try to tell her everyone applauds her actions."

"I'll see what I can do."

Later, he cornered Jennie in the packaging room. "How are you doing?" he asked pleasantly.

"Pretty well, Mr. Percell."

"You know, Jennie, God, in His infinite wisdom, created you and me decades apart. If we were the same age and unattached, you'd have to get a court order to keep me from pursuing you."

Jennie stiffened, wondering if the world had gone mad, then she saw the twinkle in her boss' eye and realized he was teasing, trying to bolster her ego.

"Mr. Percell, if we were the same age and unattached, *you'd* be the one seeking a restraining order."

He laughed, thinking she was one tough lady, then he walked away feeling better.

Chapter Six

It was Saturday, and Jennie allowed her son his first opportunity to play host. Jasmin invited Marve from across the street, Tommy Koven next door, and Guy Lovell, two houses south of them.

They romped in the backyard and were having a fine time playing games that seemed to have no rules. Then it began raining. It was a light drizzle, but Jennie called the boys into the house, anyway. At first, she thought of sending them home, but playing host was important to Jasmin, so she herded them into the porch, instead.

As the boys glumly watched the gentle rain from the porch, Jennie made hot chocolate and brought a platter of cookies.

"Wish it would rain hard," Tommy said.

"Are you crazy?" Tommy asked.

"If it rains hard, there'd be water in the streets, and I could make paper boats."

"You make hats with paper, not boats."

"I guess a hat could be a boat," Guy said.

"We could sail them clear to the corner," Jasmin added.

"If it rains hard, the paper would get soaked, and there goes your boats," Marve sneered.

As if in answer to Marve's wishes, it rained harder.

"It's raining, it's pouring," Tommy sang, "the old man is snoring."

"What old man?" Jazzy asked.

"Jeez, Dummy. The old man's your father."

"He ain't no dummy, Marve," Guy said logically. "He ain't got a father."

"Could you get some paper?" Tommy asked.

Jasmin went into his mother's bedroom while she worked in the kitchen. He opened the box where his mother kept writing supplies and took out several sheets of foolscap.

With the deftness of practice, Tommy made four paper hats that were, in reality, Spanish galleons. Ignoring the rain, the boys raced to the curb, launched their vessels, and ran along the curb to Yates Street as the ships made their journey without mishap.

When they reached the aperture of the sewer, the fleet negotiated the right turn through the teeth of the grid and dropped into the sewer system below.

Jennie, hearing silence on the porch, went to investigate and saw the boys at the corner. She quickly ended the outing.

Back inside, Jasmin asked why he didn't have a father. She explained God needed Gus in heaven and took him.

Jasmin was a bright, inquisitive child, and she replied to his questions to the best of her ability. Later, she'd explain his death as a casualty of a shooting war between rival gangs into which he innocently strolled. Always, she kept from downgrading Gus, praising him for a talented artisan who made intricate tools. In that, she was truthful.

On Jasmin's birthday, she gave him a picture of the Rhinehardt coat of arms she framed for him and hung it above his bed.

"What's that?" he asked.

"It's called a coat of arms. It belongs to all Rhinehardts. Your father was a Rhinehardt, and so are you."

"How about you, Mommy?"

"No. I'm a Jones."

"I want you to be a Rhinehardt, too."

"Well, all right. If you're really sure."

"I want to look at it, Mommy."

She took it off the wall and gave it to him, and he walked from the room. "Where are you going?"

"I want to show this to Maria."

"You don't take it outdoors. I'll call her in to see it."

From the kitchen window, she saw her neighbors in their backyard. "Maria? My son has something he wants to show you."

"I'll be right there."

"Bring Mateo with you."

When the old couple walked into the kitchen, Jasmin thrust the picture into Maria's hands. "That's our arms coat."

"Coat of arms, Jasmin," Jennie corrected.

"It's beautiful," Maria told Jasmin, then looked at Jennie. "It looks like the real thing."

"Gus told me a genealogist traced his family to the court of Charles the Sixth."

"Who's that?"

"Who knows? Truth is, if you dig back far enough, everyone can find an interesting forebear."

"Not me, Jennie. We were always peasants."

"I'm worse off. I don't know if I was born, hatched, or created. For all I know, I came from Mars."

Mateo silently admired the artistry of the coat of arms. "Martoranas have a coat of arms."

"You?" his wife asked. "Your family were peasants, too."

"What does your coat of arms look like?" Jennie asked.

"It's simple—crossed salamis on a field of garlic."

"That's funny." Jennie laughed.

"It's dumb." Maria laughed, too.

The situation with the trolley car became unbearable. Before she even set foot in it, the car was filled to capacity. The genius of Henry Ford produced a closed car, the Model A. Installment buying became easy for whatever someone desired. After Jennie bought a car, she had mobility.

Weekends were times of frolic with Jasmin on the midway of Sea Breeze and the sands of Durand Eastman Park. Jennie's vanity wouldn't allow her to don the ugly bathing suits designed for modesty. She had a tub for bathing, and she preferred the one-piece, skin-tight swimsuit exhibited by Gertrude Ederle when she swam the English Channel.

Jasmin was thrilled and terrified when his mother waded through deep water, holding him close to her bosom, while small waves lapped against his legs regularly. He was less thrilled and more terrified when she set him on her back and propelled them through the water with a respectable breast stroke.

On the beach, Jennie discouraged the advances of admirers but basked in their attentions.

The Coolidge prosperity became the Hoover prosperity, but that prosperity was short-lived. Late in 1929, the stock market, like Humpty Dumpty, had a great fall. America didn't have a blueprint for Utopia after all.

Jennie panicked, even though she'd been conservative in money matters. Factories were shutting down everywhere, and many workers were laid off. Surviving factories cut back on production, and that was what panicked her. However, she had little cause for worry.

The Rochester Button Factory continued manufacturing. They reduced inventory, cut production, and laid off a few employees, but Percell wasn't about to lose Ida Belding or Jennie. They were fixtures within the company.

Her hours were cut, which hurt her budget, but soon, the hard times blossomed into a full-fledged depression, and the deflated prices made her earnings seem more. The depression hurt the most-recent arrivals in the neighborhood the most. Those were people who boasted of modest wealth from investments.

Less affected were old neighbors who were never that far from the land that sustained them. Unlike the urban dwellers, those people had access to food from their labors in the small plots adjoining their homes, and most were mortgage-free.

Jasmin was six and in the first grade. With his fine features, gentle soul, and graceful walk, he didn't need the handicap of a name that meant a flower. It was logical to call him Jazzy, and it was Jennie who created the change.

One Saturday morning, Dora had all the boys at her house. Marve was late and was running hard on chubby legs.

"Marve," Jennie said.

He stopped and looked at her.

"When you get to the Kovens, tell Jazzy I want to see him after he eats his ice cream."

"Who?"

"My son. Tell him to come home."

Marve ran even faster. "Jazzy! Jazzy!"

Jennie awaited her son's return with some misgivings. He ran into the house, crying.

"Why'd you call me Jazzy? Everyone's laughing at me."

"I did it, because I love you, and you're special to me. Do you know what Jazzy means?"

"No, Mommy."

"It means you're exciting, like the music."

The transition came about as if people had been waiting for it. Even the old couple took the change in stride, especially Mateo, who saw the logic of it. Jasmin didn't accept it readily, but soon, he signed everything *Jazzy Rhinehardt*.

There were times when Jennie saw Maria's affection for her son with pangs of envy. The reciprocity of that outpouring was felt even more deeply. She tried not to be envious, because it was very fortunate for him to have such loving grandparents. As always, at night, she countered Maria's outpouring with a more lavish display of love of her own.

"Why?" Maria asked herself often. "Why doesn't she pick up the lad and smother him with kisses in public?"

Jennie's education at the Mansfield home had been basic, at best, and the relationship between mother and son had psychological overtones. Jennie was short on knowledge, but she was blessed with a fine, analytical mind. She understood her reserve and vowed to devote her entire life to her child.

A strong bond existed between the neighborhood boys from the start. There was Marve, Guy, Jimmy, Sam, who, with his brother, Fred, lived on Norton Street, and Jazzy. The youngster's devotion was like a sacred trust, and they, in turn, were protective of him.

Jennie tried to be her son's friend. Since she had a car, she took him to Mandel's for a lemon phosphate, and the old druggist always greeted them warmly.

Jennie was entertaining Mateo and Maria. From her pantry window to the back of the house, she saw Jazzy and the boys flying kites in the wide meadows behind the Koven house. Jazzy never owned a kite before, and Jennie planned to buy him one from the hardware store.

"Bought kites break easily," Mateo said. "If you want one that's tough and flies high without breaking in a strong wind, you have to make it. Jennie, you buy the string, and I'll make the kite."

The finished kite was a thing of beauty, and Jazzy displayed it to his friends with pride. It was the best kite they ever saw, going up quickly and climbing faster than the others.

Cock-eyed Ben Turpin was the most-feared bully in the lower grades. He was a year older than Jazzy and in the fourth grade. Certainly, plastic surgery would've rendered him less repulsive, and a good surgeon could've straightened his eyes. What Cock-eyed needed most, however, was psychiatric help. That wasn't available, because he wasn't in a life-and-death situation.

His aggressive behavior may've been the manifestation of something beyond his control. His eyes were a condition from birth and never repaired, but he earned his flattened nose.

Guy Lovell, always thinking like a lawyer, once belabored a point with Cock-eyed. Cock-eyed began his summation with a kick to the seat of Guy's pants. He was slow to follow up, and Guy ran with the speed only fear could generate. With Cock-eyed in hot pursuit, he ran down the train tracks.

Cock-eyed tripped and fell, striking his nose against a rail, and everyone knew it was only a matter of time before Guy got paid back.

The kite was a speck in the sky. Jim Logan was content to keep his closer to the ground, enjoying its spirited antics. His kite was a dancer. Marve had his kite on the ground, adding ballast to the right side with a strip of cloth so the kite wouldn't pitch left.

By the time Jazzy saw Cock-eyed coming across the meadow, it was too late to reel in his kite and run home. Marve scooped up his kite and ran off.

Jazzy heard many tales of Cock-eyed's brutality, but it was his first encounter with the bully. He was frightened, but his kite, his pride and joy, kept him from fleeing. Jim Logan pulled in his kite furiously but didn't make it.

"Well, well," Cock-eyed said. "So this is the sissy kid. How's the kite-pulling?"

"Fine," Jazzy said in a small voice.

"Let's see." Cock-eyed reached for the taut string. Between the forefinger and middle finger of his right hand was a Gem razor blade. He cut the string, and the kite flew off. A moment later, Logan's kite suffered the same fate.

When Jazzy arrived home, sobbing hysterically, Jennie was in the kitchen, having coffee with Mateo and Maria.

"What's the matter?" Jennie asked.

"Cock-eyed cut the string to my kite, and it's gone!"

"Porco Diavolo!" Mateo said.

"That sounds like swearing."

"Damn right, I'm swearing. I made that kite, and no little son of a bitch is gonna do that to the kid!"

"Please, sit down." Jennie was concerned for the man's health.

"Where are you going?" Maria asked her husband.

"To have a little talk with that bastard's father."

"Please don't," Jennie pleaded. "This is a children's affair. My boy must learn to cope. It's part of growing up."

Mateo stared at Maria, unable to understand Jennie's passivity.

"Dry your tears, Jazzy," Jennie said. "I'll buy you a new kite and string."

It was Sunday night, and Abel had no engagement that evening. Dora was content to stay home with her family and invited Jennie over for Danish and coffee. Although Jennie would've preferred driving to Sea Breeze, where a new band was playing, she agreed. Dora and Abel were family to Jennie, and she felt compelled to accept.

Abel played Rudy Vallee records when Jennie arrived.

"You said you didn't like him," Jennie said.

"Me? Like Vallee? You must be kidding."

"Don't believe him, Jennie," Dora said. "He's got all the man's records."

"I like his guts," Abel said. "Listen to him. He's got problems."

"What problems?" Dora asked, playing straight man.

"He starts somewhere around his larynx. Somehow, he propels his voice through his nose, the sound making it to the megaphone, where it rolls around, then comes out the large side."

"He *is* nasally," Jennie agreed, laughing.

Abel put away the records and joined the women at the kitchen table.

Jazzy and Tommy sat on the living room rug, playing Lotto and taking turns calling out the numbers. Jennie recounted her son's experience with Cock-eyed.

"I'm glad I had Tommy shopping with me," Dora said.

"What can we do about this bully?" Abel asked.

"Not much," Jennie admitted. "He's only one year older than Jazzy. The problem is, I can't look after him all the time. I have a job and a house to maintain. Fortunately, nothing will happen to him when he's with Mateo and Maria."

"I've been meaning to talk to you about that," Abel said. "Let the kid go."

"What do you mean?"

"For Christ's sake, Jennie, he's the only kid in his class who's still being led to school. You'll have a kid with hang-ups if you don't send him to school alone."

"Abel!" Dora said. "Mind your own business. Jazzy isn't your child. Let his mother decide what's right."

"It's all right, Dora," Jennie said. "Abel's right. Tomorrow morning, Jazzy Rhinehardt will be on his own."

Monday morning, Jazzy felt like the prisoner of Zenda, and the bridge across the moat was down at the Rhinehardt Castle. With uneasiness, he left home. Mateo and Maria hugged him close and watched him walk to school as they stood on the walk, waving, gulping hard to fight back tears. They were a sentimental pair.

Alone, Jazzy contemplated his freedom. He looked at other children, walking slowly toward school, and he was deep in thought. Marve joined him, and Jazzy spent the rest of the trip listening to his constant chatter. The bigger boy latched onto his small neighbor almost as a solemn duty, and that attachment would last a long time. Eventually, Marve would need Jazzy's guidance, but, for the moment, Marve was the teacher.

The education of the streets began. Marve was persistent, and, although Jazzy realized the Martoranas were waiting for his return home, he couldn't deter Marve from giving him a tour of the neighborhood and the wonders of the free world.

First, they went to Bricker Street, several blocks from Goodman. A strong, overpowering stench engulfed Jazzy long before they arrived. From every window, large hoses were draped over sills, emitting a dark liquid.

"What's that?" Jazzy asked.

"Hooch," Marve said.

"It smells like beer to me."

"What do you know about beer?" Marve was surprised.

"Tommy's father has it at home sometimes."

"I wonder how it tastes."

"It's bad."

"How would you know?"

"When Tommy's dad wasn't looking, Tommy made me taste it."

"I'd like to do that."

"You wouldn't drink the stuff coming from the windows?"

"No."

Jazzy knew Marve had contemplated it, anyway. "I wonder why they're throwing it out. Must be going bad."

"Don't you know anything? It's against the law to make liquor or beer."

"Did they arrest the people who own the house?"

"I heard my father tell Mom nobody knows who owns it."

Soon, other children gathered to watch the pumping operation. A few, taking advantage of the moment when no authorities were around, entered the house.

"Let's go in," Marve said.

"Not me." Jazzy was frightened.

"Come on." He pulled Jazzy along.

Inside, they looked in awe at crudely constructed vats in every room. By standing beside the vats and getting on tiptoe, they saw the contents of the vats, which were nearly empty. Vapor hung heavy in the house.

At the bottom of each vat were several large drowned rats. Jazzy ran outdoors. Whatever taste for beer he might develop later in life, it was curbed then.

They went home at his insistence, stopping at the corner of Norton and Goodman, where Marve pointed to a large building.

"Know what it is?"

"No, I don't. It's a building, that's all."

"It's a speak easily."

"Speak easily?"

"Yeah. Men and women go there at night."

"What for?"

"To have fun."

"What kind of fun?"

"You know—drinking, dancing, and eating all kinds of food."

"Why do they call it a speak easily?"

"They don't want the police to hear, Stupid. It's against the law to go there."

"I see. It's the liquor and beer they serve that's against the law."

"Yeah. That's it."

"Look! I see ladies on the second floor. They keep looking out the windows."

"They're called hers."

"Why?"

"How do I know? They're ladies, ain't they? Maybe they're called hers, because they're not hims. It's not a him house."

"What do they do with all that paint on their faces?"

"Have fun with men."

"What men?"

"The ones who pay money for the fun."

"Must be a special kind of fun if you have to pay for it."

"Don't you know anything about the fun men and women have?"

"What do they do?"

"I'm not sure. I'll bet Lefty knows."

Lefty knew many things. He had older brothers who were eager teachers, and he was deprived of the wonders of childhood. He had the look of a cynic, more like one of the little people than an eight-year-old. He didn't attend Townsend Elementary. He was one of the detested mudstompers from Irondequoit. His school was an old farmhouse remodeled to a schoolhouse. He was able to meet the Goodman boys, whom he preferred over his fellow mudstompers, because his school day ended earlier.

Jazzy's education in areas not covered by the school curriculum was a continuing process. The enterprising Lefty taught Jazzy and Marve many things, and some would've alarmed their parents.

It's said that the play of children is the preparation for manhood. Jazzy held his own in games of skill and cunning, but physical games left him lacking.

Each day was a new adventure. His love for his companions was deep, and he was an only child suddenly given a host of brothers.

There was trouble brewing in paradise. Guy Lovell and Marve Pittman were getting on each other's nerves. Marve considered himself the leader of the gang by virtue of his size, but Guy, a parliamentarian, challenged his decisions, reducing Marve to stuttering in his inability to counter Guy's logic.

Their quiet neighborhood was far removed from the sounds of the inner city, but there were times when the quiet was shattered by one of two sources.

First, there was Mr. Catina's coronet. He was a man of means, and it was his park, converted from a lavish domicile on Norton Street at Midland Avenue that some clubs and fraternal orders leased on Sundays for picnics.

He was a first-rate musician, soloing on his coronet for the Flower City Band. He practiced constantly, shattering the stillness often with his rendition of *Carnival of Venice*.

The second source of sound was the arpeggios of Miss Laura. She was a single woman whose only aim in life was to become an opera singer. She was an irritant to some neighbors, but Jennie tolerated her, because she loved music of all kinds.

The Pittmans found her a nuisance. Miss Laura lived on their side of Goodman Street, north of them across Corwin Avenue. Marve took his parents' complaints as license for a little devilment. Jazzy wisely declined to join him.

While Miss Laura trilled up and down the scales, Marve crawled under her window and interjected his own caterwauling. Miss Laura's music teacher, his mustache waxed to sharp points, came out the front door, bristling in anger, and ran Marve off.

If the neighborhood had culture, it was furnished by an accomplished musician and a tyro of an opera singer.

It was the time of year when stone fruit was ripe, waiting for young raiders. Fruit was plentiful, but it was a game of skill, cunning, and courage to steal from a worthy adversary. Old Man Browser had the best plums, and he was also the neighborhood grouch. He was troublesome, and everyone detested him. In addition, he was a worthy adversary, a man with keen ears and an instinct that told him the night the boys would come.

Marve showed where he snipped the wire holding the fence to the post for easy access to the target tree.

"We go under the fence," he ordered.

"You're an asshole," Guy said.

"I'll smack your mouth if you keep that up."

"Old Man Browser opens his front door, and sees us under the lamplight, and he'll recognize us. Come on, Gang. We'll go in from the back where it's dark. We approach the tree from that side and pick the plums in the dark. We won't even have to climb it. There's enough for all of us on the lower branches."

The others saw the wisdom of Guy's plan and followed him, forcing a fuming Marve to tag along.

They had no trouble climbing the fence and moved cautiously toward the tree. Browser's keen ears didn't fail him, though, and he heard something in the yard. He turned on the porch light, peering into the darkness, while the boys dropped down and hid in the tall grass.

Browser stood there a long time and listened. Finally, convinced no one was there, he turned off the light.

A few minutes later, the boys stood under the streetlight on the corner of Goodman and Yates and emptied their booty. They achieved their mission with dispatch, and success added more flavor to the fruit. The evening would've ended without unpleasantness if it hadn't been for Guy's persnickety nature. He wouldn't let the matter drop.

"You see, Marve?" Guy asked. "You didn't have to snip the wire. We climbed the fence without any trouble—unless you had trouble, because you're too fat."

Enraged, Marve rushed Guy, who had no intention of fighting. He never had a fight in his life. Marve hurt him, though, and Guy was forced to counterattack, flailing away with no style but some success. He fought relentlessly, becoming a windmill that confused Marve.

Jazzy had long felt Marve didn't really have the stomach for a fight, and he suddenly cowered and covered his face, content to block Guy's barrage. The boys quickly ended the fight, but news of the fracas swept the schoolyard the next day.

Chapter Seven

Father Weideman liked to entertain priests from other parishes and enjoyed being entertained in turn, especially by those who owned billiard tables and were pigeons in penny-ante three-cushion billiards, a game he played well. Unfortunately, his converted barn paled alongside the fine churches elsewhere in the city, and it had no recreation room.

There were many others who felt the need for a new church. The parish had expanded in recent years, and some of the parishioners had to stand at the back of the church during mass.

At a time of deep depression, money somehow appeared for a new church. Feelings were strong it had to have a name, too. There was confusion about the old name, Saint Fechan, a corruption of the name of an Irish saint.

Father Weideman had an idea for the new name but kept it to himself. In a grandstand play, he suggested a poll. The four most popular names would be presented at a general meeting of the parish.

Everyone had an opinion. Secretly, Father Weideman moved to stack the deck, enlisting the considerable aid of Ida Belding. He wanted to call the church, the Church of the Annunciation.

The choices were gathered, and the four most frequently named were St. Luke, St. Matthew, St. Mark, and the Church of the Annunciation.

In the runoff, the church was named as Father Weideman hoped. When asked the significance of the name, he replied smugly it was the announcement by the angel Gabriel that Mary would be the mother to the Savior. He neglected to add that his German grandparents gave his mother the Italian name Annunziata, which was the fashion among the literati of their day.

Annunciation had no school, which normally would excuse the parish from participating in the Catholic School League. An exception was made for the church, however, because they had enough sixth, seventh, and eighth graders from religious-instruction classes to field teams.

Tommy was talented at baseball. He played infield, making plays that would've been remarkable in older boys. Once, when Annunciation played St. Andrews, he raced behind second base, caught the ball, wheeled, and made a long throw to first in time for an out.

An old-timer, impressed by Tommy's play, said, "He's a regular Napoleon Lajoie."

From then on, Tommy was nicknamed Napoleon, but that seemed too long, so it was soon shortened to Nap. In time, that changed to Nippy, and the name stuck with him the rest of his life.

Despite the depression, Jennie felt God was good to her. She was employed, had a fully paid house, and her son was doing so well in school, he filled her with pride.

One day, she ventured downtown to shop at McCurdy's, and her orderly world threatened to collapse. She finished in McCurdy's and decided to explore Sibley's diagonally across Main Street.

A derelict approached her, probably ready to ask for a dime for a cup of coffee. Somehow, he seemed familiar under the grime and the white stubble on his face. When he reached her, a stiletto appeared out of nowhere, directed at her stomach.

"Mr. Martino!" she gasped.

"Yeah, it's me. No ghost. Just me, you miserable witch. Your hair looks great. No home job. Must've cost a lot. You're not wearin' your old man's rags, either. I'll bet you're not eatin' cold beans from a can."

"What do you want from me?"

"I don't know how you did it, you fuckin' bitch, but you pulled off a great pea-in-a-walnut-shell scam. Fritz and I were in a lot of stings in the old days, but nothin' like you."

"I don't know what you're talking about." She started crying and shaking.

"Wanna know what I've been doin'? I've eaten out of a can a lot, even from a garbage can. Sometimes, nothing at all. Now that I've met you, that'll change, won't it, Mrs. Rhinehardt?"

"What do you want?" she whispered.

"All the money you've got and can beg, borrow, or steal. Stealing shouldn't be too hard for you. The money from that money belt must've earned a lot of interest by now. With the dough, I'll get a new start in this asshole town. I won't waste you with Garibaldi here," he glanced at the stiletto, "because we're going to be real tight. After that, *que sera, sera.*"

Martino grabbed her arm with his left hand, and the point of the weapon dipped slightly in the process. She swung her purse and caught him alongside the head. When he staggered, she ran into the traffic, zigzagging like a quarterback running for a touchdown.

Martino stood at the curb, shrieking obscenities, not daring to make the same run. He waited for the light to change as she entered Sibley's.

Jennie took the escalator to the second floor and saw Martino walking into the store toward the escalator. *That must've been a short light,* she thought bitterly.

On the second floor, she blended with the crowd, collected herself, and felt certain she'd make it back down undetected.

Through a chink in a pile of suitcases, she saw the down escalator was empty, but she didn't want to take chances. She waited, but no one came, so she surmised Martino was scouring the building, looking for her. She stepped out and ran toward the escalator.

Suddenly, Martino stepped out ahead of her, triumph in his eyes. He'd been hiding, too. She turned as if to run, then spun back toward him as he came closer. She timed her kick with precision, dealing his crotch a vicious blow. Martino screamed, and Jennie ran for the escalator.

Martino went berserk. He no longer thought of money or a new start. No woman had ever hit him with her purse, much less kicked him in the balls, and he had to kill her for it. He threw himself at her, his speed remarkable considering his age and the blow he just received.

Jennie ducked the descending stiletto. As his torso came over her, she shouldered him hard and pushed, sending him over the guardrail.

He fell to the first floor and struck his head. Jennie watched in horror, knowing from the position of his head that his neck was broken. When she reached the first floor, a crowd formed, but no one paid her any attention.

"The guy's stone dead," an onlooker said.

Nausea overcoming her, she rushed to the Junior Miss department, grabbed a dress off the rack, and went into a fitting room, where she immediately threw up into the dress. The stench was overpowering, but she stayed long enough to compose herself, then walked home.

She never considered keeping Kroger's money as stealing, and she didn't feel accountable for Martino's death, either. The newspapers had a field day with their theories, but only Jennie knew what really happened on the metal slopes of Sibley's.

Despite Jennie's steadfast stand concerning her innocence in the theft of Kroger's money and Martino's death, she couldn't entirely exonerate herself. She knew she was involved, but she rationalized it as involvement that the Lord shared and arranged.

At night, however, her dreams had a clarity that never surfaced during the day. She recalled the terrible night of Gus' death, and her anguish made her sleep fitful. In her dreams at least, she knew that if she hadn't taken the money, Jill would still be alive, nor would she have had to face Martino. She had a lot to live with.

"Brother, can you spare a dime?" was the cry of the newly created beggar roaming the streets. The destitute entrepreneur, selling apples at every street corner in the dead of winter, was a pathetic sight, as were the long lines of hungry men, women, and children at every soup kitchen in the city. Statistics never told the full story of the devastation of the shattered economy.

Abel's shoe factory closed. Since he had no work, the pressure fell on Dora to find employment, and Maria offered a solution.

"My foreman from years ago is now an important man at Bonds," Maria suggested.

"Will he remember you?" Dora asked anxiously.

"Will he? My God, we girls worked piecework, and I was so fast my pay often matched Mr. Steiner's."

Dora prayed Maria could help. She knew Abel's music wouldn't support them, and other shoe factories were shutting down, too.

Mr. Steiner greeted Maria like an old friend, graciously saying he'd never met any woman who could match Maria's speed or quality of work. In addition, he said she could do everything, not just one or two jobs.

When the question of employment for Dora came up, his enthusiasm waned.

"We're fighting to stay in business," he told Maria. "I don't have to tell you we're in a depression. I'd have trouble placing her even if she was experienced."

"Mr. Steiner, I never asked you for a favor, not even once. I'm putting you on the spot. Please hire Mrs. Koven."

"Maria, I'd be strung up alive in the corporate office if I brought in a trainee when there are so many experienced seamstresses out there— all unemployed."

"Suppose I train her for you like in the old days."

"You have the equipment in your house?"

"No."

"How will you train her?"

"Here in the shop on Saturday afternoons."

"Impossible."

"Why? Just tell the guards I'm coming."

"I don't know," he hedged.

"Come, Mr. Steiner. What do you need most?"

"Lapels." He sighed.

"See? You do need help. I'll give you a great lapel girl."

"How long will this take?"

"As many Saturday afternoons as I need to train her right."

"OK, but I should have my head examined."

When Dora finally started work, she was as good as the others in lapels. The Kovens rode out the depression on her wages, and the pressure on Abel disappeared.

When Jazzy was in the sixth grade, the girls underwent changes not shared by the boys. Their bodies went through a metamorphosis that converted straight lines to curves. None developed as rapidly as Antoinette Dubois.

The change was dramatic. She was suddenly heavy breasted and had a derriere to match. She would've been another fat girl except for her narrow waist, giving her an hourglass figure. To the boys, she was an eleven-year-old Mae West.

Marve was in love with her. She became his obsession, and consequently the other boys felt he was no fun to be around. He incessantly talked of her, and he went out of his way to walk past her house and try to catch a glimpse of her.

Whenever he could at school, he was at her side. Sometimes, she yelled at him and told him to get lost. Most of the time, she allowed him to play the dutiful page. It flattered her to have an attendant plying her with gum and candy.

When Marve's mother added a tasty piece of pastry in his lunch bag, Antoinette accepted it as her divine right. After school, however, she broke his heart—not once, but many times. High-school boys in an old car came by and whisked her away.

Nature wasn't as kind to Carrie Evans. Her legs and arms were painfully thin. Her cheeks were sunken, making her brown eyes seem much too big for her face. Her slow development worried her mother. Carrie would soon be twelve. Mrs. Evans knew of the importance of attractiveness and being popular with one's peers. For that reason, she organized the Let's Get Together party at her house.

She limited the attendees to eight—four boys and four girls. The boys were Jazzy, Marve, Guy, and Sam, and the girls were Carrie, Belle, Pamela, and Josie, three girls from her reading group. They weren't truly friends, but they were the closest. Antoinette wasn't invited.

Jennie took great care preparing Jazzy for the party. He wore his first pair of long pants. With the blue blazer bringing out his blue eyes, he was worthy of a Kodak ad. As she looked at him, she marveled, as she always did, at what she and Gus wrought.

Maria came over, and, when she saw Jazzy, she hugged him. He endured it and wondered if his mother would hug him, too, but she didn't. She kissed his forehead.

Jazzy sat nervously on the couch, flanked by Marve and Guy, with Sam sitting on the ottoman. The girls were in a corner, giggling, excited at having their first boy-girl function and anticipating the program Mrs. Evans worked out for the initial encounter.

Although the boys were all eleven, Marve was the only one enduring the onset of puberty. While his classmates sat in their misery, unsure of what was in store, Marve tried to get Antoinette out of his mind and find some interest in the parlor games Lefty explained.

Mrs. Evans prepared hot dogs with potato salad and baked beans. Dessert was peach cobbler. Soon, the children relaxed, and their chatter began. Mostly, the girls made small talk among themselves. Then the boys joined them, and the atmosphere became even more relaxed.

After dinner, in the parlor, the girls challenged the boys to a game of charades, something they learned from their homeroom teacher. Despite little help from Marve, who couldn't concentrate on the game, both were formidable teams. Sam, Jazzy, and Guy tried to withstand the challenge from the girls. They played well, but the girls were quick, intuitive, and showed marvelous investigative powers.

The girls won, but the game accomplished its purpose. All the youngsters were talking to each other, and the segregation wasn't so absolute.

Soon came the part of the evening they'd been awaiting with nervous dread.

"How many of you know how to play Post Office?" Mrs. Evans asked.

"I do!" the girls cried.

"So do I," Marve said.

"Let's go over the rules. One girl at a time goes into the pantry and calls the name of one of the boys to say there's a letter for him in the post office. The pantry is the post office. The girl can give him the letter immediately, and he returns to his seat, or she says there's postage due. In that case, the boy must stamp her mouth with a kiss. It'll be their secret."

"Can we call any boy we want?" Belle asked.

"No, because then we'd know who was sweet on whom. We don't want that, do we?"

"Why not?" Josie asked.

"You might not mind, but the boys might feel differently if one doesn't get chosen. I have four envelopes in my hand. Each has a boy's name on it. I've shuffled them so nobody knows which is which."

She handed one envelope to each girl, although she made sure Carrie got Jazzy's.

Josie went into the pantry and said the post office had a letter for Guy Lovell. Guy walked in slowly, obviously frightened. He was in a short time, then returned with an envelope in hand, followed by a smiling Josie.

Then Pamela called Marve, who swaggered in. In that group, he was the man about town. He returned in a short time carrying an envelope, but, from the expressions on his and Pamela's faces, the others couldn't tell what happened.

When Carrie called Jazzy's name, he was petrified. Marve helped him to his feet and pushed him toward the pantry.

When Jazzy reached the post office for his letter, Carrie attacked him like a wild creature. Her thin arms were around his neck, pinning him to her. She showered his face and neck with kisses and tried to pry open his mouth with her tongue, but his lips were clamped shut.

She ran her hands over his body and clasped his testicles, making him cry out several octaves higher than his normal voice.

Mrs. Evans' hand flew to her throat at the sound. What kind of monster was Jennie Rhinehardt raising? She almost went into the pantry, then Jazzy came out, red-faced, a crumpled envelope in his hand. Carrie followed looking serious and composed, but, had her mother looked into her eyes, she would've found them alive.

Sam went in with Belle, and Marve nudged Jazzy.

"What happened?" Marve asked.

"She grabbed my crotch," Jazzy whispered back.

"Who you shitting? You put your hand on her doo-doo."

"Her doo-doo? Oh, God!"

Later, in the schoolyard, with every sixth-grade girl gathered around, Carrie carefully didn't divulge what happened in the pantry. Jazzy was perceived as a rogue.

Almost before Jennie knew it, Jazzy was her height. She suddenly had a dancing partner in her home. At first, dancing with his mother, even in the privacy of his home, embarrassed him, but soon, under her tutelage, he not only became proficient, he caught her enthusiasm.

She prepared him for any eventuality. He became adept at the waltz, the two-step, and the polka. Then she danced the Lindy with him, and he jitterbugged so well, the two of them flew about the room, like two kids at a sock hop.

Jennie also showed him the tango, the carioca, the charleston, and the black bottom, wanting him to be a complete dancer.

She still considered herself a young girl. She certainly danced and felt like one.

Changes were occurring on the dance floor. She, who'd been queen of the ballroom, experienced the frustrations of a wallflower. Jitterbugging was becoming acrobatic, and she could've done the moves, but it wasn't prudent. Girls leaped and clasped the boys around the waist with their legs, then the boys threw the girls into the air, young legs flashing, raised skirts showing panties on tight, shapely bottoms.

A widow with a son soon to attend high school didn't expose her undergarments. Jennie had done some exposing of herself in the charleston-black bottom era, and it felt like yesterday. She wondered if she could really be thirty-five.

Jennie had spells of depression, where she sat in the dark and relived her early years before Gus, surrounded by friends her own age. Life had been sweet then. At night, her dreams were ugly and precipitated depressions during the day.

It wasn't that she feared growing old. Aging wasn't so bad if she had someone who faced it with her. She missed the togetherness of Ida and Mr. Belding, or of Mateo and Maria or Abel and Dora. For all their bickering, even Mr. and Mrs. Pittman were a couple.

Jennie had a son who was the most important person in her life, but she had to share him with his classmates. Because she was alone, she also had to share him with Maria and Mateo.

Negotiations between Marve and Lefty's parents were completed, and Lefty would sleep over at Marve's house. Abel permitted the boys to stay outside until Dora and Jennie returned. They went to see *The Tale of Two Cities*. Ronald Coleman, who supplanted all Jennie's old favorites of the silent screen, played the memorable role of Sidney Carton. Death, old age, and talking pictures took their toll of the stars. It was in a silent film, with Vilma Banky, that Ronald Coleman stole Jennie's heart.

Jazzy and Nippy joined the group on Yates Street, where a game of Run, Sheep, Run was in progress. It was a popular game, consisting of hunters and sheep. The sheep hid throughout the neighborhood, while the hunter sought them. When the captain of the sheep judged the moment had come for a mad dash to home base, he shouted, "Run, sheep, run!" Jazzy enjoyed pitting his cunning and speed against the other team.

They'd been playing a short while when Marve and Lefty ran up, gasping for breath.

"Jazzy!" Marve said. "Old Man Kilty's got Antoinette!"

"Did he kidnap her?"

"No. She walked down Yates Street to the end, and he was waiting for her in his car."

"Why are you telling me?"

"She's my girl, and you're supposed to be my friend. You know what they say about Mr. Kilty."

"What do they say about him?" Jazzy asked wearily.

"He's a dirty old man who screws young girls."

"Why didn't you tell Mr. Dubois? You ran past his house."

"You're right!" Marve raced back up the street with Lefty behind him.

Reluctantly, Jazzy left the game and followed. He felt an obligation to be with Marve at such a time. Marve pounded on the Dubois door, and Mr. Dubois finally answered.

"What do you want?" he asked gruffly.

"Antoinette's with Kevin Kilty at the end of Yates Street."

Dubois' son, who still lived with his parents, was at his father's side. Both bolted down the street before Marve finished speaking. Bob picked up a baseball bat.

They arrived in a group, and Jazzy had the opportunity to look into the car. He saw three gleaming white mounds, which perplexed him until he realized they were Antoinette's exposed breasts and Kilty's bald head. His face was buried in her bare midriff.

Antoinette's blouse was raised upward, and she wore it around her neck. Her skirt was high on her hips, exposing her legs, and she fought to get rid of her panties, but she had trouble because of Kilty's considerable girth.

"You stinkin' degenerate!" Dubois roared. "Seducing my baby! I'll cut out your fuckin' heart!"

If he'd kept quiet, he would've caught Kilty, but, at the sound of Dubois' voice, Kilty rolled off Antoinette, opened the opposite car door, and hit the street running, hampered by the fact that his pants and shorts were around his knees.

He pulled on his clothes, having trouble getting them over his huge buttocks, but he eluded Bob.

Mr. Dubois yanked Antoinette from the car. She managed to pull on her panties, but her huge breasts were still exposed. Her father shook her hard, bouncing her breasts, then pulled down her blouse.

"Where's your brassiere?" he demanded.

"I didn't wear one," she sobbed in terror.

He struck the back of her head with his open hand, then dragged her toward home with a cruel grip.

"Get lost, you kids!" he shouted. "Get the hell out of here!"

He'd forgotten they were there. Marve was crying, and Jazzy was filled with a sense of sadness he couldn't explain. The boys walked back toward the others, still playing at the other end of Yates Street.

"Wow," Lefty said. "Did you see those tits without the flopper stoppers?" He cupped his hands to demonstrate.

That angered Jazzy—once a mudstomper, always a mudstomper.

In the Dubois household, there was uncontrolled anger. Father and son spoke of violent retaliation, including castration. They discussed waylaying Kevin Kilty one a dark night and stomping him to death. They even considered hiring a killer.

Finally, Mrs. Dubois stepped in. "I want this craziness stopped. I've spoken to Mrs. Kilty, and she's crushed."

Father and son looked at her in silence.

"I'd like to crush her husband," Mr. Dubois said.

"Have compassion for Mrs. Kilty. She's lived with him for years, and they've been years of humiliation for the family. She keeps praying the police will put him away or an asylum will take him. He's a sick man."

"What can we do, sit here and turn the other cheek?"

"No, but doing any of the things you and Bob have been ranting about will make you more of a beast than Mr. Kilty."

"Maybe we should call the authorities," Bob suggested.

"What would the publicity do to Antoinette? Right now, just those boys know. I'm sure the news will spread, but the shame of it will at least stay in the neighborhood. Calling the police would spread the story around the country."

"I'll die if I don't get the bastard!" Mr. Dubois raged.

"Let's be grateful we reached our little girl in time. I'll call my sister. Antoinette can live with her until she graduates from grade school. Then she can go to Franklin High with the rest of the kids."

There was no room for a lecher in the Kilty home. There would be a clean break. Mrs. Kilty would divorce him, with or without the approval of Father Weideman.

It was a close call for Kilty. If he'd been caught, Dubois and his son would've killed him. He moved cautiously back to his car. He needed it. He knew he was through in his own home, but he felt no remorse, sadness, or loss. There were many young things in the world, and he couldn't keep his mind off them. Without his wife, he had more freedom.

The chemistry between Guy Lovell and Josie and Sam Trippett and Belle in the Evans' pantry must've been right, because soon, Guy started taking casual strolls past Josie's house. He was content just to see her occasionally, and when she came to the fence to talk to him, he was ecstatic. Eventually, he progressed to sitting on the porch with her. Before long, they strolled together in the evenings, and the long trip to the library was like a stroll to the corner.

Jazzy felt abandoned. Guy was the only member of the gang who shared his love of books. Walking alone, Jazzy found the trip to the library twice as long.

Sam Trippett was more direct—he approached Belle and asked if he could carry her books. He met her in the morning at her house and escorted her home after school. When he started eating lunch with her, too, he was lost to the boys.

They were at the delicate age of balancing between childhood and adolescence. Jim Logan thought girls were a bother. His parents both worked, and he and his sister, Cathy, were more or less on their own. Jimmy, unsupervised, was slovenly. Cathy, one year younger, tried to groom him. Strangely, Viola, her friend and classmate, had a crush on Jimmy, who was cruel to her at times just to keep her from following him.

Concerning girls, Jazzy wasn't as asocial as Jimmy. He tolerated them, having an easy, friendly relationship with all his classmates. So far, he wasn't interested in girls. Just as he'd been slow walking and talking, he was slow in puberty. To him, girls were just classmates, nothing more.

Although Jazzy didn't covet Carrie Evans, Lefty did. Just as he opted to associate with the Goodman crowd, rather than those in his own school, he found Townsend girls more desirable, too.

Marve played the sad lover to the hilt, pining for Antoinette. It seemed that girls were messing up the gang's solidarity.

Lefty stood in the schoolyard, waiting for the bell to ring. Carrie came out with Pam and Josie, followed by Jimmy Logan, who was instantly corralled by Cathy and Viola.

Mr. and Mrs. Logan gave the children one key, which ensured that Jimmy, who carried the key, would have close supervision over Cathy. He had to go home immediately after school, so Cathy could get into the house to prepare supper. That galled Cathy, but Viola, who adored Jimmy, was happy with the arrangement.

Lefty hurried to Carrie and placed a hand on her shoulder.

"Get your hands off me!" she snapped.

"I just want to talk to you, Carrie," he said awkwardly. "What are you mad about? I want to be your friend."

"I don't like you touching me."

"You wouldn't mind if it was Jazzy."

"You bet! He's beautiful, and you're ugly."

Josie laughed, while Pamela covered her mouth with her hand.

Jazzy walked out of school after receiving an A on his history project, feeling nothing could spoil his exhilaration. Suddenly, a fist came out of nowhere and crashed against his cheekbone, producing excruciating pain. He was down on the ground before he saw his assailant was Lefty, and he wondered why Lefty attacked him.

"Get up!" Lefty said.

Dutifully, Jazzy got up, hoping to learn the reason for the assault, but all he got was another blow. Lefty struck above Jazzy's eye, knocking him down again.

A wall of pupils ringed them as Lefty threw himself on Jazzy, drumming his ribs fiercely. Jazzy hallucinated, imagining Marve treasonously urging Lefty on.

When Jennie got home that day, she saw Maria and Mateo tending the swelling on Jazzy's face. Maria was crying. Jennie viewed the scene without the slightest sign of emotion except for a faint quiver of her lower lip.

When the old couple left, Jennie locked the doors, ordered her son to bed, and, over his objections, had him remove his clothes. She explored his body for bruises and placed a long, hard kiss on each one, her soft body pressing against his.

If she intended to console and comfort, she failed. The treatment produced strange, disturbing sensations—and considerable embarrassment. The beating, however, proved a turning point.

There was no other boy Jazzy's age in the neighborhood so vulnerable and helpless in the give-and-take of growing up. The neighborhood wasn't exactly high society.

Jennie saw Dora's boy, Nippy, who was smaller than Jazzy, engaged in rough exchange in the heat of a game, but he was a scrapper. If anyone had told Jazzy the thrashing was for the best, he would've been hard-pressed to accept that. He hurt for days, and his face bore the evidence of the beating for weeks.

Chapter Eight

Marve was on trial. The Goodman boys had many discussions concerning his perfidy, but Marve steadfastly denied exhorting Lefty during the fight. He insisted they heard wrong, saying he'd been pleading with Lefty to stop. So often and so emphatically did he repeat his denials, Jazzy questioned his recollection of the events of that terrible afternoon. Before long, he put the matter out of his mind, and the two boys were friends again.

It was the end of Lefty in the neighborhood. He stayed in Irondequoit. School officials moved quickly after the incident, issuing a decree forbidding all but Townsend pupils on school grounds.

One afternoon, the women discussed Jazzy at lunch.

"Trouble with your boy?" Percell asked, joining them.

"Yes, but not the kind parents usually have," Jennie replied.

"Jazzy's a good boy," Ida said.

"Too good. He's a perfect gentleman, and that's the problem."

Percell was confused. "I don't follow you."

"He's helpless in the world outside his home," Jennie explained. "He got beat up by a nasty boy his own age."

"That's to be expected. There's a pecking order among kids. Some your son will beat, others he won't."

"He can't lick anybody!"

"You're being hard on him."

"Am I? I've seen him playing, pretending to fight. His friends roll on the ground laughing. He throws punches like a girl tossing a bean bag. He can't fight his way out of an empty room."

"That bad? It happens when there's no father in the house."

"I've been thinking of sending him to military school."

"No good. You'll create more problems than you solve."

"What'll I do?" Jennie asked in dismay.

"Well, Jennie, do what my sister did with her hippo."

"Her what?"

"Hippo, my lard-ass nephew. He had the same problem. Smaller kids were using him as a punching bag."

"Oh, my!"

"I told her to send him to Ozzie Solomon."

"Is he a psychiatrist?"

"No, he runs a gym downtown and makes sissy kids tougher."

"I don't know. It sounds like a gladiator school."

"Ozzie knows what he's doing. He was a good fighter once. He won't make a fighter out of your boy, but the workouts will get him in shape, and he'll learn to defend himself."

"It's worth a try," Jennie said. "I can't fight his battles. I'm no better at that than he."

Percell looked at the deceptively fragile woman and knew she could hold her own.

Jennie eyed Ozzie Solomon carefully, while Solomon eyed the good-looking boy in front of him. Neither was impressed. Jennie saw a middle-aged, paunchy man dressed in a business suit. Except for thick ears and a nose like a crooked road, there was nothing to indicate the man was a fierce warrior.

Solomon sighed and appraised his new pupil—too thin, too delicate, with classic features precluding any zest for mixing it up.

Jazzy's bright eyes swept the gym, noting many boys his age working on wall pulleys, skipping rope, and punching a bag awkwardly, not with the rat-a-tat of an expert. One thin boy struck the bag with vigor and hardly moved it.

In the ring, two overweight boys wearing headgear and oversized gloves, flailed at each other. They were quickly winded, and their gloves dropped to their sides.

"A sissy is a boy who's too thin, fat, or weak to protect himself," Solomon explained. "He's not born a sissy, and he doesn't have to stay one.

"I'll get your boy in great shape. I'll teach him footwork, defense, and how to throw a punch, not slap it. I want you to look at all this activity. Your boy will be involved with all of it. We start the class running around the building, and, if you were a rich bitch, I'd have your boy here every day, because I need the money. I can still do a job on him if you bring him every Tuesday and Thursday."

"That's fine," Jennie said. "We'll be here."

"I expect cooperation from you, Mrs. Rhinehardt."

"Me? What can I do?"

"Conditioning is the key. I want your boy running a couple miles a day."

"I'll see he does. I might even join him."

"Why not?"

Twice a week, she delayed her nightly trips to Sea Breeze. She became a regular at the pavilion once more, but Dora found sewing lapels tiring and restricted her dancing to weekends. Jennie accepted the new order at Sea Breeze reluctantly, but there were sufficient mature men who sought her out instead of the tireless young women with their gymnastics. Still, the pavilion was a wonderland to her.

She never asked about Jazzy's progress, and neither Solomon nor Jazzy volunteered any information. She vowed not to interfere. True to her word, she joined her son in his daily run. They went from Goodman to Blakesley to Bricker to Yates and back to Goodman, making one mile, then they ran it again. For someone her age, Jennie was in excellent condition.

It was their secret. She trusted Ida to remain silent about Jazzy's progress. The rest of the neighborhood simply assumed mother and son dined out frequently.

Sit-ups were agony. Solomon was big on sit-ups. The key to conditioning was a hard, flat stomach. Jazzy endured push-ups only because Solomon had an eagle eye and made malingerers suffered the consequences. Jazzy hated push-ups as much as sit-ups.

Solomon worked him hard on the pull-tension equipment to exercise every part of his body. He took to skipping rope naturally and soon became fast with it. Then Solomon viewed him with more interest.

Jazzy cut a length of rope and took it with him, skipping everywhere he could. Jennie became intrigued and asked if she could join him, which delighted her son. Soon, she matched him trick for trick.

The neighbors on either side thought mother and son had finally gone crazy. In addition to the eccentric behavior of skipping rope, they became local pied pipers, as a coterie of joggers joined them on their regular two-mile runs. Nippy Koven, in particular, ran with them, because conditioning was important to a baseball player.

Solomon seemed to be extending the learning process, but he knew what he was doing. Finally, he brought Jazzy to the punching bag. He worked the boy there for so long, Jazzy came close to rebelling. Repetition was the key to developing skills, and Solomon wouldn't let Jazzy off the hook no matter how badly his muscles ached.

Then the meat of the learning process began. Solomon showed Jazzy how to tape his hands and painstakingly showed him how to throw punches. Since that was where Jazzy was the most inept, Solomon kept him on the big bag, practicing jabs, hooks, straight rights, and uppercuts until Jazzy thought he'd die.

At that moment, Solomon commanded him to reach within for more strength, making him end with a fast flurry of both hands pumping hard. He came to resent Solomon. At time, he almost hated the man.

Looking out the pantry window one day, Jennie watched Jazzy shadow box. He threw his left hand with conviction, not like a girlish slap. Then he threw a series of imaginary punches, supposedly to the body before raising his sights to the head. All the while, his feet flashed in movement like a spirited dance. To her untrained eye, he seemed to be doing fine.

At thirteen, Jazzy's days were full. In addition to his training at the gym, he had books to read and school projects to complete. He was still growing, and all that exercise didn't produce a single bulging biceps, triceps, or deltoid. When he lolled around the house, his chest bare, Jennie was filled with motherly pride. Although he had no bulk, he had good definition. His musculature was modest, almost in bas-relief, and, to Jennie, he was a Greek god. She had the urge to run her hands over his marvelously sculpted body and kiss him all over, as she would when he was a child—but Jazzy was no longer a child.

She never considered her preoccupation with his physical attributes and her strong desire to shower him with kisses could be perceived as something sensuous. He was her son.

Puberty came to Jazzy late and without warning. Now he had a preoccupation to deal with—his mother. Unfortunately, she couldn't be easily dismissed. There were times, sitting at the kitchen table, drinking a glass of cold milk to replace the fluids he lost during an arduous workout in the backyard, when his eyes followed her about the kitchen. Her scanty housecoat delineated her figure.

Working at the kitchen sink, Jennie bent low to the cabinet underneath for a sponge, cleanser, or steel wool, and Jazzy was engulfed by distressing emotions. The movement made the hem of her housecoat rise high on her thighs, exposing much of her exquisite legs. The sight made him nervous. His mouth became dry, and the glass in his hand shook. Proper deportment dictated looking away, which he found difficult to do. To his disgust, he looked forward to those moments.

Guilt eventually overcame him, and he hastened outdoors to skip rope again. He atoned for his sins by going through his entire routine of jumping moves until he was utterly exhausted.

Finally, Jazzy was ready to spar with a live opponent. Solomon laced heavy gloves on him and sent him into the ring with a shorter, stockier boy.

The stocky boy rushed Jazzy, but he wasn't there. He danced away. Once again, the boy rushed with hands swinging, but Jazzy simply caught the wild punches on his gloves.

Then Jazzy threw a left, and the other boy went to his knees, blood spurting from his nose. With his gloved hand to his nose, he stalked toward the locker.

Solomon's gaze went to Jazzy thoughtfully. He had speed of foot *and* hand? It was time to take the boy in tow.

Solomon began keeping Jazzy long after his regular sessions were over, leaving Jennie pacing outside the gym. He explained the technique of clinching, rolling with the punch. He showed him how to slip off a punch and use the ropes as part of his offensive or defensive arsenal, stepping back from a punch instead of leaning back, because that strained the back muscles.

Solomon stressed his view that a good right-hander not lose to a lefty. A left-hander was more left-handed than a right-hander was right-handed. With lefties, a man circled clockwise.

Repeatedly, Solomon taught him to feint. It was an art that Solomon, in his heyday, brought to a science. The best feint wasn't showy and apparent. It was barely perceptible.

Jazzy was receptive to all the new moves, and his store of knowledge grew. He was hooked by then, and he was much more realistic than his mentor. He knew his fellow sissies could be had by anyone.

One would've been hard put to find anything memorable about the 1937 graduating class of Townsend Elementary School. If one delved into the school records, he would unearth a remarkable statistic—the entire graduating class, with the exception of Antoinette Dubois, who was exiled to another school district by her parents, remained intact for nine years, if one included kindergarten. That accounted for the closeness of the classmates. There were arrivals and departures at the school, but none affected the original group.

Soon, they'd go to Benjamin Franklin High School, and courses, classes, and teachers would dissolve that unity. People wondered what effect that would have on the boys from Goodman.

It was finally legal to drink alcohol again. Repeal of the Volstead Act was one of the legacies of Roosevelt's New Deal. Marve, still trying to recapture the leadership that slipped away from him, tried to organize a beer party after graduation, but wiser heads vetoed the idea.

The ship of state was still trying to right itself. That took time. Roosevelt asked the country to have faith. With repeal, bootleggers folded their operations and disappeared. The speakeasy and the girls of joy were gone almost overnight. After a flurry of rebuilding, triggering speculation of its new function, what emerged was a large pool hall with eight new tables.

Whitey came from the west side, and he owned and operated the hall. He was a huge man, his stomach so immense his lap disappeared when he sat down. He was dark, too, so it seemed natural to call him Whitey.

The second story of the old, two-story building remained as before, without the women who once lived there.

Mrs. Belding was furious at the thought of a pool hall in the neighborhood. She gathered a group of her sodality sisters, including Jennie, and marched to Father Weideman. He had no heart for such a battle. For one thing, he found nothing sinister about a pool hall unless it hid a nefarious activity. He'd shot pool in his youth and still played a fine game.

He listened to the women calmly and explained there was little anyone could do if the proprietor obtained the proper licenses to operate. He promised to investigate, then concluded by reminding them that the pool hall was an improvement over the immorality the previous owner offered.

Mrs. Belding wasn't mollified. She vowed to watch Whitey like a hawk.

Soon, each Goodman boy found his niche at Franklin High. Marve joined the wrestling club and worked hard in the weight room, striving for muscles. He was already overweight, and it was a foregone conclusion he'd make the wrestling team.

He could've had Antoinette Dubois any time he wanted her, but he, like all the others, wasn't interested anymore. Her past indiscretion wasn't any great thing, nor was she newsworthy. Her center of gravity shifted, turning her into a fat girl, not another Mae West.

Guy Lovell was already breaking away from the gang. He joined the debating team and became a thespian. He was always in rehearsal.

Nippy Koven tried all the sports. The coaches allowed it, because he wasn't that big a boy, and he finally rewarded them when baseball season came and he could show his talent.

Sam Trippett and Jim Logan walked home together. Sam had no interest in after-school activities, and Jimmy still had to get home to let his sister into the house.

Jazzy was fourteen when Ozzie Solomon was finally finished with him. Those were hard times, and Solomon could ill afford to give up Jennie's regular tuition, but he had no choice. He was in danger of losing some other good accounts. Other boys, discouraged when they didn't make progress like Jazzy, threatened to quit, and few would spar with him. That was when Solomon called Johnny Bourda.

Monday night boxing at the Elks Club was the centerpiece of Rochester's sports offerings. It was amateur boxing at its best. The Elks Club graduated the best of eastern amateurs into the ranks of the professionals.

It was a lucrative venture, too. Every card brought large crowds, and, if the fighters were paired well, they had standing room only for the audience.

In addition to showcasing the best amateur fighters around, the Elks Club produced its own fighters. It had a gymnasium, and it was always filled with local hopefuls at every stage of development. The man in charge of the fight mill was Johnny Bourda, a cagey trainer and fine judge of boxing talent.

Ozzie's call amused Bourda. To suggest one of his little Lord Fauntleroys was worth a trip to Solomon's gym was laughable, but Ozzie was a fun guy, and it might be worth a few laughs. They'd been fighters in the same era, and their paths often crossed in the old days. They never fought each other, because Bourda never reached middleweight.

Bourda's eyes swept Ozzie's gym when he arrived and saw nothing unusual about any of the boys. Looking at such a bunch of mama's boys saddened him. He agreed that American children were far behind their European counterparts in fitness.

At that point, Jazzy was still lean and trim, unlike the others. Bourda's skeptical mind skipped over him. If he noticed him at all, it was for his face, but he didn't believe anyone who looked like a combination of Taylor and Power could possibly be a warrior.

Bourda was surprised when Ozzie introduced him to Jazzy. That was the phenomenal kid Solomon trained? He was further dismayed by the boy's voice, which sounded as if he'd just left the cricket or rugby field at Eton. English fighters like Phainting Phil Scott weren't very awe-inspiring either.

Solomon cajoled a larger boy to fighting Jazzy, then let them go at it. From the beginning, Bourda saw things as they were, not as Solomon wished them to be. The boy has learned the rudiments. He threw punches in the prescribed manner and moved like a dancer, but his actions weren't synchronized. Bourda watched Jazzy's feet and had to admit the boy was light and fast.

"Jazzy," Solomon said when they finished, "I'm calling your mother tonight. I can't teach you anymore. You've come a long way and been a prize pupil. Look, let's stop the banana oil. I want you to meet Johnny Bourda, the trainer and matchmaker at the Elks Club."

"I know about you, Mr. Bourda," Jazzy said.

"Good," Bourda replied. "Since you can't continue here, why don't you come to our gym? You can work out there." He wondered if he should warn the boy.

"There's no fee?" Jazzy asked.

"Absolutely not. It's a community service of the Loyal Order of Elks, Rochester Lodge." It seemed certain his boys would kill the new kid.

"What's in it for you?"

Bourda tired to hide his annoyance. "The satisfaction of seeing a youngster develop." He almost choked on the words.

"Let's get one thing straight, Mr. Bourda. Mother has plans for me. I love boxing, but I don't want to be a boxer."

That nettled Bourda. All he wanted was to humor Solomon and get the kid to his own gym for a better look.

"I respect that, Kid. I won't pressure you into the ring. If you change your mind and want to try it, I'll be there to help." He doubted the kid would get that far.

"Fair enough. Mr. Solomon, please don't tell my mother I'll be working out at the Elks Club."

Since the gang, with diverse interests, dispersed at Franklin, Jazzy's long walks after school, down Hudson to Central Avenue and on to the club, went unnoticed.

It was said if all the corridors of Franklin High were laid end-to-end, they'd extend one mile. The school was so big, it threatened to permanently disband the gang. Whitey and his pool hall were a godsend. That was a meeting place to regroup after dark and homework. It was comfortable, exciting, and Whitey was a genial host.

At night, the boys were together like before. They shared the hall with upperclassmen and older youths, and those weren't always welcome.

Since Whitey's was open to all, a forced integration of Goodman people and mudstompers occurred. Strange friendships, previously thought impossible, sprang up. Fun-loving Moon Latuski came out of the thicket, attracted by the hall, and, before long, became a member of the Goodman crowd.

Cock-eyed came in occasionally, strutting, because he played a mean game of pool. He couldn't tell who he might beat in Whitey's, and he wasn't about to find out. Lefty came, but the gang ignored him. He, in turn, socialized only with fellow mudstompers.

Jazzy's friends had no reason to believe he was better prepared to defend himself from another attack than before, but he carried himself with an air of confidence and authority the others accepted without question. Even Cock-eyed showed him respect.

Saturday nights were special, because they were movie time. Sometimes, the girls came along. Without fail, they met after the show at the Greek's Texas Red Hot Café. Jazzy relished the white hots made of pork, found only in Rochester. The camaraderie of those late Saturday night gatherings at the Greek's would be savored for the rest of their lives.

Sundays were special, too, in a different way. Sunday was picnic time, and the Goodman area was blessed with three of the best picnic grounds in the county. The apple trees in Costach's orchard were the sequoias of the city. There was Catina Park, a favorite for the sensational finale of fireworks across Norton in Irondequoit, and no license was required.

Jennie came a long way in her life. She was a woman of influence, and, with Mrs. Belding, became Goodman's conscience. With Mrs. Belding's approval, she went to visit the owner of the pool hall.

"Are you Whitey?" Jennie asked.

"Edward Whitey Alexander, at your service. You're the dancing lady."

"What do you know about me?" Jennie asked in surprise.

"I try to know everybody in the neighborhood."

"To what end?"

"I want to know you as a friend. This'll be my home until I die."

"How dramatic. Next year, you'll probably open a gambling casino somewhere."

"No. I'm at the end of the line."

"Are you running from someone or something?" She could understand that.

"I'm going to die."

"We all are."

"I think I have another year. With luck, two. At the outside, it's four. I'll cross that stream soon enough."

"I'm sorry. There's no mistake?"

"No. My leukemia is terminal. Please, let's change the subject. What can I do for you?"

"Well, a pool hall bothers us on this street. We worry about morality and our children."

"Do you find baseball corrupting?"

"Of course not. It's the great American pastime."

"Billiards is a game not wrapped in the American flag."

"What kind of man would open a pool hall here in Goodman?"

"You're worried about atmosphere. It'll be what I make it. What kind of man am I? I'm a moral man who likes young people. Don't let my dark looks fool you. I've known criminals, but I'm not one of them. I've known degenerates, too, but I'm God-fearing. If I'm guilty of anything, it's that I've been a gambler."

"Didn't you find time for a wife and children?"

"Oh, I was married, all right. I had a son, too."

"What happened?"

"When my wife and I were both young, my gambling forced her to seek assistance from the Catholic Charities."

"How sad."

"She left me and took the boy with her."

"Can you blame her?"

"Not at all, but after all those years, you'd think she'd forgive. I don't know where they are. I never saw the boy again."

"You see? What's to keep you from teaching Jazzy to gamble?"

"If I taught him to gamble, I'd also teach him the stupidity of being a gambler. A knowledge of gambling won't hurt him. It might even save him from being skinned someday."

"I wouldn't want him to be a pool shark, either."

"Certainly, you've read Mark Twain? His famous line is, 'Show me a good pool player, and I'll show you a wasted youth.' That's hogwash. A good player is admired today just as a golfer or polo player is admired by swells. Times change, and we must change with them."

"I can't shake the notion that pool halls and criminals go hand-in-hand."

"Mrs. Rhinehardt, as long as I'm here, all the boys in this area will be the son I lost. If I prepare them to face the bad elements, it'll be with the approval of you parents."

"To my surprise, I find myself agreeing with you. My husband was big and impressive-looking, but he was a pussycat who couldn't cope. If he were alive, I probably would've left him, like your wife left you."

Whitey was there to stay. He became an integral part of the neighborhood, and Father Weideman came to know and respect him. Whitey supported the church, starting with an Annunciation bowling league held at St. Stanislaus bowling alley across the street from the high school.

Chapter Nine

Jazzy entered the Elks Club gym with trepidation. He had a moment of indecision that he finally controlled, then went inside. The clientele weren't much older than his classmates at Solomon's, but they looked older, and each went about his training with a determination that was utterly lacking at Solomon's.

He toured the gym, the walls of which were covered by many photographs of great fighters, past and present.

Johnny Bourda nurtured the Brown brothers like shoots of a very rare plant. Bobby, at sixteen, was the oldest, and Eddie was fifteen. Hughie and Hubert were fourteen-year-old twins. They were impossible to tell apart until they started throwing punches. Sweet Georgie was the fifth brother, a thin youngster who looked undernourished.

Hughie was the best of the lot. Fate was mischievous when the twins were born, because Hughie got all the talent. Hubert had nothing, and the family wouldn't allow him in the ring, not only because they feared he'd be hurt, but because his performance might reflect on Hughie. Hubert was allowed only to spar.

Bourda singled him out and sent him in the ring with Jazzy, who felt uneasy in the presence of athletes. There were no skinny or fat boys there. Hubert looked impressive.

He started cautiously, dancing lightly, throwing an occasional left. Hubert was showboating—weaving, turning from side to side, trying to fake Jazzy with broad movements. Jazzy shot a left, which landed, then he threw three more lefts. He was amazed at how slow his opponent was. Jazzy looked good against him, but Bourda wasn't impressed. He considered Hubert a punching bag.

When Jazzy walked in the next day, Bourda hid Hubert in the office and put Hughie in the ring instead. That would show him what the white boy could do against a good African-American boy. It was a dirty trick, but he had to know how that Adonis could handle the unexpected. It was better to send him home early than let him hang around.

Jazzy was bored. He didn't want to punch that slow kid again, so he threw a left without any enthusiasm. Hughie threw a series of lefts that landed, leaving Jazzy helpless. He never saw the right hand that felled him.

"That's it for Sonny Boy."

Jazzy got up, fighting back hard, and was soon being pummeled. Bourda stopped the fight.

"Stubborn bastard, but enough's enough," Bourda said.

Learning there were twins involved, and he'd been thrashed by the superior one, didn't lessen Jazzy's humiliation. Hughie was no bigger or older than he.

What was the profit in his mother spending her hard-earned money for lessons in self-defense if the result was he could beat up only sissies like himself? Quitting was unthinkable, no matter how much it hurt or how much time it took.

Jazzy was like his mother. Her drive to excel at dancing was, like Jazzy's boxing, a drive for self-worth.

War clouds gathered in European skies, and Jennie saw a striking similarity to the prewar days of her childhood. She had no faith in public officials who promised America would stay out of the European conflict. She knew it was inevitable—familiar names on the lists of dead or wounded, while crippled young men returned from overseas to walk the streets of their hometowns. Apparently, the world hadn't been made safe for democracy after all. It was likely Jazzy would be involved in the next war.

It wasn't the best of times economically, either. The New Deal hadn't solved the country's economic problems. Millions were still unemployed, and Hitler was a bad dream that refused to go away.

She didn't want to dwell on her fears, and she vowed to give her boy plenty of leeway to enjoy those precious years, because he'd never have the chance again. She wondered at his late arrival from school the previous day—she arrived home before he did—but she never questioned him. He graduated from Solomon's without diploma or ceremony.

Jazzy walked into the Elks Club gym for a workout, and Bourda was stunned. He was also angry. Although the gym was said to be open to any boxing aficionado, the program on Monday nights was Bourda's responsibility. He'd have the youngster cluttering up the gym. He'd have to put up with him awhile, but the ring would be strictly out of bounds.

Hughie was stunned, too. He'd been brutal to that white boy. It wasn't that Hughie was mean and enjoyed hurting people, but Jazzy made Hubert look bad, and he'd been getting even.

Hughie watched Jazzy approach, wondering what he intended. To his surprise, Jazzy held out his hand.

"You're a very good fighter, Hughie."

Hughie smiled, and a friendship was born.

Whenever Bourda was away, the other boys sneaked Jazzy into the ring and held back on their punches so they wouldn't hurt him. He put in many rounds with the brothers, and he developed fast. Soon, he forced them to fight back. In the heat of their exchanges, they often hurt Jazzy. He occasionally hurt them, and his foot speed made them work hard.

At Solomon's, there were times the workouts at the weights were so exhausting, Jazzy hated his mentor. Left to his own, he punished himself more than Solomon ever had.

Bourda couldn't help noticing the change in Jazzy. At Solomon's, he had to admit the boy looked to be in good condition, but now, he looked tough and menacing. That meant nothing to Bourda. Hubert was a good example of the principle, *show but no go.* He recalled the night Lou Ambers lifted the lightweight title from Canzoneri. Ambers had the most unimpressive body Bourda ever saw in a fighter.

Returning unexpectedly to the gym one day, Bourda saw Hughie sparring with Jazzy.

"What the fuck's going on?" he shouted, standing next to a small punching bag while someone pummeled it. The constant sound drowned out his words, so he decided to watch.

Jazzy was using his quick feet, while Hughie Brown stalked him. Bourda watched both boys' footwork and was impressed. Hughie was catching Jazzy, but there was no panic.

"What's been going on behind my back?" Bourda muttered.

Hughie nailed Jazzy with a right after a left. Jazzy went down and bounced back up, throwing a left Bourda had never seen him use before. It crashed through Hughie's defense, stopping him short. With Hughie rocking on his heels, Jazzy moved in with a fast right and left. He stepped back and slammed another hard left.

Bourda climbed into the ring and stopped the fight, then he went into his office feeling sheepish. Ozzie hadn't been a dreamer after all. Those kids weren't quite fifteen, but they promised a bright future for the club.

Many exciting things could come from that new development. Jazzy would never beat any of the Brown boys except Hubert, because they got their combativeness the hard way—surviving on the streets, alleys, and playgrounds of Rochester.

That didn't matter. Bourda considered fight attendance. A white boy with the matinee-idol look and proper fighting tools could draw crowds better than his best African-American. It wasn't fair, but that was how it was. The country was more redneck than it liked to admit.

Now the man who'd summarily dismissed the white boy faced the task of convincing him to participate in the Elks Club program.

Jazzy was fifteen and a sophomore in high school. There was still no indication where he'd go after school. Girls in the neighborhood saw him standing at the streetcar stop near school when it rained or snowed. Since it was Jazzy, their dream boat, his mystery trips had to mean romance.

When confronted by the boys, who accepted his affair of the heart as a fact, all the prodding and probing in the world couldn't uncover the identity of Jazzy's great love.

Jazzy joined the gang to see *You Can't Take It With You* at the theater. The crazy antics of a zany cast made for a delightful night, and the gathering at the Greek's continued the hilarity. It was a time of great contentment and well-being.

Marve, who seldom amused Jazzy with his wit, was hilarious giving an imitation of his wrestling coach. Guy Lovell, a raconteur with a variety of traveling salesman and farmer's daughter tales, had Nippy and Jazzy clutching each other as they laughed.

"I just heard one I got from Belding," Guy began.

"The barber?" Sam asked.

"Ida will kill him if she finds he's corrupting me," Jim added.

"It's dated," Guy explained, "back to horse-and-buggy days."

"Christ! What's so funny about those days?" Marve asked. "Is it the one about the chicken crossing the road?"

"You'd be surprised."

"Come on, Marve," Nippy said. "Let him get on with it."

"There was this salesman…" Guy began.

The others hooted.

"He came to town to drum up business, selling farm equipment for miles. He could've been bored stiff in the boondocks, but there was a farmer's daughter…"

They hooted again, and Guy ignored them.

"Her name was Venus, and she gave freely of her favors."

"He laid her many times," Marve felt compelled to explain.

"After several weeks, the salesman moved to the next town. One day, he got a letter from Venus' father."

There's a token of the whipstock that's broken
And footprints on the dashboard upside down
Oh, there must've been some pushin'
'Cause there's spots upon the cushion
And my little daughter Venus ain't come round.

"The salesman's response was quick. He sent a wire back to the father."

Yes, there's a token of the whipstock that's broken
I put those footprints on the dashboard upside down.
But as for your daughter Venus,
I've got pains all through my penis,
And I wish I'd never seen your goddamn town.

The resulting explosions of laughter in the café brought the Greek out of the kitchen.

Kodak Park won the world's softball title in Cleveland in 1936. They failed in two attempts to repeat, but they were still a team to beat as they prepared for another title attempt. Nippy Kuhla furnished the neighborhood with still another reason for pride. He played for the Daw's Drugs team, a good one everyone hoped would be invited to Cleveland.

Kodak, flush with success not only on the field but in the important area of publicity, was generous to the city. They supported softball programs throughout the area.

Saturday nights, the Indians took over the town. The Iroquois lacrosse team, American in origin with full-blooded American Indians on the roster, lured not only fans but an army of starry-eyed stage-door Joanies, including Carrie, Pamela, Josie, and Belle.

The Knot Hole Gang program was especially exciting. The free triple-A baseball at Red Wing Stadium filled a void.

Whitey felt poorly. The best part of his day was when the boys were all home, and he had a moment for silent contemplation. He turned the radio down low and dialed to the station offering popular ballads, wanting to wallow in nostalgia.

When Jazzy walked in, Whitey sat at the counter on a straight-backed chair, listening to a crooner sing *Harbor Lights*. It was a quiet mood, and Jazzy accepted Whitey's offer to sit beside him. The mood was soon shattered by the sound of Miss Laura working on another aria, her voice carrying across the meadow between the pool room and her house.

"Kind of late for that," Jazzy complained.

"Yes, it is. There must be an early audition tomorrow morning. That young lady will make it. Does the name Johnny Bourda mean anything to you?"

Jazzy jumped. "Why, yes. He runs the Elks fights."

"Do the names Bobby, Eddy, Hubert, and Hughie ring a bell?"

"They're Bourda's youngsters, the Brown brothers. They'll be great fighters when they grow up."

"There's a white boy from the neighborhood who mixes it up with them every day. That's you, isn't it?"

"Not every day. Where'd you get your information?"

"Jazzy, I'm a card-carrying gambler. It's my business to know people in the fight fraternity. I saw all of Bourda's fights in the old days."

"Please keep it under your hat, Whitey."

"I don't get it. If your friends knew you were sparring with the Brown brothers, you'd be a big man around here."

"It was my mother who sneaked me out of the neighborhood to Ozzie Solomon's gym. She paid good money for my lessons."

"Why would she want to make a fighter out of you?"

"She doesn't. When another boy gave me an awful beating, and I lay there, unable to do anything about it, she decided to take matters into her own hands."

"Who beat you up?"

"Lefty."

"The mudstomper? Boy, I'd like to see his surprise if he tried that again."

"It won't happen. If I engaged him, I'd be no better than he."

"You're both something."

"Who?"

"You and your mother."

When Jazzy left, the same tenor crooned, *Thanks For the Memories,* a ballad from Bob Hope's movie of the same name. It was a fine melody, but the lyrics made it pertinent to every couple in love.

Whitey was father confessor more effectively than Father Weideman. He swelled with pride at the boys' accomplishments and commiserated over their failures. Almost to a man, the neighborhood was glad to have Whitey. He loved all the boys who visited his pool room.

With each passing day, Jennie's concern for her son mounted. Soon, she'd lose him to the Armed Forces. She wanted him near, because she thrilled to look at and touch him. She increased the dancing lessons, because those made it legitimate for her to have the intimacy she craved. One night of steady rain, mother and son were both home for the evening.

After a medley of jump numbers, Jennie placed Larry Clinton's *Deep Purple* on the record player. Mother and son moved in each other's arms. For some reason, perhaps the insistent rain, that night felt different.

The rain produced a chill in the house, but Jennie felt warmth rising in her. Steadily, her hold on her son tightened. They drew so close, Jazzy's hard body almost crushed her soft breasts.

She reached up to kiss his lips, which she'd done before, but the kiss lingered, and her lips pressed hard against his. They stopped dancing. It wasn't until their lips parted, inviting an intrusion, that they sprang apart as if they'd stepped on a live wire.

Jazzy rushed to his room, mortified. He prayed his mother hadn't noticed his arousal, while Jennie busied herself in the kitchen, feeling devastated.

Each exonerated the other, accepting full responsibility for what could've been a despicable act worthy of a Greek tragedy. The incident remained dormant in both of them—it was something that never happened.

Jazzy had a special place in Whitey's heart. He was proud of Guy Lovell, too, and he knew, long before Guy's peers, that the talkative youngster was fated to do important things.

With Jazzy, there was no direction. He hung around the pool hall more than the others. Whitey wondered if the boy worried that something exciting would happen if he left. He hoped the youngster would find himself soon.

Whitey took him in hand, interpreting his talk with Jennie as permission to tutor her son in the areas of his expertise. Whitey spent hours teaching him the intricacies of card playing and impressing on him the laws of probability. Playing against the odds would bring disaster. He showed Jazzy how to organize his thinking, absorb the activities around the table, and make overt the covert.

Whitey was a fine card player. He explained the involuntary giveaways—movements of body, face, and hands, expressions shown in winning or losing. Most importantly, he explained people's moods.

"Watch how they sit," he told Jazzy. "Are they sitting any differently with a good hand than a bad one? Are they holding bad hands loosely, while good hands are gripped tighter? Facial expressions are just the most obvious."

They made a strange couple, huddled at the counter as if studying stock-market reports, laying out hands and studying the cards.

The lessons Jazzy enjoyed most were the early morning or late-evening pocket billiards sessions. Whitey was generous with Jazzy. All the pool playing in the hours when the hall was closed would've cost Jazzy more than his allowance.

Jazzy learned to be a good shotmaker.

"You're making some fantastic shots, Jazzy. What does that suggest?" Whitey asked.

"I'm getting good?"

"No. You're playing terrible position. The best pool players are those who always seem to be shooting at cripples. The best shotmaker has no chance against a player who plays good position. Now I've taught you all I know, and I warn you not to gamble what you can't afford. You might think you're good, but there are people in your own neighborhood who can whip you in pool and strip you clean at cards."

The communist picnic at the old apple orchard had a fine turnout, not from the group's small membership, but because any picnic was a fine Sunday diversion.

The event was marred by speeches that seemed inflammatory and drew "boos" from the locals, but that was a passing unpleasantness.

The Ukie picnic was coming up soon. That year, as in every year, it was judged the most fun of all the picnics.

Jennie and Jazzy joined Abel, Dora, and Nippy. In a group, they descended on Mateo and Maria. In a merry mood, they drove to Ukie Park in Jennie's car.

The grounds were already crowded when they arrived. Kid games were in progress, and the refreshment stands were three-deep with people. Beer taps flowed continuously.

Nippy, with his mother, was neatly dressed, as he usually was after church, but he wore sneakers.

The call for the men's race came over the loudspeaker. It was a short dash, and, with Nippy's quick start, Jazzy felt his friend had a chance.

The starting gun fired, and Nippy sprang into a quick lead. A tall, blond Ukrainian boy, the picnic favorite, closed the gap in a sudden burst of speed, but he missed beating Nippy to the tape.

A smiling Nippy brought his prize to his mother—a five-dollar gift certificate.

Soon, men began clearing the raised platform for dance contests. The band sat down, and the picnic chairman went to the microphone.

The first contest was a polka, the Ukie favorite. Some contestants, to enhance their chances, wore native costumes. A colorful collection of dancing partners waited for the music.

Jennie watched, wide-eyed. That was her venue. Abel waited to see if any of the musicians were good.

The band played a medley of polkas, the *Helen* and the *Too Fat*. The dancers were good, having done the polka since they were children. Jennie, who danced it often and was an expert, learned new steps from the oldsters who brought them from the Ukraine.

Although it was a ragtag band, Abel was pleased with some of the musicians. Fittingly, the first prize went to an older couple in native attire.

There was a pause before the next contest, featuring the waltz. Jennie saw the first prize was a ham.

"How'd you like to have ham dinner at my house tonight?" she asked Abel.

"Sounds like a winner."

"Where you gonna get a ham so late on Sunday?" Maria asked.

"I've got a ham," Jennie assured her.

"Hey. I'm your neighbor, and a nosy one. I looked in your icebox, and there's no ham."

"That's mine up there." Jennie pointed to the prize.

"Oh, Jennie, really! Who would you dance with?"

"I get the feeling I'm about to be asked to dance," Abel said. "I'm not a bad musician, but I'm lousy on the dance floor. Maybe Mateo…?"

"*Basta!* Not me," Mateo said. "If it was the tarantella, I'd still be no good." He sighed.

"Don't fret, Gang," Jennie said. "I've got the best partner here."

"Who?" they asked in unison.

"Jazzy."

"Oh, Mother," Jazzy said. "I couldn't. Not before all these people."

"Nonsense. You'll put Vernon Castle to shame."

A murmur went through the crowd as Jennie and Jazzy walked up the steps to the platform. Word went out quickly, and almost everyone at the picnic gathered to watch.

The band played a waltz from her past, *Meet Me Tonight in Dreamland*. She was in Jazzy's arms, and she didn't fear the eruption of passion they had on that rainy night. She was in public, and she had the cool reserve of an Englishwoman.

Jennie was pretty, but, on the dance floor, she was a thing of beauty. The pair danced so well that they didn't seem like mother and son, but Rogers and Astaire.

They started with basic moves, but even their simple steps were done with a grace that made them the focus of all eyes. Their steps were so light, their turns so graceful, the audience applauded almost immediately.

Then they offered the many nuances of the waltz, giving beautiful interpretations to a beautiful song. Their hesitations, done superbly, froze them into two statues for a second, bringing tears to Maria's eyes. Dora held her hand to her throat. The crowd watched in awe as the pair made their cross-overs. When they spun effortlessly on the balls of their feet, as if on the pedestal of a music box, the applause was deafening.

When it was over, they had trouble getting through the crowd.

"If we hurry home," Jenny suggested, "I can pop the ham in the oven, and we can have dinner at seven, not eight."

"Let's go," Abel said, leading the way to the car.

"Mrs. Rhinehardt?" a small voice called. "Is it all right if Jazzy stays behind?"

"You're Mrs. Evan's girl, Carrie, aren't you?" she asked. "If he wants to stay, it's all right with me."

Carrie didn't wait for Jazzy to speak. She handed him the blanket she carried, and he glanced at a smirking Nippy for help, but there wasn't any.

Taking Jazzy by the hand, Carrie dragged him off into the crowd. He hadn't wanted to spend the rest of the afternoon with Carrie Evans, but he couldn't balk without creating a scene.

To his astonishment, she led him from the picnic grounds to the willows. He could have taken a stand once they were free of the crowd and ended the abduction, but curiosity made him let her play out the game.

She wasn't particularly attractive, but she was a girl, and it would be a learning experience. For some time, strange and powerful urges, controlled with exhausting workouts in the gym, had been painfully suppressed.

Carrie was ecstatic. Her desire for Jazzy had simmered for years, and it was hard to believe she finally had him in tow. Although some would've called her promiscuous, she felt she'd been faithful to him over the years. She may've given her body to others, but her heart was reserved for Jazzy.

Chapter Ten

They weren't alone in the thicket of willows. Other couples, either in parked cars or concealed by shrubs and trees, shared their privacy. The willows were familiar to Carrie, and she unerringly chose the ideal location, where a square of trees was augmented by honeysuckle.

She spread out her blanket and sat down, then yanked Jazzy's belt, forcing him to his knees beside her. He sat motionless on his heels, and Carrie realized she had to take the lead. She unbuttoned her blouse sufficiently to slip his hand inside, placing it on her small breast. He recoiled from the touch and tried to rise, but she held his shirt and realized there was no great romance in his life after all. He was a virgin!

She thought of the sleepless nights, lying in bed, tearing herself up inside with visions of him in bed with some stranger. She realized she wasn't going to have the ultimate sexual experience she anticipated, but there was joy in knowing she'd be his first.

Slowly, she removed her blouse, exposing her breasts for his disturbed inspection. She reached up to unbutton his shirt, feeling his chest with shock. He had the hard, contoured body of a trained athlete.

She pulled him roughly down on her, turning him, so he was underneath. She kissed his neck, chest, and stomach savagely, then she reversed positions, and held him close, kissing him hard on the mouth.

She felt his arousal and hastened the lovemaking. She would've preferred an exquisite, leisurely foreplay, but she deftly removed the last of her clothes and helped him disrobe.

She was directing him toward her when he climaxed. It was a disaster, and Jazzy was mortified.

"Never mind, Honey," she said as she dressed. "Next time, it'll be great."

At the Democrats' picnic at the apple orchard, far enough removed from the picnic so they didn't hear anything, Carrie led Jazzy to a clearing and spread her blanket under an apple tree. That time, it was better, but she had to hurry things a bit.

The next Sunday, they were back at the willows when the Garibaldi Club rented Catina Park. They were farther from the willows than from Ukie Park.

Jazzy was learning, mastering control and timing. Now it was as exciting as Carrie dreamed.

There was no picnic on Labor Day in the neighborhood, so they arranged to meet at the willows. He walked in and found her waiting for him.

Due to her infinite patience and his fine instincts, the pacing was perfect. She felt exhilarated and was loathe to pull away. She wanted him to remain in her arms forever. She trained him well, and he'd no longer be hers exclusively.

As for Jazzy, lingering in her arms was luxurious. They languished lazily, their senses devoid of eroticism, because their sexuality was fulfilled for the moment. It was comforting being in her caring embrace. The communion was new to him. He wasn't in love with her, but she'd always be a part of him.

When Moon saw the pool hall replace the speakeasy and bordello on the corner, he knew traffic would increase. He laid out his plans for his father, and Mr. Latuski didn't hesitate. He rounded up his brothers and browbeat them into giving him an interest-free loan.

The Latuskis built a combination gas station and repair garage. Moon was already a fine mechanic, but there was the problem of manning the station. It was unseemly for the pretty Latuski girls to work there, and brother Lou was too young. That left Mr. Latuski and Moon, and they both had twelve-hour shifts.

In a short time, the station became another gathering place for the gang. That made Moon's long work shift more bearable. Late at night, when restaurants and taverns finally closed, it was comforting to drop by and chat with Moon over a cup of coffee from a large urn.

Moon was eighteen and a graduate of Irondequoit High. Hitler's ambitions made a mockery of the peace efforts of European appeasers, but Roosevelt still assured America that no American boy would fight on foreign soil. He hedged, however, and his administration instituted peacetime conscription.

The threat of military service hung over Moon's head. He hired Jay Bright, and, for a while, there were three shifts at the station, each eight hours long.

Jay moved into the neighborhood from the coal mines of West Virginia. He was a dropout, because his income from working in the mines was critical to his family's survival. When his father died of silicosis, Jay, who was still only a boy, took his mother and sister north in an old truck piled high with their belongings. When they reached Rochester, they ran out of money.

A compassionate Jimmy Logan took Jay in hand and pressured Moon into hiring him.

Jazzy's senior year was hectic. He tried to do too many things and be everywhere at once. Bobby, Eddie, and Hughie became headliners. Often, the three brothers were on the same card. Ring experience began to tell. In addition to the brothers improving, Jazzy's reduced hours in the gym took their toll.

Johnny Bourda was still hopeful about getting Jazzy to become a boxer, and he had Jazzy fight Hughie less and less. At Jazzy's present rate of development, Hughie could hurt him.

With government orders for footwear for men in the service, Abel's old shoe factory reopened. Many, like Abel, were rehired. It seemed it took a war in Europe to start many idle industries.

Abel bought a used Studebaker and taught his son to drive. Jazzy was the last one in his crowd who didn't have a driver's license.

With apprehension, he approached his mother about it, but she'd been waiting for him.

"Sure," she said. "Learn to drive anytime. You can use the car, but you have to get a teacher, because I can't do it. My nerves couldn't take it."

Jazzy asked Moon to teach him.

"Are you sure you want to learn on your mother's car?" Moon asked.

"What's wrong with it?"

"It's ten years old. How does she keep it running?"

"She takes good care of it."

"I don't know about that. Right now, it needs a lot of work."

"Why don't you tell her that, Moon?"

"Yeah. I'll have you learning on a new car." Moon winked.

Jennie brought her car in for a tune-up.

"Gee, Mrs. Rhinehardt," Moon said, "why spend more money on this heap?"

"What do you want me to do with it?"

"Trade it in and get a new one."

"Just like that?"

"The car doesn't owe you anything, Mrs. Rhinehardt. It carted you around for ten years, and that's a lot more years than most cars in snow country."

"Well, you just lost some business. If I find I can't swing a new car, I'm coming back with this heap."

"Fair enough, Mrs. Rhinehardt."

Moon didn't really talk her into buying a new car. She'd been thinking of it for some time. When Abel bought his Studebaker at the used-car lot.

There was talk that, if America entered the war, there wouldn't be any new cars available. Factories would produce nothing but military vehicles.

Jennie didn't like the style of the Chryslers, and the Plymouth, which was in her price range, looked like a box. The Ford had the reputation of being a rattletrap. The country was Chevrolet crazy, so she bought one.

To Jazzy's surprise, Jennie was generous with her new car. She worried about his future, because it was clear the country would enter the war eventually. Jazzy's generation would do all the fighting. For the present, she wanted him to enjoy his senior year.

There was a whirlwind of activities at Franklin High. There were rallies and dances, but the most exciting events were football games. After a decade of losing constantly, the Quakers found the right formula and became the league's powerhouse.

The line was big and tough, and the backfield had speed and power. It also had Marty Flood. In the Quaker single-wing attack, Marty, a rugged tailback of considerable talent, did the running, passing, and kicking.

For three years, Jazzy kept a low profile, dashing out of school after the final bell to hasten to the Elks Club. He was highly visible, and all the girls in Franklin High knew of the Greek god who danced like an instructor for Arthur Murray.

He attended all the dances, and there were times he wanted to sit out a set and talk with his friends, but girls constantly approached him, even when they didn't know him. He never refused, which added to his charm.

He worried his friends thought him aloof, but they never resented him. He was born good-looking and to dance. Had he not aborted all attempts of his friends to run for homecoming king, he might've won. As it was, the choices were predictable and traditional. Invariably, the football hero is king, and the most attractive cheerleader his queen.

The results of the student voting were announced during halftime against the school's traditional rival, East. That year, East High was but another date on the Franklin calendar. The fans were in a holiday mood, because the score was 21–0 at the half.

"Attention, please!" the loudspeaker blared. "This year, you students have voted our homecoming king to be our football phenomenon, Marty Flood!"

Marty came to the stand to receive his crown. He was a popular choice.

"Now, for the homecoming queen, you've chosen the fairest of the fair, Bonnie Cook!"

There was no doubt about how the students felt about Bonnie. She was a tall, leggy blonde with blue eyes. She had a provocative walk, and her march to the stand drew a chorus of whistles. Hers was a classic beauty, with a face that seemed molded from a priceless intaglio of a genteel lady from a fabled court.

Jimmy Logan asked for a favor. His sister, Cathy, who was a junior, was allowed to attend the homecoming dance only if under her brother's watchful eye. The family car wasn't available, so Jimmy asked Jazzy if they, with Viola, could accompany Jazzy. Once at the dance, everyone was on his own.

All the Goodman crowd attended the homecoming dance. Some brought dates, others went stag. The dance committee went over budget and hired an exceptional band.

Jazzy enjoyed dancing. He executed jump numbers as expertly as slow ones. He treated each of his partners like a queen. The band played *The Nearness of You,* an appropriate title, considering the excitement Bonnie Cook generated in him as she approached. It looked like he'd get a respite and be able to join his friends, then she appeared.

"Isn't it about time you danced with me, Jazzy?" she asked.

He was pleased she knew his name. "Where's the king?"

"Off somewhere, basking in the limelight." She moved in closer and proved to be a good dancer. Whoever chose her gown was inspired. She was lovely, and there was a murmur among the other dancers as Jazzy and Bonnie moved gracefully across the floor.

He felt her snuggle in close, and her arm tightened around his neck. Her face nestled against his neck and shoulders, and her subtle perfume was devastating.

When the dance ended, Jazzy felt someone brush past him and saw Marty Flood. Marty grabbed Bonnie's hand and pulled her roughly away.

"You're supposed to be with me, remember?" he asked her, giving Jazzy a look of hate.

Jazzy recognized the merits of Marty's claim and stepped away. Out of respect, he sought out Cathy twice, and he danced with Viola once. Then he saw Bonnie approach him again.

The sight of her excited him, as always, even from his distant seat in the stands. He saw her instantly in that row of pretty cheerleaders. Up close, she was intoxicating. Jazzy feared a confrontation with Marty.

There was no graceful way to refuse a lady, especially if she was a queen. Jazzy put his arm around her and led her onto the dance floor as the band played *The Breeze and I.* He held her close and felt her lips pass lightly across his neck.

His rapture was interrupted when Marty returned to the dance floor. He came between them, put both hands on Jazzy's chest, and pushed. Jazzy staggered back and tried to explain all he wanted was to dance with Bonnie.

A crowd gathered, and Marty dreaded a scene on the dance floor that wouldn't be judged worthy of a king.

"Outside, Fairy," he ordered. "To the parking lot."

"Please, don't do this," Jazzy pleaded. "I told you she's your girl. All she is to me is a dance partner."

"Outside!"

Marty grabbed Jazzy's arm and led him outdoors with a small crowd following. Jazzy's friends converged on the group in distress, wondering if it would be a repeat of the Lefty episode.

Marty peeled off his coat and flexed his muscles, making them bunch under his shirt. He looked formidable.

Jazzy made one last attempt at appeasement to no avail, then he saw Bonnie in the crowd. He hoped she'd stop Marty, but she remained silent as a soft smile crept across her lips.

"We don't have to do this," Jazzy told Marty.

"Fuck you, Fruitcake. I'm going to rearrange your pretty face." Marty basked in the approving shouts of his teammates.

"We can't let this guy mess up Jazzy," Guy Lovell said softly.

"No way," Nippy added.

Marve eyed the group of football players supporting Marty. "We can't start a gang fight. It's between the two of them."

"Stuff it, Marve," Nippy said. "I'm helping my friend."

The rest of the boys followed him, and Jazzy hid his exasperation with Marve. Why didn't he mind his own business? Sparring with protective headgear and padded gloves was one thing, but a bare-knuckle brawl was another. He still remembered the drubbing Lefty gave him.

"Stay out of this, Fellows," he told them. "Marve's right. This is my fight."

Slowly, he took off his coat and handed it to Jim Logan. Marty lost no time, diving in with a right and a left.

Maybe I can get him out of action, Jazzy thought, coming in under the blows and giving Marty's exposed midsection a hard punch.

Marty sank to his haunches, gasping for breath and feeling a terrible pain in his stomach. It came to him he'd made a horrible mistake. His friends laughed nervously, which made giving up impossible.

With the help of his friends, he stood and charged again, throwing a wild right. Jazzy blocked it with his left forearm, and, in the same motion, his left fist continued until it crashed against Marty's nose. A rush of relief filled Jazzy. His tormentor didn't know a left hook from a right cross! He came up to his toes, rammed in five unanswered jabs, and danced smartly away.

The sight of blood gushing from his nose and mouth gave Marty new zeal. Jazzy had to pay. He moved in again, more cautiously. Jazzy gave a slight feint, just a quiver of his left shoulder, and Marty fell for it, throwing his right hand to his face to block the anticipated blow, while his left remained low. Jazzy shot a hard right, connecting solidly with the left side of Marty's face and sending him to the ground for the last time.

Silently, the crowd trudged back to the dance. The strange Adonis had completely destroyed their football hero.

The boys in the gang were silent with shock. Was that the same Jasmin Rhinehardt they'd protected so assiduously since kindergarten? He could beat them all if he wanted.

The dance was over, so Jazzy took Logan and the girls home in Jennie's car. They rode in silence.

After his passengers were out and standing at the curb before the Logan house, Jazzy said, "Good night, Gang."

"Good night, Jazzy."

"Jazzy," Logan said, "you've got some explaining to do."

"I know."

Jennie hadn't expected Jazzy to come home so soon. She poured him a cup of coffee and asked about the dance.

"I enjoyed it," he said. "I danced most of the dances and met some nice girls."

They discussed the band and lamented the decline of traditional dances, agreeing dancing was in trouble.

Later, he was still awake when the phone rang, and he rushed to answer, fearing it would wake his mother.

"That you, Jazzy?" a girl asked.

"Yes."

"This is Bonnie."

"What's wrong, Bonnie?" He dreaded the thought of her telling him Marty was really hurt.

"You ruined my evening."

"How do you figure that?" He became angry. "Do you know what time it is?"

"Never mind that. You messed up my boyfriend, and I'm sitting home alone."

"Where are your parents?"

"In New York. Besides, I'm not *home* home. I'm at our summer cottage by the lake."

"You woke me up to tell me that?"

"Shit, I didn't wake you up. You answered on the first ring. I called to tell you that you owe me."

"Owe you what?"

"It's a hell of a way to finish my coronation, sitting here alone. The least you can do is come and keep me company."

"You're crazy."

"I'm not messing around, Jazzy. Get your ass over here. If you don't come, I'll be over. I got your address from the phone book."

"You'd better not mess with my mother."

"I'll mess with her and make so much racket, I'll wake the whole neighborhood. Try me if you think I'm bluffing."

"Wait. I'll see if I can get the car again." Jazzy walked to his mother's room and knocked on the door.

"What is it, Jazzy?" Jennie asked sleepily.

"One of the gang can't get his car started. He needs a ride."

"Well, OK. You've still got the keys. Drive carefully."

Jazzy went back to the phone. "I'll be there as soon as I can. What's the address?"

"10704 Lakeside Avenue, about three miles west of Sea Breeze."

"Got it."

Jazzy had trouble finding the cottage and drove past it twice. It was set farther from the road than the other cottages. When he finally drove down her long driveway, whatever resentment he had toward her for her bold intrusion into his life vanished. He was filled with an excitement he hadn't felt in previous trysts. He was meeting the homecoming queen.

She greeted him at the door wearing only step-ins and bra. When he saw her in the dim light, so scantily dressed, his throat went dry, and his hands shook. Hers was a cold beauty. The color of her eyes was the cold blue of a deep tarn. Her skin was white and as cold as the angry waters of the rapids. She had perfect proportions, as if cast in wax and positioned inert in a wax museum.

He followed her into the bedroom. The look in her eyes wasn't cold, and he recalled wax burned hot. He was struck by the incongruity of the elegant four-poster in a weatherbeaten summer cottage by the lake. His sexual experiences to date had been under trees, in the back seat of his mother's car, and once, in complete darkness, on the gym floor behind the temporary bandstand.

The light from the single lamp was sufficient for Jazzy's nervous stare. She was no adolescent. She was heavier-bosomed than even her scanty cheerleading outfit displayed.

She unfastened her bra with tantalizing slowness, freeing her breasts, then stepped out of her step-ins and stood before him naked. Jazzy was sure no artist or sculptor ever had more to work with.

"Are you glad you came?" she asked.

"Yes," he replied hoarsely.

"Did you vote for me, Jazzy? Am I your queen?"

"Yes." He moved to gather her in his arms.

She held him off with a hand against his shirt front. Because he made her the supplicant—for the first time in her life—she intended to bring him to heel.

"Well, Lover, you've been ogling my goodies. It's only fair I inspect yours." She moved closer and held his face in both hands to kiss him lightly.

She unbuttoned his shirt and helped him remove it, then stripped off his pants while he kicked off his loafers and peeled off his socks. She ran her hands over his body. When she reached his shorts, she yanked them off without bothering to unbutton them. His arousal showed his desire, and she became wide-eyed.

His slenderness and grace caught her eye many times before, but the fact that he was as tough and threatening as a bullwhip came as a revelation. Marty had no way of knowing what he'd antagonized.

All thoughts of reprisal for his lack of initiative vanished. The cool straw blonde with the haughty look of royalty was fever hot. She crushed herself against him, kissing him fiercely. She backed slowly to the bed until it touched the backs of her knees, then she let herself drop, falling backward and bringing him down with her.

They rolled until he was on top, their hands moving frantically over each other. They lingered too long for delightful exploration.

Their climaxes came suddenly, but they were prolonged, bringing an agony of mind and body. She bit his shoulder to muffle the cries her body forced her to make. She felt she'd wasted many years not noticing him. He'd been under her nose all the time.

Afterward, she slept in his arms.

Jennie was determined to put the gruesome business of Martino's death from her mind, but the newspapers caught the story and announced the man who died wasn't just a derelict, he'd once been the proprietor of the elegant Oasis. Then the floodgates of her mind opened, and the guilt she rejected caused her the first of several sleepless nights.

Someone from the sheriff's office had fingerprinted the dead man and sent the prints to Washington, where they lay for some time. The panhandler's identity wasn't important. Fatalists always held the moment of one's death was predetermined, but that didn't erase the onus of her actions.

She mentally kicked herself for running into Sibley's. She should've outrun the old man on Main Street, but her plan wasn't that bad. She entered the store to force Martino to choose one of its many exits.

She wondered what went wrong. Either he, too, dared the traffic, or the lights changed almost immediately. For an old codger, he'd been fast. He entered the building in time to see her stepping off the up escalator.

The police promised a complete investigation, because Martino's death was big news, but that didn't bother her.

Chapter Eleven

Marve struggled hard to establish his self-worth. He realized he didn't have Guy's flair and eloquence, Jazzy's physical attraction, or Nippy's athletic attributes. That was why he put all his time and energy into wrestling, where weight often equated to strength. To his credit, he became Franklin High's representative in school competition.

His record as a wrestler was undistinguished in the first three years. Then everything fell into place. As a senior, he lost only four matches—two to O'Brien, a sophomore from East High. O'Brien had two more years of eligibility, and he was a coach's dream.

Penner, from West, also beat Marve twice during three seasons. He, in turn, was beaten twice by O'Brien that year. The seedings for sectionals had O'Brien as the favorite, followed by Penner and Marve.

In the semifinals, O'Brien handled Penner with ease, but Penner was a wily wrestler and defending champion. Although he lost twice to O'Brien, he'd never been pinned. If O'Brien pinned Penner, he'd have the distinction of pinning all opponents, a rare feat.

As the fight progressed, time was running out. Even if Penner maintained his present position to the end of the match, he couldn't overcome O'Brien's point advantage. To win, Penner had to pin O'Brien, which he knew he couldn't do.

There was an urgency in O'Brien to escape from the hold Penner had. If he did it quickly enough, he might have time for a pin. He grabbed Penner's forearms that were around his waist and, with a supreme effort, pried them loose, then he dived forward in a standard escape. All he had to do was get off the mat, which would stop the clock and force a face-off, but that took precious time.

O'Brien took one step forward, turned, and dived at Penner, hoping to catch him by surprise. His forehead struck Penner's knee hard enough to stun him.

If there was one thing Penner knew, it was how to finish an opponent who was in trouble. He pinned O'Brien and felt overcome with joy. He never envisioned such a victory.

Penner dismissed Marve as a mere formality. He'd never lost a match to the awkward Quaker wrestler.

He was still dwelling on beating O'Brien when he faced Marve, who arrived in the finals from a weaker bracket. Penner's coach tried to make his wrestler concentrate on the job at hand, which wasn't easy.

Marve's strategy wasn't very inspired. He was a plodder, and he used his weight and strength to keep from being upended. Penner's disdain for Marve was his undoing. He neglected to fight low, getting down and holding Marve captive. On several occasions, he let Marve squirm off the mat and spent valuable time trying to pin him with furious but standardized attacks. By virtue of his size and brawn, Marve couldn't be budged.

Penner, who never before had any trouble escaping from Marve, suddenly found his timing off and balance awry. His coach shouted at him that the match was too close. Marve was riding Penner, and the crowd cheered for the underdog.

Marve held on, refusing to be thrown. Penner couldn't escape, and time ran out. His coach threw his clipboard against the wall, shattering it, and a shocked Penner realized he'd just blown the championship.

It was a red-letter day for Goodman Street. They weren't accustomed to having a genuine champion come from the neighborhood. Sam was the first to think of a victory party for Marve. When he told Whitey, Whitey took over the arrangements and paid for it himself. Sam collected money for a proper gift.

Whitey covered one of his tables with oilcloth, then placed linens on that. He was lavish with food and soft drinks and held an open house all evening.

The gift pleased Marve—a black-and-white gym bag bearing the legend, *Heavyweight Wrestling Champion 1940*.

That senior year at Franklin High was a banner year for Guy Lovell, too. Everyone rejoiced at his accomplishments, although they weren't as dramatic as winning the wrestling championship. Soon after the debating team won the county finals, led by Guy's brilliant performance, the school presented its annual play. He'd been a Thespian for four years and had an important role. Even though it wasn't the lead, it required considerable acting skill. For the second straight year, the club elected to present a Henry Carlson play called *Satin in our Midst*.

Jazzy was impressed and proud of his friend, but Marve, somewhat put out at the diversion from his great moment, was sullen.

"It's no big deal to win a debate and go on the stage when you've got a big mouth," Marve said.

Jazzy saw both plays and liked them. The previous year's performance impressed him in particular. *Wolves at Bay* had the same terrifying intensity as Sherwood's *Petrified Forest*. He had a new respect for playwrights. Moving a story by dialogue alone, without benefit of descriptive and narrative prose, was superb craftsmanship.

"There haven't been any new Carlson plays, have there?" Jazzy asked Guy.

"No. He gave up on the world. He's playing hermit someone in the boonies in the state."

"What a waste."

Before the year was out, Kodak Park won its second world softball title. For the moment, the war was forgotten. The boys chided Nippy for dropping softball and missing the excitement in Cleveland.

"I ain't missing a thing," he replied. "Softball's an abortion. Give me Shift Gears of Kodak on the mound, a good catcher, and I'll field seven girls. The worst I can get is a scoreless tie."

Secretary of the Navy Frank Knox's lottery finally caught up with Moon. He enlisted to escape being drafted, and he left Jay Bright with the responsibility of the gas station. Cock-eyed was caught in the conscription web, too. Bobby and Eddie Brown were already in the service, which left Hughie as the only fighting Brown at Bourda's stable.

Bourda pleaded with Jazzy to get on a fight card, but Jazzy was adamant. Fight trainees were getting scarce. To keep Hughie in shape, Bourda had no choice but to throw Jazzy in the practice ring with Hughie regularly.

Bourda was right—Hughie could hurt Jazzy—but all the Brown brothers were fond of him, knowing he could be trusted. Jazzy was improving, too, and he gave Hughie some much-needed workouts.

Mary Burns had been an English teacher for thirteen years and was in her mid-thirties, convinced great romance wasn't coming her way. She was still a romantic at heart and freely admitted to her class she saw all Don Ameche's films.

He was no matinee idol, and his movies weren't always first-rate. She sat in the dark recesses of the movie house, closed her eyes, and listened to his deep, resonant voice, which gave impetus to private flights of fancy.

It was that way with the Rhinehardt boy, too. He was an extraordinary young man, possessing a voice with the full, thrilling quality of Ameche and a precise way of speaking that was Ronald Coleman's hallmark.

Filled with guilt that a seventeen-year-old could affect her emotions, she wondered if she was abnormal.

She asked the class to memorize a few lines of poetry over the weekend, and Jazzy memorized Coleridge's *Rhyme of the Ancient Mariner*.

Monday, Miss Burns lost no time starting the recitations. Predictably, Marve gave a few lines from Longfellow's *Village Blacksmith*. Nippy recited the dramatic finish to *Casey at the Bat,* and Carrie Evans gave a few lines from Poe's *Annabel Lee.*

Then it was Jazzy's turn. His rendition of Coleridge, done in a voice perfect for dramatic recitation, held the class captive. They'd gone through the *Rhyme of the Ancient Mariner* in their junior year, but they listened to it as if for the first time.

Jazzy was showing off. He had no interest in the tiresome epic, but he wanted to impress his classmates. Still the need for exhibition bothered him.

A performance like that merited a closer look at the young man, or so Miss Burns told herself when she asked him to stay after school. She knew she was lying to herself. What she wanted was a chance to have him near her alone before he stepped from her life forever.

"How'd you get started reading?" she asked.

"The first book Mom read to me was *Mother Goose.*" He smirked.

"Let's update it a little, shall we?"

"Actually, my first novel was *Ramona.* Mom read that to me many times. It was kind of our family Bible. It must've had a special meaning for her."

"It's a fine novel of California's early days. You couldn't start with better."

"That's the only one Mom was involved with. She's not much of a reader. I've been on my own. The first fiction I read without the guidance of school was the entire Tarzan series. A man living with apes is a keen idea."

"Read Doyle, too. You'll feel the same about his series and will probably want to be a detective." She forced herself to sound interested.

"I'm reading Sabatini now, Miss Burns, because Errol Flynn's making great movies from his books."

"Yes, Mr. Flynn makes a wonderful swashbuckler."

"I wonder if he'll play *Scaramouche?*"

"I doubt it. He'd be out of character," she said wearily. "My brother's boy feels the same way about Sabatini. Your tastes seem to run to high adventure. Why don't you try Ferber, Twain, Alcott, Tarkington, Dickens, Lewis, Fitzgerald, Dos Passos, Steinbeck…?"

"That's a tall order, Miss Burns."

"Remember how the class read A *Tale of Two Cities?*"

"Yeah. Charles Darnay was a wimp. Carton was a real hero."

"Dickens wrote so many classics, I'd strongly advise you to read as much of him as you can."

"I liked it when the class read *Moby Dick.*"

"Try his *Billy Budd.* It might not be available at the library, though."

"Why?"

"Melville was lightly regarded in his time. Even now, he's not considered a giant. If you liked Melville, try Conrad. You'll love his *Lord Jim.* I have a high regard for Conrad. English was his fourth language."

"Imagine that!" Jazzy paused to digest that. "I'm reading Wilder's *The Bridge of San Luis Rey.* It's tough going, but I'm anxious to learn what the author is trying to say."

"I wish I could see his *Our Town* on Broadway," she sighed, realizing she'd forced her interest in books long enough. "Widen your horizons, young man." She wanted to add, "Hold me in your arms," but didn't.

Spring came, the harbinger of new adventures. Franklin High was out of the baseball race almost from the start of league play. The team had a dismal start, but they had Nippy cavorting around shortstop like Lou Boudreau with speed. He had quick hands and a strong arm, and, at bat, he was too tough to strike out.

Before final exams, the school announced the All-Scholastic team. Nippy Koven was a nearly unanimous choice as shortstop. That should've attracted baseball scouts, but high-school students, about to be drafted, weren't ideal prospects.

There was a celebration at Whitey's which surpassed Marve's. The boys began to feel Goodman Street was a special place, breeding special people. Whitey liked all the boys, but he'd been in many neighborhoods and knew none was better than any other.

There was a frantic scurrying for dates for the upcoming prom. With the exception of Jazzy and Antoinette, the pairings were within the confines of the neighborhood, which pleased all the mothers.

Jimmy Logan, protesting too loudly he had to take Viola to the prom, wore down Marve until he agreed to be Cathy's date, because Jimmy's parents wanted him to keep an eye on her. The Logan car was made available for the event, and the caravan left for the school.

Whitey was left with an empty pool hall. He took advantage of the respite and indulged in nostalgia, aided by his favorite radio station.

Sam Trippett's date was Belle, while Guy was taking Josie. When Nippy announced he was taking Carrie to the prom, Jazzy smiled. He didn't know if Nippy had lost his virginity yet, but it was his guess he hadn't. After the prom, Jazzy felt certain Carrie would direct Nippy to the willows to begin his learning process.

As for Antoinette Dubois, the memory of her meeting with Kevin Kilty hadn't faded completely. She attended the prom with her cousin, whom she passed off as a Hobart man.

Bonnie and Jazzy had been too much to each other during their senior year to consider any other date for the prom. It would be their farewell. Bonnie's father had made arrangements for her to attend Cornell, and Jazzy's future was tied to military service.

She came from wealth of several generations' maturity. Once she left for college, the ties that bound her to Jazzy would be severed. For the moment, they'd make the best of their last evening together.

Maria and Mateo came to gawk, and Maria had the privilege of fastening the white carnation to Jazzy's lapel. They eyed him critically as he stepped back for final inspection. In a tuxedo, with a white shirt, black tie, and matching cummerbund, he looked like a matinee idol.

"Mama *mia!*" they exclaimed.

Mr. Cook wasn't happy that Bonnie elected to attend her senior prom with someone from the rural Franklin High School. He couldn't understand her lack of class. There were many fine young men from good families who would've been flattered to escort his daughter.

When Mrs. Cook ushered Jazzy into the foyer, however, she gasped. He wore his evening clothes with an air of aristocracy. He moved with grace, and his voice surprised and thrilled her. He was so fair, his features so finely sculpted, she dared not look into his deep-blue eyes too long for fear of betraying her admiration. There would've been something wrong with Bonnie if she elected to go with anyone else.

Bonnie walked slowly down the stairs, presenting her parents and date with a lingering look at her elegance. Her gown was long, with a princess neckline. The short sleeves puffed at the shoulders, and the bodice was form-fitted and buttoned down the back. The dress was made of black chiffon.

She wisely decided against jewelry, making her gown a simple, effective showcase to display her loveliness. The dance floor would be swimming with gowns of holidays reds, blues, greens, and yellows, while she and her beau would be a symphony in black.

When she reached him, Jazzy pinned a corsage of white carnations to her gown. Mrs. Cook wouldn't let them go until she took several pictures of the couple. Mr. Cook grudgingly agreed they were the finest couple he'd ever seen.

Bonnie's instincts were usually right concerning self-adornment. She fought off the objections of parents and friends who tried to tell her black was somber and dreary. They were wrong. On a statuesque blonde with such a beau ideal, black was devastating, and the couple would be the focus of all eyes on the dance floor.

Some of the girls who agonized over the colors most complimentary to their attributes were chagrined when Bonnie and Jazzy walked in. Bonnie stole a march on them all—with basic black.

It was a night of exhilaration and depression. Most, except during the graduation ceremony, would never see each other again. Behind the facade of gaiety, Bonnie grieved at losing Jazzy. He could leave her weak-kneed with a glance, a touch, or a word.

Her father needn't have worried about his daughter's future. When Bonnie made a firm commitment, it would be with the right young man who could support her in grander style than he could wish.

At the moment, Bonnie had an overpowering urge for Jazzy. While the Goodman gang adjourned to the Greek's, Jazzy took Bonnie to the summer cottage by the lake. When they finally parted, she cried. Jazzy comforted her stoically, acting impassive and laid back, like Robert Donat. Ronald Coleman had his share of sad partings and never cried in public.

Always in the past, Jennie comforted him, but how could he tell her he'd just lost his steady lover and only now realized what she meant to him? There was still a desperate need for comfort. He didn't know if he should disrupt her sleep and seek consolation from her.

Timidly, he knocked on her door, and she awoke.

"Come in," she said.

He walked in and saw her lying on the covers in her nightgown, covering her thighs as he entered. Slowly and in detail, he explained his long relationship with Bonnie. As he described his misery at their parting, he began crying.

Her heart went out to him. There was no hypocrisy about her—she'd known he was sexually active for some time.

At the moment, though, she wasn't facing a maturing high-school senior but a small, weak, defenseless, hurt child. He was her boy, and she held out her hands, which he eagerly accepted.

He lay atop her as he'd done many times as a child, his chest against her breasts. She sang a childhood ditty, then stopped. Suddenly, they were both aroused. With a Herculean effort, she controlled herself and gently pushed him off.

"Go to bed," she said. "We both need our sleep."

Jazzy went to the kitchen in emotional turmoil. He cried again, but not for a lost love.

Jennie heard her bedroom door shut as he left, and she silently slipped out of bed to lock it. Then she removed her nightgown and lay naked on the bed. Soon, she was fantasizing about Jazzy. Her hand massaged her breasts, making her nerve endings come alive. She slowly stroked her rib cage, moving downward to her flat stomach. Her hand negotiated the length of her stomach to the focus of her sensuality, then she gave in to the demands of her body.

Jennie was devastated. The idea that she was fantasizing about Jazzy, not making love to him in the flesh, did little to comfort her. She, who embraced the church for what she could get from it, had a real spiritual need.

She went to church alone the next day, asking God's forgiveness directly, not through Father Weideman. She'd been aware for some time that she had buried passions that were hard to control. The one concerning Jazzy was dark and evil.

Jazzy played the role of a lover with a broken heart and stopped acting like Mr. Cool. He expanded the theme of unrequited love, hoping to lessen his shame and eradicate what transpired at his mother's bed.

He sought out Carrie and assuaged his broken heart in her arms several times, much to her delight. Having shed his mantle of *savoir-vivre*, Jazzy played the martyr. His studied depression worried his friends, but Carrie's curative powers were remarkable. Soon, he was the same old Jazzy.

Chapter Twelve

Each teacher faced the final class before graduation fighting mixed feelings. Some were happy to shed their little monsters, while others felt saddened to lose the darlings forever. To Miss Burns, the only class that mattered was the one in which Jazzy belonged. She was an intelligent, educated woman, and her preoccupation with a boy not yet out of his teens was wrong, but other, more overpowering forces within her negated such logic.

To each class, she gave her farewell address, forcing an enthusiasm with proper sadness for every class. At noon, she committed a completely irrational act. She went to the parking lot and let the air out of one of her tires.

"Rhinehardt?" she called as the class filed out.

"Yes, Miss Burns?" Jazzy asked.

"Stay behind a moment."

"Yes, Miss Burns."

"I need your help. I've got a flat tire. Will you help me change it? There's a spare in the trunk."

"Of course." He'd intended to walk home with Guy Lovell.

At the service station, the attendant examined the flat tire and said, "Someone let the air out of your tire."

"What kind of mind resorts to such pranks?" Miss Burns asked.

"Consider yourself lucky, Miss Burns. There's been a rash of tire slashings lately."

Jazzy turned toward the door. "I'd better go."

"Keep me company while I shop," she begged.

She took him while she bought whitefish.

"I'd better be going," Jazzy said firmly.

"Please, come visit with me. I want to talk to you. It's possible our paths will never cross again."

He suddenly felt uneasy and wondered what she was up to.

Her flat was functional and served her needs. No doubt the rent was just within her ability to pay. There was a small kitchen, bedroom, and living room almost too small for the large Colonial couch and matching chair.

Conversation was light and changed topics often. She regaled him with anecdotes about her college years, and he, in turn, told of some madcap antics by residents of Goodman Street.

"Miss Burns," he said finally, "I must be going. It's late, and Mother will have dinner for me soon."

"Why not have dinner with me?" She pretended the thought just occurred to her.

"Oh, I couldn't do that."

"Why not? The last day of school makes me melancholy."

"My mother..."

"Call her. Tell her I'd like to discuss your future."

She sounded so forlorn, it touched his heart. He called Jennie, who was delighted that a teacher took an interest in Jazzy's future.

He helped in the kitchen, peeling potatoes and making a chef's salad under her guidance. His nearness thrilled her, and she was happy.

It was a delightful meal. The whitefish, with Miss Burns' special sauce, was a pleasant surprise. They dined leisurely, and, when they finished, it was dark outside.

"I won't keep you much longer," she promised, sitting him on the couch. "My feet are killing me. I want to take off my shoes." She disappeared into the bedroom.

When she came out, she was barefoot. She had shed the clothes she'd been wearing all day and wore a terry cloth robe that came to her knees. It was tightly wrapped around her, and Jazzy was shocked to realize she wore nothing underneath.

Miss Burns wants to lay me! he thought, finally realizing what she intended. He was frightened and trembling, then he looked at her carefully. Her face was pretty and unlined, and she had damn good legs. It was odd he hadn't noticed that before.

Then he wondered if he could perform as expected. His interest was piqued.

She turned out all the lights except the floor lamp beside the couch where Jazzy sat. There was very little room to his right, but she squeezed into the space, crowding him, then reached over and turned out the lights.

"What are you doing, Miss Burns?" he asked, feigning surprise.

"I find the dark soothing." There was a tremor in her voice. She found his hand in the dark and guided it high up her thigh. The terry cloth robe parted, and Jazzy was galvanized to action. Excitement rose within him, but he tried to control it.

Since his left hand was captive, his right inched under her robe and found her breast. He wasn't prepared for its size or its satin-smooth feel. He was no longer humoring a lonely teacher twice his age. Empathy stole over him, seeping through his raging emotions, and he realized she was a lovely, fragile creature reaching out for someone loving. Something gallant moved within him.

He freed himself from her, knelt astride her, and unfastened her robe. He kissed her in the dark, and both were stirred by the contact. She reached for him and held him desperately. They slipped to the floor, and her robe fell off. He undressed and found her again.

With a strength he didn't expect, she turned him on his back and mounted him, kissing his entire body with wet, open-mouthed kisses. The floodgates of his memory collapsed, and, in his mind's eye, he saw his mother treating the bruises Lefty inflicted on him with the same kind of kisses.

Miss Burns moved with abandon. That, coupled with the demons Jazzy hadn't quite exorcised, made his response frenetic and intense. He mumbled incoherently.

Then it was over, and Miss Burns started crying. Jazzy wisely refrained from consolation. She wasn't proud for seducing a minor.

Joe Black, a few years younger than the rest, wasn't really a member of the Goodman gang, but he was quite enterprising for his age. From the moment the pool hall supplanted the speakeasy, he walked in and took over the custodial duties. He loved it, and so did Whitey. Every evening, at closing time, Joe sprang into action, and he made the disheveled room spotlessly clean.

He was very fond of Whitey and kept a close watch on the ailing proprietor. It worried him that Whitey had several transfusions of blood lately.

One morning, when Joe checked on Whitey, he found him slumped over the counter just as he'd left him the previous night. Near panic, he ran outside and called for help. Father Weideman was at Moon's gas station, and the two of them placed Whitey into the priest's car and rushed him to the emergency room.

Whitey recovered, but everyone knew he wouldn't live long.

It was a quiet graduation. Parents attended the exercises with a sick feeling of impending doom. No one really believed the US would stay out of the war destroying Europe. Boys who were already eighteen and had been allowed to graduate were exposed to the draft.

An announcement was made for the Franklin boys who were heading to the induction center immediately after graduating. Among them was Marty Flood and any other football players who were eighteen. It seemed fitting that Franklin heroes would be among the first to serve their country.

Marve, another Franklin hero, wasn't to be upstaged and announced he and Sam Trippett were enlisting.

It wasn't planned, but it was logical. The morning after graduation, the gang met at the pool hall. There were Guy, Nippy, Sam, Jimmy, and Jay, who already had a deferment, because he was the sole support of his mother and two sisters.

"Where's Freddy?" Nippy asked. It was a solemn occasion, and everyone should've come.

"Playing tennis at the Franklin courts," Sam explained. "Besides, he's got another year in school before he's called."

"I never figured him for tennis," Marve mused.

"You have to understand he's a horny little shit. He hangs around the courts watching those cuties with long, bronze legs bouncing around."

"Nothing wrong with that, Sam," Logan said kindly.

Jazzy felt sad. His family was breaking up.

Guy had the floor, and, as the best-informed among them, pontificated about what was in store for the country. Changes would come. People who never worked during the depression would find employment. Everyone would contribute to the war effort, and there would be sacrifices. Then he became solemn and prayed all the boys would return.

"What you gonna do for girls, Jazzy, when they put you in some hellhole?" Marve asked, having had enough enlightenment from Guy.

"It won't be so bad," Guy replied. "I hear they plan to form a women's outfit for the Army."

"What the hell for?" Marve bristled. "They can't fight."

"They can type and do a lot of other things," Nippy countered. "That could release more guys to fight."

"I sure would like to give the physicals," Sam said.

"Who's the horny little shit now?" Jay Bright asked.

"The physical's simple." Guy winked at Jazzy.

"How so?"

"As I hear it, they have the inductees strip naked, then build a bonfire. Each girl jumps over the flames, and those who don't jump high enough get defurred."

Everyone laughed, including Whitey, who'd made himself inconspicuous.

"That's dumb," Marve said.

"Marve," Guy said, "it's *defurred*, not *deferred*."

Again, everyone laughed.

"It's still dumb."

The mood was light, and there was laughter and banter like there had always been. Whitey sneaked out and returned with coffee and doughnuts.

It was time for reminiscing, and each contributed to the memories to which all were privy. They lingered, loathe to break up the sad gathering.

Finally, Marve said he had to get home. Sam walked to the door with him.

Marve turned and called out, "A river dorsey, Fellas."

"River Dorsey? What the fuck's that?" Jay asked.

"Don't you know nothin'?" Marve asked. "It's Italian for so long." With a hand on Sam's arm, he ushered his friend outdoors, bellowing, "Oh, so-lo me oh…"

Sam went into a fit of laughter.

"There go Tweedledum and Tweedledee," Guy observed dourly.

"Which one's dum?" Bright asked.

"It sure ain't Sam."

"Marve gets weirder all the time," Nippy opined.

"I guess he's been seeing foreign movies at the Strand," Jazzy explained.

"He probably likes foreign girls with big bazooms," Jay added.

Guy watched Marve and Sam from the window. "Aw reservoir, you shithead," he muttered. "That's French for get lost."

They left sadly. An era was ending. Miss Laura sang an aria from *La Boheme*. Whitey watched the boys go and knew he wouldn't live long enough to see them return, nor see Miss Laura perform at the Met.

Before long, Guy Lovell was called up, and the dominoes started falling. Jazzy was still seventeen, as were Jimmy Logan and Nippy Koven. Hughie and Hubert Brown were already gone. The gym was deserted, and there was talk that the Elks Club might cancel Monday night cards.

Whitey's condition deteriorated, and, many days, the pool hall was closed. Joe Black used his dead brother's birth certificate to enlist in the Navy. There was no replacing him at the pool hall. Logan left soon after his next birthday.

Jazzy, Nippy, and Jay Bright became inseparable. They were what was left of the Goodman boys. Jay brought a little excitement into their lives by taking them to Nick Sparta's horse room. The first time, they took the dark stairs to the second-floor betting parlor with trepidation. They soon learned Nick had the benediction of the city fathers, and no more peril existed than going to the movies.

At first, the Runyanesque characters running the horse room, along with the equally bizarre patrons, made Jazzy apprehensive. Soon, he was on speaking terms with all of them.

Jazzy gambled occasionally at cards and dice, but he wasn't hooked. Betting on horses, however, fascinated him, and he couldn't stay away from Sparta's. The races were like an Agathie Christie murder mystery. Everyone was given the clues, and, if a man had an analytical mind, he could find the solution. Jazzy's meager funds remained intact, however, and that, as Whitey pointed out, meant he was a big winner and should quit while he was in the black.

On December 7, 1941, the Japanese bombed Pearl Harbor, and the country went to war. Soon Jazzy and Nippy received draft notices from the president. Mandel, as a member of the draft board, incurred the wrath of a few families when their boys were called up so soon. Most people recognized the druggist was fair and compassionate. His deferment of Jay Bright was a case in point. Fred Trippett, not yet eighteen, received his notice later.

The movies provided therapy to a distraught Jennie. Once, in the complete darkness of the Palace Theater, she shared the trials and romance of Joan Fontaine, playing the title role in *Rebecca*. At home, in her solitude, she relived the poignant scenes.

She forced herself back to dancing, although she was almost forty-two. The bands were still superb at Sea Breeze, but she, who'd been the cynosure of all eyes, found herself on the outside looking in. The servicemen who took over the pavilion were painfully young, reminding her of her son, who was in uniform somewhere. Far younger were the girls hanging around the dance floor, some as young as thirteen. Sea Breeze had passed her by.

She heard at work of the dances promoted by the YWCA to which members of the YMCA were invited. The YMCA reciprocated by having dances of their own. It was an older crowd, and the well-chaperoned affairs served as a release for those with loved ones in distant places, for whom waiting was agony.

At a YMCA dance, Jack Werner came into Jennie's life. He was a widower, alone but for two grown daughters who had lives of their own. He was witty, kind, and, best of all, an excellent dancer. Honestly compelled her to admit Jack was a more polished dancer than Jazzy, whom she taught.

When Jack first took that undistinguished woman with the fine legs into his arms on the dance floor, she affected him strangely. He was delighted with her proficiency with fast and slow numbers. Like so many partners before him, Jack was certain she was the product of many revues.

There was no spoken agreement between them, but, from the start, they were a twosome. They were partial to the conventional dances, which were being offered less and less. Jump numbers had taken over, and the jitterbug reined king. Glen Miller's music and arrangements invaded every dance floor in the country. *Little Brown Jug* and *In the Mood* signaled a frenzy of jitterbugging wherever they were played.

They were at the coffee urn set up by the dance committee one night when Jack said, "Jennie, I'd like to take you out to a dance Saturday night."

"The YMCA has one Saturday."

"I know, but this time, it'll be different."

Jennie looked at him as if for the first time and wondered what he meant. He was tall, with sandy hair, graying at the temples, and a craggy face like Gary Cooper's. He had the elegant thinness of Randolph Scott, but he was no Valentino.

"Jack, I'm a widow with a son in the service. I want to keep my life the way it is—uncomplicated."

He looked at her and felt erotic thoughts stir in him. "Jennie, I've no sneaky plot to seduce you. My God, I'll be fifty in three years. I don't think you'll see forty again, either."

"Never mind my age," she retorted.

"Do you or don't you want to come with me Saturday?"

"Where to?"

"Mancuso in Batavia. They're featuring Billy Daniels."

"A nightclub? Out of town?"

"What's out of town? It's only thirty miles away."

"Sneaking away to a nightclub like kids with hot pants?"

"You're making a judgment, Jennie. Mancuso caters to adults. I'm dying to hear Daniels sing *That Old Black Magic.*"

"Well, OK."

"I'll pick you up at your house."

"Jack…"

"Jack, hell! If I were female, there'd be no question about picking you up. Break out of your cocoon, Jennie."

"I suppose it'll be all right, but we come right back to Rochester after the last show."

Jennie received a letter from Jazzy, who was in Camp Upton. It contained a ten-dollar bill and a letter with directions to open an account for him at the bank. He became a prolific letter writer, an indication of his love for his mother.

In addition, every letter contained a bill in increments of ten. She worried about the source of the money, and, after exhausting all possibilities, she concluded there must be widespread gambling in the Army. Whitey had taught him well.

Like all mothers, Jennie lived in constant fear for her son. The sodality had, through the years, brought unity to the women. Dora and Jennie sought each other's company constantly, not bothering to knock when entering each other's homes. When Jennie embraced Catholicism, it wasn't for a spiritual need. Dora was Greek Orthodox. Still, the two women, before going to work, made early morning mass at Annunciation, lighting candles and presenting a solid front to the saints, supplicating them with prayers.

The letters kept coming from Camp Upton, and each envelope contained money that Jennie banked for Jazzy. Nippy was already well into basic training. In one letter, Jazzy put into words his belief that he was destined to remain in Camp Upton doing all sorts of janitorial work.

Jennie prayed he was right. Jazzy was as articulate in writing as in conversation. Jennie found writing frustrating, because she couldn't adequately express her feelings and hopes. Her letters were exasperatingly terse.

Jazzy kept his mother amused, telling her stories of the officers and fellow inductees. He mentioned the chores, some unpleasant, to which he was assigned. Most of all, he told of his weekends in New York City. He named names, and the list of girls soon became too long for even a mother to remember. She had no illusions about his being chaste.

When Whitey died, Jennie fretted over how to tell Jazzy. Finally, she wrote a simple note.

Whitey died. He fooled the doctors, outlasting the predictions of all. There is talk of building a restaurant there.

Then Jennie received the first bad news since Jazzy's departure. He was ill and in the camp infirmary with pneumonia. Even that letter had a twenty-dollar bill in it.

The 65th Division left without him. When he was well enough to resume basic training, he was placed in the 106th training at Camp Attebury.

Jennie's letters followed him. Finally, at camp, he learned of the death of Mateo. He grieved openly, and, when asked whom he'd lost, he said, "My father." He was stymied, unfortunately, when he tried to attend the funeral, because the old man wasn't related.

Every letter frightened her. Jazzy's letter from Boston indicated embarkment. His latest letter came from Banbury, England.

In Belgium, Jazzy received his baptism of fire. He and his battalion were placed in trenches as replacements for a holding action. They stayed in the mud and slime for an entire month.

The German juggernaut was advancing to the Belgium towns of Liege and Namur, and the 106th moved to stop them. Much later, Jazzy learned his involvement was a historic action called the Battle of the Bugle.

The men didn't sleep and catnapped wherever they could. Clothing became a second skin. Sometimes, if there were enough K-rations, they ate. It was winter, and the weather was constantly bad. The stench of decay plagued them day and night. Casualties on both sides were staggering. All suffered from trench foot, and Jazzy's main concern was his bowel movements.

Throughout January the battle raged. At the end of that month, the German offensive was crushed, and the Battle of the Bulge was of such mind-boggling proportions, the Germans lost 230,000 men. Of Jazzy's company, only seventeen were still alive, none officers. Jazzy was promoted to corporal.

At Bastogne, debilitated and sick, in a state bordering on dementia, they were captured by the Germans and marched to Bad Orb, where they were corralled behind wire enclosures like cattle. They ate sparingly of potato soup, a slice of bread, and water. Then General Patton came, and the nightmare was over.

The ragtag prisoners were flown to France to a place with the unlikely name of Lucky Strike Camp. From there, they boarded a ship and sailed home to Camp Kilmer.

There was time and money, and poker games aboard the transport continued. Most of the players were tyros, and Jazzy won so carefully, few realized he never lost.

It felt good to have clean clothes, food, and sleep. At Camp Kilmer, Jazzy rested for two days.

Although Camp Upton was a far cry from Goodman Street, it was the next best thing. The thought of returning to his hometown sustained him throughout his odyssey.

Jennie, with the aid of Jack Werner, made some shrewd guesses about Jazzy's itinerary in Europe. She lived in constant fear for his safety. The casualties in that battle were common knowledge, but the numbers were staggering. The call from Camp Kilmer made her burst into tears of joy. She went to church with Maria, still grieving for Mateo, and lit candles.

The knowledge that God had spared her son relieved Jennie tremendously. She accepted invitations from Jack for Saturday nights in Batavia and Canandaigua. Roseland Park was similar to Sea Breeze. The dancing was mostly jump and the crowd young, but the Italian dinners by candlelight made Canandaigua special. Caruso was a genial host.

The tight embraces in intricate maneuvers on the dance floor didn't faze Jennie, but, once off the floor, she played the prude. That amused Jack, who was fond of her. She was comfortable, which, at his age, was good enough.

To Jack, she was honest and candid. She drank Rhine wine and soda so no one could take advantage of her. Discussing her marriage, she admitted Gus was too old for her. When asked why she married him, she replied, "I was starving."

Still, she didn't mention Gus was a bootlegger slain by a rival mob. She said he worked in accounts receivable at Kodak Park.

One day, Jack asked, "Are you game for a trip, Jennie?"

"It's a long ride back from the Town Casino in Buffalo. You'll fall asleep at the wheel."

"We'll do it right. Let your hair down and celebrate your son's safe return. We can see the late show, then have a snack at Spano's."

"It'll be dawn when we come home!"

"No. Pack a bag, and we'll stay over."

"Are you crazy? I'm a…"

"…widow with a son in the Army. Christ, I thought you threw those hang-ups out the window."

"Jack, I want to go, but I can't. My neighbor will see you pick me up, then bring me back the next morning. I can't do it."

"You come to my apartment in your car. We park it there and drive off in mine. Next morning, you arrive home alone."

Forces battled within her. He'd become part of her life, and she didn't want to spend Saturday night without him. "OK, but we get separate rooms."

Billy Eckstine was the new rage. His voice was deep, and the message of love came across the casino intrusively. He was an accomplished performer, and Jennie was glad she went. The band was good, too, and she and Jack danced so well, they drew the attention of other patrons— as usual.

As promised, Jack signed for separate rooms at the Statler. In her room, Jennie was beset by conflicting emotions. She showered and donned a robe, then there was a knock at her door.

She opened it and saw Jack in his robe holding a bottle of Lake Niagara and two goblets. She recalled Ogden Nash's celebrated advice to a seducer—Candy is dandy, but liquor is quicker.

"What do you think you're doing?" she asked, outraged.

"Checking to see how you're doing."

"How dare you come in here dressed like that?"

"You and I should have a nightcap."

"I know. Rhine wine and soda with a twist of lime."

"If I offered you full-strength wine from the Naples vineyards, would I be able to seduce you?"

Placing both goblets on the dresser, he opened the bottle, then filled the goblets. She looked at him over the rim of the goblet, watching him drink. She sipped slowly, enjoying her little indiscretion. The wine was cold and refreshing.

"Here's to us, Jennie."

"Here's to us."

He took the empty goblet from her, and she wondered if he'd leave. He didn't. Instead, he held her shoulders and kissed her lightly. She made no protest when he slipped the robe over her shoulders and untied the belt, letting it fall to the floor. As in a dream, she felt Jack carry her to the bed.

She spent most of the night crying. Half of her was enraged at herself for allowing a man into her bed. The other half dwelt on the sheer joy of that intimacy, one in which she was a participant. Jack brought out delightful, unknown sensations in her.

At dawn, she called Jack's room. "We need to talk."

"I'll be right over."

He came in a moment later. "What's up?"

"When do we get married?"

"Married?" He was shocked. She certainly was a no-nonsense woman.

"Yes, married."

"You want me to make an honest woman of you?"

She started crying, so he held her. "What's this all about?"

"You're the only man in years."

"What happened last night was what we both wanted."

"Where do I go from here?"

"Anywhere you wish. Nothing's changed."

"I've changed."

"Jennie, do you have any idea how often I've toyed with the idea of proposing to you?"

"You have?"

"Yes. I'm a widower with two daughters who are on their own. Living with either in my old age frightens me."

"Why didn't you speak out?"

"Everything you say and do screams at me to lay off. You treat me like a leper."

Jennie didn't answer.

"I can't ask you now. It would be too much."

"I don't understand."

"I'm moving to the west coast within a week."

"You're leaving the city? Was I your last hurrah?"

"No, no, it's not like that at all. Brother Jim's retiring. He's divorced and has no children—there's no one to carry on his insurance business. I can't afford to pass up the offer."

"Where is this business?"

"San Diego."

"San Diego!" She envisioned palm trees, beaches, and the best climate in the country. Jazzy was a grown man, and he'd marry eventually. Then did she face a lonely future, too? What if her love-'em-and-leave-'em son remained single and stayed living at home? She knew the dark passions that repression and loneliness could spawn.

"Ask me," she begged. "Ask me to marry you."

"Will you marry me, Jennie, and move west with me?"

"I will!"

The letter was very important. In it, she stressed her love for Jack and that Jazzy would have a home with them if he wished.

Jazzy read it and cried. His bunk felt like a bed of nails, and the azure skies turned ominous. His once-orderly mind was in disarray as his hopes and dreams shattered like a priceless urn.

"How dare you sell our home to strangers while I'm overseas?" he shouted. "Who's this man you married and moved away with?"

The letter remained unanswered for a long time, because he couldn't collect his thoughts in an orderly fashion. He felt as if his entire world had left him, leaving a stillness so profound, it lay heavily and painfully on him.

There was no need for eloquence. He wrote a succinct note.

I am, no doubt, the first GI in Army history to receive a Dear John letter from his mother!

Chapter Thirteen

Jazzy was on busy Central Avenue, which ran along the depot's parking lot. He walked slowly down the street, and his spirits rose. He stopped before the Greek's Texas Red Hots, that, in the days before the war, was the way station between downtown and home for the youngsters out on the town.

Jazzy sat at the counter and saw no familiar faces, but that didn't matter. He had his white hots again. He'd been to many places, but Rochester was unique with its local pork hots. The jukebox blared A *Nightingale Sang in Barkely Square,* and that reminded him of his mother. Jennie may've been an excellent dancer, but she was a horrible singer. Crosby was her favorite crooner, and she always sang along. Jazzy wondered if he'd ever see her again.

Back on the street, he leisurely took in the familiar sights. He saw the Elks Club and hoped the Brown brothers survived the war. He wondered if they were back.

On Hudson Avenue, he turned left, walking all the way to Franklin High. The sight of the school stirred him, and he wondered if the halls, laid end to end, really stretched a mile. He doubted it.

Continuing east on Norton Street, he walked toward Goodman. Excitement filled him. He'd endured many hardships for that moment. When he reached the corner of Norton and Goodman, his lassitude left him. He was home!

Goodman Street had changed. The overhead trolley line was gone, and the brick road and tracks were covered with macadam. The quaint trolley cars were gone, replaced by more functional buses.

He stood before the small, red, brick home and cried silently. He truly believed it once housed brave souls who worked the underground railroad, as it housed him and his mother. His past had been snatched away, and he faced an uncertain future. He wanted to be fair, however, and tried to see his mother's side of the situation.

She wrote she was leaving him her car. He didn't expect too much. It was parked in the Martorana yard. It looked in excellent shape, and when he read the odometer, he felt better. It had been driven only 21,000 miles in six years.

He braced himself and walked to the door to ring the bell. Maria opened the door, gasped, and threw herself at him, crying.

"He's dead, Jazzy," she sobbed. "Mateo's dead."

"Mother wrote me about it." Soon, he cried, too. "I'll miss him terribly. He was Grandpa."

"How he loved you, Jazzy. He watched over you every day as you grew up. His health was never any good after his accident, but, after you left, he went downhill fast.

"I have my own aches and pains, but the worst thing I suffer from is loneliness. I came from a large family, and all I have left is a brother in Italy."

"You have me, Maria."

She kissed him. "You saw the car. Abel starts it every two or three days, and it runs good."

"Mother wrote my clothes are here, too."

"Yes. They're in the spare room where you spent so much time when your mother worked. Your books are here, too. After you get settled, you can get everything."

Jazzy looked at the old woman and saw how thin and small she was. He wondered if she had enough food. She must be short on money.

"I have to pay for a room somewhere, Maria," he said slowly. "Why don't I stay here, where it's been my second home? I can pay you instead."

"You'd stay here? You will?" She was overjoyed. "You don't have to pay anything."

"I have to pay my way, Maria, or I won't stay."

"Whatever you say." Her eyes shone.

Jazzy walked to his new room, arranged his belongings, and lay on the familiar cot.

Dressed in civilian clothes, he walked down the street to the corner and saw more changes in the neighborhood. The pool hall was gone, replaced by Slim Broadway's Hacienda. Slim was a five-foot, roly-poly character with a checkered past. He was raised in poverty by a tyrannical parent. Born thin, he stayed that way throughout his adolescent years, because he was undernourished. The street where he clawed and scratched just to survive gave him the name he carried the rest of his life.

Broadway wasn't the name for that narrow, dirty street. It was Front Street, but, throughout his life, he referred to it as Broadway. He fought off claim jumps eager to take his newspaper territory, too.

Jennie's letter to Jazzy, telling him about Whitey's death, was short on details. If Mateo was a grandfather to Jazzy, Whitey and Abel were his fathers. There was a lot he wanted to know about the funeral, so he walked to Annunciation to talk to Father Weideman.

"Old Whitey had a fine funeral," the priest said. "It was the least I could do. The entire neighborhood owed him a fine send-off."

"Was he reunited with his family before he died?"

"No, but we did the next best thing."

"We?"

"Mrs. Belding and I. With Whitey dead, we located his son, but we had a hard time getting him to drop his hatred for his father. I was surprised."

"You couldn't find his wife?"

"She died years before, and Whitey never knew. It was probably best he didn't. He loved her until his death."

"Did the son come to the funeral?"

"Only after I shamed him. He finally came down from Cincinnati. At first, he didn't want to come, and I gave what was probably the most moving eulogy in my life."

"Did you convince him his father was a fine human being, and he missed not knowing his son?"

"I had him weeping at the grave."

As he walked back from the church, Jazzy passed the corner where the pool hall once stood. In his mind, he saw Whitey, sitting like a Buddha, his chair leaning against the sill of the big window, watching the street.

It was time to pay his respects to the Kovens. Jazzy hoped to find Nippy home.

Dora threw her arms around him. "You keep getting better looking every time I see you!"

"You're still a doll, Dora." Despite a weight problem, she maintained a semblance of her girlish charm.

"How about me?" Abel asked, wearing a robe and pajamas.

"There's something different."

Abel adjusted his ascot. "My thinning hair, no doubt."

"It's not that."

"It's my teeth. I lost them to gingivitis. My uppers make me look like Peter Rabbit. I can't play in the band anymore."

"If you were bald and toothless, I'd still love you, Abel."

"You son of a gun. You're gonna make me cry."

"Where's Nippy? You have no idea how I missed him."

"Practicing baseball with some local semipros."

"Still wants to play professionally?"

"More than ever."

"Have you seen my stepfather?"

"Oh, yes, Jazzy," Dora said. "We were in the wedding group. Abel gave away the bride."

"She wore a blue gown and looked great," Abel added.

"Blue always was a good color for her. Big affair?"

"No. Father Weideman performed an emergency ceremony, because there wasn't much time. They had to leave for California."

"She was lucky she found buyers right away," Dora said. "If she hadn't, Abel would've sold it for her eventually."

"That's funny. Father Weideman didn't mention the wedding."

"You've seen him?" Abel asked.

"Yes. I wanted to know about Whitey's funeral."

"That was the darnedest thing," Dora said. "There wasn't a dry eye in that church after the padre eulogized the dead man."

There was another pause, and Dora signaled Abel to pick up the conversation.

"Jazzy," he said slowly, "Jennie devoted her life to raising you. Don't you think she deserves a little happiness?"

"What kind of man is Jack Werner?"

"A good one. I'm giving it to you straight."

"She didn't dump you," Dora added. "Jennie loves you."

Nippy walked in, cutting the sensitive conversation short. The two young men hugged without embarrassment, then Nippy led Jazzy into the living where, years earlier, they played lotto and checkers.

When Jazzy met Slim Broadway, he liked the little man. There was no pretense about him, and he had a ready laugh. At some time in his life, he learned to cook, and customers came from all parts of the city for his food. Jazzy had to admit there was more excitement in the place than when it was a pool hall.

In addition to Nippy Koven, Jim Logan was back, as was Guy Lovell, although no one had seen him. Jay Bright left the service station and was free-lancing in his old truck. The boys of Goodman were returning, and everything would be as before.

Marve Pittman hadn't arrived, and everyone was anxious to see him again. Sam Trippett had a disability discharge and came home months earlier after his knee was shattered at Anzio. An elastic sleeve over the knee kept him mobile. He became a barber and bought Belding's shop when the old man retired.

Moon arrived in Rochester the same day as Jazzy, taking over the family business by the first afternoon as if he'd never been away. He gave Jennie's car a tune-up.

It was time for a personal inventory. Jazzy drove to the Citizen's Bank and learned Jennie had left him with $12,875.50. The amount stunned him. He'd never won that much playing cards.

"Your mother added half of the money from the sale of the house to your account," the bank manager explained.

Immediately regretting his ugly thoughts, Jazzy left the money in the bank.

In Europe, he'd been forced to endure celibacy, but now, with a car, he sought some of the girls he'd left behind. Some were married, and some moved away, but there were new girls who were little more than children when he left. Some of them were attractive, and it flattered him that they remembered him. It was gratifying to find that, for the most part, they were receptive to his advances.

He dated Belle, Pamela, and Josie, who were still single and attending the university. He felt no sense of betrayal, because school crushes were short-lived. Guy and Sam wouldn't mind.

He wanted to see Carrie Evans, but she married an Army recruiter stationed in Detroit.

Joe Black was back, and the lure of the old building was strong. He took over his old duties for a new boss.

"Who's he?" Jazzy asked, indicating a stranger with Slim.

"Chris Morgana," Joe replied.

"Looks like he can take care of himself."

"He'd better. He's in his first fight Monday."

Jazzy eyed the man with interest. His features were hard, and there wasn't an ounce of fat on him. He had large hands—he probably milked cows at one time.

Jazzy couldn't help speculating how he'd do up against the new neighbor. He made a mental note to see him fight Monday night.

Old Man Browser was having his mustache trimmed, and Jazzy was reading the latest issue of the *Police Gazette*. The neighborhood grouch sat in the chair, glowering—he hadn't changed a bit. Sam and Jazzy were worried about Marve Pittman. It had been three months, and Marve still wasn't back.

The door opened, and Marve walked in, taking his friends by surprise. He had his duffel bag slung over his shoulders, and the friends hugged each other around the barber chair.

"Knock if off," Browser said. "Stop acting like a bunch of queers."

Aware of his moods, they ignored him. They were three of the four who raided his plum tree years earlier.

After Browser left, the trio sat and drank coffee out of shaving mugs Sam boiled.

"You look bigger, Marve," Jazzy said.

"You know me. I lift weights wherever I go. At Fort Ontario, I wrestled for the fort team."

"You look tough," Sam said in admiration.

"Hey, I gotta tell you this. I was at Fort Bragg soon after I got into the service. Well, this hotshot was teaching us ju jitsu, the Japanese fighting style that's supposed to be so scientific. He picked on the men, telling them to knock him down, then, quick as a wink, he flipped them to the ground.

"Some of the kids got hurt, then he saw me and figured flipping a big guy would impress the troops. 'Come at me, big fella,' he said. 'Knock me on my ass.'

"Orders were orders. He wore a big, shit-eating grin, so I came at him and knocked him on his ass."

Sam and Jazzy laughed hard, although Jazzy had reservations about the tale's accuracy.

"It made you a big man with the boys?" Sam asked.

"No, it gave me two weeks of peeling potatoes."

Marve went home, because his parents were waiting to see him, and Jazzy looked at Sam.

"You son of a bitch." Jazzy put his arm around Sam's shoulders. "All these years we've been buddies, and I never would've guessed you'd be a barber."

"I learned in the Army, Jazzy. Did a lot of clipping after I was hit."

"Sam Trippett, a businessman with his own shop! I'm proud of you, Sam. Where'd you get the idea for the shop?"

"I always wanted to be my own boss. I see myself having five chairs someday. My old man always lectures me and Freddy to avoid becoming clock punchers."

"He worked in factories."

"Yeah, assembling cameras at Kodak and polishing lenses at Bausch. You punch a clock, you're nothing but a working stiff at the boss' mercy. You're employed until slack time, then the boss gets a bug up his ass, and presto, you're unemployed."

"Thousands of people in Rochester are in that boat."

"Yeah? Pop and I don't want to join them."

"Where does he work now?"

"At Pfaudler's. He's not happy to be still punching a clock, but at least Pfaudler has a union with progressive leaders. They've got a nice relationship with management. They're working together on an incentive plan."

"Your father's not alone. We all have broken dreams."

"Pop could've been a big man. It was my mother who always threw cold water on his ideas."

"What's she doing?"

"She works at French's. You know, the spice people. She thinks it's great. She's an eight-to-five person."

When Chris Morgana climbed into the ring, the gang made such a commotion, one would've thought he was Joe Louis. Marve said Morgana would lose, because he was too awkward. Moon, an avid fight fan, bet him five dollars.

The bell rang, and, within fifteen seconds, it was over. Morgana swung a left hook and sent his opponent sprawling across the lowest rope. Awkward or not, with a left hook like that, Morgana would be someone to reckon with every time he entered the ring.

The gang reconvened at Slim's and had clams on the half-shell.

Jazzy stayed away from hard liquor in any form, but he heeded Jennie's advice for a way to solve the problem of social drinking—with diluted wine. Jazzy stayed with Rhine wine and soda, but Marve had no moderation, and his overindulgence became a nightly ritual. It was Jazzy's task to get him home safely.

They were at the bar at the Four Seasons where a fine band was playing and the smart set from Rochester gathered. As usual, Jazzy ordered wine and soda.

"Jeez, Jazzy," Marve muttered, "don't you ever order a man's drink? I've got your number, Buddy. You're screaming for attention. You want the girls to think you've got style and culture."

Jazzy felt annoyed. He could've explained that he wanted to keep his wits about him, and, at the end of the evening, he could view his options, but he didn't.

Jazzy met Rita while Marve was in the men's room. She made room for herself at the bar and sat beside him.

"Are you alone, Miss?" he asked.

"Why, yes. Are you?"

"All alone, too, except for Pancho, who's in the john."

"You must be the Cisco Kid." She looked at him and saw how handsome he was.

"Not Cisco. I'm Jazzy."

"Is that a condition or a name?" She laughed.

"It's my name. Actually, it's Jasmin Rhinehardt."

"Nowadays, you can't trust anyone. Jasmin! That's good."

Marve returned, and his eyes looked tired. He'd reached his limit. "I'm going into the parking lot, Jazzy. I gotta get some fresh air." He walked off.

"So it *is* Jazzy," Rita said. "Well, Jazzy, I'm Rita. No big deal about that, just plain Rita. Are you buying me a drink?"

"You bet." He signaled the bartender.

The crowd at the bar kept jostling her against him. She was tall, slender, and long-legged, and her red-and-black dress failed to obscure a lovely figure. Warmth came over him. He hadn't met a woman that attractive in a long time.

"I'm waiting out the jump numbers until the band plays something slow," he said. "You were designed for close dancing."

"Are you inviting me onto the dance floor?" His voice had an exciting quality. She couldn't explain it, but she was glad she came.

"You bet." He looked into her eyes with an intensity that flustered her.

The band played *Tenderly*, and the more athletic dancers relinquished the floor to the sedate ones. Jazzy and Rita were swept up in the romance of the moment. He looked at her, approving of her dark hair, wide-set blue eyes, and full lips that tempted him to kiss. Instead, he brushed his lips lightly against her neck, and she snuggled closer into his arms.

"I want to take you home, Rita."

She was in a quandary. She wasn't an easy pick-up and never took up with strangers in a bar. If she agreed, he'd suspect a promiscuity that wasn't there. Still, her entire being cried out for him, and, if she refused, she'd lose him.

"Yes," she said softly.

Then Jazzy thought of Marve. "I have a problem."

"What is it?"

"It's Pancho. He's had it. I have to see he gets home OK."

"I'll ride with you. I can help you get him in and out of the car, then you can take me home."

"It's a deal."

They delivered Marve to his house, then quickly went to Rita's apartment building and walked to her door. She fumbled nervously with the key in the lock when Jazzy reached down to open the door for her. His hand touched hers, and she turned.

Without a word, they were in each other's arms, locked in a searing kiss.

Rita pushed him away, trembling. "Let's go inside before we set fire to the hall."

From his cot in Maria's spare room, Jazzy could see clearly through the lace curtains the roof of the red brick house next door, bright in the glare of the streetlight. At times, the lingering bitterness at the loss of his home surfaced at night.

That wasn't the reason for his restlessness that particular night—it was Rita. He wanted to see her again, but that couldn't be. In addition to her thrilling sensuality, which produced a night of sheer delight, she was beautiful, intelligent, and stylish. There had been others, particularly the fashionable New York girls he dated while stationed at Camp Upton. He had to be wary of girls like that if he was to avoid entangling alliances. He wasn't ready for a commitment that would restrict his options. It was different with the local girls. They understood a tryst was of the moment.

Jazzy finally slept, but Rita followed him into his dreams. In one, he fled from her and had trouble escaping. Then, when it seemed he'd put enough distance between them, he did a strange thing. He slowed his flight and let her draw near.

Bright sunlight woke him. He'd slept long enough, but he felt an illogical weariness. The dream flight from Rita seemed so real.

Maria was puttering around the kitchen when Jazzy left his room. He was a grown man, and Maria reminded herself he wasn't her son. She never questioned his movements, but that didn't stop her from worrying.

Maria was hungry, but she stubbornly kept her vigil, waiting for Jazzy to come out and have breakfast with her. It was a pact they made, and he knew how much it meant to her, but the morning was slipping away, and she was still waiting.

As he ate his bacon and eggs and she her cereal, they engaged in pleasant talk, drinking coffee in silent contentment. From the kitchen window, he had a better view of the only home he could remember and wondered if Mother told the owners they bought a piece of American history.

He toyed with the idea of approaching them and telling them about the slaves and Frederick Douglass, who must've been a frequent guest in the little house they just bought.

He was eager to get to the Hacienda. Living on Goodman Street was like having a season's pass to the circus. There were times he found his friends crude and their banter indelicate, but he loved them all.

Chapter Fourteen

Marve was drinking coffee at the counter when Jazzy walked into the café. The pungent smell of clams hung in the air—the cook was cutting them open outside, and it wasn't even noon. Jazzy was glad to see Marve up and around. Sleep was strong medicine, and Marve had more of that than he.

"There you are, old buddy," Marve said. "What the hell did you do to me last night?"

"What do you mean?"

"My old lady smelled perfume on my clothes this morning when she put them in the hamper."

Jim Logan and Jay Bright entered and sat with them at the counter.

"What's up?" Logan asked as Slim poured them coffee.

"Marve's mother smelled perfume on his clothes," Jazzy said.

"What's the big deal about that?"

"I didn't have a date last night," Marve said, "yet there was the strong smell of perfume on my clothes. She thinks I've got a girl, and she's already talking grandchildren."

"Going sissy on us with all that sweet-smelling stuff?" Jay asked.

"Maybe it was your aftershave?" Slim ventured.

"Why don't you tell Mother it was the girl of your wet dreams?" Jim asked, deadpan.

That set off a roar, and Slim slapped his knee.

"Very funny," Marve said. "What happened last night?"

"You don't remember?" Jazzy asked. "You got loaded, and we took you home."

"Who's we?"

"Me and a very nice girl, who smells nice and sat close to you in the front seat of my car."

"The brunette in the red dress who stood beside you at the bar?"

"I didn't think you'd remember."

"How was she?" Jay asked.

"Mighty nice."

"Jazzy, you get more by accident than the rest of us by design," Logan lamented.

"That's for sure," Marve said.

Jim and Jay were close friends, although the pair made quite a contrast. Logan, ragged in his adolescence, was impeccably dressed. He despaired of polishing his friend—a difficult task.

Jay worked hard with his truck, making regular runs to East Rochester, where the railroad people dismantled old boxcars. He loaded his truck with old lumber, drove back to the city, and delivered the wood to his customers, who used it for firewood. That lumber was also used to build Slim's clam shack, south of the café.

Jazzy walked over to Jay and Jim, sitting at a table. "How's the lumber business coming?"

"Fair to middlin'."

"Fair to middlin'?" Marve asked. "You talk like a farmer."

"Why not? The family farmed when I was a kid. When he was alive, Pop tried to keep us out of the mines with the miserable company shacks and those thieving company stores."

"How'd the farming go?" Logan asked.

"It was a different disaster every year. Poor Pop. He was forced to go back to the mines and took me with him. The mine killed him."

Jay's brief disclosure of life in West Virginia produced a silence that even Marve observed. Jazzy's heart went out to Jay, and he was proud of

Jim for having interceded for his friend and giving him employment with Moon before the war.

If one were to contemplate the tolerance of the vigilant ladies of the neighborhood, led by Ida Belding, for Slim Broadway's back-room activities, one would've concluded a strange bias existed. Whitey, a professional gambler, wouldn't have been allowed to use his pool room for gambling. Slim, who was no gambler, seemed to have an unspoken blessing for the card games in the back room. He installed a huge plate-glass mirror in the wall with the mirror on the restaurant side and plain glass inside. The room was empty, and some youngsters cleaned it out.

They opened all doors and windows for the card players, who played till dawn, leaving a stench of cigarettes and beer.

The gang gathered at the counter again, and Marve suddenly sat up straight.

"Look! It's Nippy! He's crossing the street like he's hurt."

"Must've been the game Sunday," Jazzy suggested.

"No," Slim said. "I saw that game, and nothing happened. Come to think of it, he hasn't been in all week."

"Wonder what happened?" Logan asked. "I hope it's not serious. He's the best athlete we've got. He might put us on the map someday."

"Don't know about that," Marve said. "He'll never be a pro."

"Why do you want to run him down?" Slim asked.

"Ever see Williams play basketball or Bobby Davies play football? Nippy plays baseball, basketball, and football, but he's not good enough in any one of them to become a professional."

"If he's having fun, that's all that matters," Jay said.

Nippy walked in slowly, as if each step were agony.

"Did you just come from Strong Memorial for heat treatments?" Marve asked.

"Did you have to ask that?" Jazzy asked.

"Well, look at him. He walks like he's got the clap."

"You're right, Marve," Nippy said, "I've been to the Memorial, but I had a hemmorhoidectomy."

"What's that?"

"Don't you know anything, Marve?" Logan asked. "He had his piles removed."

"The old ream job, eh? Tell me, Nippy, when the doctor was doing it, did he have both hands on your shoulders?"

"Why don't you zip up your pants, Marve?" Logan asked.

"What are you talking about? I'm zipped."

"From the back, Marve."

Everyone laughed.

Joe Black walked in with a burlap bag full of clams.

"Still got the trench coat in the back room, Jazzy," the handyman said. "The one with the flaps on the shoulders."

"Don't worry," Marve assured him. "He'll buy it. He thinks that a follow-that-man coat will make him look dashing."

"Jazzy doesn't need a coat for that," Jay said.

"Is that your aim in life, old buddy," Marve asked his old friend, "to screw as many girls as you can before you die?"

"Is that bad? You should be so lucky," Jay said.

"Didn't say it was bad. I can lay 'em or leave 'em." He looked around for a reaction to his witticism.

"You must do a lot of leaving," Nippy said.

"What's that supposed to mean?"

"When it comes to girls, you got no style."

"And you have?"

"I don't tell a girl, 'Lie down, I want to talk to you.'"

"You little shit. Who have you been talking to?"

"Another thing, Marve, you don't approach a new girl and say, 'It's a perfect day for a matinee.'"

"That isn't bad, Nippy," Jazzy said.

"You're right," Jim added. "It's got a lilt to it."

"Stay out of my affairs, Peewee," Marve growled. "You don't know shit from Shinola."

"Who you calling Peewee, Fat Ass?" Nippy asked.

"Fat ass. Know what they say?"

"What do they say?" Jay asked.

"You can't drive a tack with a sledgehammer."

"You've got it all wrong, Marve. What they say is, you can't drive a spike with a tack hammer."

"What spike?" the others chorused.

They laughed so loud and long, Slim had a coughing spell. Marve hadn't quite figured out the joke and turned to Joe, feeling he had to strike back at someone.

"Save the coat for Jazzy, Joe," Marve said. "He ain't been the same since he saw a Bogart rerun last week. Now he thinks he's Sam Spade."

"Can it, Marve." Jazzy had endured enough barbs.

Logan felt things were getting out of hand. "Who's coming to Sparta's? I've got a few bucks to blow."

"I'll come," Jazzy said.

"Me, too," Marve added.

"I'll take my truck," Joe offered.

"Jesus, how about me?" Nippy asked.

"You're always welcome with me, Nippy."

"I can't sit down. The bouncing would rip my stitches."

"We'll help you into the back of the truck."

"I'll get on the truck to keep you company," Jazzy offered. "Marve, you go with Logan."

They helped Nippy into the truck bed.

"Hold on," Jay said. "We'll take off in a cloud of heifer dust."

As each walked through the door, they waved to Charlie, the lookout man, who responded with short grunts. The room, with the pool table, was still in darkness.

They climbed the stairs with the bend in the middle. It was still too early for the poker game, and the Stooge was at the boards, earphones dangling from his head. Nick was beyond the betting windows, playing gin, while Dave and Frog were at the windows.

Dave was a one-man welcoming committee. "It's the boys from Goodman!"

The young men lightened the atmosphere. For the most part, they were two-dollar bettors.

"The rubes," Frog sneered. "They've still got straws sticking from their ears."

There was the old man and his woman, both good readers. Across the room, sitting alone, were the west-side boys, derelicts, perhaps, but they functioned well enough in horse rooms and at the track. They were hard to talk to, and Jazzy felt certain their reading skills were achieved through Sparta's library, consisting of the racing form and several newspapers that carried track coverage.

Mayor Sheldon was present, obviously a regular. His presence explained why Sparta flourished when, with police crackdowns occurring throughout the city, gambling parlors were very risky ventures.

Jazzy's friends scattered, and, when Jazzy reached for the form dangling from a chain, another hand got there first.

"Pardon me, young man, but you're Jazzy, aren't you?"

Jazzy looked up and saw Mayor Sheldon. "Yes, and you're the mayor. How do you know me?"

"Don't be modest. You have a reputation of sorts. Are you a musician? I wondered about the name."

"No. I can't play any instrument."

"I know that jazz sometimes takes on another meaning. Has it anything to do with your success with the girls?"

"No way. Whatever they say about me, I'm no Casanova."

"How'd you get a tag like Jazzy? Is it a nickname?"

"Yes and no. My mother named me Jasmin."

"After a flower?"

"No. She was crazy about jazz, and she loved Jazzman Caruthers. She didn't dare call me Jazzman, so she got sneaky."

"Caruthers? Why, sure. He came from Kansas City and used to be at Martino's in the old days. He was a genius on the horn."

"With a name like Jasmin, I naturally ended up with Jazzy."

"You know, young man, your mother couldn't have come closer naming you after him."

"How's that?"

"In the early days, the blacks called the music jass."

"That so? You're coming on strong with this third degree."

"Old codgers get humored. Besides, I'm your mayor."

Again, Jazzy reached for the racing form and was stopped by Marve.

"Jazzy, he's here!" he hissed. "It's Porky Pig!"

Jazzy turned to see a short, bald, beach ball of a man past middle age. He hadn't seen Kevin Kilty since his attempted seduction of Antoinette Dubois years earlier.

"So?"

"He gives me the creeps."

"Why? Because he likes young girls? There's no law against a man's likes or dislikes."

"There's a law against screwing them when they're kids."

"Why don't you get Kilty out of your mind? Antoinette never was your girl. She was no kid—too mature for you."

"I still don't like him."

There was little Jazzy didn't know about Kilty. When his wife threw him out of the house, he got a job as a custodian at the Saints Margaret and Mary Hospital, where he had access to every area, including the nurse's quarters. Familiarity might breed contempt, but it also let one's guard down. Menial hospital jobs were usually held by those for whom such work was a last resort, and the trainees, bored by monastic life, might find Kilty less repulsive.

Jazzy lost interested in the first race and approached the mayor. "Do you mind if I ask you something?"

"Fire away, Jazzy."

"What's with this scenario? The mayor's in a den like this? Aren't you afraid what public knowledge might do to you?"

"I've played the horses all my life, but I've been mayor only a little over two years. I have a character flaw like everyone else in this room."

"Your political opponents would have a field day."

"Not really. Politics is the science of getting along and going along. The Republicans allow me my little vice, and we Democrats say nothing about the DA."

"The DA?"

"He's a lush. Every time he needs drying out, our sheriff takes him to the county hospital as John Doe."

"How bad is he?"

"Real bad. The last time, he had delirium tremens. Tiny Indians were crawling over the windowsill to get him."

"That's big! What the papers would do with a story like that!"

"They play ball with us. In fact, the last time, they issued a news release to explain his absence, saying he was touring the southern tier, giving a series of talks. Do you know the title of those talks? Are you ready?"

"I'm ready."

"The Trials and Tribulations of a DA."

"What a touch!"

"Jazzy, talking to you, I just missed placing the bet I came in for. See you around. I like you, young man. You're more than just a pretty face." He walked out, chuckling.

Jazzy watched him go to Nick Sparta and engage him in serious conversation. A gambling mayor was bizarre, but Jazzy was sure Mayor Sheldon was good for the city.

After the mayor left, Nick took a chair from the poker table and placed it squarely in the middle of the room, then stood on it and whistled for attention.

"Listen, you guys! Tomorrow at exactly two-thirty in the afternoon, the police will raid us. Those who've never been in a raid and don't want to, stay home. If you don't mind the cops coming in here and spoiling your play, you're welcome to stay. Those who're worried about it, I can promise everything will be cool. We'll be open soon after."

Nippy waddled over to Jazzy, having won the first race on a long shot. "You gonna be here tomorrow?"

"I've never been in a raid before. It can't be that bad. I lot of folks will be here, waiting for the police. So will I."

"Not me. My rectum's throbbing. I can't wait to get home and into a hot tub."

Jay Bright fondled the bills in his hand. He worked hard for his money, but he wasn't very lucky.

Marve and Logan were waiting for the second half of the daily double. The Stooge was at the boards, earpiece strapped to his head. They were ready to go at the Fairgrounds.

Jazzy hurried to the window and placed five on the favorite to win. Marve and Logan missed out on the double, and Jay didn't bet, either. It was that kind of day. He waited for his cronies.

Eventually, they had enough. Nippy had his long shot. Marve borrowed five dollars from Jim, and Jay lost one day's pay. Jazzy was out five dollars.

As they were leaving, Kilty had his belly pressed against the pay window.

"Look at him," Logan said. "The dirty old man hit one."

"Someday, you'll read that pig has raped a child," Nippy said in disdain.

"I don't think so," Jazzy said.

"Goody two-shoes won't say shit if his mouth is full." Marve was exasperated.

"I've got no use for that bastard, either. Until Saints Margaret and Mary stop receiving tender young trainees, he won't roam the streets. The fox is guarding the hen house."

The next day, the boys at Slim's hooted at the idea of going to Sparta's to get arrested. Jazzy's curiosity was piqued, and he didn't want to miss the adventure. He talked Marve into coming, then they left to a concert of catcalls.

They arrived well before the scheduled raid and were shocked to find the place jammed with people.

"Jeez," Marve said. "There are people here I never saw before."

"Nick must've advertised," Jazzy guessed.

"What the hell for?"

"Paying the fines for this mob will cost Nick plenty. I get the picture."

"Explain it to me."

"It's for the mayor's benefit. You can bet there'll be reporters and cameramen with the police. It'll be the biggest raid in Rochester's history, and it'll prove Sheldon has a handle on the vice problem in his first term in office. This will ensure his reelection. I have to admit it's a good idea."

Nick Sparta stood at the door, greeting all arrivals and thanking them for coming. He looked at the clock and left, and Frog and Dave left the windows to be replaced by Charlie and Al.

At precisely two-thirty, there was the sound of heavy feet running up the stairs, then the police burst dramatically through the door.

Without being told, the men lined up single file at the door, but the line was so long it snaked throughout the second floor. One of the officers led the gamblers out.

They brought two buses for the occasion, and the gamblers had to run a gauntlet of cheering crowds on either side. No one knew if the cheering was for them or the police. Meanwhile, reporters clicked their cameras.

Jazzy and Marve were on the second bus. At the last second before the bus left for police headquarters, Dave hopped on carrying several large boxes filled with cups of coffee and doughnuts. There was an air of good fellowship, and someone started singing. Soon, the entire bus joined in.

On the road to Mandalay
Where the flying fishes play…

Jazzy enjoyed the outing and surmised the hilarity was as pronounced in the first bus with Frog.

When they arrived, the passengers were taken out single file and into the station. There was a small table, at which an officer sat, and Nick stood alongside it with a huge stack of five-dollar bills. As each captive came to the table, he was asked his name. The officer jotted something on a pad of paper and called for five dollars, which Nick paid.

When it was Jazzy's turn, the officer asked, "Name, please."

"Jasmin Rhinehardt."

"John Brown."

Jazzy restrained a laugh and walked off, waiting for the officer to finish with Marve. Finally, Marve walked over.

"What name did he give you?" Jazzy asked.

"Tom Collins."

They laughed until their sides hurt.

Jazzy missed his books. Except for an orgy of reading at Camp Upton, where the camp was overrun with volunteers, and there was an abundance of books, there had been little opportunity for reading in the service. Since his return, he hadn't resumed the reading that had meant so much to him.

The pace he maintained with his cronies was hectic. He'd intended, after his discharge, to register for school, but he let the deadline pass. Guy, after a quick visit to Rochester, disappeared, but he was the only gang member who wasn't there.

When Jazzy finally learned that Guy went directly from his parents' house to Pennsylvania, where he used his GI benefits for Penn State, he was furious. He hadn't even said hello to any of the Goodman boys. It was tantamount to treason.

There was a letter in the mailbox for Jazzy one day. He wondered how Jennie knew where to find him, then realized Mrs. Belding must've told her.

In the letter, Jennie boasted about the weather, the city, and her new friends. She told how content she was, and that business was good. His reply was respectful but short. He felt happy for her.

Maria hadn't started dinner, and Jazzy watched her puttering around the kitchen. He recalled the many times she and Mateo took him by the hand and walked him to the corner for a treat. Not once had he given any thought to Maria. He'd been selfish.

"Put on a nice dress, Maria. I'm taking you out to dinner."

"Oh, Jazzy, never mind me. You go. I can get something on the stove in a minute. Save your money."

"No way. You're coming with me. Come on, let's go."

Her face shone with delight, and he vowed to do that more often.

At the café, they saw Slim behind the counter. When he saw who Jazzy had with him, he smiled his approval.

"Good boy," he whispered, making an O with thumb and forefinger. "Let Jazzy find a table, Mrs. Martorana. I'll come by to take your order."

Jazzy selected a table in the rear, seating Maria against the two-way mirror so she could have a complete view of the dining area. Slim recommended they try the perch, caught in nearby Irondequoit Bay, and both ordered coffee.

When Slim returned with steaming plates of fish, fries, and cole slaw, he set a bottle of wine on the table, too. "Mrs. Martorana, a special wine for a special lady. Compliments of the Hacienda." His courtly manner showed another side to him Jazzy hadn't seen.

Jazzy saw the wine was chablis and approved. He could tolerate it. He wanted everything just right for Maria.

Jazzy walked to the jukebox, made his selection, and returned to the table. Soon, he heard *That Old Black Magic* by Johnny Mercer, which he heard when he lay on his bunk. It was funny how he could remember little things like that. It should've been a happy time, because the war was over, but his mother's letter came that day, telling him she had sold the house and married Jack Werner.

Maria's eyes sparkled as she got caught up in the excitement of the crowded restaurant. She was rehearsing in her mind how to tell the ladies of the sodality how Jazzy took her out to dinner. They'd be impressed, because they commented often how much better looking he was than Tyrone Power.

Sam Trippett came out of the back room, limping noticeably. He'd stubbornly resisted an operation, but the doctors at the veteran's hospital finally prevailed, and it was scheduled for the following week.

"Jazzy!" He nodded politely to Maria. "Marve's in back, playing poker. He asked me to tell you."

A young couple walked in looking like models from *Vogue*. Jazzy recognized Lou Latuski, Moon's younger brother. If Logan was Dapper Jim, Lou was Beau Brummell. Clothes were his fetish. With Lou around, everyone saw the latest fashions. The woman with him had style, too. She clearly wasn't from the neighborhood.

There were many youngsters who went from adolescence to young adulthood in the time it took to fight a war. Lou was one of those, as were several others who were in the Hacienda that evening. When Lou's friends saw him, they howled.

"I'm witchew, Lou!"

"Yeah, Baby!"

"Hubba hubba!"

Lou scowled and blushed.

"How awful! Poor boy, ain't it embarrassing?" Maria covered her smile with her hand.

Lou's date laughed. That made her evening.

It was supposed to be a special evening for Lou. He intended to take his date out to dinner somewhere with waiters who looked and talked like Charles Boyer. He convinced his mother he was old enough to get married, and now he had to sell Sylvia on the idea.

Lou had the evening planned to the last detail, but the car wouldn't cooperate. It broke down, leaving them stranded, so he and Sylvia walked to a phone booth and called Moon. Like a good brother, Moon dropped everything and came to help with the tow truck, then he drove them to the Hacienda. He promised to come back when he had the car running again.

Slim was no Charles Boyer, but he amused Sylvia. Everyone in the Hacienda amused her, and the fish fry was great.

They'd barely finished their dinner when Moon came by to tell Lou his car was ready.

Maria and Jazzy finished the bottle of chablis. He was glad to see her enjoying it, and quiet contentment stole over him.

Just as they were getting ready to leave, there was a commotion at the front door, and an army of blue uniforms walked in, rushing toward the back door.

Slim sneaked out the front when the cops weren't looking. The sentry, who watched through the one-way mirror, did his job and shouted, "The cops!"

Gamblers poured out of the room into the restaurant area, pushing the side door open. Policemen formed a double row to create a chute and used their nightsticks as cattle prods to herd the gamblers into the waiting paddy wagon, which was already back against the door frame. Gamblers piled into the wagon, the momentum of those behind giving impetus to the headlong flight of those in front.

When Marve walked by, enduring painful prods, he gave Jazzy a look of despair. He'd been arrested twice in one day.

The ingenious ploy of the police fascinated Maria, although she felt sorry for Marve. Her amusement turned to concern after the paddy wagon was gone, and the patrol cars disappeared.

Slim came back inside. It was cold outside, and he shivered until his teeth chattered.

Jazzy learned there was a thoroughness about the mayor that belied his casual manner. He played hardball.

Chapter Fifteen

Winter came, bringing miserable weather. Some days, the heavens dumped snow too fast, and it accumulated too rapidly for Rochester's fleet of snowplows. Then the neighborhood became isolated. Bus schedules went awry, cars got stuck and sometimes buried under mountains of snow.

Jazzy depleted the armful of books from the public library, and, since it was a long walk from home, he was left with nothing to read. In addition, unless the performance of the city snowplows improved considerably, he'd be paying late charges on the books. Eventually, it stopped snowing, and the city cleared the streets and sidewalks.

The solidarity of the Goodman boys was at its peak. Sam Trippett, his leg in a cast, joined the fellowship at the Hacienda. It was like old times with Sam around. Fred, who was growing and already taller than his brother, Sam, made a receptacle for his brother's leg. He placed him on his Flexible Flyer, wrapped a blanket tightly around him against the night's bitter cold, and pulled him to the corner.

Old Man Belding came out of retirement to work the barber shop until Sam was back on his feet. Freddy was at barber's college, and soon, there would be two chairs.

Freddy was drinking clam broth at the counter.

"How's your barbering coming along?" Jazzy asked.

"Fine."

"You must be excited about joining Sam soon."

"Am I, Jazzy? Shit. All my life I've been hearing about doing my own thing. 'Don't be a slave to industry,' the old man said. Now I'm preparing for *real* slavery."

"Being a barber is slavery?"

"What else? The shop's open at night, when the rest of the city's preparing for bed. Sam's tired at the end of the day, but is he done yet? No. He has to sweep the place, do the books, check inventory, write out checks, and, when he finally gets home, he's still thinking about the shop. You know what? He loves that shit, but not me."

"Why are you doing it? Nobody's twisting your arm."

"I don't know. Maybe I'm weak and don't have the guts to put a monkey wrench in Pop and Sam's dreams. Only Mom ever questioned the old man's wisdom."

"How does she feel about it?"

"We're adults now. She can't control us like she does the old man. What's wrong with a nice job in a factory? Eight hours, and you're through for the day, with sixteen hours to do whatever you want. Sounds pretty good to me. What's wrong with making friends at work, especially girls? What social life will I have at the shop?"

"Maybe you're not meant to do your own thing. Sam says your mother likes her job at French's."

"You bet. I never saw her happier. Imagine, at her age, joining the shop bowling league."

"A family business could give everyone a better life. I never heard anyone becoming a millionaire punching a clock."

"There's no guarantee, Jazzy. Look at my old man and his wild ideas. None of them worked. It's a good thing Mom had veto power."

Jim Logan called to Jazzy, cutting off the conversation. Jazzy wanted to tell Freddy of an old adage, *Nothing ventured, nothing gained,* and that the barber shop was a sound, stable business. He couldn't tell him what he really thought—Freddy was on a single track. Confinement in the shop would make it difficult to get laid.

Whenever Jazzy's losses at the card tables in the back room were more than was prudent, although he was supremely confident he could recoup his losses with one long shot at Sparta's, he took a respite from the boys.

Then he'd date a local lovely. In his view, a sexless date was just an exercise in character building. That was why all his dates eventually found themselves at one of the local motor courts, catering to the *hot pillow* trade. Women were a fascination that never abated. He could see his young friend's point. He'd build character in some other way.

Mayor Sheldon developed an interest in Jazzy. During the many talks they had at Sparta's empty poker table, the mayor learned of Jazzy's preoccupation with books, particularly literature, and a strong bond formed.

The mayor was certain the young man was unemployed, so how was he surviving? What was his source of money? The mayor angrily told himself it was none of his business, so he tried to help Jazzy by whetting his appetite for the classics. He succeeded to some extent, because it was books from the list Sheldon recommended that kept Jazzy occupied that winter.

"When are you registering for school, Jazzy?" the mayor asked one day.

"Soon. When I make a big hit here and the horses run true to form. I'll go back to school in style."

"You don't really believe that, do you?"

"Don't you dream of the perfect day at the track or the horse room?"

"Of course not."

"Then why bet on the nags every day?"

"We're sick, you and I. Do you think when the impossible happens, and you win a fortune, that's the end?"

"Won't it be?"

"Never. There's a theory many psychologists offer as fact that we gamblers have a compulsion to lose. If and when we get our big win, our quest is half-complete. We must go back down the incline and lose it all again. That's our fate."

"I don't buy that, Mayor," Jazzy said stubbornly.

When the mayor left, Jazzy went to Jay Bright, whose horses always ran out of the money. He was ready to go, so they rounded up Nippy and Marve.

"I don't know why I come here with you guys," Jay grumbled.

"You introduced us to the nags," Marve pointed out.

"Yeah, and I'm the guy who's always sucking hind tit. I can't pick my nose."

"Stop griping. I didn't do too good, either."

"Better luck next time, eh, Guys? Let's go," Jay said.

"In a cloud of heifer dust, Jay?" Nippy asked.

Jay smiled.

"What the hell's heifer dust?" Marve asked.

Marve met Sailor White, an ex-carnival wrestler, at the YMCA weight room. Marve was broke, begging nickels and dimes from Jazzy. Every morning, Marve awoke to find the newspaper across the foot of his bed, open to the want ads.

Sailor White came into Marve's life at the right time. He joined a guild of sorts available for exhibitions. Marve wasn't getting rich, but he made a few dollars.

Jazzy got another letter from Jennie, boasting of San Diego. She had her insurance license, and, because of her experience with middle and top management and union members, she was becoming the backbone of the group insurance division. They opened an office in Chula Vista. Jennie also offered Jazzy a home with her and Jack. He wrote back saying he was proud of her, but he refused the offer.

He followed closely the progress of the Brown brothers, who were all doing well. Hubert, of course, had yet to get his first fight. The family wouldn't allow it even if Bourda was crazy enough to place him on a card.

Chris Morgana was the toast of the town. Rochester, the mecca for amateur boxing in the state, never took a native son to its bosom as it did Chris. He was on a string of nine straight knockouts—all in the first round. The *Chronicle* one morning had a half-page spread of Morgana in the classic boxing pose. There was an insert of his shoulder muscles, blown up, and accompanying it was an explanation that it was the source of the southpaw's power.

Monday nights, everyone from Goodman found a way, regardless of weather, to the Elks Club. The lure of the ring was never far from Jazzy. He took a rest from his heavy reading, telling himself his body needed exercise.

That was the first time Bourda saw Jazzy since he returned, and he ran up to pump his hand in greeting.

"I hear you've been back for some time, and you never came into my gym," he accused.

"I was afraid you'd be after me to make me enter the ring as a contestant again."

"It's getting late, Jazzy." Bourda eyed him carefully. "Not bad. You haven't let yourself go completely. There's still time. I would've preferred to get you when you were sixteen or seventeen, but…"

"Look, you've got wall-to-wall muscle in your gym. What do you want with a skinny guy like me?"

"You might be lean, but you could be mean. You're as tough as rawhide. Your right hand is a beaut. Do you know the one thing that's special about you?"

"What?" Jazzy asked wearily.

"You've got twinkletoes. That's why the boys like you. When you spar with them, you make them put their asses in gear."

"Mind if I work out?"

"Help yourself. That's what the gym's for. Who knows? I might get you in the ring yet."

Bert Bravo came over to meet Jazzy. He was a divinity student who hoped to serve the Lord someday, just as his father and grandfather had. He was a soft-spoken young man who talked of love of his fellow man, as should anyone who had heard the call.

In the ring, Bert was dynamite with both hands, and the savagery of his attack made him the headliner on all the boxing cards. He called on the Ten Commandments as a guide to living in a manner pleasing to God. In the ring, he called on his fists.

At the moment, he coveted Chris Morgana's status as the biggest drawing card in Elks Club history. He fought against his lower billing. He was pleasant to Jazzy, who saw the mad, driving zeal of a crusader in his eyes. Jazzy was glad he wasn't a light heavyweight, too. Jazzy didn't have to see him in the ring for long to realize he had the tools and had learned his trade well. He should've turned professional, but that wouldn't do for a man of the cloth.

The Brown brothers were back—the twins, Hughie and Hubert, Eddy, Bobby, and Sweet Georgie, who, now that he was grown, bore a striking resemblance to the twins. In weight classification, they were still between light and welter. Sweet Georgie, who was then a slat-legged kid, was welter. They were interchangeable.

Jazzy watched the brothers spar for some time. They'd improved, and it was obvious the twins, Bobby, and Eddy found time for boxing even in the service.

The one thing the Brown brothers had in common was style. In ability, Hughie was still the best. Hubert, his uncanny double, was all *show but no go* as before. Bobby and Eddie were solid performers.

The professionals were eyeing Sweet Georgie. Perhaps that was because of his youth, or maybe they saw something in him they didn't see in Hughie.

For the first week, Jazzy contented himself with the big bag and worked on hand speed with the punching bag. He skipped rope and worked the wall pulleys, too.

He was anxious to spar with Morgana, although he was apprehensive of the man's vaunted punching power. He'd be somewhat protected with head gear and big gloves.

They circled each other awhile. Jazzy landed two lefts to the head, and Morgana countered with a right and left, missing both. Jazzy maneuvered the slower man with ease, and he was filled with disappointment. Was Marve right in saying Chris was too awkward? Were there set-ups in amateur boxing, too?

Morgana bulled Jazzy into a corner and dug his left hook into Jazzy's right side. Even with the big gloves, the blow drew a gasp of pain from Jazzy, and he felt paralysis along his rib cage. He couldn't believe anyone could punch that hard.

Jazzy called on all his defensive skills—slipping, blocking, weaving, and dancing lightly on the balls of his feet. He made Morgana perspire, which was what the southpaw needed.

Johnny Bourda watched Jazzy's superb footwork. "Stubborn bastard," he muttered. "I could've made him a great fighter."

Jazzy renewed old friendships with the Brown brothers. It flattered him that they argued over him, wanting to work out with him. He made them step lively.

When he sparred with Sweet Georgie, he tried to determine the unknown factor that separated him from the others. Jazzy found nothing. Hughie was still the class act in the family.

For the rest of the winter, Chris Morgana filled the seats at the Elks Club arena. He added to his string of knockouts, and eventually, it was understood, he would face one or all of the Brown brothers. Bourda was in no hurry, though. Morgana had a lot to learn.

Spring hadn't arrived. Snow was still on the ground when chinks appeared in the tight unity of the Goodman boys. Nippy went south to try out with the baseball teams in spring training. Slim Broadway gave him a dinner and baked a cake in the shape of a baseball glove. It was a good turnout and happy occasion. Enough money was collected to defray Nippy's expenses to Florida and back—if a return was necessary.

The cast came off Sam's leg almost simultaneous to the day when Freddy received his barber's license from the city. Belding was relieved of his stewardship and returned to his blessed retirement. Freddy took over the barber shop under the watchful eye of his brother, Sam. When his leg was strong enough, they bought a second chair, and then the gang saw the brothers only on Sundays, except when the boys visited the barber shop.

Jim Logan dropped out of sight. They later learned he was courting Viola, the neighbor who, as a girl, had to be stoned to keep her from following Jim around like a puppy dog. It was a very short courtship—Viola had been ready for a long time.

It came as no surprise when Jim selected Jay Bright as best man. Marve felt left out when Jazzy and Moon were chosen as ushers.

The wedding was all a bride could ask for. The bridesmaids were attractive, and the ushers were handsome. They scrubbed Jay clean, leaving him barely recognizable in his formal attire. The reception was held in the home of Viola's parents. All afternoon, the guests reveled, loathe to leave despite hints the party was over. Many lingered at the bar.

The newlyweds would leave for Niagara Falls as soon as Viola and her mother finished packing the bride's bags. Jazzy had a chance to talk to Jim alone for the first time since the wedding was announced.

"Well, Jim, you know I want to wish you and Viola the best."

"I know, old buddy."

"You're the first of the gang to get hitched."

"That's right."

"I never figured it would be Viola," Jazzy lied. "Remember how rough you were with her when we were kids?"

"Yeah. I threw stones at her. You know what? I missed every time."

Jazzy smiled, knowing Jim was about to confide something he'd already guessed.

"I loved that girl from the first day she moved next door. She was only five at the time."

"But you had to hide it from us."

"You bet. Otherwise, you would've ridden the shit out of me. When I was in the Army, the fear of her marrying someone else while I was away gave me many sleepless nights. My dream was to marry her, have a home, and father children. I don't dream big, Jazzy. If I can have a happy life, like my parents, that's all I ask. Pop was tough and strict with me and Cathy, and that's how I want to be with my kids."

"Is this Jim Logan talking? How often have I heard you bellyache about your father being a tyrant?"

"That's right. The old folks get smarter as we get older. I've learned love isn't enough. You have to protect your brood and guide them every step of the way."

Viola came downstairs and claimed Jim. Jazzy shook his head. He shouldn't be surprised. There always was a streak of no-nonsense practicality in Jim. Jazzy always suspected, even as Jim held his own in the ribald exchanges in the gang, there was an air of moral superiority about him.

"As a father," Jazzy concluded, "Jim will be a horse ball."

Jay and Cathy, who was maid of honor for her brother's wedding, hit it off so well, they married one month later. Jim Logan was best man, and Jazzy and Marve were ushers.

Jay quit the old-wood business. He went into delivery and bought a panel truck of recent vintage. With Logan's help, who was becoming a successful businessman due to his valuable contacts, he obtained contracts with several stores. Cathy, who attended business college, kept the books.

One morning, Marve was talking to Joe Black. Nippy, back from Florida, was alone at the counter.

"How'd things go down south, Nippy?" Jazzy asked.

"Actually, not too bad. They found I could field, throw, and run. In their judgment, an outfielder who can't hit is like a cowboy who can't ride."

"I don't think that's a fair judgment. Every time I see you play, you seem to be able to get a piece of the ball."

"That's not what they meant. I'm a spray hitter—not enough power to hit the ball out of there."

"You've got other qualities."

"There ain't other qualities in the outfield. They can teach anyone to catch flies. Power hitters are ready-made."

"I'm not informed on baseball, Nippy, but doesn't that hold true for infielders, too?"

"Oh, no. The best athlete on the team is the shortstop. Infielders have special skills—good arms, grace, dexterity, speed, and the qualities of a circus acrobat. If you're a good infielder, they forgive lack of power at bat."

Jazzy was silent. "Why do they call you Nippy?"

"What kind of question is that? You've known me all your life."

"Answer the question."

"It wasn't always Nippy. At first, it was Nap."

"Why Nap?"

"Remember when we were kids, and Father Weideman and the Holy Name Society formed a team and entered it in the parochial baseball league? You were on the team."

"Not for long. I didn't play much, if you recall."

"Well, I did. Some old-timer from Saint Andrew's saw me make a play at second, and he yelled I was a regular Nap Lajoie."

"Is that good?"

"Hall of Fame."

"Well, what in hell are you doing playing outfield?"

Nippy looked sheepish and didn't answer for a moment. "I wanted to be another Joe Dimaggio. It's easy for an infielder to play the outfield. An outfielder has trouble in the infield. I thought I could pull it off. The big idols today are Musial, Dimaggio, and Williams, all outfielders. They get the big dough."

"Those are big boys. You're infielder size."

"Yeah, but I'm as big as Dom Dimaggio of the Red Sox."

"Nippy, how could you be so dumb?"

"Because I am."

"Horseshit."

"I can't go to college."

"Why the hell not?"

"I've got my high-school diploma and very little else."

"I thought you were doing well at Franklin."

"I wasn't about to tell the world I wasn't a brain. Besides, I didn't take the right courses. Don't get me wrong. If my grades were great, I'd still choose baseball over college."

"We all want to be good at something."

"I know myself pretty well. I see no other field where I can make a name for myself."

"Don't give up, Nippy. You'll get another chance. If you've got to have an idol, make it Lajoie."

Chapter Sixteen

Jazzy jammed a thumb sparring with Bobby Brown. It was swollen and hurt, and he quit for a few days.

"Who's coming to Sparta's?" he asked, feeling lucky.

Marve and Nippy went with him.

Their numbers, now reduced to three, were still received with the usual hearty greeting that set them apart from others who arrived in groups. Jazzy's devotion to his friends was deep, and he truly believed they were a special breed.

The Stooge was making the final odds changes. Jazzy hurried to the betting window and placed two dollars on the nose of Persistent, a filly that folded in the stretch and beat him out of a double earlier in the month. He'd give her a chance to redeem herself.

Mayor Sheldon saw Jazzy and smiled, wondering once again why he liked the young man.

"Haven't seen you lately, Jazzy," he said. "Keeping busy?"

"I've been working out at Bourda's gym."

The mayor's eyebrows rose in surprise.

"I've been sparring with Bourda's boys since I was a kid. I jammed my thumb with Bobby Brown."

"Holy mackerel, Jazzy! Got any more surprises?"

"The surprise is that I'm still in one piece."

The Stooge called the race. Persistent didn't get a call, but, when he announced the winner, it was Persistent by a nose. Later, Jazzy went to the window and pocketed his winnings—$12.10.

The mayor called Jazzy over to the poker table. "How are you doing with your reading? That list I gave you would give you a good start for going back to school."

"Would you believe I've read twelve of those books?"

"There's a lot to be learned from those early writers."

"When I read some of them, I'm reminded of campaign promises, like doing something about pornography. Things were no different in the old days. Those ancient writers weren't Mother Goose."

"Is that all you got out of that?" The mayor expected more enthusiasm.

Jazzy was silent and hurt, for the mayor questioned the depth of his appreciation. He was surprised how deeply he was hurt. Why was it so important to him to be accepted as literate? If it was that important, why was he procrastinating about going to the university?

"I've got the winner of the next race, my boy," the mayor said, not realizing he'd upset his young friend.

"Who have you got?" Jazzy asked softly.

"Forty-niner."

"Forty-niner? He couldn't win even if he ran alone."

"Ah, but I have divine revelation."

"Just what do you have?"

"It's my wife's forty-ninth birthday."

"Mayor, if the form says he looks like a dog and runs like a dog, he's a dog."

"We walk by faith, not by sight—Corinthians."

Jazzy would've given almost anything to sprinkle fine-sounding quotations in his conversation, but he had a keen mind and excellent memory. The mayor was rising to leave, and, just in time, Jazzy recalled one of Father's Weideman's favorite platitudes. "If the blind lead the blind, both shall fall in the ditch—Matthew."

A wide smile lit the mayor's face. "Touché, Jazzy."

Jazzy watched the mayor place his bet, lingering at the window to talk to Dave. When the Stooge put on his earphones, Jazzy watched and listened, but there was no call for Forty-niner. Jazzy was fond of the mayor and admired his style, but Jazzy had his quota of human frailties, one of which was vindictiveness. He was glad the mayor was a bettor.

The mayor returned with a rueful expression. "You were right, Jazzy. That horse was a dog."

Some of the boys from the west side walked by, and one playfully slapped Jazzy's back.

"How you doing, Casanova?"

Jazzy didn't answer, but his tight mouth showed his anger.

"Don't let it get you down," the mayor said softly. "Most men would feel flattered."

"I seem to have a reputation I don't deserve. I don't like people thinking I seduce their kids. I never had an affair unless there was mutual attraction and desire."

"If it wasn't you making that statement, it would sound like a boast from a conceited ass. You state it as fact."

"There are many in this room who're copulating more."

"Many? I doubt that."

"That's true. Some are married, some have steady lays. Then there are the repeaters."

"Repeaters? You've lost me."

"I've had a few girls in my time. On occasion, I seek them out again, but not often. I feel I've got to find new ones."

"You mean every time you have sex, you drop the woman?"

"Most of the time."

"That troubles you?"

"I wonder if there's something wrong with me. I'm glad we're talking about it, though. I never had the chance to discuss my feelings with someone before."

"Are you finding the anticipation greater than the act?"

"No. I have a healthy appetite for sex."

"I'm no expert. I married the first girl I dated, and I'm still with her. I suppose I missed a lot marrying so young, but, if either of us had previous experience, our first union wouldn't have held that magic."

That amused Jazzy. Was he saying sex was like a bank account, and every time someone got laid, he made a withdrawal? "Am I looking for true love? What the hell is it?"

"I can give you only my own opinion. Sex alone isn't love. The main ingredient of love is concern for the other. When you find a woman whose needs and wants are more important than yours, then you're in love. Say, I said that rather well."

The mayor walked toward the door. Jazzy wondered if love was complicated and exhausting. Jimmy found it next door, while Jay Bright, the poorest and most disadvantaged among them, found it overnight.

It should've been a good day, but, as Whitey tried to tell Jazzy once, horses didn't read. They didn't know what was expected of them. Fortunately, he restricted himself to two-dollar bets, and, with the start he got with Persistent's close win at Tropical Park, his losses were minimal.

Marve wagered very little, because he had little to start with. Nippy had a rare day and walked out of Sparta's with a tidy sum. They still had time to kill, and Jazzy talked them into a quick visit to the gym to see Morgana.

They found Chris working on the heavy bag.

"Everything all right?" Jazzy asked.

"Fine. Bert and I had a disagreement, but we talked it out, and Bourda has it under control."

"What was it about?"

"You know Bert has always fought the main go. With all the publicity I've been getting, he was told I'd be main event on the same card he was on. His pride couldn't take it, but Bourda came up with a solution. We'll double the main event—one with a big man, the other with a little man."

"Everything's fine now?"

"Oh, sure. Me and Bert are buddies."

It was dark when Jazzy pulled into the driveway, and he sensed something wrong. He rang the doorbell, but there was no response. He knocked, but Maria didn't answer the door. Jazzy was frightened for her. He went to the driveway and saw what alerted him—there was no soft light coming from the kitchen window.

He hurried to the front door again. Finding the key Maria once gave him, but which he never used, he opened the door. The entire house was dark. His calls went unanswered, and he ran through the house, bumping into the furniture.

When Jazzy opened the door to Maria's bedroom, she lay on her back, eyes closed, her mouth in a tight smile. Jesus looked down at her from a three-dimensional icon on the wall. Dancing rays of red light came from the vigil candle.

Jazzy saw she was dead. Her shoes were neatly placed by the bed, as they always were when she took her afternoon nap. She'd died in her sleep.

He dropped to his knees beside her bed and held her cold hand, putting his head on his forearm as he cried. Finally, he composed himself. There were arrangements to make, and he wished Jennie were there. He ran to the Hacienda and called an ambulance.

Slim noted Jazzy's agitated state and left the counter to speak to him. "What's wrong, Jazzy?"

"It's Mrs. Martorana. She's dead."

"How'd it happen?"

"She died in her sleep."

"I *am* sorry."

They exchanged idle talk until they heard the wail of the ambulance, then Jazzy rushed out to meet it.

Within minutes, Maria was under a sheet and whisked out of his life. A heavy weight settled on his chest.

He went to the mailbox and found a letter from Jennie waiting. She wrote and told him they'd opened a third office, and the good news jarred him in the midst of his tragedy.

Jazzy drove to Jim Logan's house. Of all the Goodman boys, Jim was the most dependable. He shared Jazzy's grief and returned to the house with his friend.

Before strangers overran the house, they searched it carefully. There was no money or insurance policy. When they found Maria's bank book, it showed a zero balance. It was evident her small widow's pension was dissipated as soon as it arrived. Without Jazzy's rent, she would've lost her home and became a ward of the county.

Logan suggested they talk to Mrs. Belding. She might know more about Maria's affairs. At the news of Maria's death, Ida was devastated. Maria was a charter member of the sodality.

She told Jazzy that Maria had no assets but the house. She couldn't pass a physical to get health insurance. Few knew she had health problems, and Ida suspected Maria hadn't even told Mateo.

Then Mrs. Belding startled them by saying Maria was contemplating a will to leave the house to Jazzy. Her brother was too old to inherit, and there were no other relatives. All Maria intended to ask of Jazzy was a decent burial.

"Intentions mean nothing if they aren't in writing," Logan said.

"What happens to her now?" Jazzy asked.

"There's a time element, too. They might not be able to locate her brother. I don't know where he is in Italy. Do you, Jazzy?" Ida asked.

"Mrs. Belding, she never mentioned it to me or Mother."

"Well, someone has to bury her. I suppose the Health Department will step in. I don't know how this works."

Jim wanted to advise Jazzy to sit tight. It wasn't his problem. If the brother wasn't found, the house would go to the state.

Back at Maria's house, Jazzy went to his room and basked in fond memories of the old days. He saw the picture of the Rhinehardt coat of arms, a bit of whimsy he endured, thinking it meant so much to his mother. When he moved in with Maria, he took the picture with him.

He read the motto—*Honor Above All.* Suddenly, they weren't just words. He heard a call from his distant past.

"Jim," he said softly, "she was a mother to me. Her burial is my obligation."

Logan stayed with Jazzy throughout the ordeal. He accompanied him to the funeral home and made burial arrangements with the director for a fine Christian funeral.

The expense would take the last of Jazzy's money, and he would've come up short if it hadn't been for the welcome aid from an unexpected source. Abel made up the difference. He remembered Maria's role in finding employment for his wife during the depression.

With the sodality coming *en masse* for the funeral, and the boys in full attendance, the entire neighborhood said farewell to Maria in grand style. The procession was long, and Maria would've approved.

That night, Josie came by to offer her condolences. She stayed the night. When, the next evening, Jazzy received a similar visit from Belle, he realized that the three of them, inseparable and acting in concert, were making a gesture of pure friendship that was touching—if a bit bizarre.

His hunch was confirmed the third night when Pamela arrived, also full of condolences. Jazzy had no fear of commitment. Those were young women with high expectations, and to them, Jazzy's future was bleak.

Chapter Seventeen

For the first time in his life, Jazzy was alone and destitute. There was no Jennie to cater to his needs, guide him, and protect him. There was no Maria to be a surrogate mother, as she was when he returned from the war. He never knew his father.

He hadn't the slightest idea what to do. He could tough it out, as Logan suggested, until some authority figure came and chased him out of the house, then dunned him for accumulated rent. There was the possibility Maria's brother might appear and claim the house. What would be the legal ramifications of that?

His friends were of little help, having saddled themselves with responsibilities. He'd been the proverbial grasshopper, wasting away the summer with frivolity and giving no thought to the coming winter.

Marve was under more pressure from his parents to get a job. His small income from wrestling exhibitions didn't go far, and they wanted him to have more meaning to his life. That was why Marve was so receptive when Sailor White asked him to join the Mack-Schiffer carnival making its way to Niagara Falls.

Marve was very dependent on Jazzy and lacked confidence without his friend. Getting a job for Jazzy was a condition he set for the deal. Sailor contacted Mack, the carnival owner for whom he previously worked, and all that was left was for Marve to convince Jazzy to come to Niagara Falls with them.

Jazzy had no alternative to Marve's solution, and he was grateful for a way out of his dead end. Slim helped, allowing Jazzy to store the cot and dresser his mother bought years earlier when Mateo and Maria agreed to watch over her son while she worked. He'd never take the furniture from the old couple, but he owed nothing to whomever got the house.

Jazzy was never on the second floor of the building that housed the Hacienda. The rooms were always empty, even in the days of the pool hall. He recalled the earlier times when he was a child, and the building had been a speakeasy. He looked out the second-story window where he saw the painted ladies looking down on him.

He was leaving the neighborhood again. He'd wasted a lot of money, and, before he left, he made a tour of the neighborhood. He started by having clam broth with Slim and Joe Black, then he visited Jim Logan's home. Fortunately, Jay Bright was there, and he could say, "Hello," to Jay, too. Freddy and Sam were without customers at the moment, so Jazzy spent time with them, too.

He had the urge to see Father Weideman, who was sorry to see Jazzy leave. He gave the young man his benediction.

Using some of his remaining money, Jazzy took the car to Moon's for a check-up and gas. It was hard saying good-bye to Moon. Jazzy deliberately saved the Kovens for last.

Niagara Falls wasn't a city Jazzy liked. It was industrial, with too many chemical plants. His accommodations were sparse. The small room Sailor White leased in advance when it was going to be just himself and Marve was made more congested with the addition of a cot. Jazzy had slept in nothing but Army bunks and narrow cots for the last few years, and someday, he hoped to sleep in a full-sized bed.

The interview with Mack wasn't what he expected, either. He was a soft-spoken, mild-mannered businessman, not the brash, fast-talking Jack Oakie type associated with carny people.

Mack looked Jazzy over, noting his rare good looks and the interesting way he spoke, giving an effect of sophistication. As he talked, explaining the various functions of his job, Mack's mind raced. What a pitchman Jazzy would make!

"You're not a performer and don't have a special skill," Mack said. "Primarily, you'll be a roustabout. At times, you'll be a painter, electrician, or carpenter. In other words, you'll help set up tents, booths, and facilities. Then, when we move on, you'll help us tear down what we've built.

"There'll be times when a concessionaire will want to be relieved. You learn about the various booths on the lot so you can be a relief man. Sometimes, the barkers need relief. Learn what they say and how they say it so you can carry on in their absence. Don't let all this confuse you. I don't expect you to learn it all immediately."

"I'll do my best," Jazzy promised.

"Another thing. I want you to play at all the skill games on the lot as often as time allows. I want you to be proficient. When business lags, nothing will rekindle the interest of the customers like someone beating us at the booths. What you'll be doing is called shilling, but there isn't anything illegal about it.

"We exist for two reasons—to make money and provide fun for folks. Since our business is family oriented, we're concerned about morality. Even our girlie show, with pretty ladies in scanty costumes, is restricted in its performance." Mack stopped, then added, "Welcome aboard."

The first time Jazzy saw Madame Dagmar, he liked her. The medium was in her middle years, wore clothes that made her appear dowdy, and was distinguishable in a crowd with her purple hair. She wasn't the grouchy old broad the other roustabouts painted her. Where she was slovenly in her personal attire, she was fastidious in the trappings of her business.

She was proficient in all aspects of divination—palmistry, astrology, cartomancy, and necromancy. It was her clairvoyance, through the aid of a crystal ball, however, that was the main source of her income.

Knowing her proved a blessing. Sometimes, when the noise of the midway, the hurly-burly of what Madame Dagmar called, "That siren call of the suckers," overwhelmed Jazzy, he headed for her tent, drank tea with her, and discussed many things.

Mack's girlie show was called Harem Lovelies, allowing the women to wear the revealing costumes associated with women of the potentates of the Near East.

Jazzy wouldn't term them lovelies, although the flashing legs, tight pants cut so short they struggled to cover the women's buttocks, bare midriffs, and low-cut bodices were enough to lure male customers.

They wore too much makeup, and all semblance of innocence ceased with the years. The only exception was Flo, the youngster, who still looked at the world with wide-eyed wonder, and whose lovely body and sensuous posturing stirred Jazzy.

The girlie show was behind Madame Dagmar's tent, which was fortunate for Sybil, an unwed mother. During shows, Madame Dagmar watched the child, lying among the blankets in a box in the back of the tent, out of sight.

Flo lived on the grounds in a trailer she shared with the Meeker twins. The Meekers were pretty, in a dairy maid sort of way, but they were a bit heavy in calves and thighs. There were others, but the turnover of personnel was rapid but for the four regulars. No one got to know them.

Jazzy was a quick learner, and his fine coordination, inherited from Jennie, made him adept at various booths. With his looks, far removed from the carny stereotype, he made an excellent shill. More and more, he was relieved of manual chores, to the discontent of the roustabouts with years of service. He was required to wear his best clothes.

Jazzy couldn't hide his interest in Flo, although he tried. Soon, she sought him out. She hadn't seen a man so elegant and desirable in her circle before. Flo wanted him and didn't care who knew it. Whenever time from the show allowed, she followed him. With a long, black cape covering her costume, she looked like an off-duty nurse. If he went to the hot dog stand, she went. If he filled in at a booth, she watched.

Once, when he was in Madame Dagmar's tent, drinking tea, Flo came in professing to look in on the baby for Sybil. The medium poured tea, and, as they made small talk, Jazzy had the opportunity to see Flo up close. She had close-cropped black hair, eyes not quite blue but not green, a full mouth, and a long, slender neck. She straddled, rather than sat, on the chair, and she might as well have removed her cape, because she exposed her considerable charms, making Jazzy uneasy.

When Flo left, Madame Dagmar chuckled. "You'd better give her what she wants, Handsome, or she'll hound the hell out of you."

"You're a nasty old broad, Dagmar."

She laughed, then reached across the small table, held Jazzy's cheeks in her hands, and kissed his mouth.

Marve earned his keep, too. Customers liked him. His youthful face belied his twenty-three years. Somehow, they managed to find menacing-looking gargoyles to wrestle him. To the anxious fans, Marve was in a fight for survival, billed as Marvelous Marve, a freshman at a local college.

The feature of the show, however, was Sailor White. He was bald, tattooed, massively muscled, and offered fifty dollars to anyone who could stay in the ring with him for ten minutes without being pinned. He looked convincingly sinister, even to Jazzy, who learned to like him, because he was a quiet gentleman when he wasn't performing. It was all part of the master plan for the grand finale of the last night before the show moved on.

Jazzy was dispiritedly throwing baseballs at the pyramid of composition milk bottles, not feeling very proud of himself. Mack's assurance of the legality of shilling didn't cover the morality of what he saw as seduction. He felt unclean, and, in addition, he was losing his conditioning. Since Maria's death, he lived on junk food and was gaining weight. He hadn't been working out since he hurt his thumb against Bobby Brown.

Then he felt someone staring at him. Jazzy was startled when he saw the lovely woman looking at him. Racing through his mind were all the escapist movies of Jon Hall and lovely island women. No Polynesian belle could match the beauty of the one watching him.

She was part of a group from the Tuscarora Reservation, and she lagged behind to watch him. In that first glance, she affected him deeply, which made him wonder. Although he knew it wasn't possible, the thought persisted he knew her from somewhere. At the moment, she was Ramona from the pages of Helen Jackson's fine novel.

She wore culottes—that ugly garment, half pants and half shorts, that did very little for a woman. On her, the limited exposure of a well-turned ankle and well-rounded calf gave promise of a delightful pair of legs. She caught him looking at her legs.

Flustered, he turned away, took aim, and threw at the bottles on the bottom row, knocking them all off the pedestal. He motioned to the concessionaire to pull down the large teddy bear. The man frowned, then suddenly smiled.

"Why not, Pal? She's a looker."

Without a word, Jazzy handed her the teddy bear. Her smile dazzled him, and he watched her run back to her friends. When she reached them, she blew him a kiss, and he never saw her again.

Flo had been making progress with Jazzy, but his ardor cooled. She knew she'd done nothing to dampen it, so the situation distressed her.

His meeting with the American Indian woman, although brief, had a profound effect on him. He was discriminating, and his interest in Flo waned.

The band played ersatz near Eastern music that lent itself to seduction, and the lovelies were doing their part with suggestive swaying. Flo was between the Meeker twins when she saw Jazzy pass the stage, where they were giving a sample of the wonders promised within. She waved to him, but his response was a limp raising of his hand.

The Meekers laughed, which angered Flo.

"I'll get that good-looking bastard in bed yet," she told them. "You can make book on that."

Rain came, although the weatherman promised it would bypass Niagara Falls. It drenched the grounds and everything on them. Everyone got a night off. Marve, who enjoyed boozing, wanted to have a roaring good time. They'd just been paid, and there wasn't much money left for Jazzy after expenses. He was content to stay in his room, snug and dry, reading periodicals.

The rain persisted and became a torrent. Then pyrotechnics were added. Marve dreaded electrical storms, and Jazzy felt certain he'd hole up somewhere until the storm subsided.

A loud knock on the door startled him. When he opened it, he saw Flo, drenched despite her umbrella. Jazzy pulled her inside the room and helped her from her coat. Her babushka was a soggy rag, and her wet clothes clung to her desperately.

"Are you crazy, coming here in this storm?" he asked.

"I thought you'd be lonesome. The boys are either at the Rayott or the Boot and Saddle. I brought hot coffee and doughnuts."

He took the soggy bag and set it on the end table. "Go into the bathroom and take off those clothes."

"Why, Jazzy!" she said in mock horror.

Jazzy pulled the blanket from his cot. "Here. After you dry yourself, wrap this around you."

When she came out, her hair was in a tangle, and she had the blanket loosely wrapped around her.

They sat side-by-side on the cot, munching on doughnuts and drinking coffee. She was in no hurry, and she looked at him carefully. Looking at him thrilled her.

She looked wanton and terribly desirable. It was a long time since he'd been that close to a woman. He realized he hadn't been with one outside the environs of the neighborhood since the woman in the red dress at the Four Seasons, but he couldn't remember her name.

With studied deliberation, Flo took the empty bag and paper cups and dropped them in the wastebasket, then walked to the door and latched it. Then she let the blanket fall to the floor.

She paused at the door, facing him and inviting his critical appraisal. Her body was youthful. She was clean-limbed, and her hips flared out enough to escape being boyish. Her stomach had the flatness of an athlete in training, and her breasts were splendid in their recent maturity.

As she smiled, her lips parted to show strong teeth with a slight overbite. Her eyes were slits as she looked at him. She was a sleek panther, and Jazzy tried to pull her down on the cot.

"No way, Love. Not on that cot." She pulled him to his feet and led him to Marve's bed, then pushed him onto it, falling on top of him. "If we're gonna do it, we do it right."

His face was buried in her bosom.

"Do you love me, Jazzy?"

"Not really," he replied, his voice muffled, "but you sure got me sizzling."

"Screw you."

Then she slid down his body, grabbed his hair fiercely in both hands, and kissed him.

The roustabouts were dismantling structures, getting a head start on the exodus from Niagara Falls early the next day. Mack hoped for a brisk night to make up for the one he lost to the rainstorm. Ahead were small towns and small crowds until they reached Erie.

Jazzy was free of the ever-trailing Flo, but it was a temporary respite. The urges would surface again. He couldn't get the American Indian woman out of his mind. He felt the ridiculous notion that he cheated on her with Flo during the storm. In his mind, she was the Tahitian lovely in a Jon Hall movie.

The Meeker twins cornered him with a riddle. "What's as rare as a day in June?"

"How the hell would I know?" he replied, irritated.

"A night in Florence." They laughed raucously.

"Christ." He stalked off.

Jazzy shook himself from the twins to face the realities of the carnival lot. Marve made such a big hit with the crowd, he drew the same people night after night. The needling by the locals began, and Sailor White, as usual had thrown the town toughs within ten minutes. Mack's fifty dollars were safe again.

The crowd clamored for Marvelous Marve. Jazzy took a position in the crowd and let Mack know he was available. Soon, Mack nodded.

"Marve!" Jazzy shouted above the din. "Make it now!"

The calliope was loud and monotonous, the side-show barkers were irritating, and the tinny music from the Harem Lovelies merely added to the bedlam. Mack was having a great night. Around Jazzy was the musty smell of the perspiring crowd.

"I'll take him!" Marve called.

The crowd roared its approval, and a path was cleared, allowing Marve to walk to the edge of the platform. Mack leaped up first.

"Get away, Boy. Stay in your own class," he said.

"Give the kid a chance!" Jazzy shouted.

Others picked up the cry.

"Give the kid a chance!"

Mack held up his hands for silence. "The Sailor's too big, Boy. He'll kill you."

"Give the kid a chance!" Jazzy shouted, moving around the crowd, repeating his words.

Soon, it seemed like the entire carnival grounds shouted, "Give the kid a chance!"

"All right, all right," Mack said. "He has his chance, but I waive responsibility."

Jazzy lost himself in the crowd as soon as Mack left the stage. Marve would throw the Sailor as planned. There was no reason to stay and watch.

Sailor White was packing his suitcase. He and Marve would join the caravan out of town in Jazzy's car. Jazzy's suitcase was already locked in the trunk.

When Marve walked in, he made no move to pack, pacing instead.

"Let's have it, Marve," Jazzy said. "You've got something to say, so say it."

"I'm staying. I'll join the show a little later."

"What are you up to?" Sailor White asked. "We've got an act going, remember?"

"I'll only miss one day."

"What the hell is this about?" Jazzy asked.

"Two guys came to see me after the match. They want me to substitute for one of the fighters in the main event at the arena tonight."

"Main event?" Jazzy asked. "Are you talking pro?"

"Yeah."

"You laughed at them, right?"

"No, I signed. Hell, I'm here to make money."

"You're no boxer. I can lick you myself. You'll be killed. What's the matter with you? Can't I leave you alone one minute without you getting into trouble?"

"What did they look like?" the Sailor asked.

"One's tall and bald, the other's short and stocky."

"Are their names Monti and Hobbs?"

"Yeah, that's them."

"Christ! You jackass!"

"What is it?" Jazzy asked

"Those are Joe Chink's torpedoes," the Sailor said.

"Who's Joe Chink?" Jazzy asked.

"Bad news. I know this area like the back of my hand. Joe Chink's top dog in the rackets in the Falls."

"Wait a minute, you guys," Marve said. "I was told all I had to do was make a good showing, then take a dive. Who am I hurting? I'll get three fifty for doing it. I want that dough."

"You talk like a man with a paper asshole," the Sailor said in disgust. "Most of Joe's fights are fixed. He's an expert at it. You know why? He sits up front during a fight and tells you when to stay down. If you take the count before he says so, you get nothing. His boy will have instructions to destroy you. For that three fifty, you'll have the beating of your life."

Marve was silent, recalling the agony of his losing fight against Guy Lovell before the war. A trained pro could maim him for life. He was alarmed.

"What'll I do, Jazzy?" he asked plaintively.

"Pack your bag."

"Then what?"

"Catch a bus to Rochester."

"I'm broke, Jazzy. That's one reason I took the fight."

Jazzy debated with himself. He felt responsible for his friend, who'd never grown up. Reluctantly, he gave Marve two fives and a ten from his wallet. All he had left was a one-dollar bill and some coins.

"Sailor, take my car keys and drive him to the bus stop. I'll stay here in case they come back soon. I'll throw them off."

"Jazzy, they play for keeps. They'll hurt you."

"There's no other way. If I'm not here when you get back, park the car behind the gas station across the street at the front entrance to the carnival grounds. Put the key under the mat. If you hurry, you can make the caravan out of here. Tell Madame Dagmar I'm asking her to give you a ride in her car. She won't refuse."

"Take care, Jazzy." Marve hurried to the car.

Just after they drove off, a car arrived, and out stepped the two men Marve described.

"Where's Marvelous Marve?" they asked.

"He went to the store with Sailor White. He'll be back."

"I told him not to budge," the tall one said.

"One of us should've stayed with that clown, Hobbs."

They forced Jazzy inside the apartment and waited for a few minutes. The short one went to the window and looked out.

"I don't like this one damn bit."

"Monti, call the boss."

Monti went out and returned a few minutes later. He nodded to Hobbs, who took Jazzy by the arm and shoved him toward the door.

"The boss wants to see you."

Chapter Eighteen

At first glance, Jazzy thought Joe Chink was Oriental. The folds of his eyelids gave that impression. He was a big, fleshy man who tried to achieve sartorial splendor and elegant manners. He didn't mind what he considered his *nom de guerre.* Joe Chink had more muscle than Marion Beverley.

He was a gangster who wanted respectability. He fancied himself a sportsman and an entrepreneur. On the walls hung pictures of Dempsey, Tunney, and little Lou Ambers, who split two close decisions with the legendary Henry Armstrong. He was catholic in sports tastes, with photos of Red Grange and Tom Harmon.

Babe Ruth smiled down on Joe from the wall over his head. That photograph was flanked by others of Lou Gherig and Hank Greenberg. On the desk using it as a paperweight, was a heavy bronze statuette of the Boston Strong Boy, John L. Sullivan.

Joe Chink sat behind a large desk. "Well? Who are you?"

"Jazzy Rhinehardt."

"Is that supposed to mean something to me?"

"We called about him. He's Marvelous Marve's friend."

"Oh, yeah. The substitute for the main go. See the morning paper?" He showed Jazzy the sports page, prominently displaying a shot of Marve pinning Sailor White. There was the old bromide about the wrestler turned boxer, and how Marvelous Marve was no newcomer to boxing, having been boxing champion of the eastern seaboard while still in high school.

That was no chance bit of photography. It was planned.

"You can't put him on the card, Mr. Chink." Jazzy was polite, ready to plead if necessary.

"What do you mean, Punk? Your buddy is signed, sealed, and he will deliver."

"He can't fight."

"He's an ox. I saw him last night. He looked real good."

"That's wrestling. The truth is, he's not much good at that, either. In a real match, he has no chance against the Sailor."

"Look, Punk, the racket's full of guys who can't fight. Who cares?"

"I do. He's my friend, and I say it's like spearing fish in a barrel. It won't be a fight. The fans won't go for it. They'll be unhappy with the match."

"Are you trying to tell me my business? The rabble don't give a fuck. They just want blood, and I give it to them. Now get out of my sight."

"Marve hasn't a license." Jazzy felt desperate.

"That's been arranged."

"You can't make Marve fight if you can't find him."

Joe didn't answer, rolling a pencil between his fingers, staring at it as if seeing it for the first time. When he looked up, he stared at Jazzy.

"When you first walked in," he said slowly, "I said to myself, 'Joe, here's a guy who's got the stamp of a troublemaker.' It shows, just like you were wearing a badge. Now you listen carefully, Punk. I'm saying this just once. I needed your friend in the main. If he doesn't go tonight, I'll throw you to the lions."

"You can't do that. I'm not a fighter."

"Marvelous Marve told Hobbs you're pretty good."

"He's crazy! I never had a match."

"You should've thought of that before."

"You don't shanghai someone off the street and throw him in the ring. The law's specific about that."

"Did you two hear that? We got us a lawyer."

Monti and Hobbs gave the required laughter.

"Do you know what incapacitate means?" Joe asked.

"I know."

"We won't make you go into the ring against your will, but, if you don't cooperate, my boys will incapacitate you. They'll break every bone in your body."

Jazzy recalled Sailor White's admonition that those men played for keeps. He looked around desperately. Joe's girlfriend stood by the window, and there was no escape. He held a bad hand and had to play it out.

"I weigh 152."

Joe's triumphant smile galled Jazzy.

"I'm not in shape."

"A guy who talks big can spot Mendez thirteen pounds."

"How much?"

"How much what?"

"How much do I get for the dive?"

"No dive. I tell you when to stay down. Six C's to the winner, three fifty to the loser."

"Why not four seventy-five each?"

"You've got a lot of balls. Remember, get cute, and I'll put your end of the purse in the deep freeze."

"I'll remember," Jazzy said bitterly.

With time on his hands in a strange suite, Jazzy felt frightened. He cursed Marve for luring him from the safety of Goodman Street, then he cursed him for getting involved with dangerous people. Most of all, he cursed himself for acting like Don Quixote. How'd he get into such a predicament? It wasn't his business.

He read the papers and waited out the rest of the day. Mendez was a hot local favorite from across the border. He was big and strong, and even with a padded record, he would be formidable. He downed some of his opponents with one punch.

They figured Marve for a part of Mendez' record. Chopping down a heavy would look good in his stats. The scenario changed, and Jazzy was in for a beating meant for Marve.

He napped on the large couch and slept fitfully. His dreams weren't of Goodman Street, the carnival, or Marve. He didn't even dream of Joe Chink or Mendez. Instead, he dreamed of an American Indian woman.

Monti woke him bringing a tray with a ham sandwich, glass of milk, and an apple. Joe Chink called him a troublemaker, but the trouble he made was his own.

The afternoon papers were filled with stories about Jazzy, creating a boxing past for him. He was a big-city Fancy Dan out to protect Marvelous Marve from the clutches of the mean Mendez and show him a trick or two in the ring.

He was Kid Jazz, and it was clear Joe Chink was a manipulator. No one was sure who'd boxed whom, but the evening promised excitement.

Jazzy met Mendez at the weigh-in. He was on the scales when Mendez came in. He looked Jazzy over and saw his lack of conditioning. They'd just met, and already Jazzy had an enemy.

Waiting his turn in the dressing room, he was the loneliest man in the world. He wished he'd listened to Johnny Bourda and experienced real struggles on real fight cards. Sparring in the gym was a stroll in the park compared to what lay ahead.

He was taped and gloved when the door opened.

"You're next, Kid." His second, an old man with watery eyes, draped a robe over his shoulder and whispered into his ear, "This is the only chance I got to talk to you, Kid. I don't know what you did, but Chink wants you hurt bad. Protect yourself if you can. Eat up the clock by clinching."

Oh, God, Jazzy prayed. *If I get out of this alive, I'll never go near a ring again.*

The bell clanged for attention, and the din in the arena subsided.

"In this corner," the announcer said, "at 160 pounds, the pride of the eastern seaboard, Kid Jazz."

There was a smattering of polite applause, but mostly there were boos on all sides. Jazzy wondered if there was anyone in Niagara Falls who wasn't in Joe Chink's pay. Jazzy weighed in at eight pounds lighter than announced.

"His opponent, at 165 pounds, is our own Luis Mendez."

Fans shouted and screamed, and it took awhile for the noise to subside.

Jazzy sat on his stool, reviewing the tactics he must employ to stay alive. Bourda often said he had twinkle toes, and they'd better twinkle soon, but he was carrying some extra fat, too.

The bell rang, and Mendez charged across the ring, a rhinoceros of a man with the sloping shoulders of a puncher. Jazzy evaded his initial onslaught, dancing away, throwing cautious lefts. Mendez seemed content to stalk Jazzy, his right hand cocked. In the clinch, Jazzy felt the man's power and was tossed about like a rag doll.

That was the pattern for the first round—retreating, flicking his left hand repeatedly. He had to be careful. Jazzy's game plan was to survive the fight without getting badly hurt, then collect the loser's share of the purse.

Then the stamping of feet started. The chant for more action mounted until it was a litany. The referee stepped in and warned them to step up the action. Mendez crowded Jazzy, putting on the pressure.

Suddenly, a bomb exploded in his head, and Jazzy went to one knee. He heard a roar, wave upon wave, and everything was hazy. His head cleared, and he heard the count going to seven. The smart thing to do was stay down, but Joe hadn't released him from his obligation. He struggled to his feet and tied Mendez in a desperate clinch. When the bell rang, it was a sweet sound.

Jazzy was breathing hard, and he'd gone only one round. He didn't like that. At the bell, he waited for Mendez to come across the ring to him. He was hard-pressed to protect himself. Mendez swung, throwing every trick he had, and Jazzy called on his cunning to keep from having his brains scrambled. On the ropes, Mendez punished him severely. Against his wishes, he found himself trading punches.

When he finally slipped away, he was aching and weary. Again, he waited in the center of the ring, and Mendez came to him. To Jazzy's shame, he was caught by a right-hand lead. He went down and wished he could stay there.

Through the ropes, Jazzy saw Joe Chink, grim, biting hard on his cigar. The promoter was oblivious to the noise. He sat there with his thumb raised, telling Jazzy to get up. He was grading his performance. To get his money, Jazzy had to get an A for Absorption.

Jazzy got up, and the rest of the round was sheer madness. He bled from nose and mouth, and he gasped like a carp out of water. They worked furiously in his corner, because Joe wanted him out there for another round. The assistants repaired the damage as best they could, and he was forced to leave his haven, but his legs felt like water.

Mendez was eager, coming in for the *coup de grace*. He planned to pummel Jazzy to oblivion and lost no time getting started.

Mendez threw block-busters, swinging in no definite pattern or sequence. He punched furiously missing often but not often enough. Time after time, Jazzy staggered, stumbling from one side of the ring to the other.

The crowd was frenzied, wanting blood. Whenever he was able, Jazzy clinched, holding on in fierce desperation.

They were in a tight clinch on the ropes, rolling along the upper strand. Jazzy put his body hard against Mendez, pinning him to the ropes while the referee tried to pry them apart. When Jazzy looked over Mendez' shoulder at the screaming crowd, he was shocked at the hatred he saw. How easily the mantle of civilization was shed.

The referee pried Jazzy loose, and he stumbled backward toward the center of the ring. Like an enraged bull, Mendez was after him. At that moment, Jazzy was willing to die. Strange sounds came from his throat.

Mendez telegraphed his right hand. Jazzy saw it coming and tried to slip it, but he was painfully slow. He felt himself falling...

He heard the band playing a waltz. He saw his mother dancing with him at the Ukie picnic. Other dancers stopped to watch, conceding the prize to mother and son. His eyes were closed, and he opened them for a better look.

It was no Ukie picnic. Through the ropes, he saw the crowd on its feet, howling, demanding his destruction. The left side of his head was numb. Joe Chink rolled the cigar in his mouth, a faint smile on his lips. He was satisfied. If Jazzy stayed down until the bell, that was all right.

The bell rang. Assistants took Jazzy to his corner and worked on him. There was more to come.

The man in the black suit climbed into the ring with his white placard. Jazzy had been in the pit of pain for an eternity, but it was only three rounds.

He started up slowly, on legs that moved independently of each other. The next blow, authentic or contrived, would finish him. He'd certainly lived up to his part of the bargain.

Mendez stalked him relentlessly, then bulled Jazzy to the ropes, maneuvering him to the far corner and pounding a rhythmic tattoo on his ribs. Jazzy was sore all over, and each blow was agony.

Suddenly, Mendez connected with his right-hand lead. It was partly deflected, but there was still enough muscle to stagger Jazzy.

Timber! he thought in relief.

To his own surprise, he didn't go down. Mendez kept him pinned, propping him up. His opportunity was gone.

Mendez savagely stepped up the pace. He sent a solid right and left to Jazzy's head. Once again, he thought that was the end, but he stayed on his feet.

It was time to stop kidding himself. He didn't want to lose, but why? He asked himself that questions many times, but the answer was there all along. He didn't want the $600 for winning. He wanted to wipe the grin off Joe Chink's face. He wanted to humiliate the mobster in the best possible way, to make him look ridiculous even while his gorilla pummeled Jazzy's weary body.

Jazzy tied Mendez up, and the referee pulled them apart. He staggered in the center of the ring, a tired old man at the age of twenty-three.

Mendez came on again. He knew no other way except a frontal attack. Jazzy slipped, ducked, dodged, struck with his left, and blocked endlessly.

The bell ended Mendez' barrage. It was a miracle Jazzy was still conscious. Bourda once told him he was like rawhide. Had Mendez' guns lost some of their firepower? Jazzy dragged himself to his corner.

He was motionless, trying to conserve his remaining energy. With deep satisfaction, he noted the activity across the ring. Mendez' chest was heaving after throwing so many punches.

It was time for analysis. Mendez demonstrated his ability to hurt Jazzy, but could Jazzy hurt him in return? It was then that Jazzy realized that in his concern to survive, he hadn't tested Mendez even once. There were doubts his legs could carry him through the next round. It seemed futile, but he promised to show Chink a very interesting fifth round.

At the bell, he tried to meet Mendez in the center of the ring, but his legs wouldn't obey. He waited, flatfooted, his twinkle toes long gone. When Mendez charged, Jazzy timed a left jab, stiff and hard. There was no flicking of the glove to keep Mendez at bay. That punch had muscle behind it, and it stopped Mendez in his tracks.

To Jazzy's surprise, his arms weren't that tired, either. He hadn't thrown enough punches for that.

Mendez brushed off the jab, annoyed that his forward progress had been halted. He threw a flurry of punches, hurting Jazzy, who begged his legs to function again.

Again, Mendez was caught as he came in. He looked surprised. Then Jazzy sneaked in a vicious right that caught him flush on the jaw and sent him into the ropes.

Jazzy's legs refused to take him to his foe. He waited for Mendez to come back while excited, disbelieving voices shouted all around him. Joe

Chink suddenly turned gray in his seat, and he crushed out his cigar against his palm.

When Mendez came at him again, his look of consternation was plain. Jazzy was determined to find out about that.

Mendez circled Jazzy in the center of the ring, showing respect for the first time. Then, as Jazzy knew it would, it came. Mendez charged, throwing a right-hand lead, but Jazzy was prepared. The right hand was slower that time, too, and Jazzy was able to get under it. He countered with a hard right to Mendez' midsection and a left hook to the head.

It was Mendez' sturdy legs that failed. There was no mistaking the roar of the crowd. Jazzy made believers of the infidels. The sound was music to his ears, and, for the first time that day, he smiled.

Now, Joe Chink, he thought, *how's the troublemaker doing?*

It was a matter of time. He had to get Mendez before the end of the round or his legs gave out, whichever came first. He prayed Mendez wouldn't make him walk toward him, and he didn't. Mendez had to attack—it was the only way he knew how to fight.

Stay cool, Jazzy told himself. *If I get anxious, I'll blow it.*

Jazzy threw three perfectly placed left hooks, leaving Mendez teetering like an oak ready to fall. The man bled profusely, and Jazzy gave him a stiff left and hard right.

Still he came on. Jazzy faked him with the slightest movement of his shoulders—it was almost too easy—then slammed Mendez with a solid right to the chin.

Mendez went down. Because of the roar of the crowd, Jazzy couldn't hear the count and didn't know how long Mendez lay there. In his corner, he leaned heavily against the ropes, watching, his legs completely gone.

Mendez stirred and writhed to his knees, but there was no mistaking the referee's hand motion. The fight was over, and the hall pulsated with noise.

Later, Jazzy luxuriated in the shower, letting warm water soothe his aching body. He rubbed himself briskly with the towel and sat on the bench, reposing in silence. After he dressed and looked in the mirror to comb his hair, he was pleased that, but for some minor swelling above the eyes, there was no sign of the beating he'd taken.

All the Brown brothers, except Hubert, could've taken Mendez easily despite being amateurs and spotting the brute many pounds. They never would've taken such punishment. Jazzy swore he'd never put on gloves again.

When Jazzy walked into Joe's office, his girlfriend, a statuesque blonde, held Jazzy's chin in one hand and gave him a noisy kiss.

"Oooh, you were exciting tonight," she cooed.

"Cut it out, you dizzy broad!" Joe shouted. "Sit down, Punk."

Jazzy sat, noting the leather satchel with the receipts of the fight. His six hundred was inside.

"You sandbagged me, you fucking ringer!" Joe said.

"No, Mr. Chink," Jazzy said calmly. "You just don't know fighters."

That stung Joe. He threw a quick glance at his henchmen. "Monti, Hobbs, wait in the hall."

He was silent for a while, drumming his desk with the pencil. "I had friends from New York with me tonight, who came to see my boy, Mendez. They were going to buy a piece of him for fifty grand. Instead, they're laughing all the way home. Everyone will think Joe Chink's a patsy."

Joe looked at Jazzy and tried to mask his hatred. Years earlier, the great Strazzi gave him good advice. "Don't love your friend or hate your enemy." What was there about that miserable carny roustabout that got under his skin?

"You're a troublemaker, like I said the first time I saw you. I know how to take care of troublemakers. I haven't made up my mind what to do with you."

"You're going to give me that six hundred and let me go, Mr. Chink. We had an agreement."

"You get nothing, Punk. Understand me? Nothing!"

"That's not fair!"

"Not fair? Can you pay that fifty grand I lost?"

"You won't get away with this!" Jazzy got to his feet. He'd been beaten, terrorized, kidnapped, and now his life was threatened. The six hundred wasn't worth losing his life over, but Joe Chink sat there and smiled at him, and Jazzy raced around the desk, surprising the crime lord. He put his hand on Joe's face and shoved hard.

The big man fell over backward, his chair striking the floor with a thud. Jazzy took the valise, emptied the money out the window, and threw the valise after it.

The blonde laughed nervously, and that sound sent Joe over the edge. He scrambled to his feet and drew a gun from his desk drawer. Jazzy picked up the bronze John L. Sullivan and hit Chink's wrist with the heavy base.

The wrist fractured, and the gun fell to the floor. Jazzy grabbed it and tossed it past the blonde and out the window.

"Monti! Hobbs!" Joe screamed.

Monti lumbered into the room, and Jazzy hit him alongside the head with the statue. He went down.

Jazzy hurried to the corridor and saw Hobbs running toward him, long legs churning fast. Jazzy stood still as if waiting to be caught, then, when Hobbs was almost on him, he dived at the man's feet in a rolling block. Hobbs' momentum made him fall heavily to the floor, striking his head and stunning him.

Jazzy's legs, still tortured from the fight, took him down two flights of stairs and onto the street.

He ran out into a wild scene. All traffic stopped, with cars parked at angles all along the boulevard. Police tried valiantly to control traffic and failed. The street was mobbed by people scrambling for the money that fell from the sky.

What had he done? Once he'd been safe in the bosom of his own neighborhood, and now he was on the lam, running from killers and totally alone.

Chapter Nineteen

The only road open to him was the one to Buffalo, and all he had in his pockets was a dollar and seventy cents. His gas tank was low, too, but Joe Chink wouldn't give his henchmen any peace until they found Jazzy. The humiliation he'd just gotten, including the laughter from his girlfriend, wouldn't let Joe rest until his retaliation was final.

When Jazzy reached Buffalo, his gas tank was on empty. Searching for a place to park, he saw a tavern called the Serendipity with a large parking lot behind it.

He parked behind the building and fingered the change in his pants pocket. He could afford a beer, and he'd learned to drink beer if it was cold enough. The dollar bill stayed in his pocket for something to eat later. Beyond that, he had no plans.

The Serendipity was like other taverns he encountered, neither clean nor dirty, showing the wear and tear of years of heavy traffic. It was a thriving establishment.

There was a pool table, the green felt bright under the light. Someone managed to place more tables around the circular bar than Jazzy would've thought possible. The dart board at the far end of the room, near the rest rooms, was constantly in play.

Jazzy ordered a Schlitz. While he sipped his beer, he debated asking the dyspeptic bartender if he could park his car in the lot overnight. He decided to wait.

"Can I buy you a beer?" a voice asked from his right.

Jazzy turned to face the stranger and saw a dark man of medium height, slightly paunchy, with his jowls slightly drooping. His dark eyes were puppy-dog friendly, and his smile was disarming. His wide belt made an indentation in his stomach.

"There's no way I can reciprocate," Jazzy said.

"Down on your luck?"

"You might say that."

"You look like a man with troubles."

"You're a good judge."

"As they say in the song, *put your cares away for another day.* Play a game of eight ball with me."

"You don't understand. I'm flat broke."

"I do understand, and I'm far from broke. I'm inviting you." He turned to the large man beside him. "Hold the fort."

Goose was drunk. He had a W. C. Fields nose, and his face showed the red streaks of broken blood vessels like many others with a drinking problem. His shock of white hair was matted and uncombed.

There was a wide discrepancy in the ages of both men that puzzled Jazzy, since they clearly weren't related.

At the pool table, the stranger held out his hand. "I'm Carlo Gomes."

"Jazzy."

"Jazzy? I like that. Fits a good-looking guy like you."

Carlo stroked his shot softly against the far cushion, returning so close to the near cushion, Jazzy couldn't beat it. That gave Carlo the privilege of shooting first.

While he chalked up, he said, "I hate playing for nothing. I'm not working on a merit badge."

Jazzy opened his mouth to retort.

"Here's a bet you can handle. If you beat me two out of three, I'll give you a fin. If I beat you two out of three, you come to work for me in the morning."

Jazzy shook his head in astonishment. *Where'd this crazy guy come from?* he wondered.

Jazzy, who developed his skill at the neighborhood tables under Whitey's tutelage, wasn't one of the fine players back at home. Perhaps pool players in Rochester were superior to those in Buffalo, or perhaps he was better than he gave himself credit for. He'd see.

Carlo played a steady stick. He wasn't that good, but he was good enough and won often enough to be able to delude himself.

To Jazzy's amazement, when his turn came, the balls seemed to develop eyes and found their way into the pockets with ridiculous ease. He won two straight so quickly, Carlo stood silently, unbelieving.

"Here's your fin, Jazzy. You're good."

"If it's all the same to you, Carlo, keep the money. I'll take the job."

"You don't even know what it is."

"I don't care as long as it's legal."

"Goose!"

Goose staggered over to them.

"This is Jazzy. He's coming to work for us in the morning. I like the way he talks. We'll put him on the phone on the front desk."

Goose grunted, too drunk to reply.

"You got a place to stay?" Carlo asked.

"No. I just got in town, and I can't afford a room."

"Where you going to sleep?"

"In my car."

"Where's that?"

"Parked out back."

"Leave it there for the night." He turned to the bartender. "Is that OK?"

"No problem, Carlo."

"I don't know why I'm going all out for you. Must be the way you shoot pool. Come on. I'll drive you to where you can get a room." He smiled at Jazzy as if reading his mind. "Goose, tell him I'm no weirdo."

Goose grunted again and staggered toward the exit.

"Maybe you'd better see he gets home OK," Jazzy said.

"Goose is all right. He lives just down the block. He always makes it home."

Carlo bought a round for the road, and the bartender showed an interest in Jazzy.

"Down on your luck?"

"That's putting it mildly."

"You should be sitting on top of the world with looks like yours. You've got style and manners, and you speak good. When all else fails, get a broad to support you."

Jazzy laughed, making the bartender smile. "I'll work my way out."

The bartender looked quite pleasant. He had black wavy hair combed straight back, brown eyes, and a large nose resembling a plowshare.

Two mill workers became boisterous and walked up to the bartender.

"Jim, give me the horseshoes. I'm going to show this clown a thing or two about finesse."

Jim reached behind him under the bar and came up with four rubber horseshoes and two metal stakes with threaded ends. Jazzy watched with interest as the two men screwed the stakes into receptacles in the floor.

"I'll be damned," he said.

"Come on," Carlo said. "Let's get out of here. Those damn fools will pitch horseshoes all night for a few beers."

It was drizzling outside when Jazzy ran to his car, opened the trunk, and pulled out the huge suitcase containing all his possessions. His wardrobe was spare, but what he had was of quality, and, in his opinion, stylish enough to grace the pages of *Esquire*. He had two pairs of slacks, a cashmere sweater that was gray to complement any combination he chose. There was also a pin-striped suit he prized and a new pair of brown suede shoes with the ornate leather flap covering the laces, like the golfers wore on the PGA tour, which were the rage among his friends. Of course, there was the trench coat.

Marve, piqued with envy, dubbed the coat Jazzy's follow-that-man coat. That referred to the ads used extensively in all the major journals and magazines for courses in private investigation. The ads showed a private detective tailing his prey wearing that kind of coat.

Jazzy took good care of his clothes, because he knew he wouldn't be able to repair or replace them for some time. His biggest challenge at the moment was to keep from starving to death.

When Carlo led Jazzy to his car and told him to throw the suitcase in the back seat, Jazzy was impressed. Carlo owned a new Lincoln, all power, and his leather jacket shrieked of opulence. Whatever misgivings he may've had about Carlo's ability to assist him vanished.

They drove to an old neighborhood near the bar. The houses were well-kept, and blight hadn't reached the area yet. Carlo led Jazzy to the front door of a two-story brick building.

The proprietor, an old man with rimless glasses, wore bib overalls and a painter's cap, the peak coming almost down to his eyebrows.

"Hi, Carlo, What brings you here at this time of night?"

"My friend needs a room."

"Well, I've got one, but it's the studio apartment in the attic. You know the one."

"That ain't bad. He'll take it. How much per week?"

"Twelve."

"Ten."

"Eleven."

"Ten. Look, I'm paying for this."

"Ten it is." The old man grinned and led the way up two flights of stairs, then unlocked a door and gave Jazzy the key. Carlo peeled two fives from his wallet and gave them to the landlord.

When the old man left, Carlo said, "Don't think you've found a patsy. I ain't no Santa Claus. This comes out of your pay. Think you go it made? Wait until you handle the hot seat."

"I'm in no position to complain. I have to eat."

Carlo opened the door. "Wait for me in the morning."

When Carlo was gone, Jazzy looked at his new home. The walls slanted to follow the line of the roof. The apartment was little more than a large room with attached bath. One side had a single bed and highboy, the other a davenport and end table. The sole light source was the floor lamp near the davenport, controlled by a wall switch.

The bathroom was smaller, containing a commode, wash bowl, and chipped porcelain tub. He preferred a shower.

He unpacked his bag, tossing underclothing, socks, and ties in the drawer of the highboy. He carefully hung his Van Heusen shirts, sweater, short-sleeved shirts, trench coat, and suit in the tiny closet beside the bathroom, then set his shoes on the floor.

After he placed his toiletries in the medicine chest over the sink, he lay down on the bed and immediately fell asleep without removing his clothes.

Jazzy was up early, luxuriating in a warm bath before he shaved, brushed his teeth, and dressed. He selected the older pair of slacks, sport shirt, and cardigan, satisfied he'd achieved the low-profile look of Perry Como.

Carlo arrived past nine o'clock, and Jazzy wondered about the man's hours. He was plagued with grave doubts, wondering if he'd gotten involved with someone unsavory.

"What sort of business are you in?" Jazzy asked.

"The Gomes Pest and Garden Services."

"What kind of services?"

"You might find this hard to believe, but I have a large business with several divisions designed to improve your home."

"Such as?"

"We exterminate and control pests—mice, rats, moles, and nuisance birds."

"So you have a pest-control company?"

"Much more than that. We treat for weeds, care for lawns, trim shrubs, doctor trees, do landscaping, and even small cement jobs."

"Buffalo has severe winters. How long do you shut down?"

"Never. I have a fleet of snowplows and a contract with the city. If you work out, you'll have a full-time job. I have a huge lot. You'll see I've got my own nursery, and, at Christmastime, the lot's strung with lights, and we do a good business in Christmas trees."

When they arrived at Gomes Pest and Garden Services, with a large sign on a chain-link fence to identify the business, it was evident Gomes had told the truth. The lot was immense. Although most of his equipment was on the road, there were still enough units in the yard to indicate he owned a fleet of trucks, trailers, tractors, and backhoes.

Jazzy was impressed by the nursery, which carried a complete line of landscaping plants indigenous to the area. There was a greenhouse in the center of the nursery, and, in the corner of the lot, he counted fifteen snowplows. Remembering his car was almost out of gas, he ogled the large gas tank beside the plows.

The building was dilapidated, badly in need of scraping and painting. The shutters and doors hung crookedly, and the windows hadn't been washed in years. Although Jazzy dressed modestly, he was overdressed for his new job.

Carlo ushered him inside, and Jazzy stepped into a Lewis and Carrol world, peopled with workers of a subculture that was strange to him. Although it was morning, beer bottles sat on many desks, and one sported a Jim Beam bottle. There were so many phones, the size of the operation was obvious, and every room had as many desks as it could hold.

At a double desk sat two women facing each other. One was far along in her pregnancy and had to sit sideways. Her black hair was pulled back severely, gathered in back and held with a rubber band.

The blonde, facing the pregnant woman, caught Jazzy's attention. She was approaching middle years but retain a modicum of the good looks of her youth. There was a perpetual sense of being frenzied about her. That harried look proclaimed she was someone important.

"This is my wife, Nellie," Carlo said. "Nellie, this is the fellow I told you about. Try him on the hot seat."

"I hope you survive, young man." She looked him over until he felt nervous. "We certainly could use a little beauty around here."

A chorus of "boos!" came from all around.

"Animals," she said good-naturedly.

Jazzy studied husband and wife. They were ill-matched—she was fair, while he was dark, and she was clearly older.

Goose came in from a room in the back and looked no better than the previous night, although he was sober.

"Hi," Jazzy said. "You look better this morning."

"Do I know you?"

"You met him last night, remember?" Carlo asked.

Goose nodded and walked off. At a sink beside the pantry, he rinsed off a spare cup and poured a shot of Jim Beam.

"Goose!" Nellie called. "Play the trumpet for Jazzy."

A musicale, Jazzy thought. *That's all I need.*

Goose set down his cup, put his hands to his mouth with his thumbs across his lips, and gave a fairly accurate rendition of *Sugar Blues*. When he was through, everyone applauded, then Goose lumbered back into a deep recess within the building, cup in hand.

Nellie smiled triumphantly, her look conveying the impression that there was culture in Gomes Pest and Home.

Carlo turned Jazzy to a big, Sophie Tucker look-alike with the baby voice of Bonnie Baker. She went to the files and pulled out a list of duties to be performed by the man in the hot seat.

"The front desk is the hub of this organization," she said. "If you need me, whistle. I'm Rosalind."

"For a minute, I thought you were Bacall. I'm Jazzy."

"I know," she said demurely, waddling away.

Jazzy studied the sheet, wondering if he could master the job. There was a lot to do. From records of the work tickets the driver retained, he was to note cancellations, reschedules, subtractions, additions, change in services, or complaints received on the phone from irate customers. Each driver was required to call the office several times a day, and the man in the hot seat would relay the changes that occurred while he was out on his run.

All purchase requisitions had to go through Jazzy, and he'd order, by phone, from a list of providers. All distress calls from drivers went to him, too, and he, in turn, would note them and relay them to Phil Paugh, the operations manager.

New business came from yellow pages ads, flyers, house-to-house canvassers, and cold canvassers from the boiler room, and it was written up by the man in the hot seat, too.

"Rosalind?"

She came over quickly.

"What the hell is a boiler room?"

She looked at him in disbelief. "You'd better come with me."

Jazzy followed her to the back, where a large room had been created by tearing out a wall separating two bedrooms. A six-foot partition ran down the center of the room, and on each side were booths with side walls and no doors. In each was a telephone and a set of city directories, from which leads were gleaned. There were at least a dozen callers using the booths when they came in, dialing for sales.

"Are they all salespeople?" Jazzy asked.

"No, some are schedulers. They schedule regular service, like monthly or quarterly pest control or weekly lawn service. They get paid by the hour. The elite are the cold canvassers, who are on commission and are the highest paid of our employees."

"Where do they get their leads?"

"They don't. They ferret out the leads cold."

Back at Jazzy's desk, the phone was ringing. It was a new customer. Then calls came in rapidly, and Jazzy never would've survived without Rosalind's help.

Jazzy missed several meals, and all he had with him was one dollar bill. Noon was still two hours away. By that time, he felt he'd be chewing the furniture.

Someone filled the coffee urn, and Carlo came in carrying several boxes of doughnuts. It was time for a coffee break, and Jazzy, along with the others, grabbed a Styrofoam cup. The coffee was hot, and he ate a glazed doughnut.

Rosalind watched him wolf it down and offered him another.

"Thanks," he said gratefully.

A young giant walked in with heavy shoulders and huge hands. He had short curly black hair on a round head, which made his head look even rounder. He had a thick neck like a wrestler and the air of someone who wasn't afraid of anybody.

Jazzy watched as Carlo greeted the giant with the enthusiasm one would've expected if Ted Williams suddenly walked in.

The big man whispered in Carlo's ear, and Carlo laughed long and loud, then the man went to the double desk.

"Hi, Penny. When's the baby coming?"

"Anytime now, Rick."

"Hi, Nellie. Who's the dude?"

"His name's Jazzy. Carlo just hired him for the hot seat."

"What happened to Manny?"

"He skipped town."

"What the hell for?"

"He beat up on his wife."

"Hell, he's always beating on her."

"This time, her brothers heard about it, and they came into town to take care of him."

"I hope they get the creep."

"Who's the giant?" Jazzy whispered.

"That's Rick Devlin, my one-man house-to-house canvasser. He's the world's best salesman."

"World's biggest con man, you mean," Rosalind countered.

"Yeah? He's keen and has the gift of gab. Sometimes, he cuts corners."

Rosalind didn't answer as Carlo went to join Rick and Nellie.

"He's a crook," Rosalind said softly.

"Who does he steal from?" Jazzy asked.

"He has arrangements with Carlo. He's got his own customers."

"He's got a license?"

"Are you kidding? Licenses mean nothing to Rick. The truth is, the customers belong to Carlo, not Rick. Then he borrows a rig from the boss and sprays the customers' grounds with water, not chemicals."

"Carlo puts up with it?"

"I think Carlo likes to get screwed."

Carlo and Rick came into the room, laughing. Jazzy was on the phone, listening intently, his expression showing he'd encountered a big problem. He covered the receiver with his hand.

"Carlo, it's a woman who's mad as hell. She says one of our men rang her doorbell while she was out. When her eleven-year-old daughter opened the door, he pushed her aside and ran through the house, looking for the bathroom. When the woman got home, her daughter was having hysterics."

"Does she know his name?"

"No, but he's one of ours. He solicited next door."

"What does he look like?"

"Can you describe him, Mrs. Bannister?" Jazzy asked, then turned. "He's thin, with stooped shoulders and wore an Army-issue coat."

"That's Kuegy, the drunken bastard," Rick said angrily. "He can't hold his piss. Give me the phone."

He took the receiver. "Mrs. Bannister, this is Richard Devlin, vice president of Gomes Pest and Home Services. Our office manager just related to me the tragic experiences of your daughter. The behavior of our employee is outrageous and inexcusable. I assure you our anger is no less than yours. I'll take action, and we'll hold a meeting for all employees. Just a moment, Mrs. Bannister. My secretary has something for me."

He covered the mouthpiece with his huge hand, waited ten seconds, then spoke again. "Are you still there, Mrs. Bannister? The man's a war veteran from the Veteran's Hospital. When he was released, they pressured Mr. Gomes, who's a compassionate man, into giving him a job.

"No, there's nothing wrong with his mind. He has war injuries that resulted in renal problems. That means the kidneys, Mrs. Bannister. No, don't feel sorry for him. He's fired as of now. Thank you, Ma'am, for calling."

"He's the best," Carlo said, beaming.

"Send Kuegy down south from now on. I don't want that jerk anywhere near me," Rick growled.

"Shouldn't we call the Veteran's Hospital?" Jazzy asked.

Everyone laughed.

"Kuegy was never in the Army," Carlo told him. "He got that coat from the Salvation Army."

Goose came in, cup in hand, walking toward the bottle of Jim Beam. He was still fairly steady on his feet, although silent. Suddenly, Rick goosed him, and Goose let out an ear-splitting scream. Although old and in bad shape, he leaped up and out like a professional long jumper.

He scurried to the wall, and, for a split second, his eyes cleared, exposing deep hatred. Just as quickly, though, his eyes clouded over again.

Laughter rang throughout the building. Everyone ran from his cubbyhole to ask what happened.

"Now you know, Jazzy," Nellie said, wiping her eyes.

"Yes, I can see why he's called Goose."

Rick sauntered over to Rosalind's desk. "Been telling Handsome about my good qualities?"

She didn't answer.

"I find you irresistible this morning."

The room became silent.

"Get lost," she said softly.

"How do I love thee? Let me mount the ways."

"You son of a bitch!"

Carlo laughed, and Penny tittered.

"That wasn't nice, Rick," Nellie scolded.

Rick strode out triumphantly, leaving Rosalind crying.

"He's got a lot of class," Carlo said proudly.

"Yes, he has," Jazzy said. "It's all steerage."

Carlo spoke to Nellie, and they glanced at Jazzy, then Nellie came over. Jazzy expected to be fired.

"You're coming home with us to lunch."

He opened his mouth to protest.

"Don't get coy with me. Just come along."

At home, Nellie reheated leftover lamb stew and dumplings. Jazzy didn't demur when she offered him a generous second helping. She cut him a large slice of apple pie with a chunk of cheese, and the world suddenly seemed brighter.

When it was time to drive back to work, Carlo took Jazzy to the Serendipity to retrieve Jazzy's car. He got out with Jazzy and sent Nellie on ahead.

Jazzy drove cautiously, but Carlo glanced at the fuel gauge, which read almost empty.

"Going to make me walk, are you?" Carlo asked.

"Relax, Carlo. There's enough gas to get us there."

"How about you getting home? I haven't adopted you."

"I'll park in your lot and walk to the apartment."

"It's a long way."

"I'll walk," Jazzy said stubbornly.

"Look, Jazzy. For this time only, when Phil Paugh gets back from lunch, have him give you a tankful from the yard. Don't wait for me in the morning. You're on your own."

"Thanks, Carlo." That was more than Jazzy expected. "What are the hours? You never said."

"Phil gets in early and uses your desk to schedule the routes, sending the men out by seven. You don't have to come in until eight-thirty. You can have as long a lunch as you like, but you're the last man out at night. You check in the drivers, lock up everything, turn off the lights, and then you're through for the day."

Nellie was at her desk when they arrived. With a good meal in him, Jazzy's enthusiasm for his new job rose. He sat at his desk with greater confidence than earlier.

"Has Polly come in yet?" Carlo asked.

"Yes. She's in the back room. What's your concern with Polly?"

"Oh, nothing. I'm concerned for all my employees."

"Yeah, sure. It's a good thing she's not interested in you, Love, or you and I would tangle real good."

It was unsettling to Jazzy that all wasn't idyllic in the Gomes household.

A small man with the bearing of a four-star general came in, followed by the most bedraggled man Jazzy ever saw. Stealing clothes from a scarecrow would be a sartorial improvement. To add a perfectly ludicrous touch, the tatterdemalion had a huge safety pin fastening the fly of his pants, which were several sizes too large. He spoke to the small man, who responded with short, crisp sentences.

"Hi, Fellow," the small man greeted Jazzy. "No manners in this pirate's den. Doesn't anyone introduce anyone else?"

He sat on the edge of Jazzy's desk. "Let me introduce myself, since no one sees fit to do that. I'm Phil Paugh, operations manager. I understand you're Jazzy—in name, I expect. I suppose there's a story to that. Maybe you'll tell me about it someday."

"Hi, yourself. Glad to meet you." Jazzy liked him immediately and felt he'd found an oasis in the dunes of insanity. He felt better knowing Paugh would be around.

"Let me use your desk, Jazzy. Otto Grundt has misplaced his work tickets. I'll write him new ones from the schedule on your desk."

Jazzy walked toward the office urn. When Phil finished, he told Carlo, "I'm taking your new man to the yard to show him around. There are a few things I want to work out with him."

"OK, Phil. By the way, fill Jazzy's tank, will you?"

"Come outside, Jazzy. Rosalind will cover." To the pariah at his side, Phil said, "Here are your tickets, Otto, and don't lose them again. Now get! You're late."

Once outside, Phil turned toward Jazzy. "You're wondering at the menagerie in there. That's not my style. As disorganized as things seem in there, we run a tight ship out here."

"How does anything get done in there?" Jazzy asked.

"Gomes built this business up from nothing with some of the craziest methods the business community has ever seen."

"What's with all the beer and booze?"

"My drivers had better not drink on the job. There's too much at stake. Carlo lets them drink to their hearts' content after they park their trucks at night. If they come in sober in the morning, I can't complain.

"There's method to his madness. In this business, especially in pest control, turnover is high. Do you know how much it costs to train new people? You know why the office people stay? It's free drinks, no dress rules, and less rules than they'd find anywhere else. Carlo has work for them even in the winter."

"They are sure some strange people in there," Jazzy said.

"Carlo's an oddball, too, and he's drawn to oddballs. I don't ever want to take myself seriously enough to forget my place in this strange business we're in. Carlo started with one license, a general pest control license. I came in with the others. I'm an entomologist. There are times I wish I were teaching youngsters about nature and our planet's tiny inhabitants."

A dour man walked past, head down, preoccupied.

"Hello, Phil." He walked past without stopping or smiling.

"Hello, Doc," Phil said.

"Who's that?"

"You haven't met him, either?"

"I saw him in the yard, but I didn't think he was anyone I should be introduced to."

"That's Doc Rivera. He's called Doc, because he's the finest tree surgeon in the area. Carlo and I run the pest control and lawn service. The rest is Doc's."

"He must have plenty of smarts."

"He graduated from the state agricultural school. He's a botanist and horticulturist. See the nursery and greenhouse? Those are his innovation. He's in charge of Christmas tree sales, too. I'm in charge of snowplows. It keeps me active all winter."

"This is the strangest set-up I ever saw."

"Yes, it is. Although there's madness inside, Doc and I represent the stability of the company outside, although I must admit we've had a few SNAFUS, too."

"Just before you came in, Phil, there was a little tiff between Carlo and Nellie about someone called Polly."

"Do you like Rita Hayworth?"

"My favorite actress."

"Then you'll love Polly." Phil regarded Jazzy pensively, noting his classic features and grace. "She'll love you, and yes, she'll sleep with you."

"Neighborhood punch board?"

"Not really. She's been around the block a few times, and she appears to be an easy make with a strong sexual appetite, but she won't bed a man she's not strongly attracted to. She's not a lay for pay and won't do it in gratitude or for a favor, either. Her juices have to be flowing."

"You've got me curious now."

"Watch yourself, Jazzy."

"Something I should know?"

"Yes. Polly has to control the affair and call the shots. It's in her crazy make up."

When Jazzy returned to his desk, he found Rosalind had covered for him. She was handy to have around. If she hadn't had a baby-doll voice, she would've had the hot seat.

It was a little past two o'clock when Polly came out to pour a cup of coffee, and Jazzy was walking toward Nellie with a question about Malathion for pill bugs. Polly and Jazzy froze in their tracks, startled, and neither recovered gracefully. It was a lot more than the surprise of seeing someone new. It was like the awe of Adam and Eve when they first saw each other.

Polly was like a Petty pin-up girl with her extraordinary long legs. Her tailored suit hugged her softly rounded hips, and the coat was unbuttoned, revealing full, firm breasts pressing hard against her white blouse. She'd been tugging at her hair with a pencil, and it was slightly awry, but it gave her a saucy look. Jazzy was hard-pressed to describe the color of her hair and settled on the word *titian*.

It was her skin that set her apart. Jazzy had never seen such a complexion. She shattered his composure, and he hers. At a loss what to do next, she gave a half-smile, showing even white teeth, then retreated to the back of the building without bothering for coffee.

He watched her retreating figure, noting the perfection of her legs. The seams of her stockings were straight up the middle as far as he could see.

Nellie smirked and gave Penny a knowing look.

"Pretty classy chick, eh, Jazzy?" Rosalind asked.

"What's she doing here?"

"You mean, what's she doing among us gargoyles? She's a smart woman. She could get a better job, but she'd never make as much money. She's one of the best salespeople we've ever had, male or female. Anything else you want to know?"

"I'll find out myself."

"I'll bet."

Polly didn't come out again until closing time. When she emerged, her composure was back. She was aloof and ignored Jazzy, but he couldn't take his eyes off her. He liked her slightly rolling walk, which threw parts of her into a fervor of disturbing movements.

Then everyone was gone except for Rosalind, who stayed behind to help check the drivers as they arrived. She shared her Lorna Doone cookies with Jazzy, and they finished the coffee.

Chapter Twenty

Jazzy sat in his apartment. There was a public library nearby, but he didn't need books. He was hungry and loathe to spend his dollar. Carlo invited him to the tavern, saying he picked up the tab for his employees, but Jazzy wasn't in the mood for beer. Maybe there would be some pretzels. He'd settle for strays peanuts or the dregs of a discarded bag of chips.

He wondered what happened to his pride.

He thought of his mother and Maria, both good cooks, and the thought of the meals he missed filled him with bitterness.

When Jazzy walked into the bar, a friendly howl went up, which pleased him. He saw Carlo, Goose, Otto, and Phil.

"Draw one for Jazzy!" Carlo said, then turned to Jazzy. "Try a pickled pig hock between two pieces of bread. You couldn't have had time to eat."

The pickled hock was just right. Jazzy felt better after eating, and his spirits rose. The others liked and accepted him.

Phil said his good-byes and left. He was a family man. Otto went with him. They seldom loitered beyond two beers. It was evident there was a bond between them, although Jazzy was hard put to think of a more unlikely pair of friends.

There were the three of them, just as in his first night at the Serendipity. That time, Goose wasn't completely drunk or completely sober.

A young woman with flaming red hair and a plethora of freckles came by. Her legs were thin, like those of a young filly. Her breasts were small, but the low, square-cut neckline of her short dress revealed some cleavage.

Carlo left the others at the bar and followed the woman to her table. From where he stood, Jazzy could see them but couldn't hear their good-natured bantering. Carlo came back, ordered two steins of beer, and took them to the woman's table.

"You guys can order what you like," he told the others.

"I have to go, Carlo. I'm tired."

"See you in the morning."

Jazzy didn't want to watch Carlo's alley-catting.

Jazzy made it to work the next morning without a moment to spare. The three office women were waiting—Penny stared, elbows on the desk, chin cupped in her hands; Nellie wore a smile, tapping the side of her cup with a pencil; and Rosalind giggled.

"She got here before you did, Jazzy," Nellie said, wearing her smug expression again.

"Who?"

"Polly, that's who."

"Is there some significance to that?"

"Well," Rosalind said, "the lady never came in to work this early since she started working here."

"You've made an early bird out of her, you heartbreaker," Penny added. "You're the worm."

They laughed, then suddenly became silent as Polly walked into the room with a cup in her hand, walking toward the coffee machine.

"Jazzy," Nellie said, "have you met Polly Bagby? Polly, this is Jazzy Rhinehardt."

"Jazzy?" She arched a perfect eyebrow. "Dixieland or ragtime?"

"Neither," Jazzy retorted. "Try the blues from Basin Street."

"Whatever. This place gets more strange every day." With studied nonchalance, she filled her cup, then walked majestically back, giving Jazzy the full treatment with that fascinating rolling gait of hers.

"Back to the blackboard, Jazzy," Penny said.

"Don't you believe it," Nellie said. "Polly will be drinking a lot of coffee today."

Carlo came in and walked toward the coffee machine, then he was joined in the pantry by Goose, who didn't want coffee. Instead, he reached for a bottle of Jim Beam. Jazzy listened to a woman named Mrs. Tolman as she complained on the phone.

"Carlo!" he called. "It's Mrs. Tolman, a monthly regular. She says our man made a mistake and filled the tank with nutrients instead of insecticides, and the roaches are having a party all over the house, celebrating their good fortune."

"That's a good one. The broad's witty. Don't mess with her, Jazzy, just give her a respray. Write Phil a note and have him send Otto out early tomorrow morning. That'll teach the old biddy."

"Wait'll that broad sees the safety pin on Otto's fly. She'll die."

Nellie laughed.

Most of the time, Jazzy was pinned to the telephone. He didn't see or hear anyone come in. Finally, he hung up and made a note that the Broad Street Church of God would need lawn service for another week.

He looked up and was startled to see a youthful face, peppered with freckles, not two feet away, topped by a head of flaming red hair. It was Carlo's pick-up from the Serendipity.

"Pardon me," she said in a soft voice, dripping with innocence, "but are you Carlo Gomes?"

Jazzy was taken aback at her nerve. She was a cool one.

"No, Honey!" Nellie shouted. "That's Carlo!" She pointed to her husband, who sat on Rosalind's desk, drinking coffee.

The redhead walked timidly to Carlo. "Mr. Gomes, the employment office sent me for the job you have open in your office."

"What's your name, Honey?" Nellie asked.

"Bea McKenzie."

"There's some mistake, Bea. We didn't put in any request for help."

"I did, Nellie, earlier this week," Carlo said.

"What the hell for?"

"Penny's leaving next week to have her baby. We can't have someone taking over the job cold."

Nellie considered that. "You surprise me sometimes, Carlo. That's good thinking."

"Give me an application form. I'll take the young lady back, make her fill out the form, and interview her."

Jazzy followed them to the back room, telling himself he needed to visit the bathroom. Carlo took Bea to the repairs room, with its long workbench covered with tools and equipment. Jazzy watched them disappear into the closet and was amazed at Carlo's audacity.

There was no wasted space in the old building. The closets were work units, containing a plywood board across one side that served as a desk, then there was a phone, a kitchen chair, and an overhead light with a pull chain. Carlo shut the door behind them.

Jazzy continued to one of the two bathrooms, washed and dried his hands, then returned to his desk. Nellie had Penny and Rosalind on either side of her, already working on the transition to facilitate Bea's takeover. Only the wall against which she had her chair separated her from her husband.

Suddenly, there was a scraping, banging, and thumping montage of sound. Whatever activity was occurring on the other side of the wall, it was noisy. Jazzy wondered how that activity was accomplished in such close quarters. Eventually, Carlo would tell anyone who'd listen to the details.

The noise angered Nellie, who attributed the ruckus to the telephone salesmen who were bored after being on the phone for hours.

"Cut it out back there!" she shouted. "This isn't a playground. Do your horsing around somewhere else!"

When Carlo and Bea appeared before Nellie a few minutes later, Carlo carried the application, which had been filled out very carefully.

"She check out all right?" Nellie asked.

"Everything's fine."

"Check her credentials?"

"I covered everything."

"Come in at eight tomorrow, Bea," Nellie ordered.

That was a gratifying moment for Carlo. Having his girlfriend and his wife sitting across from each other every morning was a touch worthy of Rick Devlin.

Payday arrived none too soon. Jazzy didn't get another invitation to lunch at the Gomes house, which was as it should be. The initial invitation was a social gesture. Anything more would've been charity.

Jazzy still felt the same allowing Carlo to order a sandwich for him at the Serendipity. Still, he was a scavenger, subsisting on junk food left by others, sitting at his desk at night.

He found edibles in the lab, too. Doc, like Luther Burbank, experimented with hydroponics, the science of growing without soil. Tomatoes and cucumbers grew on vines on strings of loom-like frames, and they were a valuable addition to Jazzy's inadequate diet. When payday finally came, it was a godsend.

Although the pay didn't allow Jazzy any luxuries, he'd eat regularly from then on. In addition, he could pay his rent and buy gas for his car.

He missed the horse room. When he learned there was a bookie in the neighborhood, he became a regular. He'd been foolish enough to mention he was known as a fine handicapper, then he picked nothing but losers. He had no racing form, because it wasn't sold in that area.

The ridicule of his fellow workers hurt him more than the inroads to his meager funds. His explanation, that it was difficult to handicap without a form, was received with derision. He resented Rick Devlin's charge that studying forms was voodoo science and no more productive than the eenie-meenie-minie-mo approach.

Most of the conversation in the greenhouse was shop talk. His new friends were fonts of knowledge. There was a lot he didn't know about many things. The mayor had been right—knowledge was power, and to get that knowledge, he had to go back to school.

The specter of Joe Chink's bloodhounds remained with him, but Jazzy convinced himself that staying at Gomes' was the sensible thing to do for the moment. Buffalo was half again as large as Rochester. Finding him in a city of one million souls was a task worthy of Hercules.

To his surprise, he found himself liking his job. He was proud of himself, because troubleshooting while running the hot seat required tact, eloquence, and a great deal of patience. The position gave him confidence, and the skills he honed every day would stand him in good stead for the rest of his life.

Nellie eventually said he had a raise coming. Carlo congratulated himself as a keen judge of men, but, with Polly, the situation remained the same. Jazzy was sure desire smoldered in her, as it did in him, but her aloofness bothered him. On the occasions when she acknowledged his existence, her remarks were caustic.

When it came time for the employees to crowd around the double desk and say farewell to Penny on her last day, Jazzy and Polly moved forward together to get a better view of the stroller to which they contributed, and they were crushed together for a moment by the crowd. Face-to-face, the shock of the close encounter showed in their startled eyes. In confusion, Polly pulled away from the crowd and went back to her post.

Jazzy got on the phone with a persistent customer. "No, Mrs. Peevey. It's twenty-eight days since we sprayed your property for bugs. No, I don't know where you got that idea. We don't guarantee for a month. We do pest control. We don't make your place sterile for all living things. We have people we service every month, and they're not stupid people who like to throw away their money. They understand that the chemicals we're allowed to use will break up in approximately one month."

Carlo listened approvingly. He waved his hand to indicate *no*, reinforcing Jazzy's stand.

"That's the thing to do, Mrs. Peevey. The board's number is in the book. Rules are rules, Mrs. Peevey." He hung up.

"You did that well, Jazzy," Carlo said. "She's a tufor."

"What's a tufor?"

"There are plenty of them around. Every company in the business has the same names on their books. A tufor is someone who tries to get two services for the price of one. Once you give a tufor a respray, you've lost him. He'll move on to the next company."

A smiling young man with tousled black hair, wearing jeans, a cowboy hat, and a flannel shirt, came in. He seemed familiar, but Jazzy couldn't place him.

"Are you Jazzy?" he asked.

"Yes. May I help you?"

"I'm here to pick up a route."

"Carlo?"

Carlo came over quickly.

"This fellow wants to run a route."

"Hello, Bob," Carlo said. "I forgot to tell you, Jazzy, we'll be short of drivers for the rest of the week. I didn't check the vacation list. This is Bob Petrillo, Doc Rivera's landscaper. Doc's letting me use him this week."

"Hear about Kuegy?" Bob asked in a conspiratorial tone.

"What do you mean, have I heard about him? He quit when I gave him the south side. Saved me the trouble of firing him."

"Guess what? He's working for Buffalo Landscaping."

"I hope he falls off a tree. Who told you that, Bob?"

"Doc."

"Who told Doc?"

"Buffalo Landscaping called him for a recommendation."

"He tipped them off Kuegy was a fink?"

"No. You know Doc. He wouldn't hurt anybody. He told them Kuegy never worked in his division, and that he hadn't heard anything bad about him. Now Doc's mad."

"Doc, mad? Kuegy was my hemorrhoid—a regular pain in the ass."

"The last time Kuegy was in the yard, Doc was showing us the carpet sweeper he bought for his wife. Yesterday, Kuegy went to Doc's house and talked Mrs. Rivera out of it, saying Doc consented to let him borrow it so his wife could clean their apartment to save the cleaning deposit before they moved."

"Mrs. River believed it?"

"Oh, she was mad, but she kept her cool and turned the sweeper over to him. It was still in the box. Doc caught hell."

"Serves Doc right. That's how Kuegy returns a favor."

Carlo shook his head in disgust at Kuegy's depravity. "He'll never get it back."

Polly was miserable. Every time she met an attractive man, her defenses went up. She feared Jazzy more than any of the others—he was special with that lean grace, the features of a Greek god, dark locks swept back from a widow's peak, blue eyes that disconcerted her when she looked into them, and a voice that sent disturbing sensations through her. She was determined not to let him control her.

Her mother was a captive of love. Her life with Polly's father was filled with pain and sorrow. He was a drunk and a wife-beater. Her mother loved him so much, she never blamed him when he beat her. She searched within herself to determine what she'd done wrong, and each time, she vowed to be a better wife. When he died one night, Polly's mother grieved so deeply, Polly feared she'd lose her mother, too.

Polly's nerves were frayed, and she had trouble sleeping. She couldn't keep Jazzy at bay any longer. It was only a matter of time before some attractive young woman latched onto him. She couldn't stand that.

Polly approached Jazzy at his desk. When she put her hand on his shoulder, both thrilled to the touch. Jazzy looked up, puzzled, and, across the desk, Nellie nudged Bea.

"I was expecting my mother today," Polly said. "Now I've learned she can't make it until later this month. I have two fine steaks thawing, and it would be a shame to waste them."

"Are you inviting me to dinner, Polly?"

"Yes, I am."

"You bet I'll come. Can't have those steaks go to waste. When do you want me at your place?"

"What time do you get through here?"

"I never know. I'm the last one out. I have to wait for the drivers."

"Oh, dear. We'd be dining quite late."

Rosalind, who was listening did a remarkable thing. She adored Jazzy, but she was a realist and tried to be a good sister to him, because that was all she could hope for.

"No sweat, you two," Rosalind said. "I have nothing planned this evening. You can leave with the rest of the gang, Jazzy, and I'll check the drivers for you."

Nellie nodded her approval.

On his way to the apartment, Jazzy picked up a bottle of Catawba. Polly had a fine apartment, and Rosalind had to be correct in saying Polly was one of the highest-paid employees at Gomes.

There was a bedroom, bath, living room, and kitchen. The kitchen had a range, refrigerator, chrome table, and chairs, with a Formica tabletop. The living room had a floral rug, an easy chair, love seat, floor lamps, end tables, and a hi-fi unit in one corner, along with a TV set.

Jazzy sat on the easy chair while Polly put some Sinatra records on the hi-fi, then she excused herself and went into the bedroom as Sinatra sang *Full Moon and Empty Arms.*

He sat there in quiet anticipation, expecting her to come out in a flimsy nightgown, but he was wrong. Polly appeared in a house dress.

She's really going to feed me, he thought in surprise, looking her over carefully.

She wore no stockings and substituted flats for high heels. Without either, her legs were still beautiful. Her house dress was short and unadorned. It was uniform white, and the elastic at the middle pinched her waist and set off her hips to their best advantage. The pleats above the waist acted as props to hold up her breasts for display. The neckline was low and exciting.

She smiled at Jazzy and disappeared into the kitchen. Soon, he heard steaks sizzling in a pan.

Polly may've been around the block a few times, but so had Jazzy. It rankled that his well-meaning friends took what should've been a private part of his life and created the image of him as the Benjamin Spock of sexology, a master of seduction.

It was a no-frills man's meal—steak, potatoes, peas, coffee, and cherry pie. It was a long time since he had a steak, and his enjoyment was marred only by the distracting and disturbing presence of Polly across the table. They made small talk, but neither was interested in what the other said. They finished the bottle of Catawba. Perhaps, Zinfandel would've been more appropriate with steak, but wine was the furthest thing from their minds. In the living room, Sinatra sang *The Things We Did Last Summer.*

Jazzy offered to help with the dishes, but she shooed him into the living room, explaining she would clear the table and put the dishes in the sink.

He sat on the couch when she came in from the kitchen. She went to the hi-fi and turned the records over, then walked to the couch, kicked off her flats, and joined him. She faced him, legs tucked under her, sitting on her heels, which made her house dress ride higher on her legs, exposing smooth, white thighs. When she reached over to place her soft hands on his cheeks, she presented a partial but unsettling view of her full breasts.

She'd intended to kiss him lightly for starters, but it was like fanning a smoldering fire. The passions they'd both been holding in restraint erupted. He kissed her hard, crushing her soft, pliant lips as she fumbled with his shirt front. She exposed his chest, lean and hard, then pulled away from the embrace to hungrily kiss his torso.

He lifted her and carried her into the bedroom. His hands trembled as he removed her dress. He kissed each lovely breast as he lay her on the bed. Frantically stripping off his own clothes, he lay beside her and pressed his hard body against her.

His hands explored every inch of her. The feel of his hands, wherever they caressed, created delightful sensations. He softly massaged her smooth breasts, his palms making her nipples harden. To keep from crying out, she pressed her open mouth against the hollow of his neck, then thrashed, trying to press herself closer to him.

Her body demanded the *coup de grace,* and she wanted to say, "Please, Jazzy, now!" Polly, in a superhuman display of discipline, stopped the roller coaster at the top of the climb, pulled away, and walked to the kitchen.

"What the hell?" Jazzy exclaimed in agony. The shock to his nervous system was more than he could bear, and he shook. "What kind of broad is she?"

Polly returned to the bed, composed, coming to him with her rolling gait. Jazzy hadn't controlled her, and she'd make it up to him.

She climbed on him, rubbing her breasts against his chest. Her legs and torso were alive against him, and she kissed his mouth hard, then his neck, and body. He mouthed her nipples until they were hard again.

Polly brought Jazzy to the height of passion once more, and all was forgiven. Then their lovemaking became reciprocal and savage as both reveled in the glories of each other. When Jazzy came to her, his intensity matched her climactic finish.

In the other room, Sinatra sang, *Put Your Dreams Away For Another Day.*

Chapter Twenty-One

The phone rang as Jazzy arrived at work the next morning. He answered still standing, then hung up and sighed.

"She's back to her old routine," Nellie said, "coming in later in the day."

"Yeah," Bea said, taking liberties as the new girl in the office. "Poor Polly needs her sleep this morning."

That angered Jazzy. He didn't need that from her. Why were the other women keeping score? Why wouldn't they leave him alone?

"Thanks," he told Rosalind. "I'll return the favor."

"Forget it. It was my pleasure." Still, she was human and hoped their night hadn't gone well.

Carlo came to his desk and poked Jazzy's ribs. "How was it last night?" he leered, whispering.

"Fine." Jazzy assumed Nellie acted as town crier the previous night. *Does everybody know?* he wondered, keeping his anger contained.

Carlo was his boss, and he needed the job and the sanctuary for a while longer.

"You lucky bastard." Carlo's manner was friendly, but his voice had a hint of ruffled pride and envy.

The beer delivery truck arrived, and the driver asked, "Where's Manny?"

"He doesn't work here anymore," Jazzy replied.

"Couldn't stand the gaff?" The driver laughed.

"Guess not."

"This place kills me. You guys go through more beer than some of the taverns."

"We go through a lot."

"See you in a couple weeks, if not sooner."

Jazzy signed the invoice, and the driver left.

Carlo went out for doughnuts for the coffee break, and Rosalind filled the machine with fresh coffee.

Jazzy walked toward the bathroom and met Goose coming out of the boiler room. The old man was unsteady, and Jazzy realized it wasn't from drinking—he hadn't come out for his Jim Beam all morning.

"I'm sick, Jazzy. Help me."

"What's wrong?"

"I'm shaking, and I think I've got a fever."

"Want me to call a doctor?"

"No, just get me home. If I could just get to bed, I'd be all right."

"Nellie!" Jazzy called. "Goose is in bad shape. Someone needs to take him home."

Nellie came running—she was fond of the old man. She took one arm while Jazzy had the other, and they walked him to Nellie's chair and sat him down.

"See if there's a driver in the yard," she told Jazzy, but a quick look revealed only Otto was available. He'd suffered a broken hose on his rig, and Phil was repairing it.

Jazzy explained the situation to Phil, who ordered Otto to take Goose home. Since the truck wasn't ready, Jazzy loaned Otto his car keys.

When Otto returned, he assured them he put Goose to bed. Meanwhile, the phone on Jazzy's desk rang nonstop. Carlo had a small army of children distributing flyers throughout Buffalo, and it worked. Orders came in all week at a very satisfying rate.

Polly didn't come in until after lunch. She was regal again, and said one "hello" to everyone in the room, including Jazzy.

As he watched her provocative walk to the back of the building, he had to admit she was a hell of a woman.

He had never experienced a night like that with anyone before. Her hot-and-cold, on-again, off-again performance wasn't something he could take regularly, but, when she was functioning right, she was pure delight in bed.

He didn't see her again until quitting time. As she swept past, she gave him a quick smile that didn't connote anything, and a flutter of one hand to indicate good-bye.

Nellie was closing the books for the month with Bea. She kept Rosalind working late, which enabled Jazzy to accompany Carlo to the races. Horse rooms and horse tracks were familiar ground to Jazzy, and it had been a long time he attended either. He looked forward to it.

Polly walked him to the car. Each day, she became a little less distant, and soon, she'd invite him over again. Paugh was right—she controlled the relationship.

Jazzy almost salivated in anticipation of another dinner date with her, and that surprised him. Maybe he was a masochist.

Buffalo Raceway wasn't in Buffalo. It was in Hamburg, an adjacent town. It was a new track for Jazzy, one for harness racing with standardbred horses. Jazzy was on unfamiliar ground, and his vaunted skill as a handicapper wouldn't be any good.

Carlo was no better a horse player than a pool player. He never mastered the art of gleaning seemingly insignificant data from the form sheet, which was the only way one should make a choice.

The trouble with betting the trotters or the pacers was the animal's ability and condition weren't the only concern. In harness racing, the driver's ability was almost as important as that of the horse.

Jazzy was soon caught up in the excitement of the track, and Carlo was a charming host, out for a good time. Jazzy itched to place a bet. It had been a long time.

Finally, he gave up trying to handicap and bet two dollars on the double, picking the number two in the first and three in the second. Polly would be twenty-three on Sunday, and he recalled how he laughed at the mayor when he bet on a horse named Forty-niner, because his wife was forty-nine. Jazzy was luckier, though—both horses came in.

In fairness to his inspiration, he pocketed his winnings of $31.80 and planned to spend it on something extravagant for Polly. He sat back and watched the magnificent animals and drivers maneuver them through heavy traffic like Indianapolis 500 drivers.

Carlo picked a long shot in the fifth, and Jazzy accompanied him to the window, where he received his winnings. Then he saw the two men and scurried back to his seat, his face white with fear.

"What's the matter, Jazzy?" Carlo asked when he arrived. "Why'd you rush away like that?"

"Stomach cramps," he lied. Luckily, he was sure Monti and Hobbs hadn't seen him, but it was close.

Carlo nodded sympathetically. "Damn hot dogs."

Jazzy was wrong—it was possible to find a needle in a haystack. Buffalo, with all its people, wasn't big enough to hide him. He had to move on and get farther away from Niagara Falls.

Driving back afterward, Carlo kept looking at his watch, and Jazzy knew he was meeting Bea somewhere. Carlo's infidelity was his own concern.

Once Carlo dropped Jazzy off and drove away, Jazzy felt alone, and it wasn't a pleasant feeling. He went into his apartment and sat there, listening to a radio Phil loaned him as Crosby sang a strange song about a man painting a fence. It was dismal, like his mood.

The next day, despite Polly's frequent visits to his desk, was unbearably long. Jazzy was still terrified and wanted to run back to his apartment, where he felt safe. He couldn't return to Rochester, because Marve had a loose tongue, and he knew that Joe Chink knew where he came from.

He was more homesick than when he'd been in the service. He missed Rochester terribly, particularly Goodman Street and the gang at Slim Broadway's.

When Nellie finished her bookkeeping for the month, which also included the quarterly report, the figures showed Gomes was experiencing healthy growth. The news triggered a party at the Serendipity to which all were invited. Jazzy wasn't in the mood to party, but saying no would've been an insult to Gomes. When Jazzy entered the tavern, he was greeted by the usual shouts.

Nellie never came to the tavern, and Rosalind made a rare appearance, driving Goose, because of the old man's recent setback. Goose made a fine recovery. At one end of the bar, Jazzy saw Bea talking to Carlo and Rick.

Otto spoke with Bob Petrillo, who wore a Stetson perched rakishly on the back of his head. Across his back was slung a western guitar.

Phil and Doc were talking to two middle-aged men Jazzy knew from the boiler room, but he'd forgotten their names. It was rare to have both Phil and Doc there.

Jim, the bartender, called, "Everything's ready!" He carried paper plates of food to the tables—hot dogs, baked beans, and German potato salad.

Everyone jockeyed for a place to sit. Once they were seated, Carlo rose and waited while they lifted their glasses, then he toasted the company's continuing success.

While the others ate, Bob got his guitar and sang a medley of western numbers. He started with *Empty Saddles,* then did *Don't Fence Me In,* and *Peace in the Valley.* When he finished with *Deep in the Heart of Texas,* everyone applauded. In the middle of the last number, Bea hopped onto a table and did a bad hula.

"Get off the table, Mable, the two bucks are for the beer!"

It was an old joke, but they laughed, anyway.

Later, they scattered, and Jazzy joined Petrillo at the bar.

"I enjoyed your medley, Bob," Jazzy said. "Do you plan to pursue a singing career?"

"Someday, if I get a break. Meanwhile, I'd like to work in Carlo's division permanently."

"Phil's the man to ask about that."

"No. Not to drive. I want to come into the office."

Jazzy smiled. Phil was as much a martinet as Doc. All Bob really wanted was free beer all day, no deadlines or supervisors, and a chance to play his guitar.

"Office work looks pleasant from the outside, but it can get rough in there."

"Yeah, but look at the fringe benefits. All those broads…I'd sure like to get next to that." He nodded toward Bea.

Jazzy smiled again. If Bob ever made his interests known to Carlo, he'd be fired.

"I suppose you'll be starting your own business one of these days?" Bob asked.

"No. All I want is enough money to get to California."

"California? Hollywood? Maybe that's where I belong, too."

Rick approached to order a drink and overheard them. "They say California is the land of opportunity with all the aircraft industries they've got."

"Yeah," Bob said.

There was a period of drinking and bantering, and everyone had a good time. Then Phil, Doc, and Otto left. Goose, who was usually the last to leave, felt weary and asked Rosalind to take him home. Jazzy thought he didn't look well at all.

The two men from the boiler room departed, leaving Jazzy, Rick, Carlo, Bob, and Bea.

The call went out for pool players. Rick, who'd been paid, answered the call, considering himself pretty good with a stick. They organized a game of pill pool, and Jazzy, who was wary of strangers with cue sticks, stayed away. With Rick, there were five in the game, insuring some substantial pots.

After the ante, they each received a pill from a leather bottle. Each pill was numbered, and they set their cues at the string, an imaginary line just above the near cushion and across the table. Each struck the far cushion with his cue, and the order of play was determined by the closeness of each ball on its return to the near cushion.

To win the pot, a player had to sink the ball with the same number as the pill he held. The balls were played in numerical sequence.

"Rick will cream those clowns," Carlo predicted. "He shoots a pretty good stick."

Jazzy reserved judgment. He knew all the facets of pill pool, and he knew the ability to make a shot wasn't enough.

From the start, it was apparent Rick had a steady hand and good eye. It was just as apparent he was going to lose. He made longer runs than the others, but he wasn't winning. The finesse of the game dictated he keep the ball with his number moving on the table with combination shots or caroms off the object ball, but he had to do it in a way that didn't reveal the identity of his own ball.

Rick didn't have that skill. When the game broke up, with two others big losers, Rick was in an ugly mood. Carlo bought him a drink and talked to him quietly for a while, with Rick nodding. Whatever Carlo promised calmed the big man.

Jazzy took Carlo aside and asked, "What magic words did you use to tame him?"

"Money. I told him I'd make up the losses in his next paycheck. Say, maybe you should've played him."

"And make an enemy?"

Carlo laughed.

Jazzy was ready to go home. He consumed more beer than he had since his lonely weekends in the Army, stationed near towns so remote they didn't appear on road maps, where mothers kept a tight rein on their daughters.

Carlo begged him to stay a little longer, handing Jazzy another beer, which he determined was his last. Bob talked to Bea. That seemed natural, two young people with much in common, but she was close to him, looking into his dark eyes, her hand on his arm.

Rick's voice became louder. He, too, drank more than usual. Behind the bar, Jim laughed. The others gathered around, carrying their drinks.

"What's so funny?" Carlo asked.

"Rick was telling me about the housewife who bought the fishing rod he'd taken from her husband's car. She got a deal."

"Were you always a scoundrel?" Jazzy asked.

"You mean, was I always a salesman? Yep. I never did anything else from the day I got out of school."

"What was your first sales job?" Jim asked.

"Selling cleaners for Vacu-Kleen. It was a new company that paid good commissions. The sales manager was a hot dog, but he thought he was Knute Rockne. He stood on chairs, yelling at us to inspire us during sales meetings. He had a blackboard with tricky figures on it, showing us how we'd all make a million."

"I'll bet that fired you up," Carlo said sarcastically.

"You'd be surprised. He'd end with the company song, stolen from some opera. Somebody wrote company words to it."

"How'd it go?" Bob got his guitar ready. "Do you remember it?"

"Do I remember? The damn tune was the same one my high school stole for their song."

Sons of Vacu-Clean and daughters let us sell
That wonder product Vacu-Clean.
Pledge our loyalty and show fidelity
That's built in our marvel Vacu-Clean.
Onward! Forward! Selling as we go
We shall meet and make a lot of dough!

"That's from Friml's *Vagabond King,*" Jazzy explained.

"Why, that's corny," Bea said.

Rick glared at them.

"Maybe. Then the manager leaped on his table and shouted, 'What are we selling?' We'd answer, 'Vacu-Clean!' He did that three times, then added, 'Go get 'em, Men!'"

"He sounds like a real meathead," the bartender muttered.

"He had us running out the building screaming like Comanches. We scattered to the four winds, then, in less than an hour, we'd meet at the nearest bar."

The big man withdrew into a silence that didn't bode well for the one who crossed him.

Carlo grabbed Bea's arm. "Challenge you to a game of darts."

"You're on, you old horse ball." She playfully punched his arm.

They walked unsteadily to the dart board, with Bob and Rick following. At the dart board, Bea and Carlo both missed the target completely on their first throw.

"Drunken bastards," Rick growled. "Can't hit a bull's ass with a banjo." With a movement so quick no one saw it, a switchblade appeared in his hand. Without taking aim, he let fly, and it stuck dead center in the target, quivering with the impact.

Jim pretended not to notice and busied himself at the opposite end of the circular bar, wiping the surface. He didn't want a confrontation with Rick.

Jazzy took his leave without saying farewell to anyone.

The next day, his head throbbed, and he felt ready to die. He found Polly sitting at his desk, legs crossed, and the electricity was there again.

"I've got some vintage Crosby I want you to hear," she said.

"When did you want me to come over?" he whispered.

"You were out with the boys last night, weren't you?"

Perplexed, he just stared at her. "Yes. I went to Carlo's party."

"You aren't falling asleep on my couch. Make it tomorrow."

The last of the drivers checked in, and Jazzy balanced the checks and cash against the work tickets. He totaled the daily activity sheet and placed the tickets to be posted the next day on Nellie's desk. He was afraid, as he was every night at that time—not of the dark but what the darkness might conceal. He put the day's take in the safe and locked it, feeling better with the money no longer in his possession.

Noises made him apprehensive, and he hated being alone in that old building with its built-in sound effects.

A loud crash from the phone room startled him. Did someone slip past him during the night? How?

He grabbed a length of pipe from the debris in the corner, only to see Goose, bleary-eyed and unsteady, although perfectly sober for the first time since Jazzy met him. He'd passed out in a drunken stupor in his phone stall, and he must've been out a long time. It was a mystery how the phone jockeys overlooked him when they quit for the day.

Goose, frustrated, slammed desk drawers and cabinet doors. One cabinet drawer was padlocked.

"Damn it, they locked up the goodies! I need a drink real bad."

"No, you don't. Sit down."

Goose sat and eyed him sadly. "Get out of here before you become one of us."

"That's strange, coming from you, the company wag."

"You mean the court jester, the company clown. Do you think I enjoy playing the fool, performing at every royal command from Carlo or Nellie?"

"Why do you do it?"

"Why does a seal perform? The fish. Look at me, Jazzy. I have no one. I'm old and hooked on booze. I know it'll kill me. Who'd hire me? I'm no good at this job, either. I screw up orders and give drivers the wrong addresses. I do everything wrong, but Carlo keeps me on, because he's proud of this goofy operation. I'm his prize display. For me, with all that hooch available, this is heaven.

"Would you believe that this old derelict has a degree from state teachers? I once taught the sciences."

"Now that you mention it, when you're sober, your speech shows education."

"Every time I put my thumbs to my lips to play *Sugar Blues* for some visiting asshole, I'm filled with hatred you wouldn't believe."

"Why don't you tell Carlo how you feel?"

"Why would he keep me? Carlo's not so bad. He's a scoundrel, but he makes no claim of sainthood. He's crooked, but, in some ways, you can trust him. Never play cards with him, though—he's a cardsharp. Most gamblers have their own code of ethics. It's twisted, maybe, but it's better than no ethics at all."

"I often wondered why a smart man like Carlo lets Rick rob him blind."

"Carlo won't stand for stealing, but, in Rick's case, it's his guts and the crafty way he gains confidence and uses people that endears him to the boss. If Carlo has a hero, it's Rick Devlin."

"I don't find him much of a role model."

"Oh, he's witty, a great storyteller, and he's usually the life of the party. I like you, Jazzy, so I'll give you one bit of advice—stay away from Rick."

"You stay away from taverns."

"I'm broke." Goose walked to the door and disappeared into the night. Jazzy locked the door behind him and returned to his desk.

Someone rattled the locked door just as Jazzy was preparing to leave. He peered cautiously through the slit, relieved it wasn't Joe Chink's boys, but Rick's appearance gave him little solace.

"I'm glad I caught you before you took off," Rick said.

"Something I can do for you?"

"Just wanted to talk."

"Come on, Rick. You didn't come back to this hole to talk to me."

"Well, Jazzy, first I wanted to know if you were serious about going to the coast."

"Yes, I am."

"Who have you got there?"

"My mother's in San Diego." Jazzy looked at Rick. Even though he was pleasant enough and carried an air of congeniality, Jazzy had long since had a gut feeling about him that was disturbing—before Goose's warning.

"Is your car in good shape?"

"For a prewar model, yes."

"Good tires?"

"Of course. Why the interest in my car?"

"If you're thinking I want to buy it, it wouldn't do me any good. They took my license."

"What do you have in mind?"

"I'll furnish the gas, and I'll go west with you."

"I don't know. I didn't plan to go with someone."

"How could you go alone? You're broke."

"So are you, Rick."

"How do you know that?"

"Come on, Rick, it's me. I saw you drop your pay to those sharks at the Serendipity. I'm a nobody, but I can beat you at pool without half-trying."

That stung. Rick's eyes narrowed, but he managed a smile. "Well, I've got my vices, and you've got yours. When I play pool, I'm betting on my abilities, over which I have some control. When you play the horses, you bet on the performance of dumb beasts, over which you have no control."

"Why are we arguing over who has the worst vice?"

"You're right. Let's blow this town."

"I can't do it."

"Give me a ride to the Bowlodrome. There's a guy at the alleys who'll give me a tidy sum. We can take off early in the morning." There was urgency in his voice.

It would take some time to accumulate enough money to head west. True, the incident at the trotters, where he almost stumbled into Monti and Hobbs, unnerved Jazzy, but he couldn't travel nearly 2,500 miles with an unpredictable man like Rick.

"Sorry, Rick. I can't do that to Carlo and Nellie. They deserve at least two weeks' notice."

"You've always been a goody-goody. In this world, you should look out for number one." Rick tried to control his anger.

They were silent for a while, then Rick said, "Sorry we can't swing a deal, Jazzy. At least give me a lift to the Bowlodrome."

Jazzy put the key in the ignition and was about to start the car when a pair of headlights blinded him.

"It's that lard ass, Rosalind," Rick muttered in exasperation.

When the car came alongside, Jazzy rolled down his window, wondering if everyone planned to return that night. "What's up?"

"Let me in the building, Jazzy. I left an envelope in my desk."

Jazzy got out and walked her to the office, then he opened the door and escorted her inside.

"Must be valuable for you to come back to this hole."

"Just my utility bill and a check. Nellie's giving me a couple hours off in the morning to run some errands. Why in hell are you hobnobbing with that crook?"

"Rick? I'm taking him to the Bowlodrome."

"Stay away from him. He's bad news."

"I know. He offered me a deal to help me get to California. He offered to finance the trip if I agreed to drive."

"That bastard's broke, Jazzy."

"Yeah, but he has a friend at the Bowlodrome who's got money he owes Rick."

"Jazzy, how can you be so stupid? He'll steal your car and dump you in the boondocks."

Jazzy laughed. "My mother didn't raise an idiot. There's no way I'd travel with Rick Devlin."

"Then what's he doing in your car?"

"I couldn't refuse him a lift to the alleys. The Bowlodrome is across town, and he's got no transportation."

At Rick's suggestion, Jazzy parked in front of the entrance with the motor running.

"I have to pay my rent before the landlord heaves my bags into the street," Rick explained.

As he sat in the car, Jazzy studied the architecture of the building. It was a far cry from the dank, smelly alleys of his boyhood, housed in the basements of corner saloons.

He thought sadly of Whitey, who, through his generosity, introduced league bowling at Saint Stanislaus for the neighborhood. There was nothing Jazzy would like better than to be back on Goodman Street, but he wouldn't inflict his nightmare on his neighbors.

Chapter Twenty-Two

A shot rang out, snapping Jazzy from his reverie. There was a sinking feeling in the pit of his stomach, then he saw Rick run toward the car. He flung open the door and dived in.

"Move! Get this fucking crate moving!"

"What happened in there?"

"I shot the bastard."

"You lousy son of a bitch! You involved me in a shooting?"

Out of nowhere, the switchblade appeared. The sharp point pressed against Jazzy's neck, drawing blood. He sat rigidly, not daring to move his head.

"Move!"

Jazzy drove off, tires screaming.

"I had the whole bundle in an old bowling bag, then the slob snatched it away from me. I shot him in his big belly. Would you believe he lunged and knocked the gun from my hand? I wasn't expecting it, or he couldn't have done it."

"Where'd you get a gun?"

"I had it all along in my jacket pocket."

"I'll let you off. You can lose yourself in the city."

"Oh, no. It was like a premier. I performed before a full house. Don't get ideas, Pal. We're going to be real tight."

Feelings of impending doom plagued Jazzy, as bad as the night he tossed Joe Chink's valise from the window.

"Keep heading south of the city until I feel it's safe."

The night was hot, and air from the open windows felt like a blast from a Bessemer furnace. Jazzy felt sticky, and he yearned for a cold shower and cold root beer in his icebox. He thought of Polly, who, like the battery, was ever-ready.

Jazzy drove through the night, harassed alternately by whining self-pity and bitter recriminations.

When they ran out of gas, Rick got out to push. "You stay in the car. Guide this piece of crap while I push it off the road. Head for the dogwood."

"What dogwood?"

"To the left. Don't you know your trees?"

"Why don't I get out and help push?"

"Stay put. I don't want you running off into the night."

Rick put his shoulder to the task. He was big and strong, and, although it was an effort in the thick grass, he pushed the car to the dogwood, then joined Jazzy in the front seat.

"Climb into the back."

"What the hell for?"

"Get the fuck into the back seat!"

Jazzy was apprehensive. Was he about to die? For a moment, he entertained the idea of trying to run, but Rick would knife him before he could get the car door open.

Jazzy climbed over the front seat to the back of the car.

"Give me your shoelaces."

"What are you planning to do?" Jazzy asked weakly, removing the laces and watching Rick tie them together.

"I'm gonna tie your hands behind you. Turn around."

"Why are you doing this?"

"Lots of people saw me. Someone may've seen you and the car. When the law locates the car, they'll know who you are. I don't want them to get you."

"If they get me, how can they hurt you?"

"I know guys like you—a little pressure, and you develop diarrhea of the mouth. You'd give them my complete biography."

"My wrists hurt. You're cutting off the circulation."

Rick ignored him. He locked the car doors but left the windows open a little for air circulation, then nestled down.

When Jazzy heard snoring coming from the front seat, he tried to touch the buttons that locked the doors without success. He tried lowering the windows to climb out, but he couldn't grasp the handles with his shoes or head.

The only way he could get comfortable was by kneeling on the car floor and lying his head and upper body on the seat. Exhaustion finally brought sleep.

Light through the car windows woke him. There were pains in his stomach. He hadn't eaten since noon of the previous day. Perhaps he'd die of hunger.

Rick was gone. *The big bastard dumped me,* he thought hopefully.

Then Rick appeared. "Come on out so I can untie those laces."

He made no move to free Jazzy's bound wrists. Instead, in a surprise move, he shot a right to Jazzy's jaw, knocking him over backward. The back of his head struck the ground hard, and Jazzy was out cold.

Rick moved quickly, raising the hood and yanking out some of the wiring. With his knife, he cut two six-foot lengths, then he twisted them together to create a strong line. Rolling Jazzy on his back, he spread his legs twenty inches apart and placed the line under his ankles, tying each ankle tightly.

The rest of the line was wrapped around the line connecting both ankles until they met in the center, where he tied both ends tightly. Only then did he free Jazzy's wrists.

When Jazzy awoke, he asked, "Why?"

"Nothing personal, Pal. Be grateful I didn't act on my first plan to knife you. Notice you're hobbled?"

Jazzy looked down and saw what Rick had done. "You pulled out the wiring! I'll never get the car started."

"That's right. By now, the description of your heap and the license number have been broadcast all over the state. If I see your hands near your ankles, you've had it."

"You son of a bitch!"

"Get up, Pal. There's a precipice out there. We can roll the car over the edge."

Jazzy walked behind Rick with little Geisha-girl steps. "Please, that's my mother's car. Don't do it."

"What good is it without gas? We'll get another."

"You aren't going to destroy my car!"

Rick's hand went to Jazzy's throat and held him tightly. "You still don't get it. I decide whether you live or die. I don't want you or your car found around here. Give me problems, and I'll put you in the trunk of the car. Put your shoulder to the car and push. I can't manage the grade without you."

A minute later, the car tumbled to the bottom.

"We have more work to do," Rick said. "See that rise across the road? We're gonna make a rock slide, and the road will be blocked off, making the next car stop. Then we jump the occupants from behind the trees."

"Maybe you will, but I'm not a party to murder."

"You'll help me if I say so."

It was back-breaking work. Boulders finally crashed down to rest on the road, and the wires, although coated, cut into Jazzy's ankles. His head throbbed.

"Hear about the job I did last week?" Rick asked.

"Not really." Jazzy felt nauseous. "Polly said you weren't working for Carlo, because you had a job of your own."

"Yeah. I got a call from an old geezer. He knew me when I was Devlin and Son. I never had a son."

"Why the deception?"

"With a father-and-son operation, the stiffs have more confidence in you."

"I'll bet."

"The sucker complained about moles raising hell in his garden, so I offered to build him a stone wall."

"That won't keep moles out."

"I know that, and you know that, but he was sold on it. I let him Jew me down to $2,500 for the job."

"You ripped off that poor old man?"

"Yeah, but with style. If you gotta steal, do it elegantly. I ordered some sand and Portland cement, then hired some peon labor. There were plenty of field stones. In two days, we had a wall around his place fifteen inches high and ten wide."

"He bought that crap?"

"Well, not altogether. He threatened to report me."

"What did you expect?"

"It wasn't the money. He said the walls were so crooked, they seemed to be waving at him. I explained the walls were built crooked to confuse the moles."

Jazzy was speechless. "Does Carlo know?"

"You bet. When I told him, he laughed so hard, he had tears in his eyes. He made me repeat it to Jim the bartender."

"Rick!" Jazzy fought to stay awake. He feared he might have a concussion and slip into a coma.

"Yes?" Rick's eyes were thin slits as he looked into the sun.

"You aren't going to kill anyone, are you?"

"If I have to."

"It's no good. They'll get you for sure."

"You're forgetting the guy I plugged at the bowling alley. They get you the same for two as for one."

"Maybe he's all right. He might live."

"With a slug in his gut?" Rick glanced down the road, shook off his weariness, and slid downhill in a hurry, running toward the trees. He turned to look up at Jazzy. "Get your fuckin' ass down here."

"No. Please don't hurt anyone."

Rick had to keep Jazzy in sight, so he dragged him to the edge of the road and positioned him against a large oak.

"I can handle this. Just don't queer it, you hear me?"

The car came closer. Jazzy heard the smooth hum of its engine. Rick hid behind the trees. The driver went past Jazzy, then saw the roadblock and slammed on his brakes.

The driver got out, and Jazzy saw the dark clothes and white collar of a clergyman. He didn't think Rick would harm him, but Rick moved in, keeping the dark coupe between him and his victim. Even if Jazzy were inclined to defy Rick and insure his own demise, he couldn't cry out.

The stranger was Rick's height but thinner. There was an air of resignation about him. He removed his coat and black hat, revealing a bald head, then went to his car and threw the hat and coat onto the seat.

Rick picked up a rock, rushed forward, and struck hard. Jazzy, unable to run, minced down the road, babbling in protest as Rick, on his knees beside the clergyman, struck repeatedly.

When Jazzy reached them, the sight made him gag. He staggered to the trees and vomited, crying tears of rage. Finally, he steadied his body, but his mind was still wild. He rushed back as fast as his hobbled feet allowed.

"You stinking son of a bitch! You lousy animal!"

The outburst and revulsion on Jazzy's face stirred Rick to action. He threw a wild right that Jazzy easily evaded. Seeing a wide-open target, he struck back with a hard right. Rick went down, stunned, then his head cleared, and his look of amazement turned to fury.

"You little piss pot! You decked me!" He got up, intent on mayhem. He charged like an enraged rhino, but Jazzy got in two left jabs that Rick shook off.

Rick's rush became more controlled, and Jazzy's hobble prevented him from moving much. Rick struck with his shoulder, sending Jazzy crashing to the ground, then he straddled Jazzy and pummeled him cruelly.

Jazzy blacked out and was out for some time.

When he awoke, he bled from his lower lip. There were lumps on both temples, and his ears rang. He sat up and placed his back against a tree, watching Rick strip the dead body, taking great care with the clothing. He dragged the dead man to the precipice and rolled him over the edge, then he came back to Jazzy.

"You should've finished me off," Jazzy whispered.

"I gave it some thought, but I need help with the rocks." He looked at Jazzy and decided he was too weak to help. He'd be faster alone. He moved just enough rocks to clear a path for the car.

"Come here."

Jazzy came forward, no illusions left. His life hung on Rick's whim. Rick found a bottle of water in the trunk and let Jazzy have some.

"Maybe we'd better split up," Jazzy suggested.

"No. You stay with me."

Rick walked to the car, with Jazzy following, his feet burning. The soles of his everyday suede shoes were paper thin, and his shirt clung to him. He'd been knocked unconscious twice in one day.

It was eerie riding with Rick in a priest's clothes. Jazzy wondered what Rick had in mind. With his rugged, unshaven face, how could he hope to pass himself off as a cleric?

He should've listened when Goose warned him to stay away from Rick. Above all, he should've listened to Rosalind, whose predictions of disaster made her seem clairvoyant.

Rick turned down a dirt road to a creek.

This is it, Jazzy thought. I *don't want to die.*

"What are you going to do?" Jazzy asked.

"I need a shave." Rick got out and helped Jazzy out so he could watch him. He opened an overnight bag and pulled out his shaving kit, then he lathered up, shaved leisurely, applied after-shave lotion, powdered, and combed his hair.

When he returned to the car, dragging Jazzy, he was a respectable-looking minister. The smell of his lotion was strong. Jazzy held out his hands for the shaving kit.

"Not you," Rick said.

"What's wrong with me?" Jazzy's terror returned.

"You're not very bright. If we both shave, we've traveled together. If I'm clean-shaven, and you look like a bum, I'm a minister who picked up a hitchhiker."

They climbed into the car and drove on. Rick felt an elation Jazzy didn't share. He hummed hymns, amusing himself in his new role and getting in the mood for another con game. The sacrilege was something Jazzy feared would bring on new terrors.

The feeling of well-being made Rick talkative. "I remember going religious once. Just about everybody can be conned. That's what keeps guys like me solvent. This is my first time as a minister. My con was Bibles. The trick is knowledge of the Bible. It's a gold mine. The key to acceptance is a dark suit that's too big and a black hat. Remember the hat. You have to master the pious look, too."

He demonstrated it for Jazzy.

"I remember one winter I was in Pennsylvania Dutch country selling Bibles, and a severe cold spell hit. My car conked out. I saw a farmhouse in the distance."

Good Lord, Jazzy thought, sitting in his misery. *He's trotting out a Guy Lovell traveling salesman story for me.*

"Well, I just made it to the door. The grouchy farmer wouldn't let me into the house, but his wife shamed him, and she dragged me to the stove to thaw out.

"She had some knackwurst with dumplings and kraut heating on the woodstove. The smell almost drove me mad. When we sat down to supper, I dug in with gusto. I entertained them with tales of life in the big city, and the wife hung on every word. The farmer got madder by the minute.

"When I reached for a third helping of kraut, he slammed the cover on the tureen and went to the stove with it, emptying it back into the pot.

"It was so cold, if I slept in the barn, I'd die before morning. I'd be no better off in the kitchen, because the only heat was from the stove and the manure heaped alongside the house. The manure was intended to radiate heat into the house, but it must've been old, because that house sure was cold. The farmer and his wife had a terrible argument about the sleeping arrangements. Finally, he agreed I could share the bed, heaped high with blankets, if he slept in the middle.

"We couldn't sleep, because a hinge broke off the barn door, and the gale banged the door, making a racket. The woman woke her husband and browbeat him into leaving the warm bed to fix the flapping door.

"'Now's your chance, Mr. Devlin,' she whispered. I rushed out of bed, raced to the kitchen, and got another helping of kraut."

Rick laughed so hard, it didn't bother him that Jazzy didn't join in. A quick look at the gas gauge sobered him. They were far from any city.

"I've got it figured, Pal," Rick said. "This preacher fellow I knocked off—if he came this far with the gauge so low, he had to be near his destination. He was probably going to turn down one of these side roads."

"What does that mean?"

"I've got his wallet, but I ain't stayin' around here to get gas. Not with his car. Somebody around here knows him. We keep going until we run out."

They traveled some distance, and the car got good mileage. Finally, the needle went beyond *Empty*, and Jazzy hoped Rick's luck had finally run out, then the nightmare would end.

They saw a battered house off the road, and they also saw a weather-beaten gas tank in front of the barn. Rick pulled over to the side of the road and got out his knife. Every time that knife appeared, Jazzy's heart almost stopped. Then Rick reached down and cut the wires around both ankles in two places, and the hobble fell off.

"Are you letting me go?"

"If I get a tankful of gas here, why not? I'll leave you off on the highway somewhere. By the time they find you, and you spill your guts, I'll be far gone, and you can bet your ass I'll have another car."

He helped Jazzy out of the car. "Your arms and legs are free, but, like I said, we're tight."

Chapter Twenty-Three

Henry Carlson was glad to be home. The day started uneventfully. Now the chores were done, and the place was like it had been before he left. He had enough of his dreary sisters and vowed the next visit would be a long time coming.

The road had very little traffic, since it meandered to nowhere special. He didn't recognize the car and was surprised when it turned off the road and approached his home. He climbed the steps, sat on the wicker chair, and looked through the lattice work around the porch.

Although retired, the playwright in him never left. He gauged the two men analytically. They were a rare pair. He gazed, unseen, into Rick's gray eyes, which mirrored a restless spirit. In his salad years, he'd encountered many men like that, and he knew they were unpredictable. Some were ruthless, but most channeled their energies into meaningful pursuits.

The big fellow's clothing seemed incongruous, and the suit was very tight. Sherlock Holmes would deduce his parish was a poor one, and the reverend's wardrobe skimpy.

Then there was the other man. Henry didn't know what to make of him. He puzzled Carlson. There were cuts on his lower lip and bruises on his face, but there didn't seem to be any animosity between the two.

"Hello, Reverend."

Rick looked up in surprise, then saw Henry sitting behind the lattice and grinned. Jazzy could almost read Rick's mind—*No trouble here. I can knock off this hayseed with my bare hands.*

"Good morning, Neighbor," Rick replied, walking up the path to the edge of the steps.

Jazzy followed and saw the old man was slouched in a wicker chair, enjoying the shade.

"Have my sins reached the attention of the Lord?" The old man laughed heartily.

"Why, no." Rick forced a smile. "I'm sure you're a good man." He played it straight, feeling confident in his role. "I've been driving since early morning, and I was so wrapped up in a sermon I'm working on for Sunday's services, I let myself run out of gas."

He managed a sheepish grin and assumed an attitude of exasperation at his own folly.

Henry's eyes were on him, dancing in good humor, then he looked at Jazzy quizzically, as if trying to classify him. Jazzy wanted to tell him he wasn't the man to worry about.

"I can help with the gas, all right. I'm Henry Carlson."

"Reverend James Hamilton." Rick climbed the steps and shook the man's hand. "This is a fellow traveler, Henry. You might say he's a knight of the road."

"I'm Jasmin Rhinehardt," Jazzy said.

For a brief moment, Rick's face clouded in anger, but Jazzy refused to give a fictitious name, because that would mean he was involved with Rick's barbarism.

Henry smiled. That was the strangest name he'd heard in a long time. The other thing he wondered about was why a man would hitchhike in thin shoes with no laces.

"What do the boys call you?" he asked.

"Jazzy."

"That's predictable." He turned to Rick. "I offer you the hospitality of my home, Reverend. It gets lonesome around here. Grab a kitchen chair and sit down. Jazzy, you can sit on that crate. It's a hot day. Have you come a long way?"

"A good stretch."

From the moment Henry gave his name, Jazzy's mind puzzled over it. As he sat down, it came to him—Henry Carlson, the playwright. Guy Lovell told Jazzy that the man had quit the world and gone into seclusion.

Jazzy sat near the wall, against a bookcase that went halfway to the ceiling. He could see the titles and felt certain he was in the company of a playwright. Every play the man had written and produced was on one row of the case in the order of their creation.

His eyes swept the bookcase, and he saw many contemporary works. He knew all by reputation but had to admit he'd read only a few—Hellman, Williams, two Andersons, Sherwood, Rice, and Odets were there.

"I've been working hard around this place," Henry said, "getting it into shape. It got a little rundown while I visited my sisters in the city. I won't be doing another lick of work today—it's hot."

He reached behind him and came up with a gallon jug. "Nothing like Concord wine on a hot day. I keep it cool in the root cellar. Made it myself, as a matter of fact. It beats Mogen David or the Widmer stuff, made not far from here. Want to try some, Reverend?" He poured some in a tin cup he took off a nearby nail.

"No, my good man," Rick said in disapproval. "Intoxicants are the allies of the devil."

Jazzy stared at him open-mouthed. When Henry offered the cup, Jazzy didn't refuse. He was parched. It was cool, but the alcohol left him feeling giddy. Without breakfast or lunch in him, the wine was like a hot poker in his stomach.

Henry poured himself a cup, his spirits dampened.

"It's a sacrilege," Rick said, being as righteous as possible. "It's said the Lord's body was His temple, and so it may be assumed our bodies are temples, too, for we were created in His image. Man is God's ultimate triumph. To defile and deface that which is God's with vile intoxicants is to insult the name of God, our Creator."

Jazzy listened, transfixed.

Henry set down the cup on the porch floor. Rick had ruined the taste for him. Rick talked slowly, until his mind caught the rhythm of the text, then he bulldozed his way through the words that followed. He was in his element. Jazzy had no doubts about Rick's salesmanship.

Rick was good, recalling snatches of conversations and paragraphs of printed matter almost intact. He gave Henry bits from prohibition tracts and the best from the elite of the bogus sky pilots he met during a lifetime of fraud.

Spurred on by an admiring Henry, he went off the subject of drinking and lashed out at sin in general. Finally, Rick sat there, his head in his hands—partly simulated humility, part genuine weariness. The drone of flies was the only sound.

Rick felt Henry's hand on his shoulder and started. "To think my neighbors call *me* the silver-tongued orator. Sometimes, when I say something cerebral, they call me Scattergood Baines, but you, Reverend, are true blue ribbon."

The mention of Scattergood Baines, one of Jazzy's most cherished fictional characters, convinced him Henry was the playwright. He had to warn the old man.

"I wouldn't associate you with Scattergood Baines," Jazzy said. "You're more the Clarence Buddington Kelland type."

Rick scowled. Things he didn't understand worried him.

Carlson perked up. The handsome young man before him was being deliberately ambiguous. He dismissed the thought he was parading knowledge of contemporary fiction just to impress him. If Jazzy knew he was the famous playwright, why the cloak-and-dagger bit?

Carlson had to make sure. He would choose an arch villain, but he dismissed Sherwood's terrifying Duke Mantee. If the big man had seen the movie, the scheme would backfire. Then he had an inspiration—Charles Dickens' classic brute.

"Reverend Hamilton, I'm amazed at how much you resemble a friend of mine, William Sikes."

"I've never heard of him," Rick replied. "I must look middle American."

"I knew a William Sikes," Jazzy said. "I knew his girlfriend, too, named Nancy, but she's dead now."

Henry nodded at the connection the two men just made. The mention of the victim of the cruel Bill Sikes in *Oliver Twist* clinched it.

"Can't be the same," Henry said. "This one's been married forty years, and his wife's name is Sadie."

He looked at Jazzy with new respect and understood the young man's bruises. He was a hostage.

Rick was angry. If Jazzy said another word, Rick would kill him.

"You must be famished," Henry said. "Come in and have a bite with me." He walked inside.

The others followed him into the kitchen. If Rick were smart, he'd get gas and get out. Jazzy was faint with lack of food, but he still wanted to get away, and he didn't want to see the brilliant old playwright hurt.

The food influenced Rick, and he accepted. The kitchen was big, the walls covered with flowered paper, faded and torn in spots, covered with fly specks. The wide pine boards on the floor were bare and showed years of traffic. In one corner was a Kalamazoo, with a bare iron sink and short pump and handle beside it.

Rick gave the hovel close scrutiny. There were four exits—front door, bedroom door, cellar door, and attic stairway. Then there was a closet.

The electricity merely furnished light. The heat in winter came from the Kalamazoo. There was a phone mounted on the wall, and in the center of the kitchen was a round table covered by an oilcloth. The pattern had been happy in its time, but that was long past. There was a three-legged stool, a leather-bound rocker, and a kitchen chair, the mate to the one on the porch.

Then Rick saw the gun. It was a Colt, sitting on a shelf above the sink. Jazzy's hope for a quick departure vanished.

Carlson puttered around the kitchen, gathering utensils for a quick lunch.

"That's a dangerous weapon to be kept in the kitchen, Henry." Rick nodded toward the Colt.

"No. I'm very careful around guns."

"It saddens me," Rick said with a sigh, "to see evidence of violence all around us these days. Even here, in the house of a God-fearing man, one finds it. Don't you know that carrying instruments of violence invites violence? Would you use that gun?"

"As you say, Reverend, I'm a God-fearing man, but if a viper enters my house and threatens me, I'd shoot it without blinking an eye. We're isolated out here. That's why I keep that gun ready and loaded."

Henry controlled his rising terror. A dangerous confrontation was inevitable, and he didn't want to die. He stepped closer to the closet.

"Henry, I want to quote something from the Scriptures…"

"Oh, stop it, young man. It's too damn hot."

Jazzy felt a prickling sensation down the back of his neck, and he held his breath.

"I've had enough fire and brimstone for one day. You're a spellbinder, but there's nothing ministerial about you."

You fool! Jazzy thought. *You poor, brave fool! Now you've done it!*

With studied detachment, Rick reached for the gun, fondled it, and approved its balance. When he turned to face Henry, his cumbersome mask of righteousness was gone, revealing him for what he was.

"So, you stupid old man. Do you think you're clever? Don't you know there are times when it's stupid to be clever?"

Every instinct told Jazzy to run, but instead, he did a strange thing—he moved forward, pleading. "Please don't kill him."

Rick hit him with the gun, and Jazzy fell as warm blood trickled down his face. The room spun.

Desperately, he wrapped his arms around Rick's legs, and Rick pulled the trigger. He pulled it several times, but the hammer kept striking empty chambers. Dragging Jazzy with him, Rick walked toward the old man, tossing the gun aside and reaching for the switchblade. With a sudden lunge, he kicked Jazzy away.

Diving into the closet, Henry came up with a double-barreled shotgun and fired both barrels.

Jazzy felt he'd been out a long time, but, in reality, he never was completely unconscious. He tried to get to his feet, but he couldn't. Not even on the battlefields of Belgium had he been so weary. He finally sank back and surrendered to the comfort of the hard wood floor.

He was less forgiving of his mother. When Jennie sold the house, she removed the sanctuary of Goodman Street and stripped him of the protection of friends and neighbors. If she'd kept the house, Marve's stupidity wouldn't have sent him through a nightmare.

He thought he knew her. Despite her modernity, love for dance, and *avante-garde* fashions, he felt certain she'd been celibate. Why then, at her age, did she have a sudden passion for a stranger? He couldn't accept that love might've come into her life.

He wanted to be fair. Was he George Amberson Minafer, in Tarkington's *The Magnificent Ambersons,* whose arrogance and selfishness destroyed all chance for his mother to marry the man she loved?

A memory he'd hidden came to the surface. It was a rainy night, and he danced with Jennie. Her soft body was crushed against his, and their perfunctory kiss turned torrid. His arousal would plague him the rest of his life.

Henry walked closer, and Jazzy thanked God the old man was still alive. A policeman covered Rick's body with a quilt.

"Never had a chance," the trooper said.

"With a double-barreled at that range, they never do," another trooper replied.

He was older and evidently in charge. He sat on the rocker, facing Carlson, who was perched on the three-legged stool. The trooper was big, and Henry looked like a gnome by comparison.

"I want to ask you some questions, Henry."

"You know me, Ralph. I'm the Gabby Hayes of the area."

"How'd you know he wasn't a preacher like he said?"

"He lied the moment he opened his mouth in front of my porch. He said he was traveling since early morning and forgot to get gas, so why was he so clean-shaven, his skin glistened? When he came up the steps, I smelled the lie. His after-shave was strong, but that wasn't anything to me. Everyone's got a right to a little white lie occasionally, even a reverend, but it certainly made me wide awake."

"How about him?" He pointed at Jazzy.

"That was easy. The big one called him a fellow traveler, a knight of the road. Only an idiot hits the road with those thin, fancy shoes. I haven't figured the missing laces out, though."

"You used your head, all right." The young trooper came within hearing range and sensed a legend in the making.

"You know, Ralph, that man looked like a preacher and talked like one. He was slick, but something didn't ring true."

"What was that?"

"I asked myself why a man of the cloth was giving me such a humdinger of a sermon, and, the more I thought about it, the more I became certain he wasn't a preacher. He was always throwing the Bible at me. He gave prohibition talk and quoted the Bible in the same breath. You know a prohibitionist would never have the Bible on his side. All the saints drank wine. Maybe it was grape juice."

"Maybe Kool-Aid," Ralph added.

"Well, Sir," Carlson continued, like a character from one of his plays, "Saint Paul was a fine man with good advice for his friend, Timothy. In the First Epistle of Paul, he tells Timothy, 'Drink no longer water but use a little wine for thy stomach's sake and thine own infirmities.'"

"What was the young man doing?" Ralph chuckled.

"If it wasn't for him, I'd be lying there instead of that man," Carlson said seriously. "He pleaded with the brute not to kill me. The man pistol whipped him, but he wasn't quite out. When the fraud found the gun was empty, he pulled a knife, and the young man grabbed his leg and slowed him enough to enable me to reach the closet and get the shotgun."

"Look at his face," Ralph said. "He's had trouble with the dead man."

"I was lucky he was able to warn me, so I sat near the closet."

"He warned you? How?"

"It was a strange dialogue."

"How about telling me about it? You did kill the man, Henry. Killings must be thoroughly investigated."

"Of course. We spoke over the big man's head. We used names and events from fiction we'd both read."

"You being a writer, that wasn't hard."

"It had its difficulties."

"The first chance you get, Henry, stop by our office. Your complete deposition will be a dandy. I'm especially interested in your coded conversations."

As Henry watched the attendants carry the body into the ambulance, the enormity of what he'd done hit him, and he wasn't as effusive. He'd taken a life, and no amount of rationalization could alter the fact. How many times in his prolific career had he written variations of the present scene? Reality had an impact the best plays couldn't match.

They lifted Jazzy to his feet and handcuffed him.

"No, no," Henry said. "Not him. I shot the man, the kid didn't."

"This guy's been battered lately," a young trooper noted.

"Why are you cuffing him?"

"There was a murder in a bowling alley in Buffalo, and the killer took off in a waiting car, which was registered to Jasmin Rhinehardt."

When they were gone, and Henry was alone again, he paused before entering the house, reluctant to do the cleaning he knew would make him queasy.

Chapter Twenty-Four

The nearest jail in that desolate country was Naples, a prosperous town, where the people were gainfully employed in the wine-making process and farming of grapes.

Jazzy was delivered to the town constable, who didn't know what to make of the dubious honor. He placed his prisoner in the small brick building's single cell. He wasn't sure of procedure, but common sense told him a questioning was in order.

A slight woman in her early twenties came, bearing a pad, with a pencil stuck through her hair above her ear. Nervous, she took dictation slowly. Her shorthand was no faster than if she wrote in longhand.

Jazzy recounted the events leading to his arrest. He started with the moment he drove Rick Devlin to the Bowlodrome in Buffalo and ended with his arrest by the state police. He was thorough, but he doubted the woman got it all.

Reverend Hamilton's murder occurred too close to the border of Livingston and Ontario Counties, and a determination had to be made. If the crime was committed in Ontario County, then Canandaigua, as the county seat, had jurisdiction. However, if the murder was committed in Livingston County, then that county would defer all claims and allow Erie County to hold two trials simultaneously in Buffalo.

A surveyor came from the capital to supervise the unskilled crew from Naples in locating the precise county line. From Buffalo came an investigative team that joined those appointed by the town of Canandaigua.

They worked together, compiling physical evidence on the road, shoulder, and edge of the precipice. They considered the location of the vehicle and body, and they gave a clear determination—Reverend Hamilton was slain in Livingston County.

There was no air-conditioning in the building. Since it was too early for heat, Jazzy sweltered in the daytime and shivered with cold at night. The meals were substantial. The jail rarely had occupants, so the town could afford it.

Jazzy was returned to Buffalo and immediately lodged in the county jail. He barely had time to familiarize himself with his new, modern cell when he was led to a large room where he was placed against the wall with several others.

Back in his cell, he was visited by a tall man who bore a striking resemblance to the tennis great Jack Kramer. He wore white slacks and white pullover sweater, with red, white, and blue piping along the V-nick. He walked silently into the cell on white boating shoes, and the two men stared at each other curiously.

"I'm W. B. Tidwell. I'm to represent you in court."

"Why should you represent me? I've done nothing wrong."

Tidwell frowned. He'd been afraid of that. He'd hoped that his new client, with the evidence indicating complicity at least, would plead guilty, and Tidwell's responsibility would be to make the best possible deal, which wouldn't take long.

"The grand jury meets on Monday to listen to the evidence the district attorney has on you, and, if the grand jury feels it's sufficient to suggest guilt, a trial will be set."

"I've explained what happened several times. Why is it so difficult to accept I had nothing to do with either slaying? What evidence suggests my guilt?"

"A witness saw your friend run to your car after the shooting. She said you were waiting for him with the motor running."

"Is that why they had me stand against the wall with four others? Someone identified me?"

"You were in a police line-up."

"I never denied being there waiting for Devlin."

"I've read your account. Why don't you start at the beginning and tell me again?"

Getting the case at that time was an imposition. Tidwell didn't relish being against Barry Kendall.

Jazzy spoke softly and slowly, recounting the details of his ordeal with Rick. When he finished, he waited for a reaction.

Tidwell finally said, "I've inquired about bail, but you've been refused."

Jazzy wasn't upset by that. At the moment, he was better off in police custody, where Joe Chink couldn't get him. He didn't doubt his friends on Goodman Street would raise the bail money if they were asked, but, if he were free, Monti and Hobbs would be waiting, and he'd be forced to flee again. If they didn't catch him, he'd be a fugitive from justice, a guilty man for the rest of his life.

"Well, Rhinehardt, I've got all the data I need. I'll do my best. Let's see what the grand jury comes up with. I'll be in touch." He walked out without saying good-bye.

There were no veterans in the county jail, just short-term miscreants, and those, like Jazzy, awaiting decisions on future legal action. They stayed in their cells for the most part, and met only during mealtime at the small dining hall. Most were young, frightened neophytes, to whom Jazzy, by virtue of two murders, held celebrity status.

Tidwell's appearance Monday afternoon gave Jazzy a wave of relief. He felt certain the lawyer came to release him.

"Rhinehardt, the DA has sufficient evidence against you. The grand jury handed down an indictment, and you'll be arraigned Friday on a charged yet to be determined. They're certain of your involvement in the murder of the owner of the Bowlodrome and the clergyman."

Jazzy sank heavily down on his bunk. For the first time, he feared the legal system. "What about the second murder?" he asked, fearing the worst.

"That's where you're most vulnerable. You were seen driving off with Devlin that evening at the bowling hall. The next day, your car is found near the body of a man with his head bashed in. You and your traveling companion were at the home of Henry Carlson afterward, and Devlin had the reverend's car, clothing, wallet, and identity. The DA will go for murder in the second degree. It's true no one witnessed the murder, but the DA feels the circumstantial evidence is strong."

When the lawyer left, Jazzy decided it was time to pray, then he slept.

He dreamed they came for him, and there was a scaffold in the yard. There was no time for him to dress as they dragged him out into the yard naked. A hearse was waiting alongside the scaffold for the long trip back to Rochester with his remains.

His friends sat in the bleachers, wearing black arm bands. Joe Chink, Hobbs, and Monti drank beer and laughed. When the executioner placed the noose around Jazzy's neck, he saw it was Marve. The trap door sprung open, and Jazzy screamed.

He awoke in a cold sweat, then went back to sleep and dreamed something entirely different. He was back in the carnival, and the Harem Lovelies swayed seductively. The Meeker twins winked at him knowingly, and Flo stepped down from the stage to chase him. The man in the booth forced him to take a teddy bear.

In court, they were able to choose a jury in one day. Jazzy didn't know if that was good or bad. His fellow inmates were quick to tell him he was in trouble. The jury consisted of ten men and two women, most in middle age.

Henry Carlson drove to Buffalo, a city he seldom visited, because it wasn't one of his favorites. He met Barry Kendall, the district attorney, who was an imposing man with a bright future. He clasped his hands and rotated his thumbs, plainly annoyed at the visit.

"I understand your concern for the young man," Barry said. "We concede he came to your aid, but some terrible crimes were committed across this state, and it's my job to bring the perpetrator to justice."

"The perpetrator is dead," Carlson said.

"We live by rules, Mr. Carlson, and I don't hold that one good deed is like doing penance in church. I've never investigated a case like this before. I talked to witnesses at the bowling alley and the troopers who came to your house. I spoke with a constable in Naples and read Rhinehardt's statement soon after his apprehension. I read two more statements made here in two different facilities."

"That should've convinced you."

"Oh what? I can't divulge testimony. We know your young friend was at the scene, waiting for Devlin with the motor running. Do you know how often we hear the line about getting money from a mysterious friend?"

"Rhinehardt's statement in Naples were concise and differed from the wild tale he concocted in the brief time it took us to bring him to Buffalo. He must've filched it from *Argosy.*"

"What wild tale?"

"I can't divulge that, but it was as fanciful as your deposition."

"What do you mean?" Carlson bristled.

"Come, come, old fellow. My youngest was nine when he gave up Tom Mix's code ring. Sometimes, we read more into words than are there. Let's not indulge in flights of fancy." Kendall rose, letting Carlson know the interview was over.

Carlson sat there seething, unaccustomed to being treated in such a cavalier fashion. As he watched Kendall's retreating figure, he vowed to expend whatever energies and resources necessary to help Jazzy.

Carlson walked to the reception desk in the foyer. "Young lady, give me the name of the lawyer assigned to the Jasmin Rhinehardt case and direct me to his office."

She saw the stubborn set to the old man's jaw and silently wrote the information on a piece of paper.

Carlson walked into Tidwell's office without the formality of knocking. The youthful attorney was lining up his putt, then he stroked the ball smoothly and effortlessly, sending it unerringly into a small paper cup on its side.

"What can I do for you?" Tidwell waved his visitor to the chair by the desk with his putter.

"I'm Henry Carlson."

"You're the old codger who shot my client's companion."

"Yes, I'm that old codger."

"Well, well. So you're the guy? Call me Chip. Everybody does."

"I take it your short game is your forte, Chip."

"Deadly, but I tend to spray my drives at times. Is there something you wished to discuss with me?"

"Yes. May I see the list of jury choices?"

"I don't see why you're concerned about the matter. Oh, what the hell. It's not classified. Sure, I'll get it for you."

Tidwell searched the files behind him, located a file folder, and handed the list to Carlson, who looked down at it carefully.

"How'd you let Kendall sandbag you, young man?"

"What do you mean?" Tidwell became upset.

"There are ten males on this jury."

"Males, females, nowadays, it's all the same. I don't go for that time-consuming selection crap. Nobody knows how a member of the jury will react. Unless a jury prospect is openly hostile to my client, one is as good as another."

"How do you figure Rhinehardt's chances?"

"Bad. Kendall needs this one. He wants to be governor."

"Everyone says the same thing—Kendall has him dead to rights. Why bother with a trial?" Carlson asked in exasperation.

"Oh, everyone's entitled to his defense. I just wish they hadn't stuck me with it."

"Losing a sure thing to the DA can't hurt you, Chip."

"It won't. It's just that the damn trial might run into the club championships, and my game's just where I want it."

That night, Henry Carlson didn't get to sleep until almost dawn. Jasmin was in deep trouble, and it was time for old codgers to get together.

His sisters were shocked to see him so soon after his previous visit. They knew of the attempt on his life, and they hoped he was finally coming to his senses and moving back to New York City.

"See?" Ruth scolded. "They talk about crime in New York, but you go into the wilderness to get killed."

"We got a call from your son," Sarah added. "He said he'd get you out of that hovel even if he has to go to court and have you declared incompetent."

"Tell him to stay away from me if he knows what's good for him."

"What *did* you come here for?" Ruth asked.

"To see you, dear sisters."

"What are you really up to?" Sarah asked.

"I was thinking of visiting my old friend, Max Muncrief."

Jazzy was no longer in a county jail. In his new prison, security was tighter and the prisoners more hardened. Some had been caged up so long, they resembled caged predators at the zoo.

Life in prison, as depicted on stage and screen, came close to reality. There was the constant threat of assault, robbery, rape, and murder. Through the underground, Jazzy was *measured*. The finding was that he was broke, didn't smoke, had no friends, and belonged to no gang with outside connections to the narcotic trade. Despite his involvement in two murders, he was a straight arrow. Still, because of those murders, he was the current main attraction. Devlin would've been better.

Jazzy was left alone. He wasn't approached for gang membership, and, if there were rapists with him, they didn't make themselves known.

There was one man, however, who made Jazzy's life in that primeval environment unbearable. His name was George Havlik—the captain of detention for day-shift officers.

His hate for Jazzy was open, and his nightstick was ready every time their paths crossed. The heavy rappings across Jazzy's legs and buttocks were unwarranted. Even hardened veterans grumbled about it.

A sociologist would've had a field day with Havlik, but it was very simple. He punished Jazzy, because he hated himself. He'd grown fat and bald, while his wife was still attractive. He felt he was losing her to another man, and, in his mental anguish, the slick-looking newcomer with two murders hanging over his head was the embodiment of all other men who broke up happy homes. Havlik had trouble separating fact from fiction.

Jazzy felt abandoned. He hadn't heard from his mother, which rankled, although, in view of his enemies, maybe that was best. He thought his friendships in Rochester ran deep, but he hadn't received even a sympathy note in the mail. Surely, his coworkers at Gomes could've made friendly contact with him.

He was being unfair. His mother hadn't even heard of his incarceration. Murders committed more than two thousand miles away weren't considered newsworthy.

In Rochester, Goodman Street was in an uproar, and Jim Logan organized a signature-gathering crew on a petition to Buffalo's city fathers, demanding Jazzy's release.

At Gomes, Doc and Phil had several talks, planning the best way to help Jazzy. While recounting the meeting with Jazzy the night of the murder at the bowling alley, Rosalind cried. That started a chain reaction, and Bea and Nellie soon joined her.

Henry Carlson was admitted into the brownstone by his old friend and led to the back of the building, where four chairs and a small, round table sat in the center of a tiny plot of yard, heavily shrubbed. It was a surprising oasis of green encapsulated by cement walls.

Max Muncrief was working on his memoirs. After a career as celebrated as Henry's, he, too, retired. At one time, he'd been the dean of criminal lawyers. Law schools throughout the country used his textbooks.

"You have no idea how happy I am to see you, old friend," Max said, producing a pot of tea, scones, and marmalade.

The two men sat there, quite content, talking of the old days.

"There's something on your mind, Henry," Max said finally. "What is it?"

"I have a young friend who's in serious trouble. He will be tried for murder, and he's as innocent as either of us."

"You have information the authorities don't?"

"He saved my life!"

"Wait a minute. Is this the case where a bowling alley owner and a minister were slain?"

Carlson nodded.

"Damn. I never associated you with that one. They must've mentioned your name. What happened, Henry?"

Carlson took his time and stated the case from the beginning. When he finished, Muncrief sat in contemplative silence awhile.

"The evidence is damning, Henry. There must be more to it, or you wouldn't be here."

"Yes, I know. I'm not a psychologist, but every playwright worth his salt has considerable knowledge of human behavior. Max, why would that young man be an accomplice to the murder of a businessman and a man of the cloth, then risk his life to save me?"

"You make a good point, Henry. It bothers me, too. I'd like to accompany you back to Buffalo and talk to your friend. After all, this *is* my ballpark, and I find myself itching to get back into the game."

"Will you, Max?"

"I can hold off the publishers for a while, and I don't have a speaking engagement for another month. What are you waiting for? Help me clean up. We're catching a train."

They reached Buffalo and rented a room. After unpacking their bags, they took a cab to the detention center. Jazzy was allowed only one visitor at a time, so Henry stayed in the atrium while Muncrief introduced himself. Henry waited patiently for a long time. Finally, Muncrief came out.

"Let's go," Muncrief said. "We have work to do. Your friend has accepted my services, so let's pick up the necessary files from the court-appointed counselor."

They went to Chip Tidwell's office and caught him just as he was leaving. Henry introduced Max, who showed Tidwell his retaining forms. Tidwell turned over the files.

"That's a relief," Tidwell said. "I was about to withdraw from the club championships."

When word got out of the change in defense lawyers, and that Max Muncrief, the living legend, would defend Jasmin Rhinehardt, the case took on a new dimension. When it was also learned that the old recluse who coolly dispatched the murderer of two men, using a double-barreled shotgun, was Henry Carlson, the famous dramatist, the case became a *cause celebre.* It was front-page news. For the first time, doubt was injected into the assumed guilt of the handsome youth in detention.

Barry Kendall took the news hard. He depended on that case for his future plans. He cursed himself for his boorish attitude with Henry and knew how much of a foe he now faced in court.

Carlson and Muncrief made themselves comfortable, both feeling tired. They lay on their beds and spoke easily, as old friends did.

"Well, what do you think of the young man?" Henry asked.

"You're right, he's a handsome devil, and you were right to be concerned about there being ten men on the jury. We can't do anything about that now. Besides his obvious good looks, there's an air of gentility about him. He looks vulnerable, almost fragile, but I suspect there's surprising toughness about him."

"It's the men I'm worried about."

"There is that factor."

"Which one?"

"My colleagues call it the Valentino Factor."

"Who could forget him?"

"Old Rudy came on the American scene like a hurricane and made love slaves of almost every woman in the country."

"He may've been big with the ladies, but men hated his guts," Carlson added.

"Exactly. Biographers even now are trying to destroy his image. Ethnic slurs didn't work, and reference to his life as a gigolo didn't work, so they settled on a campaign to make him appear less than a man. They cite two marriages, which they claim were never consummated."

"Let's hope the jury reaches a decision on the merits of the case. We have a few things going for us, the most important of which is his innocence."

Chapter Twenty-Five

Havlik's puzzling hatred for Jazzy was out in the open. At every opportunity, he prodded, poked, and slapped him with his nightstick. Jazzy bore the pain of the physical abuse, but his outrage of the harassment grew. Each day, his self-control became less. He sorely wanted to take the stick from his tormentor and beat him with it, but that would jeopardize his chances for acquittal.

It had been a particularly trying day. Muncrief appealed for a change in venue, arguing that the immense coverage by newspaper, radio, and TV, plus the large disparity in the gender makeup of the jury, precluded a fair trial for his client. Muncrief would've liked another jury, but the appeal was denied.

Phil Paugh's visit came at a most opportune time, when Jazzy was feeling the most depressed.

"How are they treating you, Jazzy?"

"Not too bad," he lied. "It's no social club, and the chef isn't Pierre."

"All your friends at Gomes' want you to know we're pulling for you. The case against you is stupid. The DA's brains must be up his ass."

"How's the old gang?"

"A lot has happened since you left. Goose is dead."

"Oh, no! I liked the old fellow."

"He was quiet in his cubicle all afternoon, but nobody thought anything of it. You know how he dozed for long periods of time. Then he tipped over and fell to the floor. When Polly looked down at her feet, she saw Goose's dead eyes staring up at her. His head was almost in her cubicle. She screamed so loudly, Doc Rivera and I heard her out in the yard."

"Poor Polly."

"Yeah. She's had a bad time. Your problem hit her hard. She was telling everyone the two of you were going steady. With her twisted logic, she took your troubles personally, as if it were an annoyance you deliberately bestowed on her."

"That's true love," Jazzy said sarcastically.

"I really think she loved you, in her own way. Once, when Rosalind went back to the boiler room, she found Polly sitting there, staring at the phone, crying."

"She'll get over it."

"She already has. She and the blond salesman from the chemical warehouse are now a hot item."

"How's Otto doing?"

Phil looked sad. "Not so good, Jazzy. He's back in."

"Back in where?"

"Don't you know? Otto's in and out of the state hospital constantly."

"I didn't know. I thought he was as zany as anyone I ever met. That safety pin on his fly was something else."

"That's his way of protesting."

"Against what?"

"His father."

"A child beater?"

"Mr. Grundt? No way. We lived in the same neighborhood. That's why I'm so protective of Otto. Something happened to him, and he feels his father is his mortal enemy. Nothing could be further from the truth. Mr. Grundt is a successful businessman and a gentle soul who feels for his son."

"Why the scarecrow clothes and safety pin?"

"In his troubled mind, Otto feels the more he degrades himself, the more he punishes his father."

"How are Carlo and Nellie?" Jazzy wanted to change the subject.

"*Mucho* trouble. Remember Bea? What a prize she turned out to be. She ran around with that south-side crowd. While Carlo cheated on Nellie, Bea cheated on Carlo."

"Don't tell me—with Bob Petrillo, right?"

"Right. On Carlo's birthday, she gave the boss a gift."

"You mean…?"

"Gonorrhea. It was inevitable the way she spread herself around."

"I'll bet that started a war."

"It sure did. Nellie gave Carlo no peace."

"She's staying with him?"

"Nellie isn't someone to cross, but she's a practical old shrew. Without the business, she's nothing."

"Does Carlo know about Bob?"

"Oh, yes. At first, he made threats, telling anyone who'd listen what he'd do to Bob. Would you believe they're now close friends, and Bob has replaced Rick in Carlo's scheme of things? Here's the kicker—they both take the treatments."

Jazzy watched Phil leave, and a wave of sadness came over him.

In the courtroom, Muncrief turned to Jazzy. "Don't you have any relatives?"

"I have a mother."

"Where is she? Which one?" He looked around the room.

"She's not here."

"Not here? Damn it, Rhinehardt, don't you folks realize you're in deep trouble? Get her here fast. Have her here every time court's in session. I like a grieving mother seated near the jury. I want them to see her grief."

"I can't do that. She's in California."

Muncrief stared in disbelief. "Give me her address. I'll see she gets here. This is insane. Your mother's place is beside you."

"Mr. Muncrief, I don't know where she lives."

Muncrief was angry, but Jazzy didn't want Jennie where the hoods from Niagara Falls could get her. It was enough that he had a long incarceration ahead—or, if he were freed, an execution.

When he saw the woman come in and sit in the courtroom, he stared. Something nagged at his memory. She wore a stylish pantsuit, and her hair was swept back, held in place with a whalebone comb.

She had the bronzed look of a Hollywood starlet. When she took her seat, she smiled at him, and he smiled back, still wondering.

Barry Kendall built his case against Jazzy with infinite care. He established conclusively Rick ran from the bowling alley at the precise time witnesses inside the building saw him shoot the proprietor.

His witness testified she heard the shot from her car, and the man who ran out of the building was the same man in the prosecutor's photographs. In addition, she was positive the driver of the car was Jasmin Rhinehardt. She had the presence of mind to jot down the license plate number when she saw Rick dive into the car.

Her testimony was hard to discredit, but Muncrief tried. "Young lady, I went to the scene of the crime. The streetlight wasn't only across the street, it was twenty yards…"

"There was plenty of light," she replied. "I'd know him anywhere."

"How's that?"

"Because he's terribly good-looking."

Kendall smiled.

The next day, Barry Kendall had a regiment of state troopers ready to testify. They all said the same thing, telling of the discovery of Jazzy's car at the bottom of a ravine. They told of the body they found, positively identified as the reverend, near the car. In detail, they inventoried every bit of clothing found on Rick Devlin. They showed the car keys, wallet, and watch he stole, then they brought out Devlin's own clothing, found in a shallow hole by the side of the road, covered with stones and dirt.

The laundry marks, with exhaustive detective work, sealed the question of ownership. Muncrief showed considerable interest in Devlin's clothes. He asked for and received permission to view them up close before Kendall took them to the jury for viewing.

Then Kendall had the troopers testify that, in the rough terrain with its upward slope to the precipice, it would've taken two men to roll the car to the edge and push it over. Muncrief objected and was overruled.

The attractive young woman was back, sitting in the same seat as before. His curiosity and desire to know more about her mounted. He called Henry Carlson and asked if he'd find out who she was.

Henry was amused. In a courtroom, where Jazzy's freedom hung in the balance, Jazzy was interested in a girl sitting in the hall.

Jazzy saw Carlson speak with her, and, although he couldn't hear her, he saw her laugh. Henry returned to the dock.

"Her name is Rachel Springwater," he told Jazzy.

"Springwater? That sounds like an American-Indian name. Why, it's the Indian girl!" He turned and waved, and she blew him a kiss as she had at the carnival grounds.

Muncrief watched Carlson speak to the woman for his client, and he realized Rhinehardt was definitely a lady's man. The ten men on the jury, all blue-collar workers, bothered him more than they did Carlson.

"Henry," he told his friend, "the kid's just too damn good-looking."

Henry told Rachel when Jazzy's visiting hours were, and she came to see him the next Saturday. It was raining, and she wore a topcoat with raglan sleeves and a turned-up collar. No matter what she wore, it was always the height of fashion.

She unbuttoned her coat as she sat down before the telephone to talk with Jazzy. She was certainly no child. Her maturity was apparent in the delightful fit of her loose-knit but tight turtleneck sweater.

"I didn't recognize you in the courtroom, Rachel," Jazzy said. "The girl I saw at the carnival in casual clothes, romping with her young friends, isn't the dream I see before me. You're beautiful. You should've been called Ramona. That's something we can talk about when we get together."

"Are we really getting together?" she asked.

Her directness startled him. It was something he'd get used to.

"Of course we are. When you disappeared into the crowd, and I couldn't locate you, I thought I'd lost you forever."

"I'm so glad you feel that way."

"You must've come a long way each day. Is it curiosity?"

"No, it's just you I came to see."

He longed to hold her. "I want you here when the jury reaches its verdict. If it's good news, I'll fly with you wherever you wish."

Jazzy was touched when Nippy Koven came to see him.

"Miss Laura got signed by the Met," Nippy said. "She's gonna marry a famous conductor, too."

"Wow! How's the old gang, Nippy?"

"Up in arms, old buddy. Slim and Jim are spearheading a drive to get people to sign petitions to stop the trial. They say the charges are trumped up. Jim got the mayor to write a strong letter to the DA in Buffalo, criticizing your arrest."

"I know. My lawyer has a copy of it. How's Marve?"

"Not saying much. He's changed. Something's eating him."

"Does he mention me?" Jazzy asked bitterly.

"When he first came back, he said you got involved with some rough people."

Jazzy concealed his anger.

"Lou got married." Nippy was glad to change the subject.

"Moon's brother?"

"Yeah. He talked his mother into giving him her blessing."

"I'll bet it was some reception."

"Who knows? None of us were there."

"What happened?"

"The girl's parents controlled the affair, and they didn't want us lower-class people around."

"I'm surprised at Lou, letting them get away with that."

"Poor Moon. He's mortified. He apologized to each of us."

"Moon's all right. By the way, how's Chris Morgana doing?"

"I gotta tell you, the whole town demanded a fight between Chris and Hughie, but Bourda stalled."

"I agree. Chris isn't ready."

"The activities committee at the Elks Club felt differently. Interest was at a fever pitch, and they wanted that match."

"Did they fight?"

"Did they? It was a donnybrook. We were all there, and we sprung for ringside seats. It was the biggest thing in Goodman history."

"Did Chris make a good showing? Tell me he did."

"He sure did. It was the most exciting fight I ever saw. Hughie piled up so many points and cut Chris up so bad, under normal conditions, the fight would've stopped. It was a blood-letting. Chris crashed his powerful left whenever things looked their worst, and Hughie had to grab and hold to stay in. The referee was thinking of ending it when, in the fourth round, Chris brought that left hand up from somewhere near the floor, and Hughie was still out after the count."

"I hope Hughie's all right." Jazzy and Hughie were close.

"He's back in the ring, working out."

"Chris must be the toast of the town. What's next for him?"

"That ain't the end of the story. Sweet Georgie made so much noise, they gave him a match with Chris."

"What was the outcome of that?"

"Maybe Hughie took a lot out of Chris, and maybe the pros are right that Sweet Georgie has something special. He's a master, and he cut Chris up so bad, he's carrying a lot of scars. They stopped the fight in the third. Chris' left ear still rings, and he might lose part of his hearing."

"Damn it! Why didn't they listen to Bourda?"

"Chris is through. Good old Jay Bright. You know what a nice guy he is? He hired Chris to work with him. When Jay gets his second truck, Chris will drive it."

"I appreciate you coming all this way to see me, Nippy."

"It's the least I can do. I owe you a lot, Friend."

"You don't owe me a thing."

"You scolded me for playing outfield when I'm an infielder."

"I have to learn to keep my mouth shut, especially in matters I know nothing about."

"No, no. It was the best damn advice I ever got. This summer, I played for the Sodus Bay team in the Muni League, and I went back to the infield to play shortstop. There was a scout in the stands, and he liked what he saw and called his boss. The club secretary came, and I pulled off some more nifty plays in the next game, too. Now I'm a pro."

"That's great news! I'd like to celebrate with you, but I'm all tied up, as you can see. Who'd you sign with?"

"Dover of the Eastern Shore League. I go south with them in the spring."

"You'll do well. I know it."

"I might even hit one or two out of the park."

"Oh? Got a set of York barbells?"

"No. You know the old expression, *It would be over in Dover?*"

"Can't say I do."

"It's an inside joke. Anywhere in baseball, if a batter hits a long ball, and it's caught for an out, he says that. That's because the fences in Dover are short."

"I hope you hit a lot of them in Dover."

"Before I forget, I have a message for you from Bourda."

"What is it?"

"He said to tell Twinkle Toes I know. What does that mean?"

Jazzy was pleased. Bourda knew of his first, and last, fight. "It's another inside joke." Jazzy grew serious. "Heard from my mother? I haven't had one letter from her. I guess I don't exist."

"You're wrong. She made a hysterical call to Ida Belding."

"What's she hysterical about at this late date?"

"She just heard about your troubles. The case reached the coast because of your famous friends."

"I find it hard to believe."

"Yeah? Well, she climbed all over the woman."

"What in hell for?"

"For not telling your mother as soon as we got news. Ida had no way of knowing your mother didn't know."

"That's true," Jazzy said thoughtfully. "She was probably waiting for Mom to open a delicate subject."

"You have a lot of us worried back home. My mother's done some crying. Cripes, Jazz. You were my brother all those years. Dad's miserable."

The bell rang, and the visiting period was over. They looked at each other sadly.

"I'm off, Jazzy," Nippy said with forced levity, "in a cloud of…"

"…heifer dust."

In the recreation yard, Jazzy was warned that two rapists, Collins and Rourke, had him ticketed for rape. They worked as a team. The next day, he learned their identity and started watching for them.

Court would soon be in session. The judge arrived, and Jazzy took a quick look at Rachel at the back of the room. Before he could give her his usual wave, he saw Monti, Hobbs, and Joe Chink sitting among the spectators. Joe's forearm was still in a cast—he should've been out of that by then—so there must've been complications. Jazzy knew they didn't come out of idle curiosity, but to let him know he was remembered.

Jazzy looked away and didn't wave to Rachel after all. He wanted no link between him and Rachel for the mobsters to see. Later, he'd explain to her that bad men were present who constituted a danger.

Barry Kendall wanted to put Carlson on the stand. Muncrief and Carlson discussed strategy, and they decided Henry would reply simply and accurately. There was be no attempt to explain or embellish.

When it came time for rebuttal, Muncrief would pass. Later, when it was time for the defense, they'd do everything they could.

Carlson was called, and Kendall walked up to question him.

"Mr. Carlson, on the day in question, did the deceased, Richard Devlin, and the defendant, Jasmin Rhinehardt, come to your home?"

"Yes, they did."

"They came by car?"

"Yes. They were out of gas and wanted to purchase some."

"Did you notice anything different about them?"

"Different?"

"How were they dressed?"

"The big fellow, Devlin, was dressed as a clergy man, and Rhinehardt had plain trousers, a shirt, and suede shoes."

"How'd they identify themselves?"

"Richard Devlin said he was Reverend James Hamilton. The other said his name was Jasmin Rhinehardt."

"What did Rhinehardt say was his relationship with Devlin?"

"Devlin told me Rhinehardt was a hitchhiker."

"Did you give them gasoline?"

"No, I offered them hospitality first."

"What did that consist of?"

"A jug of wine I keep cool in the root cellar."

"Did they accept it?"

"The defendant did. It was a hot day, and he needed it."

"What about Devlin?"

"He refused the wine."

"Didn't you think that strange?"

"Yes, but then he began lecturing me on the evils of drinking. When I offered to make lunch, they accepted."

"Was it then that the attempt was made on your life?"

"Oh, no. I was preparing lunch when the deceased spied the revolver on the shelf above the kitchen sink."

"Did he menace you with it?"

"On the contrary. He lectured me on violence and how guns beget violence."

"What did you tell him, Mr. Carlson?"

"He asked me if I'd use the weapon on a human being, and I told him yes. I said I kept a loaded gun for my protection."

"Then?"

"He picked up the gun, fondled it, and began telling me a parable."

"When did Richard Devlin make an attempt on your life?"

"I'm telling you the sequence of events exactly as I recall them. I did a very foolish thing. I was tired of his sermons, and I told him to stop, as I knew he was a fraud."

"That wasn't very bright."

"No, it wasn't. He told me I was smart, but that it was dumb to be smart sometimes. He pulled the trigger several times. Of course, the gun was empty."

"What did you do then?"

"I rushed into the closet behind me to get my loaded shotgun."

"What was Devlin doing while you made that move?"

"He dropped the gun. His hand went for his switchblade."

"You got him first?"

"In the nick of time—with both barrels."

It went too well. No attempt was made to bring into the narrative Rhinehardt's bruises and scalp wounds. There was no testimony of Jazzy's attempt to defend Carlson, either.

To Kendall's puzzlement, Muncrief passed his chance to cross-examine, being content with Carlson's appearance later for the defense. That gave Kendall concern—Max Muncrief was once the Toscanini of the courtroom.

Chapter Twenty-Six

The judge called for a recess, and Muncrief was lost in thought.

"What is it, Max?" Carlson asked.

"I may have to go your way, Henry."

"Which way is that?"

"Put Rhinehardt on the stand."

"Why the change of heart?"

"Do you see the glaring weakness in our case? The question remains—what was Rhinehardt doing with Devlin at the bowling alley, his motor running?"

"Waiting for Devlin, who told our young friend he was getting money from someone who owed it to him."

"You know that, and I know that, because we believe him. The only one who can testify to that is Jasmin Rhinehardt."

"And the only way you can introduce the evidence is to put him on the stand?"

"If only someone else knew of Devlin's duplicity," Muncrief mused.

"There's someone else who knew all about it," Jazzy offered.

"What?" both men exclaimed.

"Rosalind knows."

"Who's Rosalind?" Muncrief asked in excitement.

"Who, Jazzy?" Carlson added.

"She worked next to me at Gomes. I locked the office that night, and Rick was with me in the car. Before I could start the motor, Rosalind came driving in and asked me to unlock the door for her, because she left her utility bill and personal check in her desk."

"What was Devlin doing?" Muncrief asked.

"He sat in the car, waiting for me."

"Did you tell her you were going to the Bowlodrome with him to pick up money from his friend?"

"Yes, I did. Rosalind yelled at me for being with Rick, because she said he was no good. I told her about Rick's proposition to go to California, too. When he suggested I contribute my car, and he'd pay the expenses, I refused."

"What did she say?" Muncrief asked.

"She asked what he was doing in my car, and I replied I couldn't refuse him a lift to the alleys."

"I'll ask you once more—did you actually tell this woman you were going to the Bowlodrome and why?"

"Yes, to give Rick a lift there."

"Young man, why didn't you tell me about her before?"

"I'm sorry. Rosalind never crossed my mind."

Muncrief was asking only for actual expenses, but Carlson found even that was becoming a financial burden. That was why he was pleasantly surprised when the character witnesses from Rochester refused any money for the trip.

First, Muncrief asked Jim Logan to the stand. He told of his long friendship with the accused and explained how the entire neighborhood held Jazzy in high esteem. He was gentle, always the arbiter in arguments among the boys of Goodman Street.

Logan gave a detailed account of his solicitation for signatures on a petition to release Jasmin Rhinehardt, because the charges were a mockery of justice. Muncrief strode up and down, flaunting the stacks of papers which, he claimed, were signatures so numerous, they constituted the voice of an entire city.

Then came Slim Broadway, dressed in a suit for the first time in Jazzy's memory. He told of Jazzy's loving care of Maria Martorana in her final days. Particularly impressive was the information that Jazzy paid for the old woman's funeral with no chance of reimbursement.

Father Weideman, round, cheerful, and exuding sincerity, spoke glowingly of the defendant's Christian ethics. He talked of Jazzy's mother, who'd been a member of the church.

The testimony of the delegation from Rochester was most impressive, and Barry Kendall's cross-examinations, hoping to uncover an off-key note in the harmony of the witnesses, came up empty.

Little Phil Paugh, speaking of his friend, Jazzy, showing the education and intelligence Jazzy admired in him, was very effective. He told the court about Richard Devlin and how the others at Gomes feared him. In addition to testimony of the giant's size and strength, he told of Devlin's skill and accuracy with a switchblade.

Muncrief put Rosalind on the stand, and Barry Kendall's intelligent eyes showed apprehension. The character witnesses were predictable. Even Phil wasn't much of a surprise, but some sixth sense told Barry that the corpulent young woman before him was an important witness and could conceivably determine the outcome of the trial.

"What is your name, please?" Muncrief began.

"Rosalind Granville." Her little-girl voice surprised everyone.

"Do you know the defendant?"

"Yes, I do. We worked at adjoining desks at Gomes Pest."

"Are you aware of the tragic affair at the Bowlodrome?"

"Yes, I am."

"Do you have some information that will shed light on this case?"

"Yes, I do."

"Good. When was the last time you saw the defendant?"

"Just before the shooting at the Bowlodrome that evening."

"What was the occasion of that meeting?"

"I left my utility bill with my personal check, with which I was to pay the bill the next morning, in my desk. After supper, I went back after the envelope with the bill and check. I was concerned about the check."

"Was the office still open when you arrived?"

"No, but Mr. Rhinehardt was still in the yard, preparing to leave for the evening. He carried all the keys to the office."

"Was he alone?"

"No. Richard Devlin was in his car with him. Before Mr. Rhinehardt could start the motor, I hailed him and told him my problem, and he agreed to let me into the building."

"While the defendant was letting you into the building, where was Mr. Devlin?"

"Sitting in the car, waiting for Rhinehardt."

"Did you and Mr. Rhinehardt have a discussion?"

"Yes, we did."

"What did you discuss?"

"I was angry with him for being with Richard. I told him Devlin was no good and to stay clear of him. I asked what Devlin was doing in his car."

"What was his reply?"

"To take Rick to the Bowlodrome."

"Did he say why?"

"I asked him point-blank what was going on. He said his desire to see his mother in San Diego was no secret, and Devlin urged him to leave with him. Rhinehardt would furnish the car, and Devlin would provide the money. When I told him Devlin was broke, he said Rick had a friend at the Bowlodrome who owed him money. I told him he was a fool. Devlin would ditch him and leave him stranded."

"What was Rhinehardt's reply?"

"He laughed and said his mother didn't raise an idiot. There was no way he'd travel cross-country with Rick Devlin."

"Was that the last time you saw either of them?"

"Yes, it was."

"Thank you, Miss Granville."

"Please stay seated," the judge said. To Kendall, he called, "Your witness."

Rosalind's testimony was a serious setback for the prosecutor. He preferred to have Jazzy take the stand. It would've been far easier to discredit the accused than a witness who wasn't personally involved with the crime.

"Miss Granville," Kendall began, "you made some rather hostile statements about the late Richard Devlin. Am I to assume you disliked him?"

"No, dislike's not the word. I hated him."

"That's strong, Miss Granville. Tell the court why you hated him."

"For the same reason everyone else did. He was evil."

"Miss Granville, if he was so evil, why was he employed at Gomes Pest and Home Services?"

"I asked myself that many times."

"Surely, you can think of some reason why Richard Devlin was on your employer's payroll."

"He was a gifted salesman. When he wanted to, he could sell anything to anyone."

Kendall smiled. "Then he could sell Jasmin Rhinehardt on anything."

"No. Only if it was moral and right!"

The judge smiled, Kendall frowned, and Muncrief chuckled. The witness was a true find.

"Miss Granville, what was your relationship with Jasmin Rhinehardt?"

"I know where you're heading, and I'll save you time. Most women are strongly attracted to the accused, but he's the kind of man who, if you can't be his girl, you're content to be a good friend."

"I take it you'd do anything for a friend?"

"Almost anything, Mr. Kendall, but I'd never lie."

Kendall retreated. It wasn't a good day for him.

The informant's warning proved valid. It was Sunday, and all the prisoners were leaving the recreation yard, heading back to their cells.

Jazzy was leaving the softball field with the others. He made use of every opportunity for physical exercise.

"Come back here, Pretty Boy!"

Jazzy heard Havlik's angry voice behind him.

"Where the hell do you think you're going? Get the damn bases and carry them to the equipment shed."

Jazzy returned and pulled hard on each base, which was anchored firmly to the ground with metal spikes. It was a clumsy job, and two men usually did it.

Havlik waited for an objection, but Jazzy managed to carry them by placing one under each arm and cradling the third before him. He entered the shed and deposited the bases, then the light from the door was suddenly blocked by the two rapists.

Jazzy couldn't believe the two, standing in the doorway, would try anything in broad daylight, but he was wrong. Collins closed the door behind him, and the only light in the shed came from a small window in the back. There was no room for Jazzy to evade a rush, but the restricted quarters also made it impossible for the two men to rush him together.

Rourke came at him first. Jazzy hit him with a hard right that felled him and knocked him out. Then he hit Collins with a left hook to his right eye. Collins screamed in pain, holding both hands over the eye that immediately started swelling. A short, straight right finished him, too.

Jazzy was standing over them when the room became bright with sunshine again. Someone had opened the door.

Then everything went black.

When he awoke, he was in the infirmary. His head throbbed, and, when he touched the lump on the side of his head, the pain was so intense, he bit his lip to keep from crying out.

A doctor poked and probed, putting him through the usual reflex tests. He looked into Jazzy's eyes with a tiny shaft of light from a small flashlight.

The skin of the scalp wasn't broken, so the nurse took him in hand, put soothing salve on the lump, and wrapped gauze around Jazzy's head. He was to be watched for twenty-four hours.

Judge Vance rapped his gavel and looked up, seeing the bandage around Jazzy's head. "What happened to your client?"

Muncrief rose. "Your Honor, this is but another moment in the continuing saga of my client's personal Stations of the Cross. What we have here is a stain on the reputation of your fair city."

"I object, Your Honor!" Kendall said.

"To what do you object, Mr. Kendall? He's answering a question I put to him. However, Mr. Muncrief, we can dispense with the bombast and get on with it."

"It has come to my attention just this morning," Muncrief explained, "that a Mr. Havlik, the chief of corrections officers, has been heaping mental and physical abuse on my client in some unexplained campaign against him.

"When my client was returning to his cell after the recreation period, he was called back by Mr. Havlik and made to return the softball bases to the shed. Two other prisoners, Collins and Rourke, both dangerous rapists, cornered my client in the shed. That in itself is a dangerous breach of security. Homosexuality is a fact of life in prisons, and the forcible rape of men by other men is common.

"The rapists attempted to attack my client, but he, fighting with the fury of a man protecting himself from beasts intent on committing acts of depravity on him, subdued them.

"Although it was obvious what transpired, Mr. Havlik laid his stick to my client's head. He may have a concussion."

"This distresses me," Judge Vance said. "Mr. Kendall, find out what this is about and report back to me."

Kendall was seething. The incident would severely hurt his standing with the jury. Before the day was out, the rapists were in solitary, and

Havlik was demoted to simple corrections officer and given two week's suspension without pay.

Later, Henry Carlson commiserated with Jazzy about his bad experience, but Muncrief took a brighter view of the attack.

"You know, Henry," Muncrief said, "this might be a plus for us. Maybe I make too much of personalities in court cases, but did you notice how mad Kendall was when I told the judge how our young friend got his head bashed? He believes impressions are important. I feel a little better about the rednecks on the jury."

"Do you think it really has a bearing?" Carlson asked hopefully.

"Who knows? Maybe, just maybe, they don't see him in a Noel Coward drawing-room comedy. They might even see him as Charles Bickford fighting crime in some metropolis."

"Or Randolph Scott cleaning up a frontier town with only his horse and six-shooter?"

"You get the picture."

The moment had come. Muncrief briefed his friend thoroughly, because Jazzy's freedom rode on the outcome.

"Mr. Carlson," he began, "you testified the deceased identified himself as Reverend James Hamilton."

"Yes, that's true," Carlson replied.

"As we all know now, he was assuming another man's identity. Tell me, Mr. Carlson, when you asked the accused for his name, what was his reply?"

"Jasmin Rhinehardt."

"Jasmin Rhinehardt? That's not an assumed name."

"No. He told the truth."

"What does that suggest to you?"

"That he had no reason to hide his identity."

"I object, Your Honor," Kendall said. "That's an assumption with no substantive basis."

"Objection sustained."

"Mr. Carlson, in your previous testimony, you said the deceased indicated he'd picked up Mr. Rhinehardt on the road, and that he was a hitchhiker. Did you believe that?"

"Oh, no. He wore fancy shoes with soles so thin, it would make walking the highways impossible."

"Then you believe the two were accomplices?"

"No. There were bruises on the defendant's face and a cut on his lip. He was with Devlin, not by choice, but in fear of his life."

The DA rose to object, and Muncrief quickly produced blow-ups of media pictures showing Jazzy's face when he was taken into custody. "Like this, Mr. Carlson?"

"I object!" Kendall said. "The witness is dealing with assumptions again."

"Sustained. Strike that from the record."

"Do you believe my client is guilty of these charges?"

"No, I don't."

Kendall stood again, but the judge waved him off.

"I have to allow a little leeway here," Judge Vance said. "I can't stifle all the testimony for the defense. You may continue, but let's deal in realities, Counselor."

"Mr. Carlson, tell the court why you believe the defendant is innocent."

"Because Jasmin Rhinehardt warned me against Richard Devlin."

There was a surprised murmur in the gallery, and Kendall became wide-eyed.

"Mr. Carlson," Judge Vance said, "there has been no indication in any previous testimony of a dialogue of that nature between the defendant and you."

"That's because the dialogue is of such a subtle and sensitive nature, Mr. Kendall wouldn't deign to pursue it."

Muncrief smiled. Everything was on schedule.

"You must explain that for us, Mr. Carlson," Muncrief said.

"Before I came to you for assistance for Mr. Rhinehardt's trial, Mr. Muncrief, I went to Barry Kendall."

"To what purpose?"

"To explain about this same dialogue I'm about to include in my testimony."

"What was the result of your visit to Barry Kendall's office?"

"He cut me off, rudely and abruptly, saying he had no time for flights of fancy."

A murmur swept the room again.

"Tell us, then, Mr. Carlson, with the bogus reverend present, how was this remarkable communication achieved?"

"I was praising Devlin of his ability to speak, and I took my hat off to him. I, in that area, was regarded as a silver-tongued orator and a regular Scattergood Baines."

"Will you explain who Scattergood Baines is?"

"He's a fictional character who seems outwardly to be a country bumpkin, but his acumen always foils the city slickers."

"Does this have a bearing on the case, Mr. Carlson?"

"Indeed, it does. Imagine my surprise when the defendant replied he didn't perceive me as Scattergood Baines, but as Clarence Buddington Kelland."

"Please explain that."

"Don't you see? Kelland created the character Scattergood Baines. The young man was telling me he knew I was Henry Carlson, the playwright. I knew something was wrong. Why would a stranger speak in a manner so oblique?"

"Won't you share the conclusion you drew from this?"

"I object to this absurd testimony," Kendall shouted.

"Oh, no, you don't, Mr. Kendall," Judge Vance said. "My curiosity is piqued, and I want to learn where this leads."

"The assumption I made," Carlson continued, "was that Rhinehardt wanted to get my attention. That could only mean he was being vague to get a message to me past the big fellow. Then I had to know. I needed a brutal character to try on the young man, who, I saw, was an avid reader of fiction. I settled on Charles Dickens' villain in the novel *Oliver Twist*."

"Wasn't that risky, engaging Rhinehardt in a dialogue if what you suspected was true?"

"Of course it was. That was why I directed my conversation to Devlin next. I told the big fellow I was struck by the resemblance he bore to someone I once knew named William Sikes. I dare not say Bill Sikes, for fear of stirring his memory to a long-forgotten high school assignment."

"Is that all?" Muncrief asked.

"Oh, no. Now I had to wait for a reply to confirm my fears. Rhinehardt came through promptly saying, 'I knew a William Sikes. He had a girlfriend named Nancy, but she's dead now.' That convinced me. In the Dickens novel, Nancy *was* Bill Sikes' girlfriend, and she died savagely at his hands."

A steady murmur filled the room.

Muncrief savored the moment and stalled. He wanted Carlson to gather himself for the final questioning. "Mr. Carlson, you testified Richard Devlin picked up your revolver. When he learned you were on to his masquerade, he attempted to open fire on you."

"That's true. The gun was empty, and the hammer struck empty chambers."

"Tell me what you did."

"Because Jasmin Rhinehardt had alerted me, Devlin's move came as no surprise. I dashed into the closet behind me, where I kept a loaded shotgun."

"What was the defendant doing while that was taking place?"

"He was saving my life!"

The crowd's mutter rose to a roar.

"Please explain, Mr. Carlson."

"He pleaded with the deceased not to kill me, but he was felled by a blow to the head from the gun. He dropped to the floor but managed to cling to Devlin's legs, forcing the giant to drag him along as he pulled out a switchblade and came at me. I never would've made it if Rhinehardt hadn't slowed him down."

"Thank you, Mr. Carlson." Muncrief was very pleased.

Kendall declined to cross-examine. There was no denying the accused came to the old man's rescue. He'd known that all along, and he refused to give the wily old man another chance to entertain the court at his expense.

Chapter Twenty-Seven

Rachel came to visit. Jazzy was anxious to see her, because the summation was next on the agenda. She wore a pair of red pedal pushers, a white blouse, and a gray sweater. The pedal pushers were snug and fell below the calf, and there was enough ankle and leg exposed to indicate shapely legs.

He marveled at her devotion and felt he'd been touched by the gods. He hadn't so much as held her hand, but he knew, in his heart, he made a commitment. Was he the Jazzy who so assiduously avoided entangling alliances throughout his entire life?

"Rachel, you look marvelous."

"Thank you," she said softly.

"I want to give you the address of my apartment. Go there and pack my bag. Do you have any money?"

"Some."

"Good. I'll reimburse you. As you can see, I can't get it to you now. If the landlord wants money, pay him."

"How much, Jazzy?"

"That depends on how greedy the old fellow is."

"The reason I ask is I have only twenty-five dollars with me."

"Twenty. He must know where I am. Everybody does. He's probably rented the apartment already. If he tries to ask for too much, see Mr. Carlson."

"Is there anything else?"

"Yes. I want you in the courtroom with my bag when the jury returns with a verdict. If the news is bad, keep my belongings. If it's good, we leave together. Do you have a vehicle?"

"I'll have a truck ready."

"Good girl." He gave her the address, and she wrote it down on the back of an envelope.

Barry Kendall was a practical man. His zeal was often mistaken for stubbornness. He was trying Jazzy's case with a vehemence not normally used by his office. He would soon use language stronger than was his custom. It wasn't for political advantage, and the scuttlebutt in the courthouse hall knew it.

The DA was certain in his heart the nice young man was a willing participant in the escapades that resulted in three deaths. In all but his terse Naples deposition, taken before he had time for creativity, the accused had an answer for everything.

He attacked the defense with ridicule and sarcasm, calling it a fiction factory and reminding the jury that histrionics were Max Muncrief's stock in trade. Henry Carlson spent years weaving plot and character.

Kendall called the witnesses loyal but short on reality. He reminded the jury how, after a heinous crime, the neighbors are often shocked and invariably testify that the perpetrator was a model young man everyone liked.

He tore into the area where he'd been hit the hardest—Rosalind's testimony that the defendant told her why he was making the trip to the Bowlodrome with Devlin. If the reason was to get money from an unnamed friend, then leave for California in the morning, why the urgency suggested by parking the car in front of the building with its motor running? The logical thing to do would've been to park the car and have a drink or two with the unnamed friend.

What credence could anyone put in Rhinehardt's testimony to Rosalind? She was forthright in her testimony, but was the defendant forthright with her? He could've been establishing an alibi should things go wrong. Perhaps the real plan had been to leave immediately, not the next morning. Murder wasn't part of the plan, and, in that, Rhinehardt wasn't guilty of murder, but of attempted grand theft.

Kendall stressed evidence. He trotted it out repeatedly until the jury was bombarded with it. He reminded them that the defendant's car, with the motor running, was waiting, with the defendant sitting behind the wheel to drive. Then there was the identification of Devlin running from the building to the waiting car and the flight from the parking lot. He emphasized finding that same car in the ravine. It had to be pushed by both.

He displayed the gruesome pictures showing the extent of the minister's wounds, graphically describing the vicious attack. He told the jury there was no testimony from anyone that showed Rhinehardt tried to stop his companion.

Devlin's clothes, which had been buried, were paraded before the jury. When Kendall made a slow pass along the front row of the jury with the rock with which the clergyman had been struck repeatedly, they recoiled at the sight, just as they had the first time they saw it.

Then he told of the visit of Devlin and Rhinehardt to the home of Henry Carlson. Kendall pointed out that, when the defendant was introduced as a hitchhiker, he didn't try to deny it. The deception was shared by both intruders and wasn't the sole province of the deceased, as Henry Carlson tried so entertainingly to testify. That testimony came under particularly heavy attack.

Kendall freely admitted the accused saved Carlson's life, but the bruises on Rhinehardt's face and head weren't the result of a falling out during the commission of their crimes. They came afterward. What the falling out was about, no one would ever know. Perhaps it changed the accused's role from accomplice to adversary.

Barry Kendall used everything in his legal arsenal in his summation, and his work earned him the grudging respect of Max Muncrief.

Jazzy had faced so many life-threatening situations in the past few months, no single peril held the full implication it deserved. True, he feared what the jury held in store for him. There was no death penalty for the charges he faced, but the possibility of long-term incarceration hung heavily on his mind with every waking moment.

Still, even that didn't bring the feeling of doom it should've. If he survived the trial and gained his freedom, there was an even greater menace awaiting him outside. At such times, he gave serious thought of quitting and handing himself over to whomever fate decreed, but there was Rachel. More than ever, he knew his struggle would continue. He wouldn't give up.

At the beginning, Max Muncrief questioned his client's depth. Jazzy had an air of unconcern over the gravity of his situation. The changing tides of the trial provoked little or no reaction. Then there was the matter of Rosalind—Muncrief learned of her only by chance. Without her testimony, his client would've been in deep trouble.

In his talks with Rhinehardt, it didn't take Muncrief long to confirm what he suspected—Jazzy wasn't only innocent, but he also had high moral standards. The lawyer knew for certain that Jazzy's equanimity wasn't the result of callous indifference or an intelligence insufficient to realize his grave situation. Jazzy was a man with many serious problems.

Henry Carlson had grown fond of the handsome young man, but it was Muncrief who wished Jazzy were his son. He wanted to get past the young man's shields and help him in every possible way to alleviate the heavy burden he carried. He vowed to give the best summation in his power.

Muncrief and Carlson relaxed over tea.

"Kendall came down hard on us," Muncrief said.

"I don't like being called a liar, no matter how well it's put."

"I was waiting for him to suggest to the jury that our man, slender and in fairly good condition, could've detached himself from Devlin sometime during the long night and day—assuming Rhinehardt's heart is as pure as we contend. He had only Devlin's knife to worry about. Running away shouldn't have presented a problem."

"Why didn't he bring it up?"

"When we kept our client off the witness stand, there was no one else around who knew the details of his strange odyssey. Who was Kendall going to interrogate to enter that point into the records? He can't just turn to the jury and say, 'Notice how the accused made no effort to escape.' He could say it in his summation and get away with it, but he didn't."

"There were Rhinehardt's statements taken by various officials. The depositions show he was forcibly detained."

"No way. To show he made no effort to escape would prove he was detained. Kendall doesn't believe any of the depositions."

"That's true. When I visited Kendall in his office, he dismissed Rhinehardt's recitations as something out of *Argosy.*"

"The hobbling didn't appear in the Naples disposition."

"That's probably what Kendall meant when he told me at that meeting that the testimonies didn't match."

"I saw the deposition taken in Naples. Devlin's ingenious containment was reduced to a simple, *bound hand and foot.* Later, in the Buffalo statements, our client's detailed explanations clearly show his being tied with his own shoelaces and hobbled with wiring taken from his own car. I, too, had trouble over that, but you said our young friend came to your house without laces in his shoes."

"That convinced you, didn't it?"

"In a way, but I confess there's a little detective in me. The first chance I got, I called the constable in Naples. I wanted to talk to the person who took down the testimony, and he put her on the phone. She was pleased with my interest in her, and she confided she was taking business courses in school, but shorthand was difficult for her. I'd already spoken to Rhinehardt, who told me that, during his narration of the dreadful events, he often had to pause to allow the young lady to catch up."

"Why didn't you confide in me, Max?"

"Does Holmes tell Watson everything?" Muncrief became pensive. "I wonder, sometimes, if we serve justice when we reduce cases to games won and lost. It bothered me that only you saw the significance of the missing shoelaces. Nor did Kendall give any thought to the missing wiring from the car."

"What will you do now?"

"Nothing, just like Kendall. I don't want to put ideas into the jury's mind that aren't there. Barry Kendall called me a charlatan, and I'll hit him hard for that."

Max Muncrief sipped from his water glass, wiped his glasses with a handkerchief, and walked slowly to the jury box. There was tenseness in the room as everyone waited for the legend to start work.

"Ladies and gentlemen of the jury," he began. "By inference, I've been portrayed as a charlatan. By insinuation, my good friend, Henry Carlson, has been called a liar in his testimony of the events that occurred at his home and almost cost him his life.

"I came out of retirement to defend Jasmin Rhinehardt. To do so, I put my memoirs on hold, incurring the wrath of my publishers. Why have I done this? Certainly not for money. The defendant is destitute. I came out of retirement, because my good friend, Henry Carlson, asked me to, and because, from the beginning, I knew, as Henry did, that Jasmin Rhinehardt is an innocent man.

"There are no rewards for me in the outcome of this trial except the knowledge, should I succeed, that I helped set an innocent man free. I don't covet the office of governor of this state!"

A roar came from the crowded courtroom. Barry Kendall rose, trembling with rage, and Judge Vance rapped his gavel before admonishing Muncrief sternly.

"In my time and my work," Muncrief said, "I saw many like Richard Devlin. He murdered twice and was thwarted in his third attempt when he was slain in an act of self-defense by a gentle man I've known all my life. I will be eternally grateful to Jasmin Rhinehardt, for, without his valiant attempt to stay the killer from a third murder, I most certainly would've lost a friend.

"Who is Jasmin Rhinehardt? More importantly, what is he? Well, according to many friends who came a long way to testify, fellow workers, and thousands of people in Rochester who petitioned this court to drop the charges against him, perceiving them as a flagrant miscarriage of justice, and finally, according to the Honorable Mayor Sheldon of Rochester, who wrote a blistering letter to your district attorney, Jasmin Rhinehardt is an exemplary young man who couldn't possibly be party to the depraved crimes of Richard Devlin.

"Now I know this is in direct contradiction to your erudite district attorney. His essay into the field of sociology is illuminating. Now, if we follow his reasoning, whenever a dastardly crime is committed, all young men of good character are suspect. Certainly, we can't accept that.

"We were told by your esteemed prosecutor the character witnesses were long on loyalty and short on reality. What does he mean? Surely, the no-nonsense testimony of Rosalind Granville wasn't short on reality. It was the one most wonderfully clear insight into the mental state and intentions of Jasmin Rhinehardt the night of the murder.

"Jasmin Rhinehardt refused Devlin's pact. He was required to furnish his car, and Devlin the money, for expenses incurred on the road. Where would that money come from? Miss Granville asked that, because she knew Devlin was without funds. My client told her of the friend at the bowling alley who owed Devlin money. His driving the deceased to the Bowlodrome was an act of kindness, because Devlin had no transportation. He felt an obligation to give Devlin a lift after refusing his pact. If my client intended to participate in a holdup, it would've been folly to divulge that to a potential witness. Ladies and gentlemen of the jury, the moment a shot was fired inside that building, Jasmin Rhinehardt became a hostage.

"The entire constabulary seems to have testified, repeatedly, to the same facts presented as evidence—clothing, a blood-stained rock, and pictures of the reverend's ugly wounds. Barry Kendall did a most thorough job, but Richard Devlin's dead and can't be tried. All that evidence has nothing to do with Jasmin Rhinehardt.

"I hope you folks were impressed with the testimony of Slim Broadway, the restauranteur, as I was. From his testimony, we learn of my client's generosity, both of time and money, to an old woman who was his neighbor. It was a fine display of magnanimity, depleting what was left of his resources to pay for the old woman's funeral. Is that the kind of man who's so greedy for money he participates in a holdup? I think not.

"Barry Kendall has attempted to link Jasmin Rhinehardt to Richard Devlin. Rhinehardt was a hostage, not an accomplice. Had my client been party to the attempted holdup and slaying of the proprietor of the bowling alley, had he been an accomplice to the murder of the reverend, had he been an accomplice to all that, why then would the attempted murder of a third party, one who was a perfect stranger, horrify him so much that he risked his life to abort the attempt. Evidently, the prosecutor's knowledge of human nature is limited.

"Your district attorney was abusive to my good friend, Henry Carlson, calling his testimony a product of a fiction factory. I must ask the jury to think back to the judge's question to Mr. Carlson about the lack of any previous testimony regarding communications between my client and Mr. Carlson. If you recall, Mr. Carlson replied that the dialogue was of such a sensitive nature that Mr. Kendall wouldn't deign to pursue it.

"Mr. Kendall isn't obtuse, but you all know the quotation from Swift's *Polite Conversation,* 'There's none so blind as they that won't see.'

"Buffalo has kept my client incarcerated far too long. You've held the sword of Damocles over his head, and his life has been one of constant fear and nightmares. Should your district attorney cut the fine thread that holds that sword, each of you will be guilty of the worst abomination—the persecution and prosecution of an innocent man. May God forgive you.

"There has been a veritable avalanche of testimony to the character of the young man sitting before you. So compelling is the testimony from

Rochester and Buffalo, one can't fail to recognize the high moral fiber of Jasmin Rhinehardt.

"What have we learned of this extraordinary young man? We've learned he's a churchgoing member of a small, closely knit community in the northeast corner of Rochester, that he is a stable, level-headed youth, whom his friends seek out as arbiter in their day-to-day squabbles. He loves his friends and neighbors, and surely, no one can doubt their love for him. He's a generous man who unhesitatingly spent his last few hundred dollars to finance the funeral of an old woman to whom he wasn't even related.

"We have the evidence of a letter from the esteemed mayor of Rochester, in which he excoriates, in vitriolic terms, the incarceration of my young client. The mayor's admiration of him is no whit less than mine.

"The signs of violence inflicted by Devlin, were there before the events at the home of Henry Carlson. It had to be not in compliance, but in defiance, he earned those bruises on his face.

"What of the heroic act in saving Henry Carlson's life? To me, this young man, sitting before you, is the prototype of all that's good and wholesome in America's youth. Ladies and gentlemen of the jury, that is the essence of Jasmin Rhinehardt!"

The die was cast, and Jazzy's fate rested in the hands of ten men and two women. If their determination was guilt, he'd be in prison for a long time. His crime was that he drove a fellow worker to meet a friend at the alleys.

If the twelve jurors deemed him innocent, he'd be free to resume his flight from two assassins. What was his crime there? He helped Marve out of a difficult situation. Clearly then, a good Samaritan was a fool.

Jazzy's long stay in prison during the trial gave him the opportunity for some soul-searching. He didn't like what he learned of himself. He was a fraud. His good standing in his neighborhood was based on false premises.

From childhood, he was deemed to possess great potential, but he squandered precious time. Upon his return from the war, which, in itself, wasn't unique, he was given a special aura for his participation in the Battle of the Bulge and for his detention in a prisoner-of-war camp.

He found himself reciting a few lines of poetry from the pen of Corporal Fredman, the camp's poet laureate.

Some men have the daring of a marinated herring
And the vision of a bat in Stygian dark.
The mundane elemental looms so monumental,
And high adventure is an outing in the park.

His prowess in the ring was overblown—Tony Zale with safeguards—a cavalier in a mock war. He enjoyed pitting his skills against others in controlled situations, with big gloves, head gear, and the knowledge his opponents were benign. The Mendez fight was forced on him. To resume his education, however, meant leaving the gang. The Trippetts had the barber shop, Moon his service station, Koven his baseball career, Lovell would practice law, and Logan and Bright were businessmen.

He avoided a commitment with any one of several fine women, because a lasting relationship would keep him from Goodman Street. He played the role of gentleman, but there, too, he was a sham. He was no gentleman. The women deserved more than *wham, bam, thank you, Ma'am.*

Was there another reason, one too painful to contemplate? Did he want a girl just like the girl who married dear old dad? Or had he yearned all those years for the girl herself? He fancied himself Leslie Howard in the movie *Of Human Bondage,* held captive with shackles of the mind—shackles far stronger than those of Joe Chink, Rick Devlin, and the entire Buffalo constabulary.

It took the jury two hours to reach a decision, which indicated unanimity one way or the other.

Depending on the verdict, there was a chance he wouldn't see his prison informer again.

"Tell me, Pal," he whispered to Jazzy, "before you go, who the hell are you?"

"Christ, Mac. The whole world knows who I am."

"You're a pro, right? They're saying the job you did on Collins and Rourke was professional."

Jazzy laughed. "Tell the guys I'm Tony Zale."

The seats in the room were quickly filled. People must've been milling around the corridors while they waited. Rachel was there, with Jazzy's bag, and Joe Chink was there with his henchmen. The cast was off his arm, but he carried it in a black sling tied around his neck. Barry Kendall arrived, accompanied by his coterie of legal assistants. Max Muncrief and Henry Carlson were already seated. Jazzy was escorted to them and sat between them.

"This will make you happy," Muncrief promised, handing Jazzy an envelope.

It was a telegram from his mother

Shed enough tears. Stop. When free come to Mother. Stop. Or Mother comes to you. Stop. Jennie.

He laughed, and his spirits lifted. Her words were terse and to the point. That was Jennie, all right.

A continuing hum of conversation ceased when Judge Vance walked into the room. Everyone stood, then sat when he did and rapped his gavel.

Judge Vance nodded to the bailiff, who went to the side door behind the court stenographer's desk. The jury filed in and took their places in the box.

"Has the jury reached a verdict?" Judge Vance asked.

"Yes, Your Honor," the foreman replied. "We find the defendant innocent on all counts."

A hot rush of relief engulfed Jazzy, and his knees turned weak. He cried quietly as he sat down.

The roar of approval behind him delighted him. He didn't like being known as one who bested the system on legal manipulations, but as one who triumphed on the force of his innocence. Henry pulled him to his feet again, hugging him, then Max reached for him, too.

Over Carlson's shoulder, he saw Rachel wiping her eyes with a handkerchief. Joe Chink and his boys were leaving, but Jazzy was glad they came, because it meant he'd have a brief respite. Buffalo wasn't Joe's bailiwick, and Jazzy's execution wouldn't take place until the crime lord was miles away to establish his noninvolvement. Jazzy would be kept on hold—for a short time.

Rachel pushed her way through the crowd and hugged Jazzy over the short rail. He lifted her over it and fiercely held her. Awkwardly, he tried to thank his benefactors, to whom he owed so much.

"No need to thank me, my boy," Muncrief said. "You're not the only one to hear from your mother."

"Oh?" He was surprised.

"She wired me a retainer, a little late, but generous. You know, I can keep the whole thing. I sure earned it." He wasn't boasting. He spoke with the confidence of a man at the top of his profession.

"Yes, you did." Jazzy didn't begrudge him whatever amount Jennie sent.

"But a deal is a deal, and I won't change the rules just because your mother came into the picture. I was charging Carlson only the amount I spent in Buffalo as personal expenses. I'll do the same with your mother. I'll send back a substantial part of the retainer, though I must say she must be living a good life. I feel like a new man, and, when I get back, I'll have something fresh for my memoirs."

Muncrief put an arm affectionately around Carlson's shoulders. "Come back with me, Henry."

"I will, Max. I never realized how much I missed the excitement of living. Retiring as a recluse is like being dead. Poor Bob Sherwood will turn green with envy. My new play will make his *Petrified Forest* seem like a Shirley Temple vehicle, and Duke Mantee will be an altar boy beside my next creation."

"You're to look me up, young man," Max told Jazzy. "If you have problems, I want to know about them, you hear?" He took a pen from his vest pocket and wrote his address and phone number on a sheet of steno paper.

Jazzy stood there, not knowing a graceful way to say good-bye.

"Go on, you two," Max said. "There's a lot ahead for both of you."

Jazzy took the bag from Rachel and walked outside to an old truck, a jarring contrast to the stylish woman.

Jack stayed home with Jennie. San Diego stations advised viewers they'd be kept abreast of the celebrated murder case in Buffalo. They interrupted a program in progress and announced the verdict. Jennie burst into tears, and Jack took her to San Diego de Alcala, the oldest mission in California.

Chapter Twenty-Eight

The shack, just outside the reservation's perimeter, depressed Jazzy. The antenna on the roof, however, reassured him somewhat. There was electricity—civilization had come to the American Indians.

There was a rough wood floor throughout. The plumbing was old, but there was a tub in the bathroom. The bedroom was an extension of the kitchen.

Rachel fried chops and potatoes. With homemade sourdough bread and a hot cup of coffee, Jazzy ate contentedly and silently. His head throbbed where Havlik struck him with a nightstick, and he was exhausted from all the sleepless nights he endured, trembling in his cell out of fear of the verdict the jury would give.

It lieu of grace, he gave silent thanks to Carlson and Muncrief, whose brilliance saved him. Carlson was no country bumpkin. He and Muncrief showed Buffalo why they were household words and bested the shrewd Barry Kendall. All the men of substance in his life were educated. There was no better evidence of that than what he'd just gone through.

They retired early. The lengthy stay in the county jail had imposed a forced celibacy on Jazzy, and his need for her was overpowering. It wasn't a time for the niceties of lovemaking. They groped desperately for each other in the dark. Her desire matched his. There was fury in their union, and, when they finished, they slept in each other's arms.

Morning came, and Rachel was gone. Jazzy looked around critically and saw it was a man's shack. That bothered him more than he cared to admit. There was nothing to indicate a woman's touch. The place was filthy.

He found a broom and swept the house. The rough counter was piled high with dishes from many meals. He set them in the sink and scrubbed the oilcloth on the table with a dishcloth that was passably cleaned, then he cleared the top of the woodstove.

Jazzy made a tour of the grounds and found it was a beautiful morning. The sun was warm on his back, but it was chilly inside the house. Firewood was stacked halfway up the back of the building. He gathered some wood and kindling and took them inside. The simple chores were therapeutic. Soon, he had a fire going.

Rachel arrived. For the first time, he saw her in something other than slacks. She wore a white blouse and flowered skirt, and her legs were gorgeous. He hadn't expected that.

He looked at her standing in the doorway, Venus in ecru, and sadness came over him. He'd leave her soon. It was inevitable. At the prison, he promised they'd go together, but, after sober reflection, he couldn't do that. She'd become a fugitive, too.

"Hi," she said.

"Hi. Where have you been?"

"At my mother's place on the reservation."

"What was your hurry?"

"I had to let her know I was using the place. If I didn't, the first time smoke came from the chimney, half a dozen friends would've told her someone was using the house. I'm surprised someone didn't tell her."

"Who owns this place?"

"My brother, Reuben."

That pleased him. His smiled dazzled. "He won't mind our using it?"

"He's my twin brother. We're very close. He'd do anything for me. That's his truck we've been using."

Jazzy was silent, dreading a confrontation. "Will he come around?"

"No. He and the boys went to the islands for muskies. It's his third year. It seems his mission in life is to catch one of those monster fish."

"To each his own." Jazzy smiled. Reuben's absence gave him a sense of relief.

The stove was hot, and Rachel made an omelet. She squeezed several oranges and tossed a piece of rind on the stove, and soon, the room was filled with an orange scent, strong enough to overcome the mustiness that prevailed.

"Breakfast will be ready soon," she said.

He went to the bathroom to wash and shave.

Rachel sat across from him, and, although he was famished, he experienced difficulty eating. His eyes were riveted to her cleavage, and, every time she turned in either direction, she exposed substantial portions of her breasts. His urges, never far removed, surfaced, and his need for her grew. There was a knot in the pit of his stomach, and his mouth was dry.

When she rose to take her plate to the sink, he gulped his coffee and went after her. He encircled her with his arms, his hands cupping her breasts. When he kissed the nape of her neck, she squealed in delight and turned, throwing her arms around his neck and pulling him against her.

She mouthed him hungrily, then she pushed him away. With trembling fingers, he unbuttoned her blouse and dropped it to the floor. One deft movement at the waist of her skirt released that, too.

Transfixed, he drank in her beauty. She had lovely shoulders, breasts so marvelously molded he was left breathless, a flat stomach that delineated a magnificent rib cage, and exquisite legs.

He pulled his T-shirt over his head and stepped out of his shorts while she stepped out of her step-ins.

She lay on her back, holding her arms out to him, and he caressed her breasts, with firm nipples, until she moaned in ecstasy.

Jazzy stroked her body slowly and sensuously. She clutched his back savagely, and soon, she thrashed under him and pleaded, "Please," she whispered hoarsely, "please."

He came to her full force, and their rapture was like Cotopaxi's fiery fountain. Then they fell back into exhaustion. She laid her breasts on his chest and buried her face in the hollow of his neck.

It was summer in late fall, a day made for lovers. It must've been such a day in Verona when Romeo first saw Juliet. *Step aside, Anthony and Cleopatra,* Jazzy thought, *and Lancelet and Guinevere. This day is for us.*

She wore a housecoat with flowered print. He hadn't gone into the woods with a girl since he was with Carrie Evans in the willows. The two were silent as they walked side-by-side, following the creek until they reached a log at the water's edge.

She removed her sandals and beckoned him to take off his shoes. They sat on the log, feet dangling lazily in the swiftly moving water. They tossed in pebbles, and a frog leaped out. Fascinated, they watched it negotiate the creek, then disappear. When he returned, he had another frog with him.

The sculpted perfection of her legs delighted Jazzy, and he took in every turn and curve as she flashed them in the sun. He noted the rise and fall of her bosom under her housecoat, surprised to find himself getting excited again.

She must've felt his gaze, because she located her sandals and stood, then slowly removed the housecoat. Holding her sandals and housecoat high overhead to keep them dry, she crossed the creek naked.

Jazzy retrieved his shoes and followed her into the creek, unconcerned that his clothes were wet. In the sunlight, she was glorious. She wasn't buxom, but her breasts were delightfully sculpted. Her rib cage, large for a slender woman, enhanced her already fine figure.

Out of so many women in his life, what made her special? The answer was there in the beginning on the carnival grounds. He looked at the unclad beauty before him as if for the first time. Wading through the swiftly flowing creek made her poetry in motion. Unbidden, an image came to him of Jennie, wading through the waters of Lake Ontario, holding him tightly to her bosom.

At an old elm, Rachel placed her housecoat on the grass and pulled him down with her. There was tenderness in their lovemaking—deliberate, agonizing, and delightful. Intruding, however, was the contemptible idea he was copulating with two women.

Later, while watching the billowing clouds, Rachel said, "My girlfriend, Susie, visited me while you were sleeping. She told me about some strangers who are looking for a guy."

Jazzy stiffened. "Did she describe them?" he asked softly.

"One was short and fat, with bushy black hair. The other was tall and thin and wore a hat."

"Jesus Christ!" He pulled her up off the grass. "It's them. They're everywhere." Fear showed in his eyes.

"Who are they?"

"Monti and Hobbs. Did Susie see me?"

"How could she? You were in bed. What do they want?"

"My life. They're killers, and they work for a mobster in Niagara Falls. I wish you'd told me earlier."

"Oh, Jazzy, does this have anything to do with your case?"

"No. It's something else."

"Please go to the police," she pleaded.

"How will that help? Nobody knows where I am. Going to the police would just make it easier for the hoods."

"I'll send word to my brother. He has friends."

"No, Rachel. Keep Reuben out of it. These people are more animal than human. They'd eat Reuben and his friends alive."

"What will you do?"

"I'll run." He saw sadness come over her, and he pulled her head against his chest. "I have to. It's my life."

They hurried back to the shack, and Rachel packed a lunch for him. From her wallet she took out a ten-dollar bill. "It's all I've got," she apologized.

He put the ten in the wallet with his lone ten. "I feel badly taking this from you. I swear, if I'm alive, I'll send you money."

She began to cry.

"Right now, I'm going to Rochester. After that, I have no idea."

She went into the bedroom and came out with a gun and a box of shells. He recoiled from them, hating weapons despite his stint in Belgium, where a gun was a man's consort.

"Take it," she said. "I sure hope you don't have to use it."

He picked it up from the table and saw it was a Smith and Wesson, a model used at the turn of the century by every police officer. It was a clumsy piece.

Jazzy carried the trench coat and slipped the gun and ammo into one of the coat's deep pockets.

"The gas tank's full," she said. "I filled it when I visited Mom."

"I won't run off with it. I don't want you to get into trouble with Reuben."

"Oh, Jazzy, I know you won't. Where will I pick it up?"

"At the Rundel Library downtown. I'll park it in the lot behind it. I'll lock the trunk and hide the key behind the front license plate. How'll you get to Rochester?"

"I'll get an early bus in the morning. I'll get there."

It was time for him to leave. They faced each other and embraced. For the first time, a woman made him cry.

"I'll return if I can," he promised.

"Sure," she lied, crying, "we'll meet again."

The trial bared Jazzy to the world. Newspapers, radio, and TV stripped him of all privacy and provided a network of information to which anyone was privy.

Both the mayor, with his scientific jargon, and Whitey with his plain talk, warned Jazzy that betting the nags was for suckers. Now he had little choice. He'd prove he was the biggest sucker of all. He would bet his life on the chance of picking two winners in a row at Nick Sparta's. How else could he raise enough money for train fare to San Diego? He could go to the Hacienda, but he wouldn't put his friends in jeopardy.

He parked the car as planned. The sky was overcast, and there was a chill in the air. He donned his trench coat and looked around cautiously.

The route from the library to Nick's was fraught with peril. Finally, he reached the building and walked in quickly, shutting the door behind him.

Charlie, the lookout man, saw Jazzy, and his face lit up. "Jazzy! We've been following your case. Glad you beat the rap. Stuck it to the DA, eh?"

Jazzy raised clasped hands over his head in friendship, then glanced around. It was as if he'd never left. The pool table was still gathering dust, and he slowly climbed the stairs with the bend in the middle. He reached the top with trepidation.

There were no strangers. The Stooge was at the boards. To the left was the card game and brutal Al. To the right was the row of betting windows and Dave with Frog. In the cubicle formed by the betting window, the outside wall, and the other two walls, was Nick Sparta, playing gin.

When they saw Jazzy, a roar went up. They greeted him like a visiting celebrity. He didn't appreciate it and didn't want the attention, but he waved.

He was relieved to see Marve. At the moment, he felt forgiving. Marve edged toward the door, and Jazzy caught him.

"It's me. Jazzy. Boy, am I glad to see you. Where you going?"

"Sorry. I've got an important date." Marve made a move toward the door again, and Jazzy came closer.

"What gives?"

"I saw them. They're here."

"Who?" He knew the answer.

"Monti and Hobbs. Joe Chink's boys."

"Where?"

"Keough's pool room. They've covered the town for you."

"You gotta help me, Marve."

"No way."

"You lousy son of a bitch! I saved your ass and went through hell because of you. You owe me!"

"No way!" Marve broke free and scurried down the stairs.

"Judas bastard!" Jazzy shouted.

Suddenly, he recalled a painful event from his past. He remembered Lefty's fists against his ribs. His classmates formed a savage, screaming ring, blocking all avenues of escape. Then he was on the ground, tearing at the short grass while Lefty kicked his head, side, and legs, and a mean voice screeched, "Kill him, Lefty! Kill the bastard!"

It was Marve. Through the years, Jazzy hadn't been sure, but now he knew.

Suddenly, he stiffened, with a prickly feeling at the nape of his neck. He didn't need to hear the presence of someone at the stairway door—he sensed it. What a fool he'd been. He was careless to forget that door, immersed in self-pity, reminiscing about Marve's perfidy from long ago. He stopped breathing and turned slowly, expecting to be gunned down on the spot.

It was Kevin Kilty, and a warm wave of relief suffused Jazzy. He even had a woman with him, little more than a child. Then Kilty did a strange thing. He stepped aside and let Jazzy have a full view of his companion. Jazzy realized that was in deference to his reputation as a Casanova—Kilty was offering the child for inspection and approval, as if they were soul mates.

He had a drink at the water cooler.

"They're off at the fairgrounds!" the Stooge called, removing his earpiece and wiping it with a handkerchief.

The betting crowd surged forward, beating the deadline. Jazzy felt as if he were embarking on a long journey and stepped closer to listen to the calls.

The Stooge had an artistic soul. He held secret contempt for his associates. When he got the signal from Dave to proceed with the description, he was calling the Preakness.

Jazzy had something else to worry about. If those hoods met Marve, they'd learn his whereabouts. He'd come in late for the fairgrounds, and time was against him.

It was close to post time at Tropical Park. The Stooge was walking the plank, marking the Santa Anita board, posting the results of the sixth race at the fairgrounds, which was history.

Jazzy ran a weary eye down the Tropical Park entries—Fire Fighter, Jezebel, Willie Will, Don't Tell, Vacuum, Goo Goo, Call Me, and Have Heart. They were nothing but names, because he'd been away too long. He grabbed the racing form and murmured, "Dogs. Nothing but dogs." Normally, he wouldn't have touched such a race.

He looked up and studied the fluctuating odds. The Stooge adjusted his earpiece, then went rapidly down the line, marking the board. Fire Fighter was 6 to 1, Jezebel 8 to 1, Willie Will stayed at 15 to 1, the house limit. Don't Tell and Vacuum were at 15 to 1, too, and Goo Goo became the favorite at 5 to 2. Call Me was at 3 to 1, and Have Heart was 4 to 1.

Have Heart was an encouraging word, and Jazzy set his analytical mind to work. He reasoned that Have Heart had been the early morning favorite. All the betting of the day, with resulting changing of odds, didn't make any horse better or worse. Jazzy knew that. There were other factors involved.

Lest he change his mind, he went to the ticket window, filled with misgivings. To be knocked out of the box on his first bet would be cruel. He handed his ticket, along with twenty dollars, to Dave.

"Twenty on the nose. You're not horsing around."

The Stooge cried out the horses as soon as the race started. "At the quarter, it's Have Heart a neck, Fire Fighter a half-length, and Goo Goo."

A tiny spark rose in Jazzy's chest, trying to ignite a little enthusiasm.

"At the half, it's Have Heart a length, Goo Goo by two, and Willie Will."

Jazzy couldn't stand still and started pacing, but he kept an eye on the door.

"In the stretch, it's Have Heart by two, Goo Goo a neck, and Call Me."

Jazzy wrung his hands, his heart pounding.

"The winner is Have Heart all the way, followed by Call Me and Jezebel!"

It was easy, Jazzy told himself. I *can do it.*

When the Stooge posted the prices on the board, Have Heart paid $8.20 to win. Jazzy had $82.00 coming, but he'd expected a better price. It was a soft 4 to 1. There was a line at the window.

"Jazzy!" someone called.

He looked down the line and saw Kevin Kilty smiling and waving a ticket stub. "Me, too, Jazz."

The young woman standing in front of Kilty waved a stub and smiled, too. Jazzy was annoyed. It seemed everyone bet on Have Heart.

Jazzy collected his money feeling angry with himself for letting Kilty distract him. He tried to smother his excitement. Now, more than ever, he had to be prudent. His life depended on one more win, but he was confident he could do it.

The feature race at the Fair Grounds was coming up. Jazzy spurred his memory and recalled an affable Sparta holding court in the White Castle, regaling the boys with tales of the old days.

"Regardless of the popular idea that races are fixed," he said, "fixed races are rare. Take Ben Adams. Most people figure the bigger the purse, the more the race is on the up and up. Not so. Nobody figures Ben to lose his cut of the purse."

Jazzy looked at the board again. The upcoming race at the Fair Grounds had a large purse, and Ben Adams was riding.

Two late scratches had thrown the race into a two-horse affair. The rest of the field didn't look like much. Jacob McQueen's Orion, with Ben Adams, was at 6 to 5 and sure to drop further. There was Revolt, however, a horse with a record every bit as good as Orion a 2 1/2 shot with Grasso riding.

Jazzy hung back and watched. Orion went to even money, then dropped lower, to 4 to 5. Meanwhile, Revolt went to 3 to 1 and stayed there. It had to be Revolt. Jazzy was sure the crooked Adams was going to do business. He handed in his ticket and the entire $82.00.

Dave looked at the ticket. "Are you sure, Jazzy? Know something?"

"I'm sure, but I don't know a damn thing."

Jazzy stood beside the old man and his woman. The woman nudged the man and asked, "Ain't we betting?"

"Are you forgetting? We don't bet anything under 2 to 1."

"How about Revolt? He's 3 to 1."

"Are you crazy? Orion is Jacob McQueen's horse."

"Yeah. I guess he means to win the big one."

"That octopus wants them all. You can't buck that stable."

"They're running at the Fair Grounds!" the Stooge shouted.

Bettors pushed toward the windows, getting their bets down before the first call.

"All right, Dave?" the Stooge asked.

"Call it out!" he said.

Adjusting the earpiece more securely, the Stooge listened intently, then he started speaking like Clem McCarthy.

"At the quarter, it's Orion by a length, Backlash by two, and Revolt."

Jazzy started to panic.

"At the half, its Orion by three, Revolt a neck, and Backlash."

"I blew it," Jazzy said bitterly. "Just another easy mark."

"In the stretch, it's Orion a neck, Revolt by two, and Gay *Señor*."

"I'm in! He's stiffening his mount. Pull, Ben! Slow him to a walk!"

"The winner…" The Stooge paused to make the most of the moment. "The winner is Orion. Revolt is second, and Ragged Edge is third."

"He was leveling!" Jazzy said. "Ben Adams was leveling!" His despair was so great, he struck his legs with his fists. He felt the gun deep in his coat pocket.

Wildly, he looked at the cubicle where Nick Sparta played cards, and his eyes rested on the cash box. A quick, crazy scheme came to mind. It was crazy, because *he* was crazy. Without cash, he was dead.

He gauged his chances of taking the box from Nick and holding him at bay. He had to get past Dave and Frog, then the patrons, then Stooge. He could hold off Al, whom he feared most, and, if his luck held, and there was no signal to Charlie downstairs, he'd have the element of surprise when he reached the street.

As if in a bad dream, Jazzy walked toward the cubicle. He was lifting the gun from his deep pocket when a hand grabbed his shoulder. He spun, the gun dropping from his fingers. His nerves couldn't take anymore, and he felt himself shaking.

Then he saw it was Mayor Sheldon, and he tried to pull himself together. The mayor was distraught.

"I'm sorry, Jazzy. You must be a bundle of nerves. That must've been hell for you in Buffalo."

He put an arm around Jazzy. The others looked at them curiously as the mayor pulled Jazzy aside.

"I want you to know I suffered with you throughout the trial. Pull yourself together. When you're ready, I have a job for you in city hall. I'll launch you on a political career."

Jazzy nodded.

"See a doctor, Jazzy."

What monstrous act had he contemplated? He wasn't Rick, Monti, or Hobbs, nor was he a barbarian like Joe chink. The fact that the gun was empty brought no solace.

The Stooge's voice blared loud and clear. "They're claiming foul at the Fair Grounds!"

Jazzy laughed hysterically, unable to hope the claim would hold up.

The mayor became alarmed. "What is it, Jazzy? Got something on that race?"

"It's just Lady Luck goosing me again. She's playing games. The old man told his woman you can't buck that stable, and I thought Ben was doing business."

He heard himself rambling and looked wildly at the door. He'd forgotten it, and it was still shut.

"The claim is disallowed!" the Stooge shouted.

The mayor commandeered a chair from a card game and sat Jazzy down. Kilty's date brought him a glass of water and supervised his drinking, making him take small sips. She produced a wet handkerchief and wiped his brow, then wiped his temples and the back of his neck. She was calm and efficient—probably a hospital trainee.

What were his options now? He had to get back to the truck and return to the reservation. For a moment, he thought of chancing it in his old neighborhood. He'd be able to borrow money to go West, but the neighborhood was undoubtedly under close surveillance by now.

His pride gone, he would have to ask Rachel to hide him.

He left the room with a heavy heart. He wouldn't see any of them again, and he wondered how many would come to his funeral. He embraced the mayor, who again admonished him to take care of himself and see a doctor, then he ran downstairs. Charlie eyed him curiously as he edged furtively out the door.

Chapter Twenty-Nine

He barely heard the reports, but the slugs, whistling past, sobered him fast. He dived back into the doorway and crouched low, reaching for the gun and box of ammo. He frantically tore the box open and grabbed some rounds without bothering to count them. His hands shook as he placed them in the cylinder.

He didn't want to kill, just buy time and hold them off long enough so he could run. He aimed and pulled the trigger, and the hammer clicked against an empty chamber. Then came two reports, and Monti and Hobbs scurried for cover, knocking over some garbage cans.

Jazzy ran to the back of the building and toward the river, moving through high weeds at a low crouch, risking injury from hidden pieces of rubble as he zigzagged. Ducking behind the shell of an old car, he listened and heard rustling noise from the right and left.

Fighting down panic, he picked up a rock and threw it. They fired toward the sound and ran in that direction.

Jazzy left his sanctuary and reached the river, shaking like an aspen. He reached for his gun as he stood on the thick concrete retaining wall, the swollen Genesee moving swiftly under him, then turned to look for them.

A bullet tore at the right shoulder of his trench coat, under the epaulet. He spun, lost his balance, and fell into the raging river.

The cold water struck like a pile driver. He went down for a long time, finally coming to rest on limbs and brambles caught by jagged rocks. The sleeve of the trench coat was caught, and he couldn't pull free. With an effort, he stayed calm, unbuttoned the coat, and slid out of it. Trying to free the coat took too much time, so he reached into the pocket to pull out the gun and ammo, tucking the gun under his belt. By then, his lungs felt tortured.

Using branches to propel him cross-current to the side of the river, fighting its pull, he reached the retaining wall. The temptation to bob to the top was overpowering. He feared his lungs would burst, and the side of his head, where Havlik struck him, throbbed.

Somehow, he stayed under long enough to pull himself along the wall until he reached a recess. He rose to the top, gulping precious air and pulling floating branches over him. The recess hid him from view.

After what seemed like an eternity, he heard a voice.

"He ain't coming up."

"He's stuck down there."

"Yeah. Look at the rubbish. The river always brings the debris up from the south after a hard rain. Notice something about this river? It's running north."

"So?"

"I read somewhere rivers in the States run south."

"This one sure as hell ain't. I think you read wrong."

"He ain't coming up. Besides, I hit the punk."

"Yeah, you did, high on the right side."

"Wish I had the cannon he was using."

"Scared the shit out of me. Must be a museum piece. If you want it bad enough, why don't you jump in after it?"

"Funny. Look at that wild river. The poor slob will reach the lake before dark if he's not stuck down there."

"Say, Monti, why don't you let me have the hit?"

"Why would I do that?"

"Chink's been pissed at me lately. It would put me solid."

"What's it worth to you?"

"Fifty?"

"Done. Let's get out of here. It's finished."

For a long time, the only sound Jazzy heard was the Genesee making its way to the lake. Working with the current, he edged along the wall and came to some steel rungs set into the concrete. He climbed out shivering.

He was cold for some time, but the trucks' engine soon spewed warm air into the cab. There was no need to go to San Diego. Jasmin Rhinehardt died in the river, and, by that time, Joe Chink had been called by his torpedoes. Someday, the river would disgorge the trench coat with his name stenciled under the collar, and everyone would know. His mother had a good thing going without him—there was no need to screw it up for her.

The miraculous deliverance made him giddy. He thought warmly of her, and her telegram indicated she cried for him. Perversely, that made him happy. The mental picture of Jennie, racing across the country, grabbing his arm and dragging him back to San Diego, made him laugh aloud. He wouldn't wait too long before seeing her. He didn't want any news reaching her that someone recovered his coat from the river.

The hum of the motor was therapeutic, and he gave himself the luxury of pleasant reveries. He thought of Polly Bagby with her undulating buttocks—classical, worthy of Bernini. He thought of haughty breasts, twin sirens that lured and invited. The truck, however, was headed for the reservation. He'd met many women who could make him want them, but Rachel was different. The ache for her was constant, and he wanted to be with her forever. He was going home to her.

He made plans as he drove. The men he'd known who had influence, strength, and substance were all educated. He would go to school and take Rachel with him, then he'd raise a family. Someday, when Joe Chink's empire crumbled, and his life was no longer in jeopardy, he'd take his family back to Rochester and show them the house on Goodman Street, made of red brick and American history. He'd talk of freedom and explain about the dark, dank cellar where the slaves were hidden on their way to

Canada. Of course, he would explain that Goodman Street was the center of his universe.

Jazzy was nearing the cottage just beyond the limits of the reservation, and his pleasant reveries came to an abrupt end. There was a car near the front door. He was some distance away and slowed fast, fear gripping him.

Perhaps it was just Reuben, back from his fishing trip, and his friends brought him home, but what if it wasn't? It had taken extraordinary luck to free him from those killers.

He drove the truck off the road into a clearing, hiding it from view, then cautiously crept among the trees toward the cottage. A cluster of maple saplings concealed him as he waited, but he didn't wait long.

The door was flung open, and a young American Indian, tall and slender, went catapulting through it, followed by Monti, brandishing his gun. Then came Hobbs dragging Rachel. Her dress was torn, and even at that distance, Jazzy saw the two of them had been struck repeatedly in the face. He saw Rachel, normally lithe and graceful, stumbling and falling, only to be dragged by the long-striding Hobbs.

Jazzy hadn't considered an attack on her. It made no sense. He'd fallen into the river, and they thought he was dead. As far as they were concerned, it was over.

It had to be Joe Chink's orders. If his body surfaced with a hole in it, there would be an investigation, and they saw Rachel in court with his suitcase. There was no subterfuge that last day—the joy of acquittal made him rash. That explained the gangsters' presence in the reservation's general store. Joe Chink knew Rachel could testify that Jazzy was running from his men.

The Jennie Jones in him told him to run. He couldn't blow it now. He had it made. There was little he could do against two professional killers.

He was cramped as he crouched amid the saplings. It brought to mind his childhood and similar hidings, and, in his state of mind, he heard Guy Lovell shouting, "Run, Sheep, run!" He was a frightened lamb.

Jazzy was bitter. He felt he had no more character than Marve. An unexpected stubbornness surfaced, like the time he fought Mendez, scrambling his senses.

It takes nobility of spirit to ride off to a crusade, slay a dragon or two, rescue a damsel in distress, and joust a few windmills. That nobility of spirit had to come from him, not the phantoms of long-dead ancestors. Never again would it take a saying authored by others to guide him.

He was angry at the deprecating view of himself. Was he no better than Marve Pittman? He couldn't accept that. No craven coward could've bearded Joe Chink in his lair. No fictional Sabatini hero could've dispatched Monti and Hobbs with more elan than in his flight from that office. Twice, he confronted the brutal Rick Devlin, albeit to his own agony.

He had to break up the interdependence of the Goodman set, more pronounced in him than the others. Did he love Rachel? What life would he have without her? The answers were clear.

Jazzy raced to the truck for the gun. There were two weapons against his one. He didn't like the odds, but he had the element of surprise.

The warm air in the cab dried his weapon. He emptied the cylinder and found the chambers dry, as was his ammo. He reloaded and put a handful of cartridges into his pocket.

He hurried back, praying he wasn't too late. Rachel and Reuben were to be executed, their bodies concealed deep in the woods. Jazzy's fictional heroes were of little use to him. He was frightened as he plunged into an act of idiocy without the sardonic laugh of Captain Blood or the gay abandon of Zorro.

Jazzy moved carefully and tentatively, wondering what he'd do if he found them. He heard the noise of the foursome moving through the woods. They reached a clearing, then he stepped on a branch. When it snapped in the stillness, it sounded like a pistol shot.

"Who the hell's out there?" Monti whispered.

"How the hell do I know?" Hobbs asked. "Take Injun Joe with you."

Monti doubled back, keeping Reuben in front of him. Reuben was being deliberately noisy, while Monti snapped branches everywhere.

Jazzy saw them but couldn't shoot Monti in the back. He'd fired many rounds in war, but there was blessed anonymity on the battlefield, and he never knew for certain if he took a life.

Then he reconsidered. Why not ambush Monti? It was logical and necessary. Jennie's toughness left him when he most needed, however, and he couldn't shoot.

Reuben came into view, and Jazzy waited. When Monti drew alongside, Jazzy sucker-punched him with a vicious hook, cracking his jaw.

Monti's eerie scream of pain reached Hobbs, but he couldn't identify it. Why hadn't Monti used his Beretta?

Monti no longer had it. Jazzy's hard punch dislodged it, and the gun fell to the ground. That was the hardest punch he ever threw.

"Monti!" Hobbs shouted. "What the fuck's going on?"

Monti was built like a fireplug, and he was as tough as old scrap iron. Like a mortally wounded animal, he crawled toward his fallen weapon. He reached for it as Jazzy tried to pull the Smith and Wesson from his pocket.

It fell from his hand. He looked at his fingers in amazement, seeing them bent grotesquely. He'd broken his hand. He broke out into a cold sweat as Monti reached for his weapon.

Reuben leaped forward and grabbed Jazzy's gun, then aimed and fired, shooting Monti through the head from behind. Calmly, he took the Beretta from Monti's hand and placed it in Jazzy's left.

"You must be Jazzy. The hoods said they killed you and dropped you in the Genesee."

"They exaggerated. I hope you're Reuben."

Reuben laughed. "Yeah, I'm her brother. We gotta get Sis. I'll get the other son of a bitch."

They spread apart, intending to come at Hobbs from two directions. Jazzy wondered if he could fire the gun with his left hand. He'd never been a marksman even with his right hand. Why hadn't he bushwhacked Monti when he had the chance? Now his right hand was useless.

He had trouble holding the Beretta, and it felt awkward in his left hand. It was Reuben who first appeared to Hobbs, walking out of the woods like a wraith. Hobbs shoved Rachel aside, intending to draw his gun.

"Over here, Hobbs!" Jazzy shouted.

Hobbs whirled to face Jazzy, somehow knowing where he'd be. With his left hand, Jazzy steadied the gun on his right arm, aimed, and fired. He missed, but slugs from Reuben's gun tore into Hobbs' upper torso with such force, he fell hard to the sward under the old tree.

Rachel ran to him, and he held her close. She sobbed and clung desperately to him. Tears came to Jazzy's eyes, too, and he shook. He'd helped kill two men, and he had to live with that the rest of his life. He'd never be the same. His hand throbbed, too, and he needed a doctor.

"Let's get out of here," Reuben said. "The nightmare's over."

"No, it's not," Jazzy said. "There's Joe Chink."

"Don't worry about him. He's all washed up. The Falls is full of young barracudas trying to get to the top. That son of a bitch just lost two top trigger men. The others will be after him—if they can beat the law getting to him."

"We have to inform the authorities."

"Not you, Jazzy."

"What do you mean? I can't let you two face this alone."

"Reuben's right," Rachel said. "You've just been acquitted of two murders. With this mess, they'd swarm all over you like honey bees."

"It's perfect, Jazzy," Reuben said. "The Smith and Wesson is registered in my name. The house and woods are mine, too. There's no question they beat us up, and their car is still parked at the house. My friends can witness the car being there when I came home. Let me be the hero in this. Besides, I did the actual killing."

"What'll I do?"

"Stay away from here. It's my guess you have my truck, right? Get in it and drive off. Get your hand fixed. I'll wipe your prints off the Beretta and put it in the short bastard's hand."

"All right. I'll come by early in the morning."

He sat in a wheelchair in the emergency room of Niagara Falls Hospital, waiting for a long time. The sign outside read *Emergency*, but that was a misnomer.

Was his being in Niagara Falls, instead of Buffalo, symbolic? No, but neither was it defiance. Rather, it was to demonstrate he was a free man in charge of his own destiny. He aged a lot in Reuben's woods, and he knew he was no hero. He had much to thank Reuben for.

He'd discard the security blanket of Goodman Street. Guy Lovell understood that life was a continuing climb, onward and upward, reaching whatever heights one's energies and abilities allowed.

Jazzy had been spared twice in one day. That lent solemnity to the resolutions he made on his way back to Rachel. He was fortunate three influential men took enough interest to help him in his recent crisis.

Perhaps he'd enter politics. With the mayor's support, he'd become a force for good in Rochester. If he entered the university, it would be to prepare himself to effectively perform as a public servant. He was filled with zeal. The thought of taking Rachel back with him to Goodman and Norton thrilled him.

There was no need for a name change. When he married Rachel Springwater, she'd become Mrs. Jasmin Rhinehardt. Jennie didn't make idle threats, either. If she said she'd come after him, she would. He looked forward to her arrival. It was time Jennie met Rachel, and he met Jack Werner.

The injury to his head was still sensitive to the touch. His broken hand throbbed. He felt a chill coming on. He'd been in the river a long time, and he might've contracted pneumonia.

Still, there was a sense of contentment and tranquillity he hadn't felt since he was a child in his old neighborhood.

Chapter Thirty

Jack and Jennie turned the operation of their burgeoning business over to trusted employees. There was no urgency. The trip was in the nature of a much-needed vacation. Jennie had always wanted to ride a train, and they left San Diego in high spirits. They took the Sante Fe to Chicago, and the New York Central to Rochester, traveling for two days and nights.

Eager to see Jazzy, Jennie and Jack took a cab from the depot and drove toward Norton and Goodman. It was a joyous reunion at the Koven house. The Kovens followed the trial, and Jazzy's acquittal filled them with unbridled elation. The mood sobered, however, when they learned neither family had seen or heard from Jazzy.

Jennie and Dora visited Ida Belding. It was logical that Ida had, despite her years, slowed very little and was still the neighborhood firebrand. Ida, too, had nothing to report.

With some adroit questioning, Marve admitted Jazzy was fleeing from the mob. Jack kept that news to himself. Since Jennie didn't know her son was still in danger, and, although she was anxious to see him, she lingered two days to renew old friendships. She, Dora, and Ida drove to the Holy Sepulcher cemetery and found the graves of Mateo, Maria, and Whitey, placing flowers at the base of each headstone. She found Gus' plot and placed flowers there, too.

The next logical move was a short trip to Buffalo. Jack and Jennie rented a car, and Jennie, on the way west, stopped at the drugstore.

Mandel was the eyes and ears of the entire ward, and perhaps he knew something. Although she had a happy visit, he couldn't tell her anything.

From the courthouse in Buffalo, they got Max Muncrief's address. At the public library, they found a phone book for New York City and called him. Luckily, Henry Carlson was visiting him.

"Mrs. Werner, Max and I have a fatherly interest in Jasmin," Henry said.

"Thank you, Mrs. Carlson. My son would be in deep trouble but for you and Mr. Muncrief. I'm in your debt."

"Nonsense. When justice triumphs, we all triumph."

"Do you know where he is? We can't find him."

"That's strange. Perhaps not, though. There's a woman involved, a fine one, I might add. She was a pillar of strength for your son throughout the trial."

"A woman? Jasmin has had many women. Is this one special?"

"You bet. Not only is she a knockout, he's really taken with her, and it seems to be mutual."

"What's her name?"

"Rachel Springwater."

"What an odd name."

"Not really. She's an American Indian from the reservation not far from you."

"An American Indian?"

"Does that upset you?"

Jennie composed herself. "Of course not, Mr. Carlson. I can't wait to meet her."

"Mrs. Werner, drive to the reservation. Go to the general store and ask for Rachel. If you find her, you'll find your son."

Jennie found herself in a strange world. With trepidation, she entered what she and Jack judged to be the general store. People tend to fear the unfamiliar, but she soon learned everyone spoke English well, which was familiarity enough. A fine rapport was established quickly with the other shoppers, and they gave her directions to Reuben's cabin, where, the woman behind the counter was certain, they'd find Rachel.

As the car wound is way through a wooded area, they caught glimpses of the cabin through curtains of saplings. It was all very rustic.

Suddenly, Jack slammed on the brakes and came to a dust-raising, sliding stop.

"What is it?" Jennie asked in apprehension.

"Look. There's a Packard in that clearing, hidden from the cabin."

"So?"

"It's big and black, and I'll bet it's bullet-proof."

"You know something, don't you?"

"Yes. Gangsters from the Falls have been dogging Jazzy."

"You knew and didn't tell me?"

"I didn't want to ruin your trip. Besides, what do I know? I don't know who or what they are."

"Don't you ever do that again, Jack. Anything to do with my boy, I want to know right away. You hear me?"

"Yes, I hear you. Right now, I sense something isn't right. Get out. We'll push the car to where that Packard is parked, then we'll tread lightly to the cabin.

"Oh, Jack, I hope you're wrong."

Reuben was mistaken. The barracudas didn't come charging in, pulling Joe Chink's empire down around him. The line of defense had been breached by a most unexpected source. Eventually, those who usurped his enterprises would, indeed, come after him.

Monti and Hobbs were irreplaceable. Soldiers like them were rare, but they didn't constitute his entire army.

Joe's future was bleak, and he knew it. His life was now at stake. He'd been declawed by a young American Indian who single-handedly disposed of Monti and Hobbs, so what did his enemies have to fear?

Joe Chink was no fool The American Indian wasn't alone, and he may not have been the killer. The crime lord knew it was the work of his Jonah. After his gunsels sent him into the turbulent waters of the Genesee, Hobbs called in, telling Joe their mission was finished. He added there was an exchange of gunfire, and the quarry fired a gun that roared.

Chink had read everything written about the loss of his men. They were slain by a Smith and Wesson of an old issue—a gun like a cannon. Etched in his mind was Monti's face in the morgue, his jaw dangling to one side. He'd seen Jazzy throw punches at the tough Mendez that could break a man's jaw.

Joe wasn't superstitious, but he accepted he had a Jonah. How could an insignificant punk wreak havoc with his life? He knew their paths had never crossed, but the name Rhinehardt haunted him and kept him awake nights.

He took a quick trip to Rochester, certain the answer was there. Enlisting the aid of both newspapers, he refreshed his memory of the Oasis and one Gus Rhinehardt.

Jasmin had to be destroyed. Not until that was done could Joe shore up his defenses and save the empire Strazzi bequeathed to him. He had to do it personally.

Jennie and Jack moved laboriously through the woods. There was no sound from the cabin. They came to the porch, and Jack, with longer and faster legs, got to the open door first.

Inside, the sight he found horrified him. A large, fleshy man held a young couple at bay with a gun. From Jennie's pictures, he recognized his stepson. He cowered with his left arm around the woman, his right in a cast.

"Now, you fuckin' troublemaker," Joe said. "You've been my dark cloud long enough. Say good-bye to your bitch. She goes first."

What Jack did was foolhardy, but there was no time for planned action. He charged the assailant and crashed into him. The big man spun and deftly pistol-whipped Jack.

Jennie burst into the room as the corpulent stranger faced the young couple.

"Want to hear something funny, Troublemaker? In a moment, a Jasmin will be pushin' up daisies. Not funny? Try this. I'll take you out like your drunk old man."

A cold chill came over her. She tried to scream in protest, but her voice was paralyzed. Her eyes swept the cabin, and she saw Reuben's fishing gear in the corner. She grabbed the heavy gaff as if it were weightless, then, in cold fury, she rushed the man who had killed her husband. He'd never get her boy, not if she could help it. Years of bitterness and hate were stored in her, and they spilled over until she became a deranged vixen bent on destruction.

Joe sensed, rather than heard, the rush, and he turned once more from his task. At that moment, she swung the gaff as hard as she could. Joe got off one shot, but the slug whistled past Jennie's ear, ricocheted off the stove, and embedded itself in the wall.

The large hook caught his huge, flaccid stomach. He turned to evade it, but that buried the hook even deeper. Beside herself with rage, Jennie pulled mightily in the opposite direction, and part of Joe Chink's stomach came away.

The gun, an ivory-handled Luger, dropped to the floor as the large man put his hands to his stomach to staunch the blood. There was an incredulous look on his face. Slowly, his features relaxed, his eyes went dull, and he fell to the floor.

The police investigation was thorough. The detectives, presenting a stern exterior, were persistent. Inside, they were pleased that a thorn had been removed from Niagara Falls' tender side.

The family was in the corridor, awaiting news of Jack's condition. As any close family would, they huddled together.

"He'll be all right," the doctor assured them. "It's a concussion, but he'll be as good as new. We'll keep him here a couple of days. You may go in now. He's wide awake."

Jennie went into the room first, followed by Jazzy and Rachel.

"Dear Jack," she said. "Jazzy and Rachel told me how you put your life on the line for them."

"They're my kids, too. The doctor tells me you're a genuine, honest-to-goodness heroine."

"Mother was incredible," Jazzy said.

Rachel hugged Jennie in agreement, then she hugged Jack.

"Never mind all that," Jennie said sternly. She knew she'd taken a life, and her violent deed in the cabin would haunt her forever. She tried not to dwell on her actions. It was enough that, in one moment, she avenged Gus' slaying and rescued her son and future daughter-in-law from a similar fate. Martino's death was God's work.

Joe Chink was no mullet, either. He was the largest, fiercest, most voracious of the barracudas roiling the waters of Niagara Falls. Jennie wasn't a heroine, but, if Gus were alive to witness her confrontation with the vice lord, he would've conceded no Rhinehardt antecedent could've deported himself with more valor.

Her son was certain to ask about the cryptic reference to his father. She'd answer honestly when it came. She looked at him lovingly, feeling concerned. In the few years she lived in San Diego and out of his life, he seemed to have drifted from one peril to another.

Jazzy's pride in his mother showed in his eyes. She retained her youthful appearance a long time, but he detected bits of evidence that the years were beginning to take their toll. She'd grow old gracefully, and she was still an attractive woman. He recalled a quotation Mayor Sheldon tossed at him with grand elan, "To everything there is a season, and a time to every purpose under heaven."

Rachel met with Jennie's approval. She was a lovely young woman, and she was certain to be a stabilizing influence on Jazzy. At the moment, Jennie wanted to mother both of them

"Jack, tell them we want them with us in San Diego."

"I don't think so," Jack replied.

"Jack!"

"They'll fare better in the house on Goodman Street."

"We don't own that house anymore."

"The present owners are putting it up for sale."

"Where'd you hear that?"

"Gump told me."

"Oh, Jack! Let's buy it!"

"I already did. I commissioned Gump to do it."

"You've been keeping a lot of secrets from me, lately, haven't you?" She smiled broadly.

"When are you two getting married?" Jack asked Jazzy.

"Soon." Jazzy received a confirming nod from Rachel.

"Any reason it can't be right away?" He was deliberately pressuring Jazzy. He'd known for some time the man was a procrastinator—important decisions tended to overwhelm him.

It didn't take a genius to arrive at that conclusion. There was his failure to enroll at the university, obtain gainful employment in his hometown, and start a new life when he returned from the war. Instead, he scurried to the haven offered by Maria. However, Jack knew enough not to point those things out to Jennie.

The question seemed to disconcert Jazzy, but he recovered quickly. "No reason at all! We'll see Father Weideman as soon as we get back to Rochester." He gave no indication he'd just made that decision.

Rachel smiled, giving the impression it was a decision she and Jazzy made after careful consideration.

"Then Jennie and I will stay for the wedding," Jack said, feeling pleased with himself.

"And…?" Jennie asked, following the conversation with keen interest.

"The house will be your first wedding gift." Jack beamed.

Jazzy and Rachel were wide-eyed at the magnanimous gift. They ran to Jack, then Jennie, hugging them both hard.

"What a rental that will make!" Jazzy said.

"Rental?" Jennie asked.

"An investment that can make a difference in hard times," Rachel added, surprising Jack with an unexpected display of good sense.

"What are you talking about, Jazzy?" Jack asked. "I was sure you'd be eager to spend your years on Goodman Street."

"Mayor Sheldon offered me a job in city hall. He wants me to get into politics. I called him long distance this morning to accept the job."

"We want to live downtown, near his work," Rachel explained.

Jennie was right. Rachel *would* be good for Jazzy.

"Mother, I'll always love my friends and neighbors. I couldn't have picked a better place than Goodman and Norton to be raised, but you have time to sort things out in prison. I know my neighborhood was my crutch. There are challenges to be met and successes to pursue out there."

Jazzy was pontificating, which made her smile. He was beginning to sound like Guy Lovell.

Jennie looked at the couple with pride. Her son seemed taller, and she was singing inside. She hadn't done a bad job of raising the boy.

Jack beamed his approval, which pleased Jennie. When Jazzy left her to go to war, he was a fine-looking lad of eighteen. The sisters of the sodality were right—he *was* better looking than Tyrone Power.

As for Rachel, Helen Jackson wrote about her long before she was born, then named her Ramona.

Soon, they'd have each other to have and to hold until death do them part. Jennie hadn't done badly at all, either—she had Gary Cooper.